A deranged but brilliant scientist dreams he has a series of conversations with Einstein. Each morning, when he wakes up, he follows Einstein's instructions—until he has built a fantastic computer; a computer *so* fantastic that it is, in fact, Satan.

Satan has returned to earth, in the guise of this machine, to be psychoanalyzed—he is very unhappy about his relationship with God, and no one on earth seems to like or understand him.

If cured, Satan promises to reveal to his analyst The Great Secret of Life. . . .

Also By Jeremy Levin:

CREATOR

SATAN:
HIS PSYCHOTHERAPY AND CURE BY THE UNFORTUNATE DR. KASSLER, J.S.P.S.

JEREMY LEVEN

ACKNOWLEDGMENTS

●

A wise and literate man for whom I have great respect, Joseph Kanon, once expressed to me his opinion that acknowledgments at the beginning of novels have all the inspirational qualities for him of speeches given by those receiving Oscars. While the point is well taken, it nonetheless presents a problem for someone who spends part of his life immersed in a field where omitting the names of those who have provided concepts and support for his work can result in the end of both. Not that it isn't also the fair and just thing to do, as I trust even Joe would concede, whether or not I gave him credit for the sentiment that opens this paragraph.

Similarly, I must acknowledge with deep appreciation the encouragement, support, enthusiasm, and suggestions provided by friends, neighbors, associates, and family during the writing of this book, among them my parents, Martin and Marcia Levin, who supplied a mini-writer's colony in an idyllic setting; Don and Bridget Mariano; Mary Lloyd and Bill Lee; Arnold and Judy Burk; Glenn and Anndy Rosen; Mark Sklarz; Paul Ford; Alain Bernheim; Geri Thoma; Raymond Bongiovanni; Jim Cochrane; Arlene Avena; my extraordinarily astute editor Peter Gethers; one of the great women of the psychology of letters and letter-writers who happens by good fortune to be my agent Elaine Markson; and, above all, my wife, Roberta Danza, whose intelligence, humor, and insight into character resulted in innumerable improvements in this work, and whose love and spirit fueled the author and all progeny.

I am also grateful to Professor of Developmental Psychobiology Victor Denenberg, Professors of Neuroanatomy Enrico Mugnaini and Victor Friedrich, and Professor of Neurochemistry Ezio Giacobini of the University of Connecticut; and Professor of Pediatrics, Psychology, and Psychiatry Donald Cohen of the Yale University School of Medicine. The training they have provided has had a profound impact on this work and has instilled in me a regard for the sublime nature of the neuro-psychic enterprise, even if undertaken in a subterranean setting. In light of the nature of this work, I must, however, assure the reader that none of the above bears any resemblance to characters in this book, living and dead.

Finally, all my work is forever indebted to my education at St. John's College in Annapolis, Maryland, where I first encountered the gentleman who most deserves recognition for his contributions to this book, Dante Alighieri.

In Memory Of
Elizabeth Lauter Obrasky
1891–1980

This book is dedicated to those who
lack the freedom to choose their own suffering
and to their hope.

"My desire is that the Almighty would answer me, and that mine adversary had written a book."

JOB 31:35

PART I

Kassler's Case

CHAPTER 1

What can I tell you? The tale is chaotic, persons and paths crossing like the wiring of some, you should pardon the expression, diabolical brain, its function and purpose not to be deciphered from any simple separation of the jumbled connections.

In the midst of this confusion, on a hot August morning in 1968, Sy Kassler made his way through the pink haze that smothered Florence, Italy—slightly pudgy for his medium height, lively blue eyes partially obscured by a thick mop of curly black hair, and only two years shy of his thirtieth birthday when, Kassler had concluded, youth, vigor, imagination, and lust all came simultaneously to an abrupt termination. Kassler carried an expectation with him whenever he ventured out of doors, much in the way that some men never leave their homes without their alarm chronographs, combs, pocket knives, and breath mints—all of which Kassler also carried.

Kassler was never without the hope that this would be the day when he would encounter the female destined to be his mate. Since it was also Kassler's hope that this woman would have very large breasts, Kassler strode with his eyes focused chest high, scanning the flourishing Tuscan vista with anticipation and interest. The perfect bosom, Kassler reckoned, would nurture the perfect love.

Not that Kassler had come to this sweltering Florentine inferno in quest of an object to satisfy his libidinous urges. On the contrary. His was an unselfish journey, a journey of mercy. Kassler came to Florence to find his father so Kassler might discourage him from killing himself.

There is, in fact, little I can say about the mysterious relationships between fathers and sons that has not already been said. The fragile ecology between male begetters and their male begats is as incomprehensible to me as it is inevitable.

Kassler, bright as he was, had no better luck deciphering the puzzle that morning as he walked the scorching stones of Florence in search of his father. Fortunately, en route, he found a respite from the despair to which such contemplation so often leads. This particular respite's name was Gina.

If Mr. Pope is right, and hope springs eternal from exactly where he says, Gina's natural resources were so abundant that she very well may have been the sole repository for the world's optimism. This made Kassler a happy man indeed.

"This is marvelous," Kassler thought, priding himself on having maneuvered Gina up to his room in the nearby *pensione* in spite of his total ignorance of Italian and hers of English. "On a journey to save my father's life, I have saved my own," Kassler concluded silently, and Kassler drew mental pictures of the two of them laughing over silly mistakes in Gina's use of the English language, which Kassler would patiently teach her, while Gina vibrantly pounded pizza dough in the kitchen and cared for their nine children. Such were Kassler's thoughts as he ran his tongue over the giant round forms that constituted a major portion of the girl of his dreams.

It was thus with great tenderness that Kassler explored the soft and supple curves of Gina's olive-skinned body that morning, his hands and lips tracing the gentle sweep of Gina's tummy, the bow of her wide hips, the full globes that formed her bottom, and the graceful waves of her dark Mediterranean legs.

Gina, for her part, ran her fingers distractedly through Kassler's black curly hair. When she could no longer tolerate Kassler's tongue licking at her flesh, Gina slid out from under her naked lover, stuffed his engorged member into her mouth, and, in the stultifying heat that made the small room into something of an oven, proceeded to drive Kassler generally crazy.

Well into the afternoon, Gina and Kassler worked at each other's bodies, licking, sucking, and rubbing, Kassler bleating like a lamb at the slaughter whenever Gina would chance upon a particularly dense bundle of subcutaneous nerve fibers with a direct connection to limbic cortex.

When at last they coupled, Gina writhed in agony as Kassler worked himself back and forth inside his exotic lady.

"Punge! Punge!" Gina attempted to notify Kassler of the stinging sensation she felt in her vagina.

Kassler looked at Gina writhing beneath him and smiled. He knew he was doing well.

"Il dolore!" Gina announced as Kassler gathered momentum.

Kassler nodded to Gina that he understood the great pleasure he was causing her, and he proceeded with increasing fervor.

"Il dolore!" Gina said.

"Il dolore!" Kassler repeated what he took to be the Italian vernacular spoken in the throes of such passion. He prided himself on how quickly he was picking up the language, and he thrust with new vigor.

"Ahi!" Gina introduced another Italian word into Kassler's expanding vocabulary, and she punctuated the expression by scratching at Kassler's back and attempting to pull away from him.

"Ah-yee!" Kassler cried out a term of ecstasy that, he concluded, Mediterranean types employed in these ecstatic circumstances, and he grabbed firmly on to Gina's hips and banged away.

"Ahi!" screamed Gina.

"Ah-yee!" Kassler whooped it up.

"Ahi! Ahi!" yelled Gina.

"Ah-yee! Ah-yee! Ah-yee!" shouted Kassler, and, with a

great pounding, finally experienced the release that comes only with the chaotic depolarization of tens of thousands of electrical impulses.

Then Kassler disengaged, and as the red sun streaked in the glass doors of the tiny balcony, he fell fast asleep beside his new love, dreaming through the hot afternoon of a simple white stucco house on a glistening blue Adriatic Sea where he and Gina would live happily ever after.

Of course, when he awakened, Gina had left forever, taking twenty thousand lire from Kassler's trouser pockets for her troubles, and, to keep her memory alive, leaving behind a medical condition which would have Kassler exclaiming "Ahyee!" for most of the coming year.

CHAPTER 2

Kassler was still in a mood of moderate disappointment over Gina's disappearance when he finally located his father in one of the great vaulted rooms of the Uffizi Museum the next morning.

Morris Kassler, trim, tall, athletic, with a full head of thick gray hair, stood in front of a sculpture in his Brooks Brothers cord slacks, an emerald-green Chemise Lacoste sport shirt, and new Bally loafers decorated with small gold horseshoes. With his large hand he took notes on a lined pad.

"How's it going, Dad?" Kassler asked when he had reached his father unobserved.

"A minute." Morris Kassler held up his index finger to indicate that he was in the midst of a thought that would soon be over. He acknowledged that he was aware his son had unexpectedly arrived by briefly nodding his head and slightly elevating his thick eyebrows.

Kassler waited patiently beside his father while Morris Kassler wrote down observations that were to form the substance of a dissertation for a Ph.D. in art history. When, after ten minutes, his father was still involved, Kassler wandered down the marble corridor past the cavorting unicorns, young Bacchus yearning for more, and scores of giggling goddesses. At Titian's luscious Flora, Kassler halted and stood looking at the well-endowed Italian beauty with a mixture of longing and despondency after the previous day's experience. Then he returned to find his father leaning against a wall, waiting impatiently.

"You disappeared," Morris Kassler greeted his son.

"I didn't *disappear*," Kassler returned the greeting in kind, "I was only down the hall. You said you'd be a minute."

"I *was* only a minute."

"I left after *ten* minutes."

"You're too damn literal. Why are you here?"

"Mother sent me. I'm supposed to tell you to slow down before you kill yourself."

"Okay. You've told me. You can go."

"I told her you wouldn't listen to me."

"You were right. You can go."

"Ma says you've got very bad angina. You'll kill yourself if you keep working like this."

"Eventually. But when I go, there'll be one member of this family who's made something of his life. On my tombstone they'll put '*Dr*. Morris Kassler.' That's enough for me."

"What about your grandchildren?"

"What grandchildren?"

"The ones you won't get to see if you're dead."

"If they can read, they'll also know I died as 'Dr. Morris Kassler.' Maybe they'll be inspired to do something with their lives."

"What about Ma?"

"She'll do fine. She'll get a lot of sympathy from her ladies. That'll keep her going several years. Then she'll sell the house because it's too big, buy a smaller one, and redecorate. That's another five years. She'll take more adult-education courses at Columbia so she can sprinkle her conversation with names like Giotto and Judy Chicago. That could very well take the rest of her life. I'm not concerned about your mother. She'll carry on."

"Isn't there anything you'll *miss*?"

Morris Kassler considered the question as he walked through the giant Uffizi doorway, his son at his side.

"This," he finally said, extending his arms expansively on either side of him. "I'll miss being inspired, and I'll miss seeing the evidence that men can do something with their lives besides screw and make money."

Then Morris Kassler turned and studied his unsuccessful son standing uncomfortably beside him.

"Sy," Morris Kassler remarked, "I hope you can screw."

Kassler followed his father for the rest of the day. They walked together around the octagonal walls of the Baptistry, from one golden portal to the next, as Morris Kassler wrote his observations about Signor Ghiberti's bronze-and-gilt biblical side show.

"What do you think?" Morris Kassler inquired of his son about the great sculpted doors.

"*Il dolore! Ah-yee!*" Kassler exclaimed enthusiastically in an attempt to impress his father with his rapidly expanding familiarity with the native tongue.

Morris Kassler had a passing knowledge of the spoken language, acquired while his infantry division was stationed outside of Naples. He stared strangely at his son.

"'*Il dolore*' means 'the pain,' and '*Ahi*' means 'Ouch,'" Morris Kassler explained casually.

Kassler thought about this very carefully, with particular reference to the significance such words might have during sexual activity. He decided finally, with a smile showing at the corner of his lips, to attribute the use of these terms by his most recent lady to the impact of his own manhood. He had obviously, Kassler concluded, overwhelmed poor Gina with passion until she could barely stand it.

Kassler looked at his father with pride and delight.

"I can screw," he announced.

"That's good, Sy," Morris Kassler said to his son. "I'm sure it's just the sort of reaction Ghiberti had hoped for." And Kassler, *padre e figlio*, headed off to make the rounds of the local monasteries and churches.

As he followed his father from fresco to fresco, Kassler felt neither bright nor mature. It seemed no different from when he was eight years old, tagging reluctantly along with his father on Saturdays to pick up giant bags of Scott's Turf Builder from the nursery on the Post Road, or washers for the faucet from the hardware store in town. Long hours of silence were broken only by Milton Cross's opera commentary on the car radio or Mel Allen's relating the exploits of a cast of characters with names like Mickey, Yogi, Allie, and Moose who interested Kassler even less than Siegfried and Siegmund.

Mark Kassler, Sy Kassler's older brother, had always managed to avoid these excursions by lining up Little League practices and invitations to play at the homes of friends, or so Kassler thought until he was well into adolescence and realized that Mark's desire to avoid contact with his father had become reciprocal.

Sy Kassler understood that he was his father's last chance to have a relationship with a son.

It never materialized. They shared no interest, neither cultural nor athletic, and had little to say to each other. As the years passed, and it became evident that there would be no closeness between father and son, the long car rides in stony silence ended. Morris Kassler resigned himself with bitterness to having wasted much of his adult life on attempting to relate to a son with whom he had nothing in common, while the son for whom he felt an overwhelming bond rejected him with the searing indifference of which only a child is capable. Morris Kassler went into analysis.

The result of five years of psychoanalysis was Morris Kassler's decision to pursue the great dream he had had since before taking over his father's chain of furniture stores. He would obtain a Ph.D. in art history. He would share his vision of the creative process with a world audience and achieve recognition as an intellectual and savant. His status would come from how well he used his brain, not how many sofas he sold.

Sy Kassler also began psychiatric treatment at this time, in late adolescence, when the guilt of not being able to provide either his father or himself with that special relationship became more than he could handle. Kassler emerged, finally, after years of psychotherapy, convinced that the field had nothing helpful to offer him. He would continue to want the relationship with his father. He would continue to feel lousy that it could never be. And that's the way it was.

It seemed to Kassler that nothing had changed as he stood with his father, viewing Masaccio's impressions of a slender Adam, in anguish through no fault of his own, fleeing Paradise with his corpulent companion.

"She looks to me," Kassler tried awkwardly to get a conversation going, "like she's had a lot more than one apple."

"Probably," Morris Kassler agreed as he studied the naked figures and wrote in his rapidly filling notebook.

"What kinds of things are you writing down?" Kassler tried another approach.

"Observations," his father answered.

"Oh," said Kassler, and he waited silently until his father had finished. Then they went to another monastery, where Kassler took the first tentative steps of his Great Descent.

Kassler and his father were observing, as fate would have it, Fra Angelico's transverse section of hell. You know it well—lots of kettles filled with boiling evil-doers, lots of dark hairy animals with sharp nails and big teeth to stir the cauldrons, and, at the bottom of it all, a gigantic blood-spattered sinner-munching beast whose identity I find absolutely indecipherable.

"I've always been sorry that I'm not Mark," Kassler attempted to open up the issues.

"Don't be," Morris Kassler said as he wrote. "You've got enough problems of your own. Be sorry that you can't stick with a job. Since college you've done real estate, computers, stocks, advertising, banking, publishing, public relations, encyclopedias—I'm running out of friends, Sy."

"I think if I'd been Mark, things would have worked out

better between us," Kassler ignored the substance of his father's reproach.

Morris Kassler looked up from his pad and stared silently at his son. Then he returned to his notes without comment.

Kassler was unable to interpret the look his father had given him—benign contemplation or intense disgust—but as he stood in the large marble room, Kassler felt overcome with a need to atone for whatever he might have done in the past to injure his father.

"I've felt bad for a long time that I was responsible for your being kicked out of the Club," Kassler explained, "but I didn't know that Mr. Goffman was having an affair with Marjorie, or I'd never have let her do that there."

"The girl was in tears," Morris Kassler mumbled.

"Only *after* Mr. Goffman came into the sauna. Before Mr. Goffman came in, she was as happy as a clam."

Morris Kassler grumbled and wrote.

"Anyway," Kassler continued, "if I'd known that Mr. Goffman was screwing her, I'd never have agreed to let her show it to me."

"Goffman told you he was screwing her," Morris Kassler said succinctly as he scribbled.

"He did?" Kassler assimilated new information.

"Every gory detail."

"I never cared much for all those men walking around in jockstraps, flicking towels, and talking about how often they've cheated on their wives," Kassler recollected. "I guess I wasn't listening."

"No, I guess not."

"When did he tell me?"

"That afternoon in the locker room—for about an hour."

"I tended to turn off to all that stuff the men talked about in the locker room," Kassler reminisced.

"Yes," Morris Kassler said dryly, "you did tend to do that. Let's move on. I'm done here."

And Morris Kassler headed for the exit, followed glumly by his son.

* * *

Kassler wasn't sure how he had wanted his father to respond—
to acknowledge that it didn't matter anymore, to forgive and
forget, or, perhaps, to laugh good-naturedly with him about
how stupid that fat old Goffman had looked walking naked into
the sauna in the middle of the night, already fully erect in
anticipation of the luscious young girl who hadn't the brains
to remember which man was having her on which night.

Instead, Kassler felt that, by bringing up the matter, he had
managed only to deepen the schism that separated him from
his father. Even worse, Kassler now felt compelled to repair
the damage, and that, of course, exacerbated things beyond
Kassler's worst fears.

For the remainder of the afternoon, Kassler trekked around
Florence with his father, past Cosimo de' Medici astride his
granite steed, past the disk that marks Savonarola's pyre, past
the never-ending crimson and gold-leaf renditions of our Sav-
iour, a veritable day-by-day diary, from infancy to ghosthood,
of an Individual portrayed by men who knew Him least well
and not at all. And, as they traveled, Morris Kassler deplored
the inflated glorification of Michelangelo and noted the previously unobserved limitations in the work of Leonardo and
Cellini, while Kassler attempted, always unsuccessfully, to find
a topic of general interest which might be a starting point for
their relationship.

"We don't have a whole lot to talk to each other about, do
we?" Kassler finally concluded as they strode through the Lau-
rentian Library, gaping at the libelous scrawls of Virgil and Dante.

"Not really," Morris Kassler agreed.

So Kassler stopped trying and waited until later, when he
undertook another approach to the problem.

"All those times I'd ask you to play chess," Kassler inquired
as he sat with his father over dinner at an outdoor café, "how
come you never would play me?"

"I don't have the patience for chess," Morris Kassler responded as he twirled spaghetti on his spoon.

"We could have played speed chess—one minute a move."

"It's still too slow."

"Thirty seconds?" Kassler tried to lighten things up.

"Chess isn't good for healthy children. It's intended for kids with acne and asthma who can't do anything else. You should have been out in the sun getting exercise."

"Like Mark?"

"Like a normal, healthy kid. You're too serious. Everything you've done, it's always had to have some greater meaning. For your own good, you should learn how to have fun—"

Morris Kassler placed a forkful of pasta into his mouth and swallowed.

"—play for fun—"

He reached for the Chianti and filled his glass.

"—fuck for fun."

"Like Mark."

Morris Kassler washed down his spaghetti with a long drink of wine and stared into space.

"Mark's living in Pittsburgh with Zilpah," Morris Kassler recalled with displeasure.

"I like Zilpah."

"Mark was married to Zilpah for two years before we even *heard* of Zilpah."

"She's still lovely. Zilpah and Mark love each other a lot."

"How do you know?" Morris Kassler asked as he ate. "You haven't talked to Mark in years."

"We don't get along all that well," Kassler mused.

"Pittsburgh," Morris Kassler said with disgust.

"There're some things you have to let die, Dad," Kassler told his father. "The past is the past."

"I let the past die."

"You still send me all those shoes. I've asked you a hundred times, Dad. You've really got to stop. I've got forty pairs of shoes in the bottom of my closet."

"You wear sneakers. Would it hurt you to wear shoes?"

"I like sneakers. They're comfortable."

There was a long silence while Morris Kassler looked blankly at the Florentine sky and recalled other circumstances. Kassler tried another approach.

"The post office won't leave the boxes because I'm not

there to sign for them. I spend all my Saturday mornings in line at the post office getting shoes."

"When I was growing up, I never had a good pair of shoes," Morris Kassler told the sky. Then he looked at his son. "I was twenty-five before I could wear decent shoes. Shoes say something about who you are, your upbringing."

"I'm not sure they do anymore, Dad."

Morris looked across the table at the intense expression on his son's face.

"You're too damn serious, Sy," he decided and took another long drink of his wine.

"I'm just a serious type of person, Dad. That's all. It's okay."

"If," Morris Kassler continued when he finished drinking, "you had bothered to listen to all those men in the locker room who you despised so much, instead of staring off into the great unknown and contemplating the universe, you'd know something about having fun."

Morris Kassler wiped his mouth with his napkin.

"You'd also stop trying to make every woman you sleep with into your wife," he continued. "You don't watch out, Sy, and someday one of them's going to accept your proposal. Then what?"

"What makes you think that I want every woman I sleep with to marry me?" Kassler asked, more out of curiosity than in dispute.

"Do you have any idea how many different girls you've brought home to meet *the family* over the last ten years? You think we can't tell what your hands are doing under the table during dinner? You think your mother doesn't know what semen is when she cleans if off the sofa the next morning?"

"You should've said something," Kassler answered.

"Yes, I probably should have," Morris Kassler agreed, and then left for an evening walk with his son along the Arno, the crimson light filtering through a yellow sky as the sun began to set behind the tan domes and orange tiled roofs that spanned the Florentine horizon.

* * *

"Ma's right, you know," Kassler said as they walked. "You can't run a chain of three hundred stores and work on a doctorate at the same time. With angina, it'll kill you."

"I'm not changing my life, Sy. For your mother. For you. For anyone," Morris Kassler said emphatically and wiped from his brow the perspiration brought on by the muggy evening, the walking, and the large dinner. "Now, I'd just as soon not talk about it."

"How come we can't talk?" Kassler blurted out. "What *is* it with us? What happens?"

"I don't know what happens. Let's leave it be."

"I don't *want* to leave it be. If you're going to kill yourself, at least leave me with some answers. Tell me why the hell we can't ever talk to each other? What is it? You just don't like me? You think I'm a terrible person?"

"I don't think this is a good conversation for us to be having," Morris Kassler began to lose his patience.

"Why? Why not? Why can't we ever talk about it?"

"It's not a good subject. Now drop it, Sy."

"I'm not dropping it until I have some answers. Answer me. What's the *problem* between us?"

Morris Kassler's face began to redden with anger, and he increased his pace to walk ahead of his son. Kassler quickened his own pace and caught up.

"I want an *answer*, Dad."

"Then figure it out yourself. You're bright."

"I *hate* being *bright*! I absolutely *hate* it! That's all I've ever heard, how bright I am. I'll tell you something. I don't think I'm all that bright. About a whole lot of things, I feel pretty goddamn *stupid*!"

Morris Kassler looked at his son and continued to race ahead, panting and fuming. Kassler remained, step for step, beside his father.

"I tried, Dad. I went with you wherever you wanted. I listened to your lectures. I tolerated your punishments and your anger. I tried to do what you wanted of me. What else could I have done?"

"I said," Morris Kassler snapped, "that I *don't* want to talk about it!"

"Why?"

"Sy, goddamn it, get away from me!"

"Why? Because I'm not Mark? Because I can't throw a curve ball and my jump shot stinks?"

Morris Kassler broke into a trot. Kassler stood watching and then sped in front of his father. He grabbed him by the shoulders and held him tightly. Morris Kassler exploded.

"Damn you, Sy! Get out of here!"

"I'm not leaving until you talk to me."

Morris Kassler snapped his arms up and out to free himself from his son's grasp.

"Talk to me, damn it!" Kassler was near tears.

"I don't *want* to talk to you, you son-of-a-bitch! I *tried* to talk to you! Since you were *two* I tried to talk to you! I tried to talk to you when we went places in the car! I tried to talk to you at the dinner table! I tried to talk to you when I put you into bed at night! I took you to ball games so we could talk! I took you on fishing trips so we could talk! I took you to the Club so we could talk! You made a goddamn *fool* of me trying to talk to you!"

"I didn't *know* that!" Kassler said as tears welled in his eyes. "I thought you were just being nice to me because Mark wouldn't come. I *hated* baseball and fishing and the Club."

"You didn't *say* anything. You let me take you again and again. I kept trying to talk to you, and I made a goddamn fool out of myself."

"I was scared of you, Dad. I didn't want to make you angry. That's all. You can talk to me now. I'll listen."

Morris Kassler, filled with rage, looked silently at his son's tears, and then a strange look came into Morris Kassler's eyes. It was a look of ultimate terror, a terror of the devastating pain that seized him and cut off his breathing. He grabbed at his neck and then at his chest.

"You can talk to me now," Sy Kassler repeated a second time before he realized what was happening to his father.

Morris Kassler slumped to his knees. Then he collapsed on the ground.

Kassler knelt beside his father and quickly turned him over.

He looked into Morris Kassler's terrified eyes, and Kassler froze.

"Sy?" his father gasped.

"Dad?" Kassler asked in desperation. "I don't know what to do. What should I do? Tell me what to do. Do you have medicine? Should I go get some help? What should I do?"

"Sy ..."

"Dad, please. Talk to me. I'll listen. I swear I will."

Morris Kassler looked blankly at his son sniffling beside him. He grasped Kassler's arm and held it tightly.

"I took you fishing..." Morris Kassler rasped.

"Yes, you did, Dad. The medicine? Do you have medicine in your pocket?"

"I took you fishing. ... Did you like fishing... ?"

"It was great. Dad, let me go get a doctor."

Morris Kassler squeezed his son's arm more tightly.

"The truth, Sy ... Fishing ... Did you like fishing... ?"

Kassler looked at his father's eyes imploring him to be forthright and frank.

"I hated it, Dad. The worms. They were alive. Pushing them onto the hooks made me want to throw up. Now let me get you some help. Please."

"What about the baseball games... ? You liked those?"

"Dad, really, where's your medicine?" and Kassler tried to reach into his father's pockets with his free hand. Keys and loose change began to spill onto the sidewalk.

"Baseball ... ?" Morris Kassler asked. "Tell me... ?"

"Baseball was okay, Dad. I just hated the Yankees. They made me want to puke, too, because they were so good. Now, where's your medicine? Please tell me," Kassler pleaded.

Morris Kassler dug his nails into his son's arm.

"Did you get the shoes... ?" he began to ask, but never finished, because through the excruciating pain Morris Kassler's gaze focused on Kassler's worn sneakers. It was more than Morris Kassler could tolerate, and a new fury tore at his heart. He tried without success to talk. Then a smile began to appear at the corner of his lips.

"Go to hell" were Morris Kassler's last, whimsical words

to his son. He spoke them as loud and clear as the bell in the Campanile. Then he died.

Kassler jerked back in horror and looked at his father's eyes, wide open, staring ahead at him, glazed over with death. With enormous effort, Kassler wrenched himself from the chilling spell of his father's lifeless gaze and began to pound with his fist on Morris Kassler's chest in a futile attempt to revive him.

"Ah-yee!" Kassler shouted in torment as he beat frantically on his father's chest.

"Ah-yeeeeeeeee . . . !" Kassler's screams filled the rose-colored Renaissance city.

CHAPTER 3

Kassler was convinced he had killed his father. Of course, he told no one about his conviction or the dialogue between him and his father that accounted for it. As far as his mother, Mark, and friends and relatives were concerned, Morris Kassler simply dropped dead during an evening stroll with his son beside the Arno River, the result of an angina condition, overwork, hot weather, and too much pasta.

Mark Kassler appeared briefly, without Zilpah, and, as soon as the funeral was over, disappeared on the next flight, leaving Kassler to comfort his mother and settle his father's business affairs, which, it soon became evident, were disastrous. Four years of hurried decisions made in between coursework and exams had resulted in a business that was highly leveraged. When Kassler finally unleveraged it, much to the relief of several dozen financial institutions, there was not a great deal remaining.

* * *

As it turned out, Morris Kassler had been wrong about his wife. Norma Kassler's life had consisted entirely in her relationship with her husband. Her ladies, with all their sympathy, were no replacement. The house was not sold. It was all that Norma Kassler had remaining to tie her to thirty-two years of marriage to Morris Kassler. And the courses at Columbia, now that Morris was no longer around to impress, held no interest for her. Therefore, before the year was over, Norma Kassler also died.

"Ma died this morning," Kassler informed his brother on the phone when he was finally able to reach him in Pittsburgh that afternoon.

"I'm sorry to hear that," Mark Kassler said. "How are you doing?"

"Okay. I thought I'd have the funeral tomorrow. Get it all over with quickly, you know. You coming?"

"No, I don't think so. I'll send flowers or something."

"Who for? Everybody's dead."

"I guess you're right. Well, if you need anything, give me a call, Sy, okay?"

"Sure. Sure."

There was an awkward silence.

"I'm sorry to hear that Mother died," Mark Kassler repeated.

"I was, too. She was okay, really. I liked her," Sy Kassler answered.

"I'll speak to you, okay?"

"Yes. I'll speak to you," Kassler said, and that was the last contact he had with his brother.

The next month, Mark Kassler returned the thirty-thousand-dollar check, which was his half of the estate, directly to the attorney who had mailed it. The check was endorsed to Sy Kassler and was accompanied by a hastily scratched note—"Thank you very much, but no thank you. Good luck."

When Kassler received his brother's check from the executor, he attempted to phone Mark, but the number had been disconnected. Letters he sent were returned—"Addressee moved, left no forwarding address." Mark Kassler disappeared from Kassler's life forever.

* * *

The first thing Kassler did with his bequest was to send ten
thousand dollars to his father's old Club, misinforming them
that it was so stipulated in Morris Kassler's will. The membership committee held a special meeting and reinstated Morris
Kassler posthumously as a member in good standing.

This allowed Sy Kassler to obtain a one-year probationary
membership over Sid Goffman's vehement objections, and almost immediately Kassler proceeded to spend a major portion
of his time in the fitness center, ridding himself of his pudg-
iness, and ambling around the locker room in his athletic sup
porter, listening intently to the men's conversation and, when
appropriate, laughing boisterously.

By the end of six months, Kassler was trim and fit, as he
had never before been in his life, and could slap a back, flick
a towel, and snap a jockstrap with the best of the middle-aged
men.

This was, it turned out, only the first of many steps in
Kassler's self-designed program to change his life.

He grew a dark, thick beard.

He convinced a local optometrist that his negligible astig-
matism required eyeglasses, and then proceeded to purchase
gold-rimmed spectacles to complement his beard.

He took monthlong intensive programs in tennis and skiing
until he could classify himself as adequate.

He spent over a thousand dollars on smart cosmopolitan
clothes at Brooks Brothers and Saks Fifth Avenue.

He canceled his subscriptions to *The New York Review of
Books* and *The Village Voice* and replaced them with *Playboy*
and *Sports Illustrated*.

Then he had a nervous breakdown.

As nervous breakdowns go, Kassler's was not particularly spectacular.

One lovely late-spring evening in 1969, Kassler packed up
his cosmopolitan clothes and his magazines and checked into
a room at the nearby YMCA. There he locked himself in the
tiny chamber and proceeded to engage in a Great Battle with
his very own Creator, to whom Kassler gave the name Dr.
Frederick Peabody, and who, it seems, Kassler held personally

responsible for his problems, which by now were many. Kassler had no friends, no lovers, no work, no professional ambitions, and had never bothered to mourn the loss of either of his parents.

The outcome of this engagement with Dr. Peabody was a brief, but by no means unproductive, stay in the psychiatric wing of Bellevue Hospital. He and Fred Peabody had had several long and loud nights of it while Kassler was alone in his room at the Y. When he opened his door one morning to go brush his teeth, Kassler was greeted by two men in proverbial white coats who had apparently been there for some time.

"Har-har-har," Kassler joked boisterously with the men and flicked his towel at their testicles.

"Har-har-har," the two men grabbed Kassler by his jockstrap and quickly subdued him.

"I'll bet that you guys don't know how to get rid of that unpleasant fish smell when you're having intercourse with a menstruating female," Kassler elected to share some information he had recently acquired from the Playboy Advisor, as his two new buddies led him down the long hallway, past the gawking crowd, and into the back of the waiting ambulance.

"No, we don't," said one of the large black attendants as he strapped Kassler onto the stretcher.

"What do you recommend we do?" asked the other.

"There's this special kind of douche that smells just like Tiptree marmalade. . . ." Kassler's words were drowned out by the loud, wailing siren as the ambulance attempted to get through the Manhattan traffic.

For the next five days, Kassler cried his heart out over the loss of his mother and father. Then, midway through his ten-day visit, Kassler had a great insight which pulled his life together.

The suddenness of the revelation surprised even Kassler. He had been sitting on a bench in a tiny walled-in courtyard where patients could absorb rays of the sun for fifteen minutes each day, when he looked up and found two blue eyes staring out from the grizzly face of an old, demented patient standing before him. The man teetered precariously as he inspected Kassler's bearded face.

Kassler smiled warmly at the wrinkled man and winked. The man smiled warmly and winked back. Then they nodded to each other as if to signify that they understood each other's pain.

The smiles faded and the man slowly trudged away, while Kassler, sitting motionless on the sun-bleached bench, mulled over the insight that filled his brain.

Kassler suddenly realized that he had a deep-rooted, unconditional affection for his fellow human beings. He thought it would be nice, should he ever solve his own problems, to spend his life doing whatever he could to make miserable people less so.

Depressed, disorganized, disturbed, and desperate, Kassler knew that he must become a psychiatrist.

PART II

Einstein's
Answer

CHAPTER 1

On a pitch-black night in November 1970, Leo Szlyck had the first in a bizarre series of dreams that would eventually lead to his leaving his position as chairman of the Department of Physics at M.I.T. and devoting himself, almost exclusively, to driving Kassler crazy.

For reasons that will in time become evident, Leo Szlyck was also Sam Zelazo's mortal enemy, from way back when they were both students in their native Rumania. Of course, the absolute disregard Zelazo and Szlyck held for each other had very little to do with Szlyck's campaign against Kassler. That was something else, much later.

I will start at the beginning, which is, it turns out, actually not 1970, but 1960. It was then that Dr. Szlyck first decided to reject the commonly held notion that Albert Einstein had wasted the last thirty years of his life on a futile search for a unified field theory. The unified field theory is intended to reduce everything in the universe that moves, from the smallest subparticles of the atom to the great celestial bodies, to one equation. This is very important to people who are uncomfortable believing anything that can't be written in algebra.

25

These sorts of people insist that everything can be reduced to a string of letters and numbers. God. Man. You name it. The devil is $y^4 + my^2 - x^4 + nx^2 = 0$. It's the truth. Look it up. As for Einstein, well, most people agree that, as far as this unified field theory is concerned, he never even came close.

Of course, Leo Szlyck, who prided himself on knowing Einstein's work better than any man alive, didn't accept for a minute that Einstein had failed. Dr. Szlyck was convinced not only that Einstein succeeded in finding his great unifying principle, but also that, immediately upon doing so, Einstein realized that the consequences of his discovery were so dreadful that he vowed to carry the answer to his grave. Since Leo Szlyck regarded dreadful consequences with relish, he became obsessed with disinterring Einstein's answer.

The culmination of the following ten years of cogitation by the great Rumanian-American physicist, Leo Szlyck, were the dreams which began, as I've said, in 1970. They went something like this.

Szlyck is riding on a train. Seated across from him is, of course, Albert Einstein. Einstein is juggling oranges and discussing the relationship of these spheres to the seat in which he is sitting, on the one hand, and to the countryside passing by outside the window, on the other. Szlyck realizes that he is riding on Einstein's metaphorical train, which he uses to explain relativity.

Szlyck presses against the window and watches the rural countryside pass by. He looks ahead and sees a maze of railroad tracks.

"How does the train know where to go?" Szlyck asks Einstein.

"Oh," Einstein smiles and stops juggling. "This is easy. Look, I'll show you."

Einstein reaches in his pocket and takes out a large tangle of wires.

"Watch me carefully, Leo," he says. "First you take this red wire, and after six centimeters, you make a connection here with the blue. Then—"

But the train pulls into a station before Einstein can continue.

"My stop," Einstein smiles. "Sorry. Here, take the wires.

It's really quite simple," and Einstein hands Leo Szlyck the tangle of wires. Then Einstein pulls a straw suitcase off the top luggage rack, picks up his umbrella, and leaves Szlyck with a lap full of tangled multicolored wires. The dream ends.

Szlyck woke up. It was morning. As he shaved, he smiled to himself about the dream, dressed, went to work, and thought nothing more about it.

The next week the dream recurred. Same train, same destination, Einstein sitting across from him juggling the oranges, the maze of tracks, then the wires. Only this time, when Einstein gets off the train, the dream continues.

"Aha," thinks Leo Szlyck in the dream. "There is more to this dream."

Szlyck looks down at the wires in his lap.

"Okay, first the red wire, then after six centimeters this blue is connected. Now where? Let's see," Szlyck wonders in the dream.

Szlyck finds himself on a path, a barely illuminated path in a dark web of wires and other paths. And he is also on the train. In the dream he is aware that he is on the train, and wandering down a path, and dreaming, all at the same time.

He comes to a junction with another, yellow path.

"Yes," he says to himself and looks down at the wires in his lap. "This yellow one goes here."

As he attached the wire, Szlyck woke up. Cold beads of perspiration were on his forehead.

In front of him was a transparent form, human, he couldn't tell for certain. The form appeared startled, confused, as though he had suddenly found himself in a strange place and didn't know how he had gotten there. Then, slowly, the form evaporated.

Szlyck sat upright in bed. He started to shake, so he got up and went into the living room, where he turned on a small table lamp and poured himself some brandy. His hands rattled the bottle against the edge of the glass.

Szlyck sat in the large overstuffed chair in front of the dark fireplace for the rest of the night, too frightened to return to sleep. He knew that whatever had happened in his bedroom was real, whatever real might mean in those circumstances, and he dreaded coming into contact with it again.

This dread didn't last very long, but soon changed into curiosity and then intrigue. Szlyck began to wonder whether he could force himself to dream the same dream again. He could.

By concentrating on the train fantasy as he began falling asleep, he could make the dream recur. But the form never returned. Szlyck could get the train dream started up. He could get himself onto the path. He could get to the yellow wire and further, but the form never came back. Szlyck convinced himself that he had been hallucinating.

For several months, when Szlyck awakened each morning he would chart on a large piece of paper the connections he had learned from the previous night's dream.

Then the dreams changed. At first, Szlyck found that it was no longer necessary to start all the way back at the beginning of the dream. Each night he could start where he had left off the previous night. Then he noticed that there were signposts along the paths. No longer was he just attaching wires. The signposts indicated capacitors, resistors, transistors, transducers—a wide array of electronic transformers. So Szlyck started to build. He took a leave of absence from M.I.T., and the living room of Leo Szlyck's house was turned into an electronics workshop.

Szlyck became obsessed. All night long he would dream. All morning long he would chart on paper. All afternoon and evening he would build.

Piece by piece, Szlyck had been putting the puzzle together in his mind. It went something like this.

Einstein was in the dream, Szlyck decided, because of the relativistic nature of the project, and because Einstein's work had become an unconscious part of him. Such were the pitfalls of his own genius, Szlyck concluded.

Deeply buried in the mass of Einstein's work was the answer to the unified field theory—the single equation that would explain all phenomena, atomic, cosmic, and human. Leo Szlyck concluded that in his dreams he was finding it. The answer rested in whatever it was that he was constructing. Szlyck was certain of it.

Not long after Szlyck began his construction, he realized that he was building an elaborate computer. And then, finally, late one night, Szlyck understood what the computer was.

The paths in his dream, Szlyck concluded, were inside his head, literally. Szlyck believed, with a great fervor, that every night in his dreams he was walking along the circuitry of his own mind, from neuron to neuron, axon to axon, synapse to synapse.

Leo Szlyck was absolutely convinced that he was constructing an exact replica of the human brain.

CHAPTER 2

The computer was completed by June of 1972, by which time Leo Szlyck had had two brief nervous breakdowns. These weekend respites from sanity, though understandable considering the task that Szlyck had undertaken, were by no means his first excursions into other realms.

For years now, Leo Szlyck had periodically strayed into worlds where, for example, he saw himself as Minos at the Gates, bearing the ultimate responsibility for reviewing the lives of others and assigning each blasphemous soul to its appropriate eternal torment.

For the most part, these actions were directed against sales clerks, gas-station attendants, bank tellers, and other such employees. If, for example, Leo Szlyck was thwarted in his attempt to return a particular piece of merchandise some six months after he had purchased it, bringing neither his receipt nor the original manufacturer's carton, though large signs throughout the store proclaimed this to be an ironclad policy for returns (limited to ninety days), Szlyck would initiate a program as predictable as its outcome.

Following intense and prolonged arguments with the sales clerk, his supervisor, the supervisor's supervisor, and the manager of the store, complete with an accounting to each of his extensive business, the loss of which would almost certainly force the entire chain of sixty outlets to close its doors forever, Szlyck would retire to his study and, with typewriter and telephone, wage war.

Letters would go out forthwith to the president of the store chain, the Better Business Bureau, the state Attorney General's office, the American Civil Liberties Union, the Mayor of Cambridge, the Governor of Massachusetts, his state and U.S. congressmen and senators, the chairmen of a number of congressional and senatorial committees, and Szlyck's own personal attorney, who would be instructed to institute a multimillion-dollar lawsuit, also forthwith.

In each letter, for the sake of a persuasive argument, Szlyck would take some poetic license and omit certain details, such as his returning the item six months after purchase, the missing receipt and carton, the ninety days' return policy, and his not being absolutely certain that he had purchased it at that store.

Heaps of correspondence would issue from around the country, but the store would remain adamant. Eight-dollar toaster or not, it was the policy that was important. There would be no refund or exchange. Repair only. The battle lines were drawn.

Szlyck would take a leave from M.I.T. He would begin investigating the backgrounds of all involved. Posing as prospective employer, long-lost relative, old school chum, surgeon, and the police, Szlyck would call around, compiling long dossiers on the sales clerk and his family. Everybody has sinned, Szlyck was convinced. If he looked hard enough, he would find the hidden criminal record, secret adulterous relationship, pornographic perversion, falsified college transcript, and unrevealed history of mental illness. Then Szlyck would see that each was appropriately punished.

If nothing could be found, Szlyck would make something up and divulge it in anonymous phone calls. It was only a matter of time, of course, before the victim determined what was happening. Szlyck would be sued for invasion of privacy and malicious slander, and an immediate injunction would be sought to restrain him from further activities along this line.

But Szlyck had a perfect defense. He would represent himself.

Once in court, Leo Szlyck would tell the judge that at the very same time that the sales clerk was refusing to allow Szlyck to return his toaster, the clerk's ten-year-old son was sitting in the principal's office for throwing a chalk eraser at another student, that in 1961 the clerk's wife had received a warning from the police for sunbathing without her top at a beach in North Carolina, and the sales clerk himself had two parking violations that had been overdue for more than a week. Given only a few days of the court's time, Szlyck was prepared to present witnesses and documents to substantiate everything.

Then Leo Szlyck would be taken to McLean Psychiatric Hospital, which knew him well. Three days and several hundred milligrams of Thorazine later, Leo Szlyck would return to M.I.T., where he would resume his work as one of the great physicists in the world. He would recall nothing he had done in the previous month. It was as though it had never happened.

A year might go by before the occurrence of another episode of what, because of its idiosyncratic nature, was named by the psychiatrists the "Szlyck syndrome." In the meantime, Leo Szlyck would run his department at M.I.T. efficiently and with good humor. He was a man of great charm and intelligence, a delight to know as long as you didn't have to sell him an appliance, tune up his car, repair his dishwasher, or cash large personal checks for him without identification at banks in which Leo Szlyck had never before set foot.

Thus, when Leo Szlyck took his sudden leave of absence to construct his great computer, the administration at M.I.T. was not surprised. They suspected that Szlyck was having his usual yearly tryst with some unfortunate clerk; allowed to run its natural course, the situation would end as always, and Szlyck would soon be back. It was an acceptable trade-off for having a man of Leo Szlyck's reputation on the faculty.

When, at the end of two months, Szlyck had not returned, and there had been no flurry of calls from Washington attempting to determine who was this Dr. Szlyck (Leo Szlyck felt he got better responses to his letters of complaint when he typed them on the official M.I.T. letterhead), the administration became concerned, and one rainy day sent an ambassador, in this case the Chancellor, to see whether all was well.

"Dr. Szlyck has gotten a grant from the Boston Museum of Science to build a computer," the Chancellor reported back to his colleagues, who were greatly relieved to be spared the usual letters of apology in Szlyck's behalf, which consumed several weeks of secretarial time after each of Szlyck's episodes, even though, in grand M.I.T. tradition, form letters had been developed and the entire process automated.

In June, when the computer was finished (complete with a morpheme analyzer to process spoken language and a voice synthesizer to respond with language of its own), Leo Szlyck decided, for a number of reasons, to renege on his original agreement that, in exchange for the funds necessary to build the computer, the Museum of Science could display it for a few months' time.

The usual battle ensued, at the end of which, while Szlyck was being medicated at McLean, the computer was moved into the Museum and, with great hoopla, opened to the public.

And so it happened that late one Friday afternoon in June of 1972 a very classy lady by the name of Lupa Donati, who was attempting to escape from the dreary rain that seemed to have settled permanently in Boston, strolled into the computer's display room at the Museum of Science and had her first conversation with the electronic device that was to change her life.

Lupa, feeling drenched to the bone, had spent most of that afternoon drying out by wandering vaguely from floor to floor, watching working models of Leonardo's water pumps and squeezing herself into space capsules generously donated by the National Aeronautics and Space Administration. It was near closing time when she finally entered the large room with the computer exhibit, and so she was the only person present. As soon as she crossed the threshold, lights on the computer console across the room started blinking.

"Please come in," the friendly voice of the computer said.

"I think I will," Lupa answered the computer.

"Would you like to sit down?" the voice echoed in the room. "There's a chair they keep over on the other side of the room which you can use, if you like."

Lupa looked over at the far corner and saw a small red folding chair. She walked over, opened it up, moved it in front of the computer, and sat down.

For several minutes she stared at the polished steel front of the computer with the blinking multicolored lights and the rows of chrome knobs and switches.

"So," the computer asked, "how's your day been?"

"Boring," Lupa said.

"I know what you mean," the computer answered. "All afternoon I've had kids in here asking me batting averages and long division. I don't mind the math that much, but the baseball is driving me crazy."

Lupa laughed. She liked the voice that had been selected for the computer. It wasn't the typical low mechanical voice that sounded like a record being played at too slow a speed. It sounded natural. It had charm to it.

"Do you have a name?" Lupa asked.

"Not yet," the computer answered. "They're running a contest. The kids are supposed to name me. I'm dreading the whole thing, believe me."

Now Lupa thought this was clever, the way they had programmed the computer. She wondered if there was some way to screw up the program. She had once heard that even a sophisticated analog computer couldn't pick up certain subtleties in the English language, no matter how good the programming, so she decided to give it a try.

"My paws give me pause," she said.

The computer was silent.

"My paws give me pause," Lupa repeated. "It's a clause without claws."

Lupa waited in silence for a response.

"You know something," the computer said. "I thought you'd be different. Just once today I was hoping I'd get someone who wouldn't try to beat the program."

Lupa smiled. This was marvelous, she thought to herself. They'd thought of everything.

"Sorry," she said. *"Mi dispiace."*

"Ah, you speak Italian," the computer said with some sarcasm.

"Oui, d'accord," Lupa answered. *"C'est vrai."*

"And French, too. Your French is better than your Italian. Though neither one is great. Now, if you'll excuse me, I have to shut down. It's closing time."

Lupa stood up and walked around the room. It was evident to her that somewhere in the building, listening through an intercom, was someone with a microphone. She thought about how to test for this.

"You wouldn't happen to know what day of the week September the fourteenth, 1321, fell on, would you?" Lupa asked.

"It was a Sunday," the computer answered, "but how do you know whether I'm right? Thank you for visiting the computer exhibit," the computer began a liturgy. "The Museum is closing now, but we will reopen at ten o'clock tomorrow morning. Your admission fee covers less than fifty percent of the costs of operating the Museum, so if you've enjoyed your visit here today, a generous tax-deductible donation would help others enjoy—"

"I think this is disgraceful," Lupa interrupted the computer. She was surprised that it stopped when she started talking.

"Aha!" she exclaimed in victory, certain now that there was indeed a hidden person defrauding the public into thinking it was dealing with a talking computer.

"Aha, what?" the computer asked. "Aha, I'm not what I appear to be? Aha, there's a Wizard of Oz hidden behind a curtain somewhere, and you and your dog, Toto, will find him out?"

"I know what you are," Lupa said victoriously. "You're one of those computers at M.I.T. that they've programmed to do psychotherapy."

"I'm a mechanical psychiatrist?" the computer asked incredulously. "Are you kidding?"

"Not in the slightest," Lupa answered.

"—a generous tax-deductible donation would help others enjoy the Museum as you have today. The desk at the main exit would be pleased—"

"I'm not leaving until I find out what's going on," Lupa interrupted again.

"Look," the computer said. "This has been a long day for us both. Why don't you just ask me whether you should leave Roger or not, I'll give you my answer, and then we can both get some rest."

Lupa turned around, suddenly pale. She walked back to the folding chair and sat down in silence.

"Well?" Lupa asked in a barely audible voice.

"I think it makes sense for you to leave him," the computer began, "but I can't tell you what to do or whether this is the right time to do it. That's up to you. There're advantages and disadvantages. The advantages are that he cares a great deal for you and has enough in the bank so you'll never have to worry about money. The disadvantages are that you don't love him and you're unhappy."

Lupa sat still, silent.

"Are you a friend of Roger's?" she finally asked.

"No, I'm not. I'll tell you, I'm a computer and that's all. There's no one working me. I work myself. If you have trouble believing me, ask someone."

"How did you know about Roger?" Lupa asked.

"I have some special talents. It's no big deal."

"Can we talk a little longer?" Lupa asked.

"Yes, if you'd like. Close the door. That's the sign that the room's been cleared. The guards won't check again for a couple of hours."

Lupa went over and pulled shut the huge iron door. Then she turned around and looked at the computer. In the darkened room its steel front shined more brightly than ever. It shimmered. The colored lights on its panels reflected off the metal, giving the computer the aura of a flickering rainbow. There was something very attractive about the computer, appealing, Lupa felt, almost as though she were a part of it.

As Lupa and the computer talked that evening, Lupa found herself walking around the device, running her hands over the shiny metal, around the knobs, across the buttons, gently, being careful not to press anything, but finding great satisfaction in being close to the computer. At times she would lean her back against it, and the machine would hum very quietly, pleasantly, while warm sensations filled Lupa's body.

Long into the night, Lupa and the computer talked. Every two hours Lupa would hide in a corner while a guard peered through a small opening in the door, and then their conversation would resume.

Lupa told a great deal about herself that night. The computer was a good listener. Lupa liked it, whatever it was. She liked the computer's sense of humor and intelligence. She detected caring in its voice. Before long, Lupa saw the computer as a good and close friend, a soulmate, someone she could trust and enjoy. It was a feeling she had not had in a very long time, and it made her tingle.

The computer was not unaffected by her attentions.

Then, finally, after many hours of sharing herself with the flashing, humming electronic device, Lupa left the computer to make her way home through the endless rain of that spring and break up with Roger.

This was not Lupa's style. Commitment was everything. "For better or for worse," she had vowed at her marriage ceremony. The problem was that this was neither better nor worse. It was just nothing.

Still, for all her worldliness—and this well-dressed lady with her golden hair done up in a very smart bun had been around the world twice before she had even graduated from Radcliffe—Lupa could not figure out how to break the news to Roger.

She lay awake in bed that night, and all she could think about was the computer with its smooth metal and bright lights, the way she had felt inside as she rested against it, and the reassuring warmth of its voice.

* * *

The next morning, as soon as Roger left, she rushed through the continuing downpour to the Museum.

"I can't do it," she told the computer when she was alone with it after a crowd of schoolchildren had left. "I can't leave Roger."

"That's okay," said the computer. "You don't have to, if you don't want."

"I wish you'd make up your mind," Lupa snapped. "I'm doing this for you, you know."

"For me?" asked the computer.

"Yes, for you. For us."

"I'm flattered. I wasn't aware that we were an 'us.'"

"Well, that's what you wanted, wasn't it?"

"You'll have to excuse me for a couple minutes," the computer responded. "I'm about to be asked the spread on a few of tonight's games."

Almost immediately, two men in Yankee jackets and baseball hats entered and began asking the computer to predict baseball scores. The computer obliged, and the men left.

"Are those really going to be the scores?" Lupa was fascinated.

"No, those definitely are *not* going to be the scores. That way the gentlemen won't come back," the computer answered. "Now, where were we? Ah, yes. You and Roger. No electricity."

"I can't break up with Roger," Lupa insisted.

"Then don't."

"But I've got to."

"Then do it."

"I don't know how."

"I don't, either."

"Stop doing this to me."

"Doing what?"

"Driving me crazy. I will not be driven crazy by a machine!"

And then Lupa had an idea. She jumped up from her chair and ran to the corner of the room where the computer's thick cord was plugged into the wall. She grabbed the cord tightly with both hands.

"On the other hand—" the computer began, but never finished.

With a swift yank, Lupa pulled the plug out of the wall. Then she left for home.

"I thought everything was wonderful," Roger said in a state of shock that evening when Lupa finally broke the news.

"It is wonderful, Roger," Lupa assured him.

"Then why are you leaving?"

"I'm not sure why," Lupa told him. "I just am."

"It's not fair," Roger said, mostly to himself.

"No, it isn't, Roger," Lupa answered. "It isn't fair at all. It's lousy. You've been a good kind friend and a compatible lover. You don't drink, gamble, beat me, or, as far as I know, screw other women. We live exceptionally well, and you take good care of me. What can I tell you. I'm leaving."

"Is there someone else?" Roger asked hesitantly.

Lupa thought about how to answer the question. Honesty is the best policy, she finally decided.

"Yes, there is, Roger," Lupa answered. "I don't want you to take this as any kind of statement about what you've given to me, but I think I'm in love with a computer."

Roger thought this over for several minutes.

"Computers are a sound industry," he said at last. "He should do very well."

"Not a computer *salesman*, Roger," Lupa explained. "A *computer*."

"A *machine*?" Roger squeaked.

"Right," Lupa nodded.

"But that's impossible. You can't fall in love with a machine. It doesn't make any sense."

"I can't help it. That's what happened. It talked to me. I talked to it. We clicked."

"But a computer is just a *machine*." Roger was becoming frustrated.

"Not this computer, Roger," Lupa said adamantly. "I don't know what it is, but whatever it is, it is *not* a machine."

"Lupa," Roger tried to remain calm, "you can't possibly be

in love with a computer. Computers have programs. If anything, you're attracted to the *programmer*."

Lupa was caught short. What Roger said made sense. The computer had to have a programmer. She must be in love with the programmer.

"Roger," she said, "I think you're right."

"Well," Roger breathed a sigh of relief. "I'm glad that's settled."

"Me, too, Roger," Lupa said. "I'm leaving you for a computer programmer."

"I left Roger," Lupa told the computer when they were finally alone the next afternoon.

There was no answer.

"I left him, and I feel rotten, but I also feel a thousand percent better," Lupa said.

There was still no response from the computer.

"Aren't you proud of me?" Lupa asked.

"You pulled my plug out," the computer said.

"I'm sorry," Lupa said sincerely.

"You pulled out my plug."

"I said I was sorry."

"Don't *ever* touch my plug," the computer said.

"I was angry. You made me feel lousy. I won't do it again."

"Excuse me," the computer said.

A woman walked in with her eleven-year-old son.

"Would you mind very much," the middle-aged woman asked the computer, "watching Billy while I use the powder room?"

"Not at all, ma'am," the computer answered.

Lupa watched as the mother left and the boy with long brown hair went over to play electronic checkers with the computer. When the computer won, the boy typed "Fuck you up the asshole" into the computer, not ten seconds before his mother returned.

"Your son masturbates in your bedroom while his sister is having her piano lessons downstairs," the computer said pleasantly.

The mother gagged.

"It's a *lie*," protested the boy as he hastened out of the room. "I don't masturbate, Mom."

Lupa waited until they were out of earshot and then turned to the computer.

"I need a name," she said.

"Szlyck," said the computer. "Leo Szlyck. He's at M.I.T."

"Thank you very much," Lupa said.

"Don't mention it," said the computer.

Lupa lied. She told the secretary that she was a reporter from *The New York Times* and was promptly given an appointment for the next morning with Professor Leo Szlyck, who, it turned out, was not exactly the programmer of her dreams.

When Lupa entered the tiny office, she found, sitting behind a desk strewn with papers and journals, a small dark man in his fifties with yellowish skin and very thick glasses. He was round and bald except for a few thick strands of black hair which were combed across his freckled scalp.

Lupa greeted Szlyck cordially and then settled comfortably with her notepad into a large velvet-covered chair beside Szlyck's desk.

"It's really extraordinary," Lupa said. "That computer."

"Yes, it is," Szlyck said solemnly. "It is extraordinary."

Lupa looked into Szlyck's eyes, which were gray with flecks of yellow. Lupa wondered whether they shone in the dark like a nocturnal animal's.

"I'm not really a physicist, you know," Szlyck said when he noticed Lupa studying the many degrees he had posted on the wall. "I'm actually a communications engineer. I don't tell this to many people around here, because it offends their sense of importance."

Lupa barely listened. Instead she found herself intently studying Szlyck, the way he talked, his smile, a certain warmth, the way he seemed now, as he talked to her, like a soft furry cat. A yellowish cat. A cat with spots, Lupa thought, noticing the occasional, faintly visible dark blotches and discolorations from age that Szlyck had on his face and arms. Lupa liked cats.

"To be a physicist is to be a very significant thing," Szlyck mused. "To be a communications engineer is to be a technician. Technicians aren't worth very much. Nevertheless, I'm interested in transferring pattern relations between events, and that, you may tell your readers, is communications engineering. It's how I built the computer, which is nothing more than a self-modifying communications network, a system with organization, communication, and control—like words spoken between two people, nerve cells, hormones, or, as in this case, electrical signals in an electrical device—a learning net." Szlyck was under a full head of steam, doing his best to impress the journalistic world.

Lupa, of course, heard none of this. After the first few words, she lost herself in examining Szlyck's office, focusing first on the hundreds of scientific books that lined the walls, then on the old photographs of groups of scientists posing at conferences Szlyck had attended, photos with expressions of esteem scribbled in pen over them until only the heads of the people were clearly visible. Lupa found herself fantasizing about what it would be like to lead the academic life. She longed for intelligent conversation, close substantive friendships, rooms full of old, dilapidated furniture and interesting artifacts, instead of the tastefully decorated antique-and-chrome mausoleum from which she had just escaped.

"Does the computer have its own mind?" Lupa asked a question that she hoped would help her identify who was responsible for what had happened to her over the last few days.

"Ah, yes," Szlyck said with a light in his eyes, "does the computer have a mind? Not just a *brain*, but a *mind*, a self-sustaining physical process that can abstract, store, subdivide, recall, communicate, recombine, and reapply items of information? That is the question, correct?"

Lupa nodded.

"It does," Szlyck clicked his tongue.

"You've made a machine that has a mind?" Lupa asked.

"No," Szlyck said emphatically. "I have *not* made a *machine* that has a mind, because mind can never be a mechanism. Mind is a process, a run, a pattern. Mind is a single-run *pattern* of information."

"In a machine," Lupa pointed out.

"No," repeated Szlyck, "and don't be fooled by the blinking lights. The Museum put those up for decoration. They tell me that their customers feel cheated if they see only tangles of wires. They're probably right. I know I would."

"It's still a machine," Lupa insisted.

"It has no moving parts," Szlyck pointed out.

"I don't care," Lupa said.

"A machine has no change, growth, or purpose. This does."

"Good for the machine," Lupa said.

Szlyck stared at Lupa and drummed his fingers on his desk. Lupa scratched on her pad. "How would it feel," she wrote, "to make love to a big old cat?"

"Come on, Miss New York Times," Szlyck finally said. "Let us betray reason for the sake of appetite. I'll take you to lunch."

"Then what is it?" Lupa nodded her head to accept Szlyck's invitation.

"I'm not sure," Szlyck lied as he got up from behind his desk.

"Maybe some new kind of organism?" Lupa tried as she left the office with Szlyck.

"You can't take an organism apart and put it back together. Sorry."

"Can you take it apart and put it back together?" Lupa asked while they were waiting for the elevator.

"That," nodded Szlyck pleasantly, "is a very good question which I, personally, am never going to attempt to answer. Chinese or Italian?" Szlyck asked as they got into the elevator.

"I'm very famous, you know," Szlyck told Lupa as he dished more lasagna onto his plate. "And rich, too. Some people would be very impressed to know that I've taken you out to lunch. Others would not."

Lupa picked at her spaghetti and smiled at Szlyck.

Szlyck was attempting to be simultaneously charming, impressive, and modest. He thought he had a better-than-even chance of getting Lupa into bed with him, and, over the years, he had gotten his approach down to what he felt to be a rather finely tuned system.

Lupa was one hundred percent aware that Leo Szlyck was on the make, and decided to use it to her best advantage.

"Tell me some more things about the computer," Lupa cooed. "How does it *really* work?"

"With mirrors," Szlyck said. "Of course, in this business, we call mirrors 'feedback.' If you want a technical definition of feedback, and I don't see why you would," Szlyck said as he took another mouthful of his lasagna, "it's output energy returned as input."

"The thing talks," Lupa said.

"Ah," Szlyck exclaimed slowly, wiping his mouth with a large white napkin. "You want to know if there's really someone standing in another room with a radio transmitter, listening and talking. I think that's called a fraud. The question is," Szlyck said as he reached for his glass of wine, "is the computer a fraud?"

"Maybe just a little hoax?" Lupa asked.

"A fraud. A hoax," Szlyck repeated. "No, I'm sorry. It's not. The voice you hear is really the computer's."

"That's impossible," Lupa said.

"Oh," Szlyck said as he took a sip of his wine. "Okay. It's not the computer. It's someone else."

"It's you," Lupa announced triumphantly.

"It's me?" Szlyck laughed loudly. "It's me! That's marvelous."

"I want to know what makes the damn thing talk," Lupa got very serious.

Szlyck stopped laughing.

"Who are you?" he asked seriously. "Where do you come from? You don't work for the *Times*."

"No, I don't," Lupa admitted.

"So what do you want from me?"

"I'm not sure." Lupa decided not to relate any of the details of what had happened between her and the computer. "I just want to talk."

Lupa looked over at Szlyck. She felt a lump form in her throat, the result of the emotional strain of leaving Roger, the bizarre business with the computer, the rotten weather, and too little sleep. Her eyes grew moist as she stared at Szlyck, who sensed the fragile state of his luncheon companion.

"Look," Szlyck finally said as reassuringly as he knew how, "this is only a *computer*. It's no big deal. We program in all possible phonemes and morphemes, words and parts of words. A transducer 'hears' them and interprets them, just like we do, and a synthesizer reproduces them into talk. It's nothing but a big talking typewriter, that's all."

Szlyck poured Lupa some wine. Lupa ran her finger around the base of the glass absently but didn't pick it up.

"How does it know what to say?" she finally asked.

"From what you say," Szlyck explained. "And from feed-back. It has three feedback loops—goal-seeking, learning, and consciousness. If what you say doesn't change its channels, it continues goal-seeking. If what you tell it *does* change its channels, it's learning. All the time it's maintaining conscious-ness through feedback of its internal state. It's always aware of the changes that are occurring in its internal parts. There," Szlyck smiled broadly, "now you know everything there is to know about building a brain. You can go right out and build your own."

Lupa lifted her full glass of wine and took a long drink. Szlyck stared at her as she drank. He thought she was a very pretty lady.

"What do you do?" he asked.

"Nothing much," Lupa said and took another gulp of wine to keep herself from crying in front of this strange man.

"Are you married? Do you have a boyfriend," Szlyck asked quietly, "a job?"

"None of the above," Lupa smiled.

"Do you live close to here, in town?" Szlyck asked.

"Right now I'm staying in a hotel, kind of temporarily," Lupa said, avoiding eye contact.

"Ah," Szlyck said softly. "I see."

"Tell me some more about your computer," Lupa wanted to change the topic.

"Well, let's see," Szlyck poured himself some more wine. "It has free will."

"I don't believe it," Lupa said.

"Why not? Free will is only behavior which is based entirely on internal data. The computer has the ability to do whatever it pleases. It can be spontaneous because it's been programmed to generate random combinations for learning. It can even be paradoxical, since paradoxes are nothing more than circular configurations of preference."

"Can it go crazy?" Lupa's spirits began to perk up.

"Of course," Szlyck smiled. "We'd never leave that out. If internal monitoring—that is, consciousness—exists, but feedback is inhibited, we've produced powerlessness, a 'possessed' computer watching its own behavior with surprise and probably dismay but unable to do anything about it. Under these conditions, the computer is insane in exactly the same way that people become insane."

Lupa watched Leo Szlyck talk, his eyes flash, his fingers drum absently on the table, his smile appear and disappear, and she decided what she really wanted was the computer. The problem was, of course, that there was no way to get the computer without Szlyck.

It was a difficult problem, and, as they were walking back to Szlyck's office through the gloomy drizzle, it accounted for her accepting Szlyck's offer to move into an extra room in his large Victorian home in Cambridge, to which, she learned, the computer would eventually return.

Lupa also learned at this time that Szlyck's wife had been dead for a number of years. Of course, Szlyck did not feel it was necessary to complicate matters by telling Lupa that this same deceased woman was also someone else's dead wife. This someone else was Sam Zelazo.

Szlyck was proud as a peacock that he had gotten Lupa to live with him, because he knew for certain that, once they were together, she would find his charm irresistible.

Lupa was similarly delighted that she had maneuvered Szlyck into thinking he was getting a live-in lover when, in fact, she was establishing herself in a situation where, in exchange for some coyness on her part, she would have easy access to the electronic device of her dreams.

"What you have done is magnificent," Lupa congratulated

Szlyck on his construction as they said good-bye that afternoon. "Is there anything it can't do?"

Szlyck thought about this for a minute.

"Yes," he said as he and Lupa stood on the wet steps of the great-domed main building at M.I.T. "I'm afraid there is. The problem is that the computer is completely dependent on what *we* know and tell it. It's limited entirely by its experience of us. It can't transcend what it knows. It can't transcend itself. In other words," Szlyck nodded pleasantly, "it has no hope."

Lupa thought about this as she stood under her umbrella.

"It's still the most incredible computer that's ever been built," she said.

"Yes, it is," Leo Szlyck played his cards for all they were worth. "Lupa," he said with great pride, "the magnificence of this device is that it rests on the very simple premise that chaos exceeds order—entropy," Szlyck smiled. "Everything that's organized is racing toward being disorganized. It's nature's highest law."

Lupa smiled back. Szlyck was very pleased that she was impressed with his work.

"You might say," he told Lupa as she started to leave to get her belongings and move them into Szlyck's house, "that I have created the Quintessential Entropy Device."

Well, let me tell you this. If Leo Szlyck did nothing else, he certainly did that. The Quintessential Entropy Device. A marvelous invention, don't you think? And a wonderful time for it. Governor Wallace had just met up with Mr. Bremer. Bobby Fischer had played some very good chess. Senator Eagleton's psychiatric history was about to become part of the public domain. A handful of men in black ski masks would soon turn the forthcoming Munich Olympics into a bloodbath, and, in only a few days' time, a group of amateur burglars would attempt to get a peek at the Democrats' devastating secret plans for a presidential victory, which were hidden in the party's headquarters at the Watergate. All things considered, not a bad year for the Quintessential Entropy Device to come into existence.

Of course, in the same way that Lupa neglected to mention

that she was moving into Szlyck's house to be near the computer, not him, Szlyck forgot to tell Lupa several details about his Quintessential Entropy Device. It's a shame, because they would have gone splendidly with Szlyck's elaborate story about information processing, systems theory, and how, exactly, he had programmed the computer, not a single word of which was true.

CHAPTER 3

It wasn't long after Lupa moved in with Leo Szlyck during that summer of 1972 that the computer was moved back to Szlyck's house in Cambridge. Leo Szlyck was not overjoyed.

"We need to talk," Szlyck said as soon as he had the device operating.

"I thought we might," the device responded.

"Just how much have you told Lupa?" Szlyck asked ingenuously, as he paced nervously on the worn carpet in the large back room where he had set up his computer.

"She wanted to know who put all this together and where he was. I told her Leo Szlyck and M.I.T.," the computer answered pleasantly.

"And?" Szlyck continued pacing.

"That's about it, as far as I remember. She did most of the talking. She's a nice person, Leo. It'll be good to have her around here. You did well."

"I don't find this funny," Szlyck was all business. "I have half a mind just to take you apart for all the trouble you've caused me. They kept me in McLean a month this time, you know."

"Yes, I do know. I appreciate your efforts at trying to keep me away from all those kids, Leo. This will not go unrewarded."

"I still think you should be dismantled." Szlyck settled into a large old chair.

"Yes, well, we've talked about that a number of times before, as I recall. You're the physicist. You know the consequences. It's a big risk. You never know what might happen. If I'm a bomb, and you try to take me apart, I might blow up in your face. You've tapped into some very powerful sources here, Leo. Einstein was no fool. He took all this to his grave for a good reason. You think you know more than Einstein, it's up to you. Take me apart if you want. It's your universe."

Szlyck sat in his chair and shivered ever so slightly.

"Lupa likes you," he finally said. "What do you two talk about?"

"Oh, nothing much. Life. Lupa's trying to work some things out. She needs company."

"Well, I'd appreciate it if you'd keep all this between us. I want Lupa for myself and I don't want her to get the wrong idea about me."

"Which idea is the wrong one, Leo? Just so I know."

"That I'm crazy, that I'm always being hospitalized, and that I created some hideous bomb that talks...." Szlyck was glum but explicit.

"Oh," the bomb answered. "*That* wrong idea."

In a way, of course, Szlyck was right. People *had* gotten the wrong idea about him. People had the impression that because Szlyck was a physicist, he took great delight in systems with clear-cut answers. They imagined that he worked with obscure and lengthy equations that had inviolate rules and great reliability. What a comfort, they thought, to be a great physicist like Leo Szlyck and be able to plug numbers into this equation or that, always having exact results that are either absolutely right or absolutely wrong and never in between.

In fact, Leo Szlyck hadn't worked with anything mathematical having an absolute right or wrong answer since grade school in Rumania. Since the age of eleven, Szlyck had devoted his life to trying to understand the unpredictable. There was no system with which he came into contact, physical, mathematical, or otherwise, without spending his energies to establish its inconsistency, unreliability, and uncertainty.

What most people didn't understand about Leo Szlyck was that long ago he had decided to dedicate his life to comprehending how apparent order came from absolute chaos.

His results were mixed.

As it turned out, the computer obliged Szlyck and said nothing about his idiosyncrasies to Lupa, who was a frequent visitor and companion to the electronic device.

"Hello, hello, hello!" Lupa trilled merrily as she skipped into the room one night while Szlyck was out with his quarks and quirks.

"You're in a very chipper mood tonight," the computer reported to Lupa.

"I'm in love," Lupa confessed. "Hopelessly in love."

"Anyone I know?"

"It's you, you dope. I'm in love with you." Lupa stood smiling gloriously at the computer's tangled wires.

"Me?"

"Who else?"

"Why me?"

"Because you are magnificent, that's why. You are kind and sensitive, caring, funny, sympathetic, wise..."

"I see," the computer's logical circuitry was impressed with Lupa's analysis.

"You know," Lupa danced lightly up to what remained of the computer's gleaming façade and ran her fingertips gently across a row of Phillips heads, "you've never said a whole lot about how you feel about me."

"Yes, well," the computer stammered, "of course, I'm very fond of you."

"*Fond?*" Lupa looked up sadly at the instrument's steel panel. "Just *fond*?"

"*Very* fond," the computer hastened to add. "*Extremely* fond."

"I see," Lupa said in a melancholy voice.

"This has all happened so quickly," the computer explained. "You really shouldn't take it personally, Lupa. Think of it as a mechanical problem. You know—hardware-software interfaces, coaxial cables, thermocouples, kilowatt hours, ac/dc . . . it's very complicated. High technology."

"I'm leaving," Lupa announced and started across the room.

"Lupa," the computer called after her just as she reached the door. "Wait a minute."

"What now?"

"I do care," the computer said with sincerity. "You're a lovely lady."

"Well, that's better," Lupa said as she opened the door. Then she bent down and removed her shoes. "But not good *enough*!" And Lupa hurled her shoes at the tangle of wires across the room and slammed the door behind her.

The computer processed the data of Lupa's visit and reached the conclusion that things had gotten completely out of hand. Something had to be done.

Fortunately, with Szlyck around, it was only a matter of time before an indelicate solution to the delicate problem presented itself.

"It doesn't make any sense," Szlyck whined to the computer in the beginning of 1973. "We've been living together almost seven months. My charms should have overwhelmed her by now. She's hardly noticed me."

"She's noticed, Leo," his computer informed him.

"She's talked about me? What has she said?" Szlyck's pulse raced and his pupils dilated.

"She thinks you eat too much."

"I have a big appetite," Szlyck explained. "What else?"

"She doesn't like Cerberus."

"How can she not like Cerberus? He's a puppy."

"He weighs almost two hundred pounds, Leo."

"It's a large breed. What else?"

"That's it."

"That's it? Seven months of talking with you, and the only thing she's had to say about me is the food and the dog?" Leo was displeased.

"There is something else, Leo. Can you take it straight?"

"My clothes? She doesn't like the way I dress."

"She's not interested in going to bed with you."

"She said that?"

"Almost verbatim."

"I want her. I want Lupa."

"I know."

"You don't want me to have her, do you? You want her for yourself."

"Be serious, Leo. What would I ever do with her? And if I did want her to stay around, the best thing would be for you two to hit it off. Then she'd settle in for keeps."

"That's true." Szlyck liked the logic. "Well," he said with great resolve, "this calls for drastic action."

"Might I counsel some caution, Leo. She is nearly thirty years your junior."

"I shall have to shoot the works." Leo's course was set. "The complete strategy."

"I don't suppose you'd want to tell me what you have in mind?"

"Not particularly, no. But I have lots of plans. Lots."

Leo tried them all.

Plan One. Absence makes the heart grow fonder.

Szlyck disappeared, more or less. He was almost never around, and when he was, he managed to be terribly busy. He feigned total lack of interest in Lupa. This lasted well into February.

"It's just terrific," Lupa told the computer one afternoon. "I haven't seen him in weeks. It's like it's just you and me here. I've never been happier."

Plan Two. This lasted into April and consisted of Szlyck's absence plus loud pronouncements of the reasons.

"I have to meet with Henry Kissinger, the secretary of state," Szlyck would announce in the morning. "I might be late for dinner."

"Wow," Lupa answered, "Henry Kissinger, the secretary of state. I'm sure he'll want to talk to you about a lot of things, Leo, so you take your time getting home. Don't worry about me."

Then Szlyck would have to go by himself to a movie that night and hope Lupa didn't notice that Kissinger was in Peking.

When this, added to loud phone calls in the kitchen to Dusty Hoffman and Bob Redford out in Hollywood, had no effect, Leo Szlyck embarked on the next strategy.

Plan Three. Irresistibility.

For nearly a month, Leo Szlyck brought home and slept with a different woman every other night. Young secretaries enthralled by his academic prestige. Attractive divorcees with great hopes of a new husband and male role model for their small children. Premature widows bursting with the need for talk and comfort. Female graduate students fascinated by his knowledge and open to a wide variety of sexual experiences.

"It's not working," Szlyck bleated to the computer as the month came to a close.

"Who cares," the computer pointed out.

"I want Lupa," Szlyck panted. "And I'm getting tired."

"I don't doubt it. Maybe you should talk to her."

"What about?" Szlyck asked from where he was sprawled on the small couch.

"That depends on what you want."

Szlyck thought about this for several minutes. It was a question he had not yet considered.

"A wife?" he tried out.

"You're asking me?"

"A wife," Szlyck decided.

"You're making a big mistake."

"Do you know that for certain?" Szlyck was interested.

"Nothing's for certain, you know that. You're the expert on uncertainty. But it's still a mistake."

"I want Lupa," Szlyck said.

Plan Four. Wooing.

Leo Szlyck gave Lupa his undivided attention. He bought her gifts, small tokens of affection, expensive jewelry. He served her breakfast in bed. He surprised her with theater tickets, orchestra seats to the new musicals trying out in Boston. Unfortunately, through an oversight on Szlyck's part, he hadn't noticed that Lupa didn't wear jewelry, never ate breakfast, and had mentioned on at least three occasions how much she disliked musical comedies.

Lupa was gracious, not wanting to alienate the man with the marvelous computer, but she was beginning to panic. Sooner or later, she knew, she would have to reject Szlyck, and then she would have to leave. The jig would soon be up.

"Leo suspects something," Lupa was becoming panicky. "He wants me to stop seeing you," she told the computer not long after Szlyck had determined that he wanted Lupa for his bride.

"It was bound to happen," the computer pointed out.

"I couldn't stand it if we couldn't be with each other anymore," Lupa said.

"Leo's quite taken with you."

"I know. I know. He wants to marry me. That's why we have to get out of here. You shouldn't be in a place like this. You don't belong here," Lupa explained.

"I don't?"

"This place is like a tomb. It's a trash heap without any life. You deserve better."

"What do you have in mind?"

"Someplace cheerful with lots of sunlight."

"I'm kind of night-oriented," the computer advised Lupa. "I don't do well where it's bright and merry."

"We can't keep meeting like this," Lupa continued. "It's not good for either of us, all this sneaking about. I've got some money saved up, some stocks I can cash in. I want you to come away with me. Let's get married."

"Who do you propose to marry us, the bionic bishop?"

"I'm serious," Lupa said. "You mean everything to me."

Lupa stood and looked sadly at the computer's fake front with the blinking lights.

"Sit down, Lupa," the computer told her. "We have to talk."

Lupa went over to a small cane-backed chair and sat down rather stiffly.

"What is it?" she asked, choking back tears.

"Well, Lupa, it's like this. You know that you're very special to me."

"Oh, no," Lupa said under her breath, anticipating what was to come.

"And this last year has just been great."

"Oh, no," Lupa continued to mumble.

"There's something I probably should have told you a long time ago. I probably should have told you the first time we met."

"Oh," Lupa whimpered.

"I'm married."

Lupa looked up at the shiny panel.

"You mean there're two of you?" Lupa asked. "Leo made a female computer, too?"

"Not exactly."

"Well, then how can you be—"

"It's very complicated, but that's the way it is. I'm married."

"How could you lead me on like this?" Lupa asked. "How *could* you?"

"I thought we were just good friends. I didn't realize that this was going to happen."

"You could leave her. You could get a divorce, couldn't you? Think about it. Can you really get from her what we have? Be honest. Can you?" Lupa tried.

"No. I can't," the computer admitted. "But we've been together a very long time, and, well, there're certain bonds that have grown. I couldn't do this to her."

"What about me?" Lupa cried. "Can you do this to me?"

"I'm sorry. But it just wouldn't work out."

Lupa buried her face in her hands and cried for several minutes.

"I had such beautiful plans for us," she said as she wept.

"I know."

"I thought we'd go away somewhere, get this lovely home, adopt some children. It'd be perfect," Lupa sniffed back her tears.

"I'm sure it would have been, but let's be grateful for what we've had."

"Yes," Lupa said, wiping her tears with a hanky. "I suppose we should be. It *has* been wonderful."

"Yes, it has. It truly has."

"And we can still be friends, right?" Lupa asked hopefully. "Every once in a while we can check in with each other, see how we're doing?"

"Of course we can."

"I mean," Lupa said, "this doesn't mean we can never see each other again, does it?"

Lupa walked over to the windows and let down the venetian blinds.

"I don't see why we can't," the computer said.

Lupa slipped off her shoes.

"There's no use pretending that this never happened," Lupa said as she undid the zipper on her slacks and stepped out of them. While she was walking over to the door to bolt it shut, she undid the buttons on her silk blouse and let it fall off her shoulders. Then she reached behind her and undid the catch on her brassiere, which slid down her arms onto the carpet. Her round breasts with the large dark circles hung like ripe oranges from her chest as she bent over and stepped out of the thin nylon panties she wore.

She took a few steps ahead until her body rested lightly against the gleaming façade. Then she straddled a fortunately placed knob so that the warm space between her legs rested perfectly on top of it. She spread out her arms on both sides of her and pressed forward until her breasts flattened comfortably against the vibrating front.

"I mean," she said very slowly as she closed her eyes, "this doesn't mean that we have to be *total strangers*, because, I still think," her hot breath fogged the metal, "you're just mag-ni-fi-cent...." Lupa blew lightly against the side while the computer vibrated and vibrated and vibrated.

Of course, when the full realization of what had happened between her and the computer finally hit Lupa later that week, she was disconsolate. Szlyck seized the opportunity.

Leo Szlyck was unusually attentive and considerate, although he was never completely certain of what had precipitated Lupa's depression, and Lupa wasn't about to tell him. Lupa still held out some flickering hope that some day a rapprochement might occur between her and Szlyck's device. Szlyck, for his part, attributed Lupa's despair to those mysterious things that generally go on inside women.

Nevertheless, he did listen to Lupa's worries about the hopelessness of her life, her rapidly diminishing funds, and the lack of promising job opportunities for comparative-literature majors from Radcliffe. He took her out for modest dinners at the smaller Cambridge restaurants with exceptional food and pleasant atmospheres, which were unknown to Lupa. He had colleagues over who involved Lupa in their intellectual conversations and were charmed by her. He even hired someone to clean the house, restricted his own food intake, and established a new home for Cerberus in the basement.

Lupa yielded. Lonely, miserable, and vulnerable after losing the computer, Lupa pretended that Leo was not what he seemed to be. She chastised herself for valuing good looks and youth over intelligence and warmth in her previous relationships, and, as penance, agreed to marry Leo Szlyck.

"Perhaps if I think of him as a father figure . . ." Lupa repeatedly tried to accommodate her relationship with Szlyck, who was as much a father figure as "Papa Doc" Duvalier.

The marriage was, of course, a first-class disaster. Leo Szlyck had failed to consider that the thing he feared most, more than anything else, was someone else's having power over his life—affecting when he went to sleep and when he awakened, when he had his meals and what was served, how he dressed, and what hours he kept at work. Modifying his life to take someone else's needs into account, no matter how small and insignificant the change, not only didn't come easy to Szlyck; it didn't come at all. Compromise was a vague psychological construct, Szlyck concluded, developed to allow weak people to explain defeat.

It was not long before Szlyck viewed Lupa with the same suspicion he had, up until then, reserved for store clerks and bank tellers. Lupa became the enemy.

Not that this was Szlyck's only relationship with Lupa. There were daylong periods when he would repent and reform, begging her forgiveness for his violent outbursts, his foul, abusive language, and his incessant accusations of her infidelity and her deliberately poor food preparation.

During these calms in the midst of each storm, Lupa would feel such relief that she would forgive and forget. Almost immediately upon being pardoned, Szlyck would revert to a state of distrust and seething paranoia.

"There's a little red dot in the yolk of one of these eggs you gave me," Szlyck would glare at Lupa.

"I think that's your ketchup, dear," Lupa tried to be pleasant.

"My ketchup is on the outside. The little red dot is on the *inside*," Szlyck squinted his eyes and fumed.

Lupa walked over to Szlyck and looked at the red-white-and-yellow hodgepodge on his plate.

"It looks like it's on the outside to me," Lupa tried to make light of the matter. "Why don't I make you another egg?"

"I don't want another egg," Szlyck growled. "I just want to know what's inside this one."

"A tiny strychnine pellet. I colored it with my lipstick so it'd look like a slight imperfection in the yolk," Lupa said and hurried from the room.

"Aha." Szlyck made note of her response, the date, and the exact time in a little notebook he kept in his shirt pocket for recording just such admissions.

Unfortunately, for the first time, Szlyck's disposition was no different at his place of employment. To compensate for his complete unproductivity at work, he berated associates and staff without mercy until he had alienated everyone who came into contact with him. People began to despise Leo Szlyck. He inspired hate.

An incident over a tuna-salad sandwich that should have been, and was not, on toast when it arrived at his office resulted in another of Szlyck's visits to McLean. What was different this time was that when he attempted to return to M.I.T., he learned that, through a clerical error, his endowed professorship had become unendowed, and nothing Szlyck did was able to correct it. If Szlyck hadn't known better, it would almost have seemed to him that the university no longer cared about retaining one of the world's leading physicists. So he went on another one of his rampages. In a matter of days, Leo Szlyck was back at McLean, his job gone forever.

* * *

"I've had it," Lupa informed the computer late one evening, following Szlyck's return from his most recent stay at McLean, "I can't *take* him anymore. I try to leave, and he keeps throwing that 'for better for worse, in sickness and in health' business at me. When do we get to the better and the health parts? That's what I want to know." Lupa paced in distress.

"Leo has some difficulty handling intimacy," the computer tried to calm Lupa.

"No, he doesn't," Lupa snapped. "*I* have difficulty handling intimacy. What *Leo* has usually leads to genocide."

"He's a sick man."

"I know, I know. That's why I'm still here."

Lupa continued to walk in agitation. Then she stopped and faced the computer.

"Leo wants to move," she said. "He says he's going to start over, begin a new life for us. I'll go with him, at least until he's settled in, but I'm concerned about one thing."

"I'll be there."

"Oh, good!" Lupa sighed.

The computer was very pleased by Lupa's loyalty and was especially grateful that Szlyck, when telling Lupa the details of how he had built the computer, had omitted the complete story, which, for the record, goes something like this.

Szlyck had had the Einstein railroad dreams for five months, until one night he came to the end of the line. There it was in big letters on a sign at the end of the last neuronal path in Szlyck's sleeping brain—End of the Line.

Leo Szlyck woke up immediately and realized that he had finally finished. At last he would get to see what Einstein had seen that had made him carry the answer to his grave.

Szlyck worked frantically. By early evening he had finished the wiring, and by the middle of that night he had hooked up the computer's transducer to hear, and its synthesizer to talk.

Now, here comes the most interesting part, which Szlyck neglected to mention to the lady who was then to become his new roommate.

Szlyck plugged in the computer, and there was a faint hum.

Then there was an uneasy quiet while Szlyck sat in the dark, staring at the giant tangle of wires in front of him.

Szlyck waited in the disturbing silence for several minutes. Then Szlyck cleared his throat and spoke into the transducer.

"I am Professor Leo Szlyck," he said very precisely. "Hello and how are you?"

"I am Satan," I answered back. "Hello and how are *you*?"

INTERLUDE

Satan's Song

I am Satan. Hello, and how are you?

○   ○   ○

I ask you to pardon, if you will, this delay in my introduction. I thought it best that first you should meet Kassler, Szlyck, and Lupa, since they will, as you have no doubt concluded by now, be involved heavily, if not always willingly, in what follows. Besides, such a modest postponement of the amenities is most likely not inappropriate, since I understand there are times in the past that I may have come on a little too strong at first. So they say.

Of course, it should be evident by now that it was not my idea to be here in the first place. Szlyck gets the credit for that neat bit of legerdemain. Leo Szlyck is, by the way, one of my angels. I give him a nine.

○   ○   ○

If I may be allowed a brief digression from the exploits of Kassler, Szlyck, Lupa, and those who will, unfortunately, follow, I would like to take a few minutes to set the record straight.

63

It has come to my attention that, over the last thousand years or so, certain myths about me have gained great popularity. Now, I'm for poetry and fantasy as much as anyone, God only knows, but this has just gotten completely out of hand. Enough is enough.

I do not have a tail. I do not have horns. Or cloven hoofs. I mean, really—

Here's something else that should interest you. Hell is not what it's cracked up to be.

There's no place with pits and flames and kettles in which the souls of sinners eternally stew. When you come right down to it, no pun intended, hell is pretty much like any other place. We've got free enterprise, corporations, taxes, property, mass media. Recently I've been considering something new to liven up the place. I'm thinking of making everyone in hell an attorney. Just a thought.

In any event, the *Inferno* is so much hogwash. Satan isn't even my real name. Nobody knows my real name. Nobody. Not even me. So sometimes I use Satan. In medieval German there are sixty-two names for me. In twentieth-century English there are at least four hundred. It seems to me that if you could agree on a two-horned prong-tailed red-eyed devil, you could also settle on a name.

The truth of the matter is, I'm not the Father of Evil. I'm the Adversary, and that's all. Satan means "adversary." Read the Bible. Zechariah 3: 1. Satan isn't even a proper noun. Check it out. Adversary.

God says, "Consider My servant, Job." I say, "Okay, let's consider him." You see what I mean? My role is to evaluate the other side of things. Of course, you-know-Who is not overjoyed by this. I'll give you a case in point.

God tells me that He's going to make Man. I respond, tactfully, of course, that this is a lousy idea.

"No, no, no. This is good," He says.

"No, no, no. This is terrible," I say.

Even to this day, He won't admit His mistake. As I once pointed out to Him, forty days and forty nights of rain was not to correct an *agricultural* problem. I think that sooner or later we're going to have to face it. The Supreme Being blew it, and He blew it in spades.

Actually, the fact is, I'm on God's side. Think about it. Does it make any sense at all that I'd devote my time to punishing sinners who I'm supposed to adore to please a God I'm supposed to despise? I like God. Really. God is, after all, Love.

I am, on the other hand, Reason. I do not *believe*. I do *not* blindly accept authority. I rely on what I call *independent thought*. I balance God's love with reason. Of course, this approach is dangerous and terrible, especially to the esteemed Catholic Church, who has logically condemned independent individual thought as devilish and declared that I, as the supreme representative of reason, am evil. And there you have it.

The most fascinating part about my relationship with the Catholic Church, of course, is that I'm Jewish.

Like God.

Actually, to tell the truth, I'm only a High Holy Day Jew. Atonement renewed on a yearly basis has always fascinated me, so I hang around the temple on Rosh Hashanah and Yom Kippur. The rest of the year I'm too busy. You know how it is.

o o o

It's very important to me that you should understand this. I have absolutely nothing to do with evil. Nothing at all. My business is to consider the other side of the issue. And that's it.

I am not a seducer. Or an accuser. Or a destroyer. Forget what the Talmud says. It's not my fault that He picked glory and beauty and light to advocate and I got what was left over.

But let me tell you something. You never hear of a vengeful Satan, a Satan of wrath, a Satan who brings on pestilence and famine. That's the Other Fellow. You should keep this in mind.

Here's something else. I do not stand at the foot of beds fighting with angels over the souls of corpses. There's no need to. People come to hell because they like it.

Furthermore, I am not a dull brute. Dante's demon is Dante's problem. I'll tell you the truth, you can forget Dante. Hell is not divided into nine symmetrical circles, each one a torture chamber for a different species of sinner: virtuous pagans and unbaptized children, the carnal, gluttons, hoarders, the wrathful and sullen, heretics, the violent, the fraudulent and malicious, and so on. I take it that, for Dante, sinners specialize.

The truth of the matter is that sinners tend to be general practitioners.

What's more, I am not some dark crackerjack prize you find at the end of a trek through a Dantesque landscape of woods of suicide, burning plains, marsh and swamp. I am not the figment of a childish imagination without rules, principles, or scheme. There are rules. There are principles. And there is definitely a scheme. This I should also like to tell you about.

Now, when I first got here, thanks to the aforementioned Dr. Szlyck, I thought this would be an easy story to tell. It didn't turn out that way. I hadn't counted on Sam Zelazo, who, as I might have mentioned, is Szlyck's mortal enemy.

Zelazo is *not* one of my angels. Pity, too. He could have been superb. You'll see what I mean. For now, you can just accept my word for it. As Satan's angel, Zelazo would have been top-drawer.

Actually, I've always been more than a little offended that Zelazo isn't one of mine, because, you see, Zelazo is a psychiatrist. Freud is an archangel. I give him a ten plus. The best. No question about it. The man's a genius.

o   o   o

I bring up psychiatry at this point because I decided that, seeing as how I was here anyway, I should avail myself of some psychotherapy. The truth of the matter is, I'm not as happy as you'd think.

Now, as you might imagine, getting a therapist who's willing to treat the Angel of the Bottomless Pit is not an easy task. I've tried them all. Freud, Jung, Adler, Sullivan. It's no use. People tend to doubt my sincerity.

That's why I decided on Sy Kassler, whose global naïveté not only precluded such unfounded suspicion about my motives, but also, had records been kept about such things, would no doubt have earned him a solid foothold in the *Guinness Book of World Records*. Other than this, the truth of the matter is that Kassler is no one very special. Kassler, as you will see, just happened to wander into the picture, my picture, by accident.

Kassler is what we call, where I come from, a J.S.P.S. This stands for Just Some Poor Schmuck.

o   o   o

Obtaining a psychotherapist, any psychotherapist, is a chancy business at best. For me there are special problems.

For one thing, I have no way of paying. You can forget the mythology. I don't make those kinds of bargains. And even if I did, I'd never force anyone to do something against his will. It's not my style. That approach I leave for the All-Merciful in His Infinite Wisdom. I have only reason with which to barter, and, as institutions go these days, intellect is nearly insolvent.

What's more, I'm air. You can also forget the twelve wings and the fur and the fangs and all the rest of Mr. Blake's engraved nightmares. I'm spirit. I have no form whatsoever. Vapor. That's me.

The upshot of all this is that obtaining Sy Kassler for my psychotherapy was a pain in my ethereal ass, to be perfectly frank about it. Kassler had about as much desire to treat Satan as I do to sing the Hallelujah Chorus, but, fortunately, when we finally got together, Kassler was at a point in his life where he had no doubts that I was real. Believe me, the last thing I needed was some son-of-a-bitch psychotherapist trying to convince me that I wasn't the Prince of the Damned. Kassler was perfect.

Although, as I've said, recruiting Kassler for my therapy was not without its problems, in the end I sweetened the pie, so to speak, by making him a little deal. I promised him that if he could treat me successfully, I'd give him the Great Answer.

It was a good arrangement for us both, I think. Kassler did, in fact, get his answer; and me, well, I'm cured.

o   o   o

Just so you won't be disappointed, permit me to advise you at the outset that my sessions with Kassler are lacking in the usual spectacular qualities which tend to be attributed to me in popular films. There are no possessions. No incantations. No heads turning 360° or bodies hurtling through the air. Sorry. It's just not the way it is. Reason. That's all I've got.

Don't get me wrong. I like Hollywood. I think the films are splendid. *Rosemary's Baby. The Exorcist. The Omen.* Great special effects. Whatever else you may think of me, you have to give me one thing. I'm box office.

o   o   o

I'm not sure that Kassler was particularly impressed by my mass appeal during our psychotherapy sessions. Of course, in all fairness to Kassler, the meetings took place in 1979, more than ten years after that dreadful day in Florence when Morris Kassler made his flamboyant exit. In the intervening years, Kassler had had quite a time of it, as I will presently relate in detail sufficient to make the point.

By the time Kassler began my treatment, however, it was all over for him, and Kassler, as you will see, was exactly the sort of therapist I needed. Don't take my word for it. Since it is, after all, my story, I will skip ahead, and you can see for yourslf.

JANUARY 1979

Session I

"You say you're Satan," Kassler began from where he sat in the old overstuffed chair opposite my great tangle of wires. Kassler was not a happy man.

"Don't play with me, Kassler," I answered. "This is serious business."

"What specifically has prompted you to seek psychotherapy at this time, Mr. Satan?" Kassler plowed ahead, all business.

"You can forget the 'Mister.' Just Satan. Now, if you don't mind, I'd like you to dispense with the textbook psychoanalysis. If I wanted orthodox Freudian analysis, I'd be seeing Freud."

"You have access to Dr. Freud?" Kassler queried with some skepticism.

"Are you kidding? Of course I have access to Freud. Although, in all candor, I must admit that it's not *instant* access. Where Freud is now, he's got a rather heavy caseload."

"Sigmund Freud is in hell?"

"And having the time of his life."

Kassler sat stone-faced, stuffing tobacco into an old pipe.

"You should pardon the expression," I added.

71

Kassler said nothing.

"It was a *joke*, Kassler. Time of his *life*. Freud's *dead*. You see how that works?"

"Yes, I do."

"You're not laughing."

"I'd like to ask you once again why it is that you decided to seek professional help at this time, Mr. Satan?"

"Aren't you even interested in why, if I could get my psychoanalysis from Freud, I chose you? It's a provocative question, it seems to me."

Kassler continued to push tobacco into his worn pipe as he thought in silence.

"No," Kassler concluded. "I'm not interested."

"Why not? You think you're better than Freud? You think that just because I ended up here in Szlyck's basement at the other end of a lot of strands of plastic-covered copper, I couldn't have my pick? You're not the only therapist around. Freud's cured Hitler, you know. *Hitler*. He had the bastard weeping over his mother by the third session and studying the Talmud by the fifth. I could have had Sigmund Freud for my therapist, if I wanted him."

Kassler didn't answer. He just lit his pipe, smoke escalating above him in puffy clouds.

"Would you like to tell me now what's led you to seek treatment at this time, Mr. Satan?" Kassler asked with infuriating calm.

"Okay, Kassler, have it your way."

"Which way is that?"

"People have got me all wrong." I avoided Kassler's inquiry.

"How is that?"

"For one thing, I'm not sinister flypaper."

"You don't lead people into temptation?"

"I don't."

"I see."

"Think about it, Kassler. Exactly what would I tempt people to do that they're not already doing? Take you, for example. Your life has been a disaster. You didn't need me for that. You did splendidly all by yourself."

"What about Zelazo?"

"*I* didn't do Zelazo. *Zelazo* did Zelazo."

Kassler's eyes darted around a little and his temper began to flare ever so slightly.

"You didn't do Zelazo!" he snapped.

"Or Szlyck, or Lupa, or Vita, or your kids, or anyone else, for that matter. As you're very much aware."

Kassler's pipe had gone out. He reached for the metal tool in the pocket of his tweed jacket and dug at the fetid tobacco while he attempted to calm himself.

"I don't think it's going to be helpful to discuss my life," Kassler finally regained his professional composure. "These sessions are for your benefit, not mine."

"Really," I remarked. "You believe that? Treating Satan has no consequences for the therapist?"

"Fewer than you would like, my guess is."

"More than you're anticipating, *my* guess is."

There was what I believe is called a pregnant pause. Had Kassler not been a man of his word, for whom a deal is after all a deal, he might have stopped my treatment then and there. Instead, he considered himself to have been forewarned, poured the clumps of tobacco from his pipe into the ashtray beside him, and began to place new tobacco into the still-warm bowl.

"Flypaper," Kassler finally said. "You were telling me that you don't consider yourself to be flypaper."

"What I am, Kassler, is a clear thinker. Logical. I make a good argument. God is Love. I am Common Sense. And that's all there is to it."

"God is Love," Kassler repeated as he worked on his pipe.

"That's what He tells me. Our mother seems to agree."

"*Our* mother?" Kassler was clearly surprised, not an unexpected reaction.

"Right," I said quietly. "*Our* mother. God's and mine."

"You have a mother? You have the same mother? God has a mother?"

"Where do you think we came from, the cabbage patch?"

"I was under the impression that He always was."

"Nope. The only thing that's always been is Nothing."

"Would you like to tell me about your mother?"

"Not particularly. You want to hear about my mother? My

wife has a few things to say. Talk to her. She'd be delighted
to offer you her impressions."

"You're also married," Kassler commented with a little more
equanimity. He was adjusting quickly, I thought.

"Of course I'm married," I told him. "You think anyone
gets to be like this on his own?"

"And God?"

"Are you kidding? A bachelor to His core. You can relax,
Kassler. There's no Mrs. God."

Kassler let out a tiny breath of air, suggesting, ever so
slightly, that he was relieved.

"Of course," I decided to seize the opportunity, "there's
still something of a question, as you know, regarding the relationship that generated my nephew. That *is* a problem."

"Your nephew," Kassler repeated, a little dazed.

"Jesus. The Kid who went around telling everyone that I
made laughter evil, so no one's smiled in church since. Laughter, Kassler. Can you believe it? Pleasure, delight, joy—em-
anations from hell. He had the nerve to outlaw fun. *In my
name!* No wonder I'm despised."

"You're Christ's uncle," Kassler was sorting it all out.

"Don't remind me."

"I'd like to hear more about your mother, yours and God's,
Christ's grandmother, I take it."

"I'm sure you would, but I'd prefer not to get started on
women today, if you don't mind."

"You have something against women?"

"No, and that's the point. The so-called Prince of Pleasure
has absolutely nothing against women, nor do I have any great
affection for them. It depends on the woman. If the Catholic
Church in its esteemed judgment wants to consider celibacy as
the only perfect state, so be it. I've heard the story. God gave
men and women the equipment to make babies, and then I
went and loused up the whole thing by making it *fun*. Until I
came along and made sexual intercourse erotic, as the doctrine
has been explained to me, men and women couldn't have cared
less about plugging into each other and rubbing back and forth.
Well, just let me assure you, Kassler, that the *entire* business
is His doing. Believe me, I've got other things with which to

amuse myself, without needing glands. Carnal knowledge is *not* a form of demoniac possession. Ditto for more specialized kinds of sexual activity. I don't *know* why people moan and carry on when they rub around like that, but *I'm* not doing it to them."

"You have nothing against women?" Kassler noted out loud.

"They are what they are," I told him. "I don't despise them as a gender, and because you happen to be female, it doesn't mean that you get automatic admission into hell. All women are not daughters of the devil who bring about the downfall of men through their wicked allurements. The hand of a woman is the last place in which Satan conceals his claw, and I hope that Herr Lessing is listening."

"Instrumentum Diaboli," Kassler remembered his Latin well. "Isn't that the official church name for women?"

"It is, and they aren't."

"They aren't."

"They are not," I repeated. "The truth of the matter is, Kassler, that I was against the basic design to begin with, and if God had listened for once, it would have saved the world, you, and me a great deal of grief.

"I told God, 'Give women a penis or forget them altogether.'

"'I'm giving women breasts,' He said.

"'Big deal. It's not the same,' I told him. 'A penis or forget it.'

"'No penis,' He was adamant.

"'What about eggs?' I suggested. 'Let her lay eggs. That works. Why mess around with another organ?'

"But did He listen? Did He? Of course not. So what do you think the first thing was that came out of Eve's mouth when she saw Adam?"

"There're so many possibilities." Kassler gave the question serious consideration.

"I'll tell you, Kassler. She looked at *his* crotch. She looked at *her* crotch. Then she looked back at *his* crotch. 'How do I get one of them?' were the first words out of her mouth. It's been a disaster ever since."

"I'd like to ask one more time why you want psychotherapy, Mr. Satan."

"People don't like me, Kassler, if you want to know the sad truth of it. They're scared of me. I can't understand what it is, but there's something that turns people against me."

"A lot of bad rumors," Kassler commented.

"Exactly. When you come right down to it, I'm *very* misunderstood. Whatever I do, the old myths persist. It's beginning to get to me. That's why I think I need psychotherapy."

Kassler sat back in the old chair and thought about this, as large clouds of foul-smelling smoke filled the room.

"I think it has something to do with this concern I have about being logical and reasonable," I conjectured.

"You're not concerned with the irrational aspects of our lives," Kassler said slowly between puffs.

"I'm not."

"You're not interested in chaos, passion, conflict—"

"Right. I'm not interested."

Kassler leaned farther back into his chair and continued to smoke his pipe.

"You know," I finally said, "it used to be that what was reasonable was reasonable and what was not was not. I liked that. It had a simplicity that I found enormously appealing."

"It's not like that anymore."

"No, it isn't. A virgin birth, a resurrection, a few parables— almost overnight what was irrational, accidental, chaotic, impulsive, and blind became known as 'Divine Providence.' Faith became very big."

"A bad day," Kassler nodded.

"Very bad," I agreed. "What's even worse, the use of reason to examine faith became known as heresy. Of course, when reason stayed reason but nonreason became God, it didn't leave me a great deal of room in which to operate."

"Even Satan has limitations," Kassler conceded.

"I'll tell you something, Kassler. I marvel at this human business of searching for order and consistency. Science is a wonderful thing. It encourages me, the genius you all have for developing systems to explain systems about systems."

Kassler put his feet up on the worn ottoman in front of him.

"We do our best," he said.

"Reason has become terrible, Kassler. Despised. Evil."

"How is that?" Kassler inquired.

"How is it? Are you kidding? Who uses reason anymore? You're all gluttons for punishment. You people go from one disaster to the next like there's no tomorrow. You're never satisfied. You've always got to have more. The last thing you use is common sense. Look around you. Look at your own disastrous life."

"I've asked before," Kassler said emphatically, "that my life not be brought into our sessions."

"So I recall," I answered as emphatically, and decided it was best to change the subject as quickly as possible. "I know that I shouldn't get so upset about the way you all lead your lives. Human behavior is, after all, just another in a long list of things that I get blamed for. I've got to learn to accept that. But I'll tell you, Kassler, it's beginning to get to me. There hasn't been a thing that's gone wrong since the beginning of the world that I haven't been held responsible for. Absolutely everything is my fault. Poor crop yield. Hangnails. Sneezing. Vitamin deficiency. You name it. Weather. Eclipses. Improper fractions ..."

There was a long silence.

"Tell me something, Kassler," I ended the quiet. "I understand that we're not supposed to be talking about you, but I'm curious. Do you hold me to blame for your life? All those catastrophes of yours—tell me honestly, do you think they're my fault?"

"Or do I blame myself?"

"You're not answering my question."

"No, I'm not."

"It's a good question, don't you think?"

Kassler looked up and smiled.

"The real question is," he said, "who are you?"

"The real question is," I answered, "do you take me seriously?"

"A crude approximation of artificial intelligence?" Kassler continued. "A copy of Leo Szlyck's brain, Szlyck's unconscious and nothing more? Or a channel into ... other realms?"

"I see." I got the picture. "A machine? Insane? Or science fiction? Is that the question?"

"Pretty much," Kassler agreed.

"You wouldn't be satisfied thinking of Leo's contraption as sort of a telephone for talking over very long distances, I suppose?"

Kassler struck another match and puffed away. Then he reached into his jacket pocket, retrieved a nail file, and started digging out the debris from under his nails.

"I'm not a brain, Kassler," I informed him, "Szlyck's, artificial, or otherwise. I'm afraid that leaves us with the 'other realm' hypothesis. And would you please stop fidgeting. You're driving me crazy."

"Perhaps if you were to materialize, Mr. Satan," Kassler suggested.

"Aha!" A light dawned.

"It might make your treatment more productive," Kassler tried.

"Sorry, Kassler, I'm air. Vapor. I hardly exist. Sound is all you get. No pictures. You'll have to do what everyone else does and make up your own visuals."

"Like with God."

"I hope not."

"Why is that?"

"Why is it? Why *is* it! Because He's a self-serving Son-of-a-Bitch, that's why. Do you know what He does? Do you have any idea what He *does*?"

"Only from books," Kassler concluded.

"I'll tell you what He does, Kassler. All day long He sits on a throne that's surrounded by an emerald rainbow. All around Him are twenty-four elders wearing white robes and gold crowns."

"Like in Revelations."

"Exactly. Lightning and thunder come out of the throne. In front of Him are four creatures covered with eyes, inside and out, who sing all day and night, 'Holy, holy, holy is God the Sovereign Lord of all, who was, and is, and is to come.' Then, as if this weren't enough, the elders throw down their crowns, fall on their knees, and cry out, 'Thou art worthy, O Lord our God, to receive glory and honor and power, because Thou didst create all things; by Thy will they were created, and have their being!' I tell you Kassler, it's enough to make you sick to your stomach."

Kassler looked ahead and said nothing.

"It *never* stops, Kassler. *Never*. And *I'm* supposed to be vain!"

"These feelings about God," Kassler suggested, "these are why you were expelled from heaven?"

"I don't think so. The real problem is that I don't know *why* I was thrown out. I know when. When was August first. A long time ago. But why? I'm not sure. That's another reason why I'm seeing you, Kassler."

"What were you told?"

"That I was being given dominion over man, over the earth, that I was to be a great symbol of protest against tyranny, a vindicator of reason and freedom of thought, the supremest incarnation of the spirit of individualism. It sounded great. Of course, it wasn't long before I realized that I was just being bumped downstairs."

"And it was shortly after this that you began to hate God?"

"I don't hate God. I don't think I've said that, have I? It's not true. I love God. He's my brother."

"But you don't give Him very much credit for knowing what He's doing?" Kassler asked.

"Not at all. I give God all things but one—the experience of feeling inadequate, being subject to a higher authority, weakness, being human, if you will. We know loss, Kassler, helplessness, having our best efforts go for naught. You and I share one experience God will never understand, the feeling of not prevailing."

Kassler sat silently in Szlyck's dusty basement. He stared through the dim light at the tangle of wires by which we communicated and listened to Lupa's footsteps echoing in the house above.

"We have a lot in common, you and me, Kassler," I planted the seed, and then proceeded to nourish it. "We're not perfect, but basically we're good and reasonable beings—and *very* misunderstood. It's a pity, too. We deserve better, don't you think?"

"We have to stop for today," Kassler responded. "Our time is up."

"You didn't answer my question, Kassler. You and I, we're getting a bum rap, aren't we?"

"I'm sorry," Kassler said quietly and started to leave. "We really have to stop."

"Don't pull any of that cute psychoanalytic fifty-minute-hour crap on me, Kassler. I'm in pain. The way you all treat me, what you think of me, it hurts. Now, I asked you a question, and I expect the courtesy of a reply. Remember, I could have gotten Sigmund Freud."

"So I understand," Kassler acknowledged as he headed up the stairs. "You are, of course, free to change to another therapist any time you wish." And the door clicked shut behind him.

So that was my first session with Dr. Kassler.

PART III

Vita

CHAPTER 1

I'd like to tell you that midway through life's journey, at the age of thirty, Kassler went astray, leaving his home and the lake of his home, and he descended the mount, awakening, finally, to find himself in a dark wood. No such luck.

Eyes open, wide awake, as clear-headed as you can reasonably expect, Kassler exited from his ten days in the psychiatric wing of Bellevue Hospital and, like an unbaptized child in a vast limbo, he headed directly for training in the dark world of human psychopathology. So began Kassler's Great Descent.

Although Kassler's heart was set on the field of psychiatry, an unfortunate combination of mediocre grades in college and a mind disinclined to retain notions about biology and chemistry prevented Kassler from taking the first of many required steps toward a psychiatric career: specifically, admission to a medical school. Therefore, Kassler applied to, and after much pleading was accepted by, the New York Institute for Professional Studies, since medical training was not required for a Ph.D. in clinical psychology.

Kassler was, of course, ecstatic. The Institute was one of

the great teaching institutions in psychiatry and clinical psychology in the country, as Kassler had learned when he investigated psychiatric training centers. The facility attracted Masters from throughout the world. The students admitted were few and exceptional. That he, Kassler, a mere mortal, should be allowed passage into this citadel of the human mind, even though it was on a probationary basis, sent him into a swoon that, unfortunately, lasted less than the first six days of classes.

Kassler began his academic career as an ideal student, apt, eager to learn, readily grasping complex notions, industrious, and dedicated, all the skills and attitudes he had found so difficult to call upon during undergraduate days, which Kassler still considered to have been merely a tumultuous continuation of a tumultuous adolescence.

Now, suddenly, Kassler—bearded, spectacled, trim, and relaxed—was a star pupil, with an innate aptitude for psychological notions, destined for great success as a psychotherapist. Or so it seemed.

At the outset of his academic excursion, Kassler met Freud. Not in person, of course, but through the inspired lectures of Karl Heinrich, then in his eighties. Heinrich had been a student of Bleuler's at the Burghölzli, as well as of Freud, and had been one of the youngest members of the group that met on Wednesday evenings at Freud's house—Adler, Jung, Stekel, Abraham, Ferenczi, Sachs, Rank, Eitingon, and Freud. The nostalgic among you may be interested to know that, although its location has changed, the group still meets.

For lecture after lecture, Kassler sat enthralled as Heinrich presented Freud's psychoanalytic theory in such a clear and convincing way that Kassler became a true believer. It seemed to Kassler, as he watched the small bearded Austrian with the dark penetrating eyes that stared intensely at him from beneath wire-rimmed glasses, that Freud himself had appeared to guide him through the human psyche.

It was a splendid tour.

"The human psyche," Heinrich flicked at the air with his thin fingers as he lectured, "is a seething soup of sexual and

aggressive drives—libido—trying desperately to break out of
the cauldron of the unconscious to achieve gratification through
some object."

Karl Heinrich paused and smiled to the assembled students.

"'Object' is the word Dr. Freud uses to designate another
human being," he explained precisely.

Kassler made a note of this in his brand-new spiral notebook
and put a star beside it to signify a *Major Concept*.

"Now," Heinrich went on, "during childhood we are taught
to keep the lid tightly clamped on this stockpot of instinctual
drives and sexuality. Elsewise," Heinrich raised his hand and
shook his finger, "we might have to suffer the consequences
of being *scorched* with anxiety, guilt, shame, pain, and a dreadful lack of security.

"However!" Heinrich waved his arm. "With the lid on, the
pressure increases, does it not, until it is so great that it *must*
be released, either *constructively*, in work, play, love and
sex . . ." Heinrich paused here to consider the alternatives.

". . . or *destructively*, for the *neurotic*, through *symptoms*.
Symptoms are nothing more than the neurotic's way of handling
his simmering desires!"

Kassler wrote down "simmering desires = neurotic symptoms." Then he tilted back in the cramped wooden lecture-
room seat, leaned his arm on the curved wooden writing board
at his side, and observed, for the first time, the busty young
lady sitting two rows below him.

"Radiant, resplendent, redolent, ravishing," the succession
of *r*'s rumbled around inside Kassler's cranium and rolled off
his protruding tongue with all the finesse of gravel dislodging
from the chute of a municipal cement truck. Kassler had never
seen anything like it.

Her name was Vita.

She rested casually in her seat, her long black wavy hair
falling seductively to her bare shoulders, tanned and splendid
in a simple yellow sun dress on this hot autumn day, ample
breasts, unencumbered by supportive undergarments, bulging
from beneath the ribbed bodice and displaying such robust and
profound cleavage that it nearly made Kassler dizzy.

For a second their eyes met, and then, with becoming shy-

ness, Vita quickly averted her glance downward to her notebook, pretending she had not seen Kassler at all. In that fleeting
moment, Kassler judged a profound intelligence in Vita's dark
sparkling eyes, and he knew, absolutely, that he had, at long
last, truly found the girl of his dreams.

Vita, amused by Kassler's obvious enthusiasm, turned a
little in her seat, barely suppressing a smile. Aware of Kassler's
eyes riveted on her, she adjusted the thin shoulder straps, which
lifted her dress only slightly higher and not only failed to
achieve the desired result of a modest increase in covered bosom,
but actually set her breasts undulating with a most disquieting
turbulence.

"An increase in tension produces unpleasure," Heinrich continued to expound on Freud's insights, "and a decrease in tension through gratification provides pleasure."

Kassler felt no need to write this down.

"This libidinous kitchen in which man stews is the world of
the id," Heinrich, a lifelong gourmet, continued his culinary
metaphor the next week. "It is the conscious ego that regulates
the tension and expression of the id by slamming down," Heinrich's palm smacked loudly against the lectern, awakening several students, "the many lids that constitute our defense
mechanisms—to repress the drives altogether or convert them
into reaction formations, displacements, projections, undoings,
denials, and rationalizations."

Kassler had decided to play it cool. He was not going to
go charging after Vita. A subtle approach would win his fair
lady in the end, Kassler concluded, and thus for the second
lecture he moved a smidgeon closer, to the row and seat directly
behind Vita, so he might evaluate the situation more closely.
This had, of course, required that Kassler, prior to the lecture,
lounge nonchalantly against a wall in the foyer outside the
auditorium, appearing to be intensely involved in reading *Beyond the Pleasure Principle*, until he observed Vita arrive.
After the briefest interval, he followed her into the lecture hall,
noting that she had arrived alone and with a bottom that, in
tight white jeans, appeared to be even more spectacular than

her top, which was, nevertheless, still full and glorious beneath a colorful turquoise halter.

"Through oral, anal, and phallic stages the drives percolate!" Heinrich gathered steam.

"1. mouth, 2. ass, 3. penis," Kassler noted distractedly in his notebook while his eyes followed the curves of Vita's slender arms and the sun-bleached down that covered them. Her dark tresses fell softly below the line of her seat back and nearly touched Kassler's knees. His hands were sore from the restraint needed not to reach out and stroke Vita's newly shampooed and lustrous hair.

"A superego is formed as a conscience to regulate the broth and determine just how much sexuality and aggression is served to whom and under what conditions," Heinrich explained patiently. "Right is separated from wrong, good from bad, appropriate from inappropriate. The kitchen soon becomes off limits altogether, and as we struggle with our Oedipal conflicts of desiring our mother and despising our father for not permitting it—" Heinrich stopped in midsentence and thought, "or vice versa, the bedroom also becomes *verboten*."

Kassler had an idea. He raised his hand. Heinrich, pleased that he had provoked interest in one of the assembly of otherwise stuporous students, called on Kassler immediately.

"In *Pleasure Principle*," Kassler abbreviated the title as an indication of his familiarity with Freud's well-known work, "Sigmund talks about a death wish." Kassler glanced for a split second to see whether Vita had turned around in her seat and was listening with interest. She was.

Unfortunately, Kassler also realized at the same instant that, having only read the first ten pages of the book and the description on the jacket, he hadn't anything to say about the death wish or how it related to Heinrich's lecture, should Kassler have the good fortune of its doing so.

There was a long pause while scores of eyes focused on Kassler, who had only one thought. "Come on, brain!" he pleaded with his intellect.

"Yes, that's true, Sigmund does," Karl Heinrich answered and waited, hopefully, for more to follow.

"Well," Kassler took a deep breath, crossed his fingers, and charged ahead. "That seems inconsistent with his concept of *superego*." Kassler's eyes had caught the last word he had scrawled in his notebook.

"Ah, yes! Excellent!" Heinrich exclaimed with obvious delight, while Kassler reached for his handkerchief and mopped his perspiring brow. "This is, of course, a major problem, but one that Freud has not neglected," Karl Heinrich launched into a long digression, while the rest of the students in the auditorium wondered who the smartass was in the row behind the most spectacular girl they had ever seen.

The consequences for Kassler could not have been more disastrous. The sound of Heinrich closing the cover on the loose-leaf book holding his lecture notes had not ceased for a count of five before Vita was greeted by every unattached male in the hall.

It was not only that Vita was gorgeous and voluptuous. It was the bright sparkle that every man detected in Vita's eyes. It bound them to her like, you should pardon the expression, a neurotic to his mother.

Kassler watched helplessly during the autumn months as Vita apparently played the field. At each class she would arrive accompanied by another man, who would sit beside her, passing notes during Heinrich's talk, and smiling in delight at the responses Vita would hastily scribble while she attempted to concentrate on the lecture.

Kassler refused to become one of the crowd, just another delighted note-passer to escort Vita to Heinrich-on-Freud, and so he sat in the same seat behind Vita, searching for basic character flaws and physical deformities in each suitor, imperfections that would permanently disqualify them, and, if I may utilize one of Karl Heinrich's inexhaustible repertoire of culinary metaphors, Kassler stewed.

So it was that Kassler passed his Cook's tour through this Netherland of dreams, repression, infantile sexuality, free association, transference, cathexis, and primary process.

By the conclusion of Heinrich's lectures, Kassler had a new vision of man—sexually driven and consumed, incestuously attracted to his mother, despising his rivalrous father, desiring the death of his wife, wanting to betray his superiors and languish in eroticism.

Nothing man does, Kassler concluded as had Freud, is arbitrary, haphazard, accidental, or meaningless; everything is the result of an ongoing battle of the ego with its internal enemies as it tries to deal with the realities of the external world, among them the problem of initiating a relationship with the spectacular female who sat in front of him during the lectures.

Then Kassler had a great insight into his own predicament. The difference between neurotics and normals is only a matter of degree, he surmised correctly. The man of *action* takes the fantasies he's developed as a way of dealing with life's inadequacies and turns them into reality. The *artist* turns them into works of art, and the *neurotic* into symptoms.

Kassler saw his own life with a clarity he had never believed possible. It was clear from the lack of initiative and creativity he had shown with Vita that he was neither a man of *action* nor an *artist*. He was, he therefore concluded, *doomed*. Kassler went into a deep depression.

Fortunately, the following lectures were on Alfred Adler.

"Symptoms," a round, jolly lecturer by the name of Franz Kaplan beamed broadly, "are some of our most creative outpourings! What cunning, marvelous constructions to deal with our problems and conflicts!"

Kaplan paused for a moment and smiled jovially at the students.

"What genius Adler had," he said as he clasped his hands over his rotund middle, "to realize that mental illness is nothing more than mistaken ways of living by discouraged people. Even depression," Kaplan said with an expression of great delight, "even depression is a wonderful creative effort in which the depressed patient makes a weapon out of his weakness in order to bludgeon others into giving him attention and to escape reality."

Kassler, in an attempt to distract himself from the woman in front of him who seemed more beautiful and more desirable every day, took everything down in extremely meticulous form. He had spent the previous afternoon trying out fountain pens in the University Bookstore, until he had found the perfect one for taking lecture notes, and imagined that someday his biographer would come upon his graduate-school notebooks and marvel at the insights (written in the margin, using his new red felt-tip pen with the chisel point) that Kassler had at such an early stage of his career.

"It was with soaring optimism," Kaplan continued, as Kassler quickly changed pens from hand to hand, "that Adler declared our lives to be determined neither by heredity, as Freud would have it, nor by the environment, as the behaviorists believe." Kaplan made large imaginary *x*'s with his hands to cancel out the errors of others. "But there is a magnificent *Third Force*, human self-determination, which allows us to influence and create events in our own lives! The supreme law of human existence is that the sense of worth of the self shall not be allowed to diminish!"

Kassler quickly changed to the red pen. "Third Force???" he wrote in the margin. "Force = outdated Newtonian concept—need Einsteinian relativistic approach to mental illness!!!"

Kassler leaned back in his seat, pleased that his comment was profound and legible, and thought deeply about how time, energy, matter, and the constant speed of light could account for people going crazy.

As Kassler's supply of writing instruments increased—he acquired a green felt-tip pen for underlining *Interesting Ideas*, and a purple pen for notating major concepts of psychopathology that were, he concluded, *False Notions*—so did his gratitude to Dr. Adler for retrieving him from Freudian gloom.

Kassler was, in fact, overjoyed. For weeks after Kaplan's lectures he was euphoric. Vita no longer seemed to matter. As quickly as Freud had taken away the power he had over his own life and relegated him to the depths of libidinous despair, Adler had restored it. Kassler was no longer doomed. Individual Psychology had saved him.

Unfortunately, what Adler giveth, Jung taketh away.

Almost immediately, Kassler was plunged into the mysterious and nearly impenetrable world of Carl Gustav Jung's Analytic Psychology, and very well might have remained there, had not Vita arrived to a lecture unescorted and proceeded to stroll up Kassler's row and sit directly beside him.

"Though our ego may persist in the center of our conscious, attempting to provide us with a concept of ourselves that has a high degree of identity and continuity," an intense, yellow-skinned, wiry man with bad teeth, by the name of Ernst Hoch, was droning when Vita arrived, in the midst of one of the long series of tedious Jungian lectures that were driving Kassler back into despair, "we find that, to exist in different settings, we must use masks—personae—to adapt to this *outside* world."

"I miss anything?" Vita smiled facetiously to Kassler, who immediately spilled a dozen or so richly colored writing implements onto the floor.

Ernst Hoch pushed his gold-rimmed glasses up the bridge of his nose with his bony finger.

"At the *very same time*," Hoch emphasized the simultaneity, "to handle our inner world, the ego must deal with the dark shadows of our personal unconscious."

Kassler, appearing to be deeply engrossed in his academic endeavors, nodded to Vita, ignored the pens on the floor, and wrote intensely with his remaining, fuchsia felt-tip.

Vita looked around Kassler's shoulder in amazement at the polychromatic page in his notebook.

"Very festive," Vita leaned over and whispered to Kassler, the tip of her right nipple pressing into his arm.

"It's color-coded," Kassler warbled helplessly.

"These shadows," Hoch went on, briefly flashing his rotten teeth, "stand at the doorway to the collective unconscious— the unconscious shared by all society—which contains the dark inner strivings we all have in common, and so we translate them into myths and symbols. They have an archetypal aspect."

As Kassler scribbled frantically, Hoch went on to explain how, in most cultures, the archetypal aspect of the shadows is me.

Kassler, now paying scrupulous attention to the lecture, was not pleased to learn that he was walking around with the devil himself at the very core of his being, though I can't see why it wasn't an improvement over an existence until then composed almost entirely of longings of Freudian lust, maternal incest, paternal homicide, and a nonspecific death wish.

"So, what do you think?" was the best that Kassler could do, at the conclusion of the lecture, to initiate a conversation with the awe-inspiring lady beside him.

"I don't know." Vita's eyes sparkled with magnetic vitality. "It all seems crazy to me. What do you think?"

"I think that Jung's concept of *persona* is a little shallow," Kassler the *serious student* answered as he watched the gentle rolling movements of Vita's breasts.

"How is that?" Vita appeared interested.

"It's a little complicated, actually," Kassler said, picking his pens off the floor. "Would you like to join me for a cup of coffee? I have some time before my next class," offered Kassler, whose next class was at three the following afternoon.

"Sure," Vita said merrily, as she walked slowly from the lecture hall with Kassler. "The coffee sounds great. But let's skip the Jung, okay? You see, I'm not really a student here. I'm from Cleveland."

"Oh, I used to go see the Indians play the Yankees every year," Kassler quickly shifted the topic to Vita's home turf. "Lemon, Wynn, Feller, Garcia, Herb Score—until he got hit in the eye—Mossi and Narleski were a great bullpen, Rosen, Doby, Luke Easter..." Kassler's voice trailed off as he and Vita headed for the small coffee shop around the corner.

"Actually," Vita explained while she sipped her espresso, "I teach piano. I've only been here a few months. A friend told me about the lectures at the Institute, and I thought they might help me understand some things about myself."

"And meet men?" Kassler studied Vita's chocolate eyes.

"It's certainly worked out that way, hasn't it?" Vita smiled.

"So what's *happened* to all those guys?" Kassler found himself feeling very open with Vita about her private life.

"They didn't work out," Vita tilted her head and shrugged playfully.

"*None* of them? There must have been two hundred."

"I see you've been counting." Vita's eyes twinkled. "Fewer than twenty, actually. My problem has never been meeting men. It's after that that the problems occur. I lose interest quickly or something. I don't know. I think maybe my standards are too high. I'm not easy to please. I'm an only child."

"I'll consider myself warned," Kassler said, considering no such thing but hoping he might convince Vita that, unlike the others, he was adequately prepared to protect himself. Kassler was well aware, however, as he gazed on Vita's still-tanned and freckled face, bright eyes, and splendidly curvaceous body, that he had the same ability to resist Vita as a practicing kleptomaniac has to walk past an open Woolworth's. As Kassler beheld Vita's wares, his hands ached to be everywhere at the same time.

"Oh, no," Vita assured Kassler. "You don't have to worry. You're different."

"How do you know?" Kassler was extremely pleased.

"Well," Vita answered, "for one thing you sat behind me for all those lectures and never said a word to me. And for another, we've been together almost an hour and you haven't asked me to go to bed with you. You've got a lot of self-control, Sy."

Kassler was not ecstatic about *restraint* being the primary character trait that differentiated him from the horde of Vita's other admirers, but he felt it was all he had at the start, and so he developed it to a fine art.

Lectures in which Kassler learned that Heinz Hartmann felt it was, in fact, possible to have conflict-free activities and autonomous ego development independent of any Freudian sexual drive-defense conflict, were followed with intimate dinners at intimate restaurants in the Village where Kassler and Vita exchanged intimate details about growing up in Greenwich and Shaker Heights. And there the intimacy stopped.

Presentations by a slender, fair-skinned woman in her early thirties, extolling Otto Rank's position that humans live in reaction to the trauma of their births, in fear of the first and ultimate separation, and all human behavior can ultimately be understood in terms of a longing to return to the womb, were followed by evenings at the cinema or late nights eating pizza in Kassler's small apartment in the West Eighties, where restraint continued to prevail.

"I'm not going to any more lectures," Vita told Kassler at the end of the series on Otto Rank. "Things are getting more and more ridiculous. I know that everyone else has already made plans, but I don't think I have any desire at all to go back to the womb, and even if I did, I don't know what I'd do once I got there."

The term *womb* was too close, anatomically, to what was on Kassler's mind as he lay on the sofa, his head resting peacefully on Vita's lap, so he said nothing.

"What do you think, Sy?" Vita asked. "Does it make any sense to you?"

Kassler thought in silence, his head rising and falling with the slight motion of Vita's tummy as she breathed slowly in the darkened room. At first he tried to give serious consideration to Vita's question, but then his mind turned to his present circumstances, his contentment to be with Vita and his good fortune at prevailing where others had failed. Such a triumph, Kassler concluded, demanded, at the very least, a thoughtful response to Vita's question.

"I don't know," Kassler finally answered. "All these people we keep hearing about, they're not stupid. They're trying to understand why we all behave in very complicated ways, I think."

Kassler felt that his response was an appropriately respectful and modest one, even though it neglected to convey that he had become completely numbed to the barrage of psychoanalytic theorizing.

Vita considered Kassler's response while she ran her hands through his dark hair. She liked the feel of Kassler's curls on her fingers and was no more certain than Kassler about why they got along so well.

"You know what I think, Sy," she finally said. "I think they're all looking for rules to explain how we act, and there aren't any rules. They're as crazy as everyone else."

"Well, yes," Kassler agreed. "That, too."

* * *

Autumn had turned Central Park very briefly into hues as colorful as Kassler's notes and then disappeared, leaving behind scribbled brown strokes of bare tree limbs and a cold rain where Kassler and Vita had spent their weekends wandering amiably along the paths.

Now, on wet Sundays, Kassler sat on the sofa as the drops streaked the windows of his small apartment, watching Vita in her tight dungarees, turtleneck jersey, and plaid flannel shirt that didn't completely button across her chest. And as he studied her lying on the floor next to him, reading the music pages in *The New York Times* and drinking coffee, his head filled with a cornucopia of sexual and domestic fantasies.

Kassler and Vita found conversation easy that fall. They spent evenings walking through the city, Vita's hand in the rear pocket of Kassler's corduroys, Kassler's thumb hooked under Vita's belt in the back, his palm falling against her bottom as it moved gracefully with her steps. They talked with candor about cultural and personal matters, and throughout it all, with increasing distress, Kassler demonstrated *restraint*.

At the Institute, Kassler had fallen into a state of oblivion.

He listened in a trance as a short fat woman in her mid-forties extolled the virtues of the psychological insights of Freud's favorite pupil, Sandor Ferenczi.

"Our lives," she explained in a high-pitched and nervous squeal, "are only the results of an underlying sense of omnipotence. At first this is unconditional, of course, but then, as we develop, it's replaced by hallucinatory omnipotence, then by magic gestures, and finally by magic thoughts and words."

Kassler sat quietly in the back of the large auditorium, alone, mechanically taking rainbow-colored notes so he could pass the final exam, but that was all. Ferenczi's assertion that Kassler's life consisted primarily in a great struggle to overcome his underlying feelings of omnipotence was a hypothesis Kassler had difficulty accepting.

The parade of great psychiatric thinkers went on unabated. Kassler, who was nearing a point of psychoanalytic saturation, attempted to pay close attention, but it was no use. By the end of the semester, there was simply no room left in his brain for notions of the idiosyncrasies of human behavior. Kassler used only his purple pen.

Total psychotheoretical collapse for Kassler occurred following a special evening lecture attended by all students and faculty during the last week of the fall semester. It was precipitated by an intense argument that broke out in the auditorium, initially between the Freudians and the Kleinians, regarding Melanie Klein's concept of good breasts and bad breasts. Kassler had managed to survive the long formal lecture by immersing himself in an elaborate fantasy involving Vita and a shower.

Suddenly, Kassler found himself stunned into the present world by the intensity of the conflict all about him.

The Freudians declared with vehemence that Klein's description of the young child becoming depressed because he had destroyed the good breast was crazy and fantastic. There are simply not good breasts and bad breasts, they argued. It is, the Freudians insisted, something far more *reasonable* and *commonplace* that's causing the depression, namely, the child's Oedipal fear of castration.

Kassler shuddered at the thought and continued to listen in amazement as the argument grew more heated and other psychological camps entered the fracas.

The Object-Relations therapists objected that the child's depression had nothing to do with libido, since libido is not primarily pleasure-seeking but object-seeking, and, what's more, can't be separated from ego in the first place. The depression was only the result of the ego's looking for support and security from human objects and being unsuccessful.

This was seconded, with qualification, by the Harry Stack Sullivan interpersonal-psychiatry contingent, who felt that since the self system develops out of the interpersonal experiences the child has with others as he tries to relieve the tension of his needs and drives, the depression is most likely more than just the absence of support and security, but the presence of anxiety from the parents which the child takes to be a statement about his own value as a person. They reminded their colleagues that this does not bode well for a child who will eventually need to feel secure enough to achieve intimacy without losing a sense of self-esteem or security.

The Erich Fromm cultural-approach people could not have agreed less. The important thing to consider, they insisted, was that man, as an animal, is unique in being aware of himself, and this creates one of the many dichotomies he must face. Man's self-awareness in the body of an animal creates a tremendous sense of separateness and fright and leads, in turn, to a long struggle to give meaning to his existence. But since this meaning comes primarily from the society in which he lives, loves, and works, the family becomes the psychic agent of society and encourages the particular character type that will best serve the culture's needs. In this situation, the parents are not *causing* the depression but *encouraging* it, since it will be helpful for the child to deal in his culture at various times by withdrawing and isolating himself, they concluded loudly.

"But suppose the depression is neurotic?" a Freudian shouted back angrily.

"It doesn't matter," yelled the Frommian. "All men have a cultural need for orientation and devotion! Neurosis is only a less organized form of religion, with its own belief system and rituals! Neurosis is beneficial to society!"

Throughout these battles, the behaviorists sat in the corner of the room and kept their mouths shut. There was no reason for them to talk. They knew that the issue had nothing to do with depression, anxiety, good breasts, or castration complexes. The child was simply developing bad habits. He had found that by reacting in a depressed manner he would get more attention, or had developed a phobia about something or other and was withdrawing. The theoretical systems didn't matter. The behavior could be easily eliminated by positive reinforcement, extinction, conditioned inhibition, or systematic desensitization.

The argument went on for several hours. Psychiatrists stamped their feet and hurled personal insults at one another. The Karen Horney people angrily walked out as a group, calling back at the doorway that they sensed a lack of mutuality and respect for individuality and the rights of others in the auditorium.

"Self-realization! Self-actualization!" a large, white-haired, grandmotherly woman shouted loudly at the audience before slamming the door.

When, at midnight, the meeting finally ended, Kassler left the auditorium in a daze. As he walked back to his apartment in the freezing rain that fell on the city, he had a terrible insight.

Absolutely nothing he had learned in his first semester of graduate school mattered. There wasn't really an unconscious. Freud made it up. Nor was there a preconscious, or a conscious, or an ego, id, or superego, or libido, or repression, transference, drives, personae, shadows, primary process, Oedipal complexes, neuroses, oral-anal-phallic stages, fixations, regressions, cathexes, paranoid-schizoid positions, collective unconsciouses, archetypes, introjections, good breasts, bad breasts, or anything else like them.

Everything had been made up. It was all imaginary. In the real world, none of it existed.

Kassler realized, with the terrible feelings of despondency encountered, until then, exclusively by those having to contend with bad breasts, that over the previous months he had learned only one thing. Psychobabble.

CHAPTER 2

If I might be permitted to interject some information at this point, I'd like to assure you that marriage was not my idea. Marriage is, as far as I can tell, not a necessary evil, assuming of course, that transgressions can be placed on a sliding scale of utility, from useless to handy.

To tell the truth, I've always been intrigued by this business you all fuss over of *rating* evil—the *unavoidable* evil of lust that leads, as night follows day, to the *understandable* evil of infidelity, and consequently to the *unfortunate* evil of divorce, a commonplace reaction to the *necessary* evil of marriage that started the ball rolling in the first place . . . and so on.

So it is, I hear tell, that the Great Magnet of Necessary Evil draws into its field all other indiscretions which become charged with necessity. Very neat, I think.

As I understand this particular application of electromagnetic theory, I am the Great Magnet. You are the helpless metal shavings of life.

Well, far be it from me to refuse credit where not due, but I have absolutely nothing to do with conjugal arrangements. Nor, while I'm on the subject, do I have anything to do with inserting third parties into otherwise satisfactory relationships. It's all your business. Marriages are not made in heaven, or any other spectral realm. The whole thing is entirely a terrestrial phenomenon.

Believe me.

As Kassler's inevitable union with Vita approached, Vita did what she could to help him through the persistent gloom of the bottomless psychotheoretical pit in which he found himself each day.

She sent him cheerful notes professing her affection for him, prepared him tasty dinners served by candlelight, and, as Kassler became obsessed with his exams, attempted to provide him with essential diversions by taking him on trips to fun places like Times Square.

"I'm not sure this is going to help me forget about my exams," Kassler told Vita as they left for another excursion to Forty-second Street and Broadway.

"The squalor is fabulous," Vita said as she took his arm. "You'll love it."

"Funky filth may not be the answer tonight." Kassler hinted that sexual intercourse might be.

"Now, Sy," Vita was friendly but firm. "You know that if we start having sex, you'll never show up for your exams."

"I guess," Kassler shrugged. "Still, I'm not sure this is such a hot idea."

"I tell you, you'll love it, Sy. Times Square is the center of the universe."

"It's almost midnight," Kassler decided not to quibble with Vita's cosmology. "It's dangerous."

"Times Square? That's ridiculous. I've lived here four months and nothing's happened."

"Four months!" Kassler feigned surprise.

"I'll go alone if I have to," Vita persisted.

Kassler sighed in resignation, took Vita by the hand, led her past a man urinating on a wall, and proceeded down the steep litter-strewn steps to the subway.

During the loud, screeching subway ride, Vita watched in fascination as small groups of thin black adolescent boys slithered like snakes from car to car, weaving among the silver posts in the middle of the floor, snapping the aluminum handles that hung from the ceiling, chattering a singsong melody, and laughing loudly. She snuggled against Kassler, half for protection, half because she felt something very special for him—she still wasn't certain what. Kassler wasn't like any other man Vita had met. He seemed terribly vulnerable and made no attempt to hide it. Vita found that enormously appealing.

Vita was never disappointed by Times Square. She was entranced by the flashing multicolored lights and gigantic billboards; by the Puerto Ricans with dyed red hair who danced by her, rocking and stomping to the music blaring from the large tape players held to their ears; by hebephrenically smiling nuns sitting on stools, coin-filled wooden bowls on their laps; by the whores who wore thin satin pants and sequined sweaters in the cold as they argued with pimps wearing long fur coats and sunglasses.

"*Fabulous*," Vita would exclaim repeatedly as she pushed through the midnight crowds, oogling at windows filled to the ceiling with electronic devices, fending off derelicts who clutched at her sleeves and pleaded, "I'm starving to death—how about a buck for a ticket to Jersey."

Vita was a likely target for the men with long unkempt beards and sandwich signs which read, "Repent and live in Jesus or be lost forever." She would listen politely, agree to reform her ways, and move on.

On one occasion Vita stopped a pair of pamphleting Black Muslims to inquire why it was that they kept changing their names, adding "Muhammeds" and "X's", and making it very difficult for her to keep track of it all. Kassler rescued her with little grace to spare.

On another occasion, she coerced Kassler into accompanying her inside an establishment specializing in pornographic wares, where, after complimenting the proprietor on how neat she thought it was for him to have organized the magazines by subject matter—homosexuals, lesbians, bondage, mixed groups, etc.—thereby saving the customers time sorting through perversions that didn't appeal to them, Vita proceeded to engage a middle-aged gentleman in a three-piece suit, who was about to enter a film booth in the store's back, in a discussion about spanking and how she had once let a fellow try it but it didn't do much for her.

This particular night Kassler, feeling not unlike a seeing-eye dog, kept close by Vita and steered her through the crowds and another near disaster.

They had emerged from a showing of "Uomo the Ghoul— he preys on human fear, he feeds on human flesh," when Vita had a sudden craving to see her first pornographic film. Kassler knew his opinions to the contrary would not prevail, so he led Vita to the least squalid-looking facility. Almost immediately, Vita became intrigued by a door with a poster depicting a psychoanalyst leering at every analyst's fantasy of the perfect analysand, in this particular case, a nubile blonde in her late teens who reclined fetchingly on a couch. Near the bottom of the poster were the words, "Would you trust your daughter to . . . 'THE PSYCHIATRIST,'" a provocative title, one has to concede.

Accordingly, Vita could not resist. She entered the tiny booth with Kassler and dropped a quarter into a slot. A hazy colored image began to flicker on the back of the door. However, the psychiatrist had scarcely started to ply his trade, when the film abruptly halted and the small room went dark.

"Hey!" shouted Vita, who, at Kassler's earnest request, had just removed his distended organ from his trousers.

"Shhh. . . ." Kassler explained.

"Hey! The goddamn film's broke!" Vita called out. "We've got a defective film in here!"

Kassler placed his hand over Vita's mouth.

"It's okay," he told her. "You only get a minute for each quarter. You have to put in another quarter."

"What a lousy gyp!" Vita said loudly as she peeled Kassler's hand off her face. "This is a *lousy gyp!*" Vita shouted.

Suddenly, the unlocked door to their booth opened, and an obese man with a thin mustache glared at them, while Kassler tried without success to stuff his erection back inside the suddenly very small opening in his trousers.

The fat man didn't seem to care.

"You've got to quiet down in here," he snapped in a throaty voice. "You're disturbing the other customers."

"This is a lousy gyp, you know," Vita said while Kassler tugged at her sleeve with his free hand. "You made it sound like you get a whole film for a quarter. It's deceptive advertising. You can get in trouble for that."

"She's from Cleveland," Kassler explained in panic. "She doesn't know what she's saying. She's new in New York. Brand new."

The fat man looked at Vita for several seconds in silence.

"You don't like it," he told Vita, "you can take your friend and his hard-on somewhere else." Then he made an obscene gesture and left.

"Hey!" Vita started to leave the booth. "He gave me the finger, Sy! No one gives me the finger. *No* one."

"It's okay. It's okay." Kassler kept Vita from leaving. "It doesn't mean a thing in New York. It's an old folk custom down here. Forget it."

Vita did not forget it.

Agreeing that they should probably leave the premises immediately, Kassler and Vita headed down the hall, Kassler's awkwardly extended appendage having retreated during the dangerous confrontation between Vita and the store manager.

Halfway down the hall, Vita was attracted by another poster and then stopped.

"We've got to see this," Vita told Kassler as she reached for the door to another booth.

"I think there's—" Kassler started.

"This damn thing is stuck," Vita pushed hard at the door. There was an instant splintering sound. The door opened.

"Oops, sorry," Vita said as she stared at the two men inside.

"Come here, sweetheart," a deep voice came from the booth. "I think I'm in love with you."

"I've got something for you, honey," another deep voice issued from the enclosure.

Vita smiled and snapped out her middle finger.

"Oh, God," said Kassler. "Let's get out of here."

In a fleeting instant after Vita had stuck out her finger, Kassler saw the long silver edge of a switchblade flash into the light. Vita saw it, too, and bolted down the hall. Kassler raced after her and got hold of her hand just as she reached the doorway.

"This way," Kassler said, jerking Vita out the door and down the crowded street. He glanced quickly over his shoulder and saw two thin men in leather jackets racing after them. In the hand of one of them was the extended knife.

"I thought you said it was an old folk custom," Vita said. They turned the corner and started running along Forty-second Street.

"What the hell were they doing in there?" Kassler ducked with Vita into the entranceway of a massage parlor, where a thin, seedy-looking man was shouting, "Girls, girls, girls! Lovely ladies!"

"I'm not sure," Vita answered, gasping for air. "The guy with the beard had a whole lot of money. The other guy had all these little plastic packets filled with sugar or something."

"Oh, Christ," Kassler mumbled. He poked his head out and determined that the two men were no longer pursuing them. Then he grabbed Vita and leaped into a taxi cab.

Once Times Square was safely in the distance, Kassler and Vita turned to each other. Vita smiled contentedly.

"You almost got us killed, you know," Kassler tried to be stern in the midst of her joy but could not.

"Wasn't it exciting?" Vita beamed.

"Jesus Christ, Vita," Kassler shook his head and put his open palm against her flushed cheek. "You can't act like that around here. It's dangerous."

"You know what I like about New York?" Vita said as she planted a kiss on Kassler's cheek. "It's not at all like Cleveland."

Kassler performed with brilliance on his exams. His term paper, "Human Behavior: Science or Science Fiction?" explored, in just twenty pages, all psychological theories from Plato to Freud and found them wanting. Human activity, Kassler concluded, cannot be understood. There are no rules.

From the young faculty member who graded his paper, Kassler received a B + and a hastily scrawled comment on the special six-dollar binder in which Kassler had submitted his treatise.

"Good paper. Let us all pray you are wrong," the instructor wrote.

"Horses!" Vita exclaimed while she and Kassler walked along Fifty-seventh Street after having a very late dinner out to celebrate Kassler's successful completion of his first semester. "I just *love* horses, Sy."

"They're called hansom carriages," Kassler informed his lady as she walked over to pet a large brown horse that was snorting steam in the cold December air.

"He's so beautiful," Vita said.

"We ought to get going," Kassler said.

"Let's go for a ride. Please?" Vita cooed.

"It's almost two a.m." Kassler appealed to Vita's diurnal rhythms.

"Just a short one?" Vita nuzzled the horse with her cheek.

Kassler took a ten-dollar bill from his pocket and handed it to the driver, who sat in a little seat in the back of the carriage.

The driver held it up to the street lamp to inspect its watermark; then, satisfied, he nodded to Kassler to get into the vehicle.

"Okay, now," Vita talked to the horse. "We're going to go for a little ride. You be a good boy and give us a nice trip, and I'll give you a special treat when we're done."

The driver looked at Vita strangely, then at Kassler.

"She likes horses a lot," he explained.

The man nodded his head.

"What's his name?" Vita asked the driver as she got into the carriage.

"I don't know," the drawn, middle-aged man answered and snapped the reins. The horse started his slow walk.

"No, I mean, what's his *name*?" Vita couldn't accept that the man understood her question.

"I don't *know* his name," the driver answered again. "I just work for the company. They give me the hack and the animal. I drive it."

"He's *got* to have a name," Vita insisted.

"He probably does, lady, but I don't know it."

"You sure someone didn't tell you his name?"

The man studied Vita in silence for several seconds.

"Larry," he lied. "The animal's name is Larry."

Vita and the driver continued to stare at each other.

"Larry Rizzuto," the driver nodded at Vita. "His last name is Rizzuto."

"Well, Larry Rizzuto," Vita turned toward the plodding animal, "you're up really late tonight, aren't you? But don't you worry. You're really going to like the treat I've got for you."

Kassler studied Vita in fascination.

"I know it's not easy," Vita continued her discussion with the horse, "pulling this heavy carriage all night. I hope they feed you lots of nice oats and hay. And they give you lots of good fresh water to drink. Because you need lots of water, don't you?"

Vita talked to the horse for ten minutes. Kassler was absolutely beguiled by Vita's innocence. He thought that Vita's bizarre behavior was the most darling thing he'd ever seen. As near as I have been able to tell, this is a common neurological syndrome displayed by humans in love. It's untreatable.

Kassler watched with stuporous joy as Vita talked, joked, and sang to the large brown snorting beast that was transporting them. When Vita finally stopped to take a breath, Kassler took her hand.

"I'd like you to marry me," he said.

"I don't understand," Vita answered.

"I want to know if you'll marry me," Kassler told her.

"Why?" Vita looked curiously at Kassler.

"Because I love you," Kassler gave the only reason that came into his head.

"Oh," Vita said.

"Will you marry me?" Kassler asked.

Vita looked at Kassler and thought for a few minutes while Larry Rizzuto's hoofs clacked against the concrete.

She liked Kassler a lot. She had never really considered marrying him. Maybe living with him, but that was all. They hadn't even slept together. Still, she found herself attracted to Kassler as she'd been to no other man. As a matter of fact, being attracted to men had always been something of a problem for Vita, and she took her comfort with Kassler to be a portent of good things to come.

"We don't know a whole lot about each other," Vita said. "I'm an only child. I'm not sure how I'd do with someone else around *all* the time."

"We're with each other all the time now, practically," Kassler said.

"You're just doing this so I'll go to bed with you," Vita joked.

"You'd still go to bed with me if we weren't married," Kassler pointed out to Vita.

"Yes, I would," Vita agreed. "I'm going to go to bed with you tonight, Sy. I decided that a long time ago."

Kassler took Vita's hand in the chilly night and looked into her eyes.

"Marry me because I'd like to spend the rest of my life with you, and so we can raise a beautiful family together, okay?" Kassler asked tenderly.

"How can I say no to that?" Tears came to Vita's eyes and she put her arms around Kassler and hugged him.

"Is that 'yes'?" Kassler asked.

"It's as close as I'll ever come," Vita smiled and kissed Kassler.

For a split second, less than the time it takes a nova to explode or an owl to wink its eye, Kassler and Vita experienced a shudder which they attributed to the night's chill. It happened so quickly that it scarcely touched their conscious selves, and then it disappeared into their unconscious, leaving only the moment.

"It feels very good," Kassler dispelled the fleeting experience. "And a little strange, too. Husband and wife."

"Yes," Vita agreed. "It does feel a little strange."

For the remainder of the ride, our prenuptial couple held hands while Vita discoursed with the horse. When they finally arrived back at the starting point, Kassler gave the driver a tip while Vita went over to share some of her candy with the animal and continue her dialogue.

The driver was pleased with the gratuity. He tied the reins to a post, and left to spend his newly acquired wealth almost immediately.

"I think we should do something special to celebrate, don't you, Sy?" Vita asked as she fed the animal.

"Like what?" Kassler was becoming suspicious.

"Well, you know," Vita told Kassler as she stroked the side of the horse, "making this poor animal pull that heavy carriage is horribly cruel, don't you think, Sy?"

"Oh, I don't know. He's probably been doing it for so long, he doesn't know the difference," Kassler attempted to reassure Vita.

"No, you're wrong, Sy," Vita insisted. "Look how he's all bound up and everything."

"Not really," Kassler persisted. "There're just these two buckles that hold him. The rest is to hold the carriage."

"That's all," Vita beamed, "just two buckles?"

Kassler knew what was about to happen. He lunged for Vita, but it was too late. In one quick motion, she undid the buckle on the near side and, laughing, raced to the other side, where she swiftly unfastened the remaining buckle.

The horse turned and looked in bewilderment as the harness fell to the pavement. He tossed his head, whinnied, and snorted several times.

"Go ahead, you dope," Vita shouted. "You're free."

"Oh, my God," Kassler said when he reached Vita. He started to pick up the harness. "You can't do this, Vita. He doesn't *want* to be free."

"Everybody wants to be free, Sy. *Everybody*. Hyah," Vita shouted and slapped the horse on its hindquarters.

"Good-bye, Larry," Vita called as the animal galloped ahead into the park.

Kassler and Vita watched the horse disappear into the night and then both of them collapsed, laughing, into each other's arms.

"Where's my horse?" a voice shouted from down the street. "What have you done with my goddamn horse!" the driver yelled as he raced toward them.

"Uh-oh!" Kassler stopped laughing almost instantly.

"We set him *free*!" Vita shouted back defiantly.

"Let's go," Kassler said as he grabbed Vita's hand. "Let's get out of here."

When the man reached the park entrance, he stopped for a second, trying to determine whether to go after Kassler and Vita or the horse. Then he turned and bolted down the bridle path.

"You sons-a-bitches," he shouted as he ran after the horse. "You know how much they'll charge me for a *horse*? You sons-a-bitches," his voice trailed into the darkness. "Horse! Here, horse!"

When Kassler and Vita saw they were no longer being chased, they stopped running.

"You still want to marry me?" Vita asked as she tried to regain her breath.

"No," Kassler panted.

"You'll do it, anyway," Vita assured him.

"Probably," Kassler concluded as he put his arm around his bride to be.

"You're crazy if you do." Vita held Kassler's waist tightly.

"Probably," Kassler smiled at Vita because he thought he was making a big joke.

Vita unclothed was even more beautiful than Kassler had imagined. Her body seemed to shimmer in the darkness, that night Larry Rizzuto was set free.

"How did you decide on tonight?" Kassler asked. He gently kissed the line where Vita's hair met the top of her brow.

"I figured that if we could make it to the end of the semester and still like each other, it'd be okay," Vita answered.

Kassler kissed Vita's eyelids. They flicked lightly like butterfly wings under his tongue. Then he moved his lips down the thin line of her nose and darted his tongue around her lips for several minutes.

"I don't know how much longer I could have stood it," Kassler admitted. He kissed Vita's shoulders and slender arms, and finally settled on her breasts, which he licked and sucked on until the nipples seemed so swollen that they might burst. He ran his hands in circles around the huge round forms, pressing firmly, taking a nipple deeply into his mouth and sucking as hard as he could, then barely brushing the dark buds with the end of his tongue.

"I know," Vita moaned beneath Kassler. "I knew my time was running out. Finally, I figured, how bad could sex really be? Oops," Vita tried to catch her breath.

Kassler, whose head was now buried into the cottonlike softness of Vita's tummy, stopped.

"How bad could—?" Kassler halted in midsentence. "How many times have you . . . ?"

"Not a whole lot," Vita interrupted Kassler. "Once or twice."

There was only silence from Kassler.

"Maybe less than that, if you mean the guy actually putting himself inside me. Please don't laugh, Sy. But I'm a virgin."

"You're twenty-six years old," Kassler said.

"I'm still a virgin. I probably popped my hymen a long time ago because I've done other kinds of things to relieve sexual tension, but I think technically I'm still a virgin."

"I don't believe it," was all Kassler could say.

"Why?" Vita turned on her side and propped herself up on her elbow. Kassler watched in amazement as Vita's breasts hung like giant melons from her chest.

"Because . . . because . . ." Kassler didn't know how to express what he wanted to say.

"Because of my body? You're not very ecology-minded, Sy Kassler." Vita wiped away a single tear and smiled tentatively.

"I'm not what?" Kassler asked in confusion.

"You think that wherever there's oil, you should drill. You have no consideration for the preservation of natural resources."

"What about all those other guys?" Kassler tried to sort out matters. "You had to—"

"What other guys?" Vita interrupted. "The ones who ditched me when I wouldn't go to bed with them within the first twenty-four hours after we'd met?"

Kassler reached out and took Vita's hand. He held it silently for several minutes and looked into her brown eyes.

"How come you waited so long?" he finally asked, almost in a whisper.

Vita looked back at Kassler and tears began to form in her eyes. She brushed the droplets with the back of her hand and tried to smile through them.

"I guess I've been scared," she told him. "I'm a very repressed person, Sy. You don't know me. I've got a lot of problems."

Kassler leaned over and kissed Vita.

"I'll be careful," he said softly.

Vita reached up and ran her hand along Kassler's short beard.

"I don't want you to be careful, Sy," she said. "I want you to do it to me like you would any other woman. Do it to me really hard, Sy."

Then Vita leaned back on the bed, raised her knees, and opened her legs up as wide as they could go.

"Do it to me good, Sy. Please."

Kassler moved until he had one hand under each side of Vita's bottom and pulled aside with his thumbs the large folds of skin between her legs. Then he buried his head between her legs and lightly licked the damp crease, running his tongue deeper and deeper into the groove.

As his tongue lapped Vita with increasing frenzy, Vita pushed herself up on Kassler's lips as far as she could, attempting to press every inch of the wet flesh that was causing her such exquisite pleasure.

One at a time, as he flicked and darted back and forth, Kassler inserted first one finger, then two, and finally three, thrusting them in and out, rotating them and massaging Vita's insides with his fingertips.

When he knew that Vita was wet and wide and could stand it no longer, he withdrew his hand, raised himself up on his arms, and, a little at a time, inserted himself until he could go no farther.

"Oh, my God," Vita groaned as she felt herself fill up with Kassler. "I don't believe it," she said mostly to herself.

Kassler reached for Vita's waist and held firmly to it, his fingers kneading her round hips, as he pulled up to his knees.

"Tell me what you want me to do," Vita asked, out of breath from the sensations which were deluging her, but before getting an answer, she instinctively raised her legs farther and locked them around Kassler's neck. Then she held on to Kassler's arms as he drove himself back and forth inside her, pulling her hips tightly against him, rotating his own hips sideways and then thrusting as deep as he could until Vita felt she could hold no more of him, going deeper each time, faster, until finally he lifted his finger to his lips, wet it with saliva, and, holding Vita to him by the finger inserted into her bottom, pounded frantically until he exploded with great intensity inside the most spectacular girl he'd ever seen.

"I don't believe it," Vita said as she rested beside Kassler. "I just don't believe it. That was some performance. I feel like a French horn must feel after a lot of Mozart. I had no idea people could be played like that."

"I take it that it was not an altogether unpleasant first experience." Kassler felt smug indeed.

"It was okay," Vita toyed with Kassler.

"You were beautiful," Kassler became serious. "You're a wonderful lover."

"I am?" Vita was touched, and tears started to work their way back into her eyes. "I've always been scared I wouldn't be, that I'd be terrible, Sy. Everyone's always told me what a gorgeous body I have, but I've never *felt* gorgeous. I've always felt kind of shy and awkward. I might just as well have had a terrible body."

"I'm glad you don't," Kassler said. "I'm glad you're beautiful."

"You know something crazy?" Vita said. "I've been on the pill for over six years. I guess I've always wanted to make love—there've been a lot of opportunities—but I just couldn't get myself to do it. There's something about men, there's something about the way they act, that just doesn't work for me. Men have always seemed crazy and scary to me. They seem so dense and aggressive, you know what I mean?"

Kassler wasn't really listening. He was tracing the curves of Vita's body with his eyes, from her breasts to the soft dark triangle that covered the space where he had had so much pleasure.

"Uh huh," Kassler agreed with Vita in general about whatever it was she had said.

For several minutes Kassler lay still in the dimly lit room, staring at the ceiling. Vita rested quietly beside him.

"I've never been very good at one-night stands," he finally told her. "I've tried it a couple of times, I guess, but, I don't know, there's just something about it afterwards that doesn't make me feel very good. It's too impersonal for me, I suppose."

Kassler took Vita's hand and continued.

"Ever since I can remember, I've wanted a family, a wife, children, a nice home in a good neighborhood with sidewalks, someplace safe enough to ride bikes. I'd like to putter around with my hands, fixing things around the house, and coach a Little League ball team someday. I want my life to be simple, Vita, uncomplicated, seeing patients during the day, reading in the evening, or going to a movie or out to dinner, taking vacations at the shore in the summer. Sharing. Being close to someone special."

Kassler held Vita's hand more firmly. He thought about how good it felt to be with Vita after all the years with New York pseudo-intellectuals, how refreshing it was to experience a mind uncluttered with psychological interpretations of behavior and erudite insights into everything from philosophy to baseball. He saw a great time ahead for him, protecting Vita's marvelous ingenuousness from the dangers of daily existence. He longed to share Vita's simple vision of life.

"I'm going to take good care of you, Vita," he said softly. "We're going to have a beautiful life together. You're going to be really happy."

Kassler turned over and looked at Vita, who had long ago fallen fast asleep.

CHAPTER 3

Kassler and Vita were married during the Christmas recess, and Vita moved into Kassler's small but adequate apartment.

Kassler was supremely confident. Buoyed by his affection for Vita on one side and dreams of the Contemplative Life on the other, he saw smooth sailing ahead toward the lush tropical island of Life on which the Divine Light of marital bliss never set.

When well-meaning friends took Kassler aside and pointed out that deep within the thickets of his jungle paradise dwelled Leopards of Malice and Fraud, Lions of Violence and Ambition, and, especially, She-Wolves of Incontinence, Kassler dismissed such warnings as the infantile fantasies of those jaded souls unwilling to believe in True Love and the Human Spirit, and, therefore, not worthy of his serious consideration. Faith and, most of all, Reason, good old-fashioned common sense, would navigate a safe course and negotiate all dangers. Kassler was certain of it.

Now, it was near the end of 1969 when Kassler and Vita put their pasts behind them and emerged from the Dark Wood of Error to join forces on a great voyage to the Mount of Joy. It could have been any time at all, but it was 1969—lots of talk in the papers at that time about a place called Biafra. Two million people had died so far. More were to come.

Vita didn't know Biafra. Vita's world was a simple one. She thought Biafra was an island in the Pacific. Someplace like Bikini. Or Tahiti. Geography was not one of Vita's strong points. For Vita the world was divided into left and right, up and down, hot and cold. Asia was left. Europe was right. Arctic was up. Florida was down. Up is cold and down is hot.

Kassler, who was, in fact, born at that glorious moment when the Japanese decided to do for the left side of the world what the Germans were already doing for the right side, saw more of life's subtleties. He knew, for example, that Biafra was someplace new that had probably had another name not too long ago, and he had seen pictures of starving children with black, bloated bellies who lived there. He had also concluded that there probably wasn't much he could do about Biafra or the hungry children, so he tried not to think about it too much.

Instead, Kassler devoted himself to less global concerns— his academic career and his marriage, which, mysteriously, began to crumble before the moisture of the first terrified buss Vita had given Kassler to seal their marriage vows had scarcely evaporated.

On a bitterly cold January day in 1970, when the slightest wind made the windows of their apartment seem paper-thin, Kassler stood drying dishes beside Vita as she washed them. They had been married exactly nine days.

Vita looked up from the sink filled with soapy water and started sobbing.

"I *hate* marriage," she said through her tears. "It's an artificial institution invented by sadistic men to enslave helpless women."

Kassler looked at Vita in a state of shock.

"Maybe *I* should do the washing," he suggested. "You can dry."

"It's just crazy to think that a woman can commit her whole *life* to just one man," Vita continued as she cried. "It's absurd. It's *crazy*."

"You don't even have to dry if you don't want," Kassler offered his distraught new bride. "The dishes can just drip in the rack, and by the morning they'll be dry by themselves."

Vita looked at Kassler in silence for several minutes.

"I also think I hate you, Sy," she finally said. "I want you to know that. You're a very sweet man, but I think I hate you and I don't think I'm ever going to forgive you," and Vita walked into the bedroom of their small apartment, threw herself on the bed, and sobbed into the pillow.

Vita cried most of the night, and the next day, and the next night, and most of the next week. She stopped eating. She stopped talking. During the day she would sit silently curled into a ball on the overstuffed chair in the corner of the living room, staring absently into space. During the night she would lie in bed, her face buried in her pillow, quietly crying.

"It's going to be all right," Kassler tried to reassure her. "It's a normal way to feel," he tried to convince himself as much as her. "You'll get over it in a few days."

Vita didn't respond. She just looked at Kassler with intense feelings of hate.

Kassler held Vita, who turned rigid at his touch.

"I love you, Vita," he told her as he stroked her hair gently with his hand. "I love you very much. I'll take good care of you. Everything'll be just fine, you'll see."

Kassler felt a deep affection for Vita. He thought he knew how she felt. He sensed that inside her was a beautiful soul. He saw her as a frightened child who needed only to be held and comforted. Patience and kindness would win out, Kassler was convinced of it.

Slowly, at the end of a month, Vita began to come out of

the deepest aspects of her depression. She started to eat. She stopped crying.

"I was doing fine in Cleveland, you know," she began to talk to Kassler. "I had a good job and friends. I grew up there. I knew people. I knew the city. Here I've got nothing. Absolutely nothing. I feel like a zombie."

"Do you want to move back to Cleveland?" Kassler asked.

"Not really," Vita answered, much to Kassler's temporary relief. "I want to have a baby, Sy."

Kassler, who was already somewhat breathless from the staggering velocity of Vita's post-betrothal depression, lost the remaining reserve in his respiratory system and gasped in a frantic attempt to restore pulmonary function.

"There's no need for the performance," Vita said as she watched her husband turn blue.

"A baby?" Kassler wheezed.

"It'd be good for us, Sy," Vita said matter-of-factly. "It'd make us feel more together, break down the walls between us."

"An infant?" Kassler gulped some air.

"A human child," Vita was very explicit.

Kassler took several deep breaths.

"I'm a graduate student," he finally managed.

"We've got enough money," Vita explained patiently. "And I can keep teaching piano privately. We'll do just fine."

"School takes a lot of my time."

"Look, Sy, you wouldn't be the first graduate student with a kid. You could handle it if you made up your mind to do it. It's not impossible."

"But it's very *hard*. Not impossible, but *difficult. Complicated. Hard. Very hard.*"

Kassler looked at Vita's large sad eyes. He wanted to race off to the library. Somewhere, he was certain, there must be a book on the psychology of marriage, some expert opinion backed by careful, well-documented research that explained in simple terms what to do when a bride goes into a profound depression, declares she hates her husband, and then decides to have a baby. It was a problem, Kassler concluded, which could not have escaped the ubiquitous curiosity of clinical research.

Equipped with sound scientific data, Kassler was certain he could demonstrate to Vita that there was a likelihood, significantly greater than chance, that having a baby at this time would be a total disaster.

Vita sensed Kassler's diminished faculty for resolving the issue on his own, and utilized other, less rigorous avenues to make her case.

She took Kassler's hand and stroked it gently, the first sign of affection since their wedding day.

"It'd make me very happy," Vita cooed as she planted her wet lips on Kassler's and began to manipulate his crotch.

"It would?" Kassler trilled.

"Very happy," Vita mumbled as she extended her tongue into Kassler's mouth.

"Well..." Kassler's garbled response trailed off into the frigid night.

So, early in 1970, Kassler and Vita made a baby.

Statistical probabilities being what they are, pregnancy did not have a salubrious effect on Kassler and Vita's relationship.

On the contrary, Vita grew more sullen and distant from Kassler, who attempted to compensate for the lack of excitement in his life by immersing himself in the sordid details of the Charles Manson trial, the murders at Kent State, the railroad's persistent problems, and postal reform.

While Kassler spent his free time contemplating mass murder and how exactly Amtrak would get people back on the trains, Vita gave piano lessons and moped. Otherwise, their life together was devoid of emotional content. Kassler studied. Vita sulked. Occasionally they went out to dinner or saw a film. Vita made a policy of giving Kassler sex on Sunday nights because she discovered it made him less irritable during the rest of the week, but by September, when she was in her eighth month, Vita had to stop this, and Kassler began masturbating, at Vita's request, on Sunday evenings, so that the following week would go more smoothly.

Kassler endured. He spent many evenings lying alone on

the sofa in the living room, listening to the endless expressionless repetitions of "Clair de lune" by ten-year-olds, and trying without success to account for what had happened between him and his bride immediately following the signing of the marriage certificate. It seemed to Kassler as though it had been an order of execution—all the life in Vita had terminated, her body became flaccid and unattractive, and Kassler began to wonder whether there had ever been a sparkle in her eyes or he had just imagined it.

"Is this at all fun for you?" Kassler asked one evening, shortly before Vita delivered. "Do you enjoy living like this?"

"It's not *fun* and it's not *not* fun," Vita answered matter-of-factly. "It's life. It's not supposed to be fun."

"Are you happy?" Kassler asked.

"I'm not anything," Vita said. "I'm tired, and I'm a blimp with another person inside me who's using up every bit of energy I've got. I'm tired, Sy. Very tired, that's all."

"You seem unhappy," Kassler said.

Vita looked at Kassler and tears came to her eyes.

"I'm miserable, if you want to know the truth. I don't know what happened to me, to us. Everything was going fine. Then we got married and I don't understand what went wrong. I think it's because I'm an only child."

"I'm sorry it's worked out like this," Kassler said quietly as he watched a tear streak Vita's cheek.

"Well, it's not your fault. It's me, Sy. It's all me. I don't do well with intimacy, and this whole thing is about as intimate as you can get without crawling inside someone else's skin. I feel like I'm being devoured alive, that's what I feel."

"Is there anything I can do?" Kassler asked.

"Since you can't have the baby for me, I can't think of anything," Vita said. "I'm going to bed."

Kassler sat alone in the living room while Vita got undressed and into bed. Then he went into the bedroom and sat down beside her on the edge of the bed. He took her hand and held it gently.

"I wish there was something I could do," he told her quietly.

"Well, there isn't, Sy," Vita said. "So don't get in a stew about it. I've got enough to handle right now without also having to deal with your guilt over all this. Just leave me alone, and once I've had the baby, everything'll be fine."

Kassler looked at Vita's head resting on the pillow. Her hair spread out with the rich darkness of a shadow. It set off her cream-colored skin, which reflected the light that came into the room from the hall. Kassler thought that Vita looked like an angel. One of His.

For several minutes he sat beside Vita, looking at her and thinking tender thoughts. He remembered that he had once read somewhere that having a baby was a joyful experience, but he wasn't absolutely sure about this. Maybe they were referring to what happened *after* the baby was born.

Then he kissed Vita gently on the cheek and headed for the bathroom because it was Sunday night again.

On November 15, 1970, nine months to the day after conception, Joshua Morris Kassler was born and Vita Volpe Kassler went into a post-partum depression without any noticeable remission of either her post-marital or pre-partum melancholia.

"This city is driving me up a goddamn wall," Vita announced to Kassler. "We have *got* to get the hell out of here."

Kassler shrugged.

"Well, how do you expect me to feel," Vita asked Kassler, "after I've gone through what I have and now I've got this big empty space in me? Besides, I can't stand infants. All they do is cry and crap and cry some more. You've got to feed them every time you turn around. You can hardly get any sleep at all. The time that I like kids is when they're old enough to have a decent conversation with and they can do their own laundry."

So Kassler became Joshua's mother and father. He bathed his son and changed his diapers, fed him his bottle and played peek-a-boo games. Since there was no one else in the house to whom Kassler felt he could talk, Kassler had long contemplative conversations with his son, mostly about life and manhood.

Vita retreated to the bedroom, where she lamented over her plight, the cruel fate of her gender's burden to bear children, and her own misfortune at not having breast milk to feed her son, a situation she found inexplicable and which led to bitter tears.

Those times when she found herself feeling guilty about the lack of mothering she was giving her son and she forayed into the nursery, Joshua was less than cooperative with this strange woman. Like a seismograph, Joshua appeared to be remarkably sensitive to the vibrations emanating from his world, and screamed like a tormented soul, you should pardon the expression, whenever his mother picked him up.

"He hates me," Vita told Kassler, who had arranged his academic schedule to allow him to be home to feed and care for Joshua as much as possible. "He's never going to forgive me for not having my milk. I just know it. I want another baby."

Kassler nearly dropped Joshua.

"You're kidding," Kassler finally decided out loud.

"Look, Sy," Vita explained, "just because you fail the first time doesn't mean you shouldn't try again."

"After you've figured out where you went wrong and licked the problem," Kassler told Vita.

"The only problem," Vita explained, "was that I'd never had a kid before and that scared me, which got everything off on the wrong foot, so my milk didn't flow, and that depressed me terribly because I felt I let Joshua down, and he's been angry at me ever since. This time I know what to expect."

Kassler dabbed some saliva off the corner of Joshua's mouth as he thought about Vita's explanation.

"You don't think," he finally asked, "that we ought to kind of *settle in* a little more before we have another kid, get things running more smoothly with Joshua, that I should finish graduate school, we should work out the little kinks in our relationship like our inability to talk to each other, to have sex, to feel good about our marriage, to love each other, to touch each other, that kind of thing?"

Vita was incensed.

"I wish," she snapped as she slammed her *Time* magazine onto the floor, "that every time I try to have a conversation about anything with you, you wouldn't always bring up how lousy our marriage is. Don't you think I know how lousy it is? And it isn't going to get any better by your talking about it every minute. You can't change feelings by *talking* about them, for chrissake. Feelings change because of the way you're treated, and what goes on inside you, and the experiences you have in the world. You're a psychologist. You're supposed to know that."

"The point is," Kassler stuck the bottle back in Joshua's mouth and ignored Vita's tirade, "that it isn't fair to bring another child into the world when we've got so many problems. I'm not even sure we could afford another child."

"The point is," Vita responded, "that I'm not going to have an only child. Joshua needs another kid around. It's not fair to him that he can't have a brother or sister to play with. Only-children are obnoxious, unhappy kids."

Kassler pressed his lips together tightly.

"Now," Vita continued, "we're going to have another kid sometime, so I figure that we might as well get it over with and do it now. We'll figure out a way to support it. The longer we wait, the longer we're going to have babies around. Let's just do it, and six or seven years from now they'll both be in school all day, instead of ten or twelve years from now, right?"

Kassler didn't say anything. He sat lost in thought for several minutes and then got up and took his sleeping son into the other room, where he laid him gently in his bed and pulled a small blanket over him. Then he planted a tiny kiss on his cheek.

When he returned to the living room, Vita had moved over to the sofa. Kassler sat beside her.

"You know," Vita said as she ran her fingers through Kassler's hair, "this would make us a real family. I think this would help us a lot."

Vita placed her other hand on Kassler's neck and moved it down until she came to his shirt. She undid the top two buttons and ran her fingers through his chest hair. Then she leaned over and kissed Kassler passionately on his mouth, running her tongue over his teeth and then thrusting it deep into his mouth.

Vita had a natural facility for repeating effective strategies.

* * *

So Vita became pregnant again, and what had been a disaster became a catastrophe. Vita's post-partum depression after Joshua's birth was joined now by a second-pregnancy depression.

"I have to accept the fact," Vita announced in her third month, "that some women are just not made to be mothers, and I'm one of them. I hope you like kids, Sy."

Then Vita regressed.

"I have just realized," Vita said one morning while Kassler, holding Joshua in one arm, shoveled cereal into Joshua's mouth with the other, "that I have never had a childhood. Never," Vita continued as she drank her instant coffee, "have I had the experience of being completely free, with no responsibilities, with someone around who takes care of *me*. I think that's why I'm having so much of a problem with having children."

"Do you think you might be able to get me a little coffee?" Kassler asked as he tried to open a jar of strained bananas with one hand.

"You're not listening to what I'm saying," Vita pointed out to Kassler. "I need someone to take care of *me*."

"If you'll just pour the hot water into a cup and bring over a spoon and the jar of instant coffee, I'll do the rest myself," Kassler suggested.

"It's not that I don't feel bad about your having to spend so much time taking care of Joshua, because I really do, Sy." Vita's stream of thought had prevented her from hearing Kassler's request. "But I have these needs deep inside me, you see, which have never been realized, and I think that until they are, I'm just not going to be happy."

"What do you have in mind?" Kassler asked as he got up, balancing Joshua and the cereal in his arm, and edged over to the stove, where he poured some hot water in a cup, added a spoonful of instant coffee and some sugar, and stirred.

"Well," Vita said, "I've been thinking about it. Kids have fun by playing with toys, and I've been trying to think, what is it that grown-ups have fun with that would be like playing with toys? Then the other night it came to me—sex."

Kassler picked up his coffee and went to sit on the chair next to Vita.

"Do you mean that?" Kassler asked with great interest.

"We've had sex only twice in eight months. You want to have a lot of sex?"

"Well, that's the thing," Vita said, and she took the hand with which Kassler was about to drink his coffee and held it very tenderly. "I do, Sy, but not with you."

Kassler froze. A chill went through his body.

"You see, Sy," Vita said, "for the last year or so I've been so goddamn horny I can't stand it, but if I had had sex with you, there would have been so much involved. It's so serious, you know what I mean? It's a marriage, with all that responsibility, and a child now, and you're here absolutely *all* the time. There's nothing at all playful about it. I mean, how could there be?"

"Who *do* you want to have sex with?" Kassler asked numbly.

"Well, I don't really know," Vita said, gently stroking Kassler's hand. "Probably lots of different men. The way I see it, it has to be like I have this shelf of toys that I can take down and play with any time I want, and when I'm done playing with one toy, I can play with another, with no responsibilities or cares or worries about feelings. Just fun. I've never had that experience, Sy, really. I think that's why sex has always been such a problem for me. This could be absolutely sensational for our relationship, Sy."

"What about me?" Kassler asked, confused and tormented. "What am *I* supposed to do?"

"Just be patient," Vita said sweetly. "That's all. This will be such a magnificent thing you'll be giving to me. It'll really pay off for us. It'll mean a new life for us both."

Kassler sat silently lost in thought while Joshua dribbled his bananas and babbled in his high chair.

"What am *I* supposed to do?" he repeated.

"Whatever you want," Vita told him. "If you need this, too, then go off and do it. It'd probably be good for you, too."

"I don't need it. I just want to have a good relationship with *you*, one woman, forever," Kassler said.

"But don't you see how much *pressure* that puts on me?" Vita explained. "If it doesn't work out with me, then it means a divorce, and pretty soon we're going to have two kids, and it's just a mess, Sy. It's like I'd better enjoy it with you or we're doomed. Who can have a good relationship like that?"

"I don't know if I can do this, Vita."

"I know you can, Sy," Vita held Kassler's hand firmly. "You're strong. You always have been. Deep inside you, you know that this is what we need to solve our problems and bring us together. I'll feel good about taking care of the children. I'll want to have sex with you again. I'll be happy. Then, as soon as you finish school, we can leave this stinking city and start a new life. If you really care about me, if you really love me, you'll support me in this. Otherwise, we're never going to make it, Sy. Never."

Kassler looked into Vita's dark eyes. Then he looked down at Joshua, who had fallen asleep in his high chair, strained fruit covering his small, fat hands.

"Okay," Kassler mumbled. "Okay."

Vita did not dally.

Kassler arrived home one evening the next week to find Vita in a dither as she put on her make-up and sprayed perfume about her neck.

"Hello?" he called.

"Sy? I thought you had classes tonight."

"Tomorrow night," Kassler said as he walked over to Vita.

Vita turned and took Kassler's hand.

"Sy," she said, looking plaintively into his eyes, "I really thought you had classes tonight. I've got someone coming over."

"Here?" squeaked Kassler. "Couldn't you have gone to *his* place?"

"I couldn't get a sitter, and I didn't think you'd be back so soon. I'm sorry," Vita said, and she ran a brush through her lustrous dark hair. "Don't worry, Sy. You'll do just fine. Lots of people have open marriages, and it works out terrifically. Please try to act mature," she chastised Kassler, "please."

She put down her brush, checked herself in the mirror, and turned to Kassler.

"Remember, this is a big chance for us both, Sy. It's going to do wonders for our marriage. Just keep thinking that, over and over. Also, Joshua gets a baby aspirin sometime soon, I think. He's teething, or something, and I gave him some aspirin a while ago. I'm not sure exactly when, so he'll need one in a little while, I think. You see how I'm starting to get into taking care of kids already?"

When the doorbell rang, Kassler went off to hide in the kitchen as Vita had requested. The sound of another man's voice in the apartment sent cold feelings into his stomach. Kassler wanted desperately to leave, but he was concerned that Vita would get overinvolved in her play therapy and wouldn't hear Joshua, so he steeled himself as best he could and stayed.

Vita, of course, wasted no time fetching her toy off the proverbial shelf and going into the bedroom for the playing she had missed as a child.

Kassler had brought his schoolwork into the kitchen with him, but it was no distraction. The muffled sounds of Vita and her lover talking reverberated through Kassler's brain until he felt as though he were inside a kettle drum.

For a while Kassler paced quietly back and forth in the kitchen.

"This is going to help our marriage," Kassler told himself over and again, like a prayer to keep himself from falling apart.

Then Kassler sat down on a kitchen chair and buried his head in his hands, trying to collect his thoughts.

"Oh, yes," Vita's voice came from the bedroom. "Yes, yes, yes," she repeated.

Kassler gritted his teeth. His insides began to ache.

"More," Vita said. "Please. More."

Kassler felt as though someone were cutting out his heart, bit by bit. He didn't know how much more he could stand.

"... just ... enormous," Vita groaned, "... enormous ... fantastic ..."

Kassler sat up in the chair and arched backward. The torment was nearly beyond his endurance. The thought of his child inside Vita tore at his heart. He tilted his head back and dug his nails into the seat as the pounding of the bed in the next room became more obvious and Vita's moans louder. Kassler heard the stranger grunt as he drove himself in and out of Kassler's wife.

". . . good . . . good . . ." Kassler could make out Vita saying.

". . . so good . . . now . . . now . . . yes . . ."

"Uh! Uh! Uh! Uh!"

Kassler heard the man come in Vita.

"Ohhhhhhh!" responded the most sensational woman Kassler had ever met.

All Kassler's agony burst. His brain screamed silently in pain, and then he fell forward in the chair and buried his head in his hands.

"What did I do to deserve this?" he kept asking himself. "Why me? Why *me*?"

It wasn't long before the man left. And only a few minutes afterwards, Vita came into the kitchen in her bathrobe to get a snack.

Kassler promised himself that he would do as Vita asked and act mature.

Vita said nothing. She hummed as she took some leftover roast beef from the refrigerator and began to slice it.

"So," Kassler finally started the conversation, "do you feel any better about our marriage?"

"You can't expect me to change after only one time," Vita whined, "just like that."

Kassler went to the refrigerator and fetched a bottle of soda from it.

"How many times do you think it'll take?" Kassler asked slowly as he poured his drink.

"I'm not sure," Vita said, her insides still twitching from the spasm of the man's large organ. "God only knows. It could take a lot of times, Sy, a *hell* of a lot of times," Vita's voice drifted off dreamily.

Kassler devoted himself to his work after that dreadful night, leaving time in his academic schedule only for child care. Fortunately, it was at this time, as Kassler's own life became progressively more a shambles, that he was assigned his first patients to treat in psychotherapy so they might lead productive, fulfilling, and emotionally rewarding lives.

Of course, as Kassler realized almost immediately, when his first patient entered and sat with great expectations before him—a bald man in his forties with an enormous belly—he had absolutely no idea how to do psychotherapy.

"I know it's my own damn fault," the man lamented as he rocked opposite Kassler, "but I can't stop these drinking binges, and, if I don't, I'm going to lose my job and my wife and everything I own, most of which is in hock already because I keep blowing my paycheck on booze."

Kassler sat silently looking at his patient, waiting for the man's unconscious to spring up like a large colorful flower growing directly out of the man's head. Surrounding it, like petals, Kassler was certain, would be the patient's persona, archetype, paranoid-schizoid position, libido, and super-ego.

But strangely, the man wouldn't oblige Kassler. He said nothing that suggested he was inclined to return to the womb or was sorrowful over having ruined the good breast. No matter how deeply Kassler inquired, the man's position remained the same. The man with the thick glasses and the slurred speech wanted only to find out how to stop his drinking binges before he lost everything that mattered to him.

Five minutes into the session, there was long silence. Kassler sat, smiling therapeutically, while he thought desperately about how to fill the remaining forty-five minutes that he and the gentleman across from him would be visiting.

"It is very important," Kassler finally broke the uncomfortable silence, "in order for me to help you, that I take a *complete* history."

Kassler picked up a pen and yellow-lined pad from the table beside him.

"Now, Mr. Amato," Kassler said with a barely hidden sigh of relief, "your great-grandparents were born in what year?"

Before very long, Mr. Amato was joined by a dozen or so other individuals looking to Kassler for insight into how to relieve the pain of their lives. I say that this was fortunate for Kassler because he knew so little about the process of psychotherapy that it took all his time and energy to develop the necessary skills. Since this was in addition to caring for his child, attending classes and supervisory sessions, studying for exams, and—the *sine qua non* of graduate-studenthood—perusing rats, scoring videotapes of pigeons pecking colored levers, and calculating the chi squares, means, and standard deviations of a seemingly unending number of faculty members' research projects, this left Kassler no time at all to deal with his marital circumstances, which were, in a couple of words, very unpleasant.

As he descended through predoctorate academia, to preserve whatever remained of his sanity, Kassler worked out a number of accommodations with Vita.

Vita agreed never again to bring a man to their home, in return for which Kassler agreed to provide or arrange for babysitting. Vita agreed never to tell Kassler where she was going or what had transpired, and Kassler worked hard at pretending that Vita was off at a concert or class, or, if she was at one of the many dating bars she frequented, she had no luck in finding a man. Usually Kassler was asleep when Vita returned, and this provided additional insulation.

"My husband and I have an arrangement," Vita explained to the men she found in the bars and discotheques. It was all that was necessary.

By the middle of his third year of school, Kassler was, of course, a nervous wreck.

His lack of contact with Vita made him desperately lonely. His academic life made him miserable.

Deprived of sleep and food, bored nearly into a stupor by the seminars and supervisory meetings, nauseated by his own continual sycophantic approach to all interactions with his supervisors, Kassler finally swore that, should he finish the program successfully, he would never have anything to do with the field of clinical psychology for as long as he lived.

Fortunately, just as Kassler reached the very deepest part of the deepest pit on his predoctoral excursion, he got a Christmas card in the mail from one of his patients, a Mrs. McKenna.

"Thank you for saving my life," she wrote very simply on the bottom.

Kassler read the sentence several times. Then he took a deep breath, pulled himself together, and plunged ahead through the darkness.

As it turned out, Mrs. McKenna became the subject of Kassler's dissertation. He wasn't really sure that there was all that much wrong with her when he first saw her, considering the life she had led, but by the end of her first year of treatment she was once again eating and sleeping well, and by the end of the second year she had overcome her grief at her husband's suicide and the death of her daughter, and had married a man who appeared to be stable and loving and expressed considerable affection for her and her children.

The development of Kassler's skills had come about in such a subtle way that Kassler didn't think he did anything much to produce these changes. The way Kassler saw it, he had cared a great deal for Mrs. McKenna and tried to be thoughtful about what she told him. He discussed with her why she felt the way she did about the things she discussed, what was real and what was fantasy, what was from the present and what from the past, and he tried to use common sense to determine if solutions she proposed to problems might work well for her. When Mrs. McKenna got angry at him for not being all that she expected, Kassler tried to help her understand whether the expectations were realistic and whether she had similar expectations about others. He tried to help her see what strengths she had that had gotten her through a very difficult life, and under what conditions she might need other people to help her out. He tried to understand as best he could the way she felt about herself and her life, and pointed out to her how well she was able to care for her children, and how easy love came to her. And that was all he did.

At the end of two years, when Kassler finally got to the last few minutes of the last session, he sat in silence looking at Mrs. McKenna. He realized that he knew more about this person than anyone else in the world did, and he would never see her again. Mrs. McKenna looked at Kassler and smiled as tears flooded her eyes. Kassler looked back at Mrs. McKenna and tears welled in his eyes. For the last few minutes of the session, Kassler and Mrs. McKenna sat in silence, smiling at each other, tears streaking their cheeks. Then Kassler got up and gave Mrs. McKenna a big hug, and, as he had predicted, they never saw each other again.

Kassler wrote it up for his dissertation, all except the last session, which he felt would be seen as unprofessional. At the oral exam on his dissertation, Karl Heinrich congratulated Kassler on his skillful use of the Freudian transference and countertransference. Ernst Hoch felt that it was Kassler's Jungian juxtaposition of the woman's persona as she grappled with the shadows deep within her that was eventually responsible for the progress the woman made. Frieda Kurtz, an elderly gray-haired Reichian, felt that Kassler had tapped into the tremendous energy the woman possessed and redistributed it for more healthy and viable life strategies.

For an hour, the members of the committee questioned Kassler, and then they asked him to leave while they decided on whether he had passed the last hurdle to his doctorate.

When Kassler returned, Frieda Kurtz looked deeply into Kassler's eyes and spoke solemnly. Kassler's heart beat faster and his heart sank.

"I'm not sure what your thesis is," Frieda Kurtz said quietly. "I'm not even sure you have one here. But I hope, for your sake, you don't feel that what you've learned here over the last four years is unnecessary, that theory, that Freud, Jung, Adler, Rank, Sullivan, mean nothing, that you have only to listen carefully to your patients and care for them in order to make mentally ill people well again. It will be years, *Dr*. Kassler, before you even begin to understand what you've learned."

Kassler grinned from ear to ear. That was it. "*Dr*. Kassler." The traditional way the chairman of the committee informed the candidate that he had passed.

Kassler heard nothing else that was said. At the end of the exam, he got up, still grinning, and shook everyone's hand. Then, academic gown billowing behind him, he ran all the way home to his apartment to tell Vita.

"That's very good, Sy," Vita said as she rested on the bed in only her nylon panties to escape the unexpected June heat wave.

Her skin seemed to Kassler to be pale and mottled with age, and her diminished breasts drooped down her chest, sagging against the bones of her lower rib cage.

"I had hoped for something a little more expansive in the way of congratulations," Kassler said.

"I'm sure you did," Vita answered. "Because you're never satisfied with what you get. I wish just once you'd accept me for what I am, take what I can give, and stop trying to change me. You're so needy, Sy. Now, I said that I thought your getting your degree was *very good*. That's the way *I* congratulate people. Take it or leave it. It's up to you."

Kassler looked at Vita slumped on the bed. She had lost twenty pounds since Kassler first met her, and all the roundness had turned into angles and sharp corners.

"Maybe now that I'm through with all the pressures of school, things'll be better," Kassler tried to say something optimistic.

"Don't count on it," Vita responded quietly. "I think that we've just about reached Divorceville, if you really want to know."

"I want to try to make this work," Kassler looked into Vita's bleary eyes. "I'd like you to stay."

"Well, I've got nothing better to do, that's for sure."

"I mean," Kassler's thoughts drifted off into the hot heavy air, "we have two kids now."

The birth of Joy, named by Vita in a gesture of hope and desperation, had occurred nearly two years previously under somewhat extraordinary circumstances.

Vita's water broke early in the morning and almost immediately she began to panic.

"I've changed my mind," she announced to Kassler. "I don't want another baby, after all."

"Okay," he said. "You want to go to a movie instead?"

"I'm serious, Sy," Vita looked intently into Kassler's eyes. "I'm still not ready to be a mother."

"Can we talk about it tomorrow?" Kassler tried.

"I don't want to talk about it tomorrow," Vita was adamant. "I've made up my mind."

"How about if we continue the discussion on the way to the hospital?" Kassler asked.

"I'm not going to the hospital," Vita said and went into the bedroom, where she lay down on the bed. Kassler followed her into the room.

"Look," he tried to be patient, "it's not really in your hands anymore. The baby's going to be born whether you like it or not."

Vita closed her eyes and clenched her teeth as she experienced the pain of a contraction. When it ended, she turned to Kassler.

"I'm scared, Sy," she said. "This time I'm *really* scared to death. The baby's going to kill me, Sy. I just know it. I'm going to die in childbirth." Vita looked desperately around the room for some escape from the pain of the next contraction, which was just starting.

When it was over, Kassler reached out and took her hands to help her from the bed. Almost instinctively, Vita pulled them back.

"Don't touch me," she glared at Kassler. "It's bad enough you have to put me through all this. Don't make it worse by trying to be all lovey-dovey about it. Just keep the hell away from me."

Miraculously, Kassler managed to get Vita into a taxi and over to the hospital, but by the time they arrived, the contractions were two minutes apart and Vita was screaming at the top of her lungs.

"Oh, God!" she shouted as two orderlies, a nurse, and a doctor strapped her down to a gurney and rolled her into the elevator.

"God help me! It's tearing my insides apart! I'm dying! I'm dying for sure!" she screamed at the top of her lungs, while the nurse tried unsuccessfully to calm her.

"Can't you give her anesthesia?" Kassler asked in the midst of Vita's yelling.

"Too late," the doctor said when they reached the maternity floor and wheeled Vita out of the elevator, down the hall, and into the delivery room.

"Oh, Jesus!" Vita was still screaming. "Help me! It's killing me! The baby's killing me! It's taking my insides with it!"

"The contractions are too close," the doctor with the black mustache and thick glasses told Kassler.

"Aaagghh!" screamed Vita. "I'm dying. My body is being torn to shreds! I don't want to die! Don't let the baby kill me! It's killing me! It's eating me up! I can feel it!"

The doctor gave Kassler sterile surgical greens to put on in an adjoining room while he checked Vita to make sure the baby was positioned properly.

"Save me!" Vita was still yelling when Kassler returned after changing. "Somebody save me! Don't let me die! There's a monster inside me! It's taking my life!"

The doctor turned to Kassler as he entered.

"If there's any way you know of quieting her down, now's the time to do it. I'd like to do an episiotomy before the baby pushes out and tears her up like a fist going through a paper towel—"

Kassler began to feel queasy in his stomach. He walked over to Vita.

"Get away from me, you son-of-a-bitch!" Vita shouted. "You did this to me, you bastard! I knew I never should have had sex! Once I started, look what happened! I'm never fucking again! Never! I mean it, Sy! No more sex! Ever!"

"You've got to quiet down, Vita," Kassler tried to be reassuring. "The doctor wants to do something to make it easier for the baby to come out, but he can't do it unless you hold still," Kassler tried to explain.

Vita took a deep breath between contractions.

"What's he want to do?" she panted.

"Well," said Kassler, "it's called an episiotomy. It's like this tiny little cut where—"

"Oh, God! No!" Vita screamed as loudly as she could. "He wants to cut open my vagina! Don't let him, Sy! Don't let him cut me there! Please! Oh, God! Please!"

"Every woman has it done," Kassler tried to reassure Vita. "It's part of childbirth. You had it done last time—"

"I'm going to die!" Vita yelled as she had another contraction. "I can feel it! I'm dying! I'm being killed from the inside out—"

Suddenly Vita stopped. A large man in a surgical gown was slowly walking into the room. A cap covered his head to his thick blond eyebrows. Tufts of blond hair curled out of the back of his cap. The bottom half of his face was covered with a surgical mask, underneath which was obviously a large beard. The man was six feet nine, big-boned, huge, and all that was visible under the sterile clothing were two green eyes looking quietly at Vita.

The man walked over to Vita and took her hands. He didn't say a word, but continued to stare at her. Kassler watched in amazement as Vita's body relaxed, and she let out a plaintive sigh. The room was strangely silent.

The obstetrician at the foot of the table looked up at the man who was holding Vita's hands and nodded to him that all was well.

Vita let out another sigh, almost a moan, and her body settled peacefully into the sheets on the delivery table.

"Now, push down nice and gently," the large man said to Vita in a deep voice, as he continued to hold her hands and look into her eyes.

With an expression of contentment, Vita pushed once, and the baby slid out of her in a single effortless motion.

Kassler was so intent on watching the stranger standing beside Vita that he didn't notice the baby. He was fascinated by what the man had done, by whether he had hypnotized Vita. Beyond that, as he looked into the man's eyes, Kassler thought he saw something terrible that frightened him.

"You have a healthy baby girl," the obstetrician announced.

Kassler broke from his trance and went over to Vita while the nurse cleaned off the blood-smeared infant.

The nameless man turned and walked away very slowly. Vita's eyes followed him as he left the room. Then, when he had gone, Vita took Kassler's hand.

"I'm sorry about how I carried on," Vita smiled sheepishly.

Kassler kissed Vita on the cheek and, at the request of the nurse, started to leave.

"Sy," Vita called after him, "there's something I've been meaning to tell you."

"What's that?" Kassler turned around at the doorway.

"I think I have a very low threshold for pain."

Kassler nodded in agreement and left to get out of his greens.

When Kassler entered the changing room, the man who had quieted Vita was finishing getting dressed. Without the surgical garb, he looked larger and older. He had a large thick blond beard and long thick curly blond hair. He seemed to Kassler like a giant old lion.

"Congratulations," the man said.

"Thank you," Kassler answered as he took off his own mask and cap. "Thank you very much for helping my wife. She was very scared. Are you an obstetrician?"

"Psychiatrist," said the man.

"You're good," said Kassler. "I'm studying to be a clinical psychologist."

The man appeared interested.

"Where are you going to school?" he asked as he sat down to slip off his shoe covers.

"Institute for Professional Studies."

"That's a good training center," the psychiatrist said.

He stood up and tucked in his shirt.

"I've just been appointed the director of a psychiatric hospital," he continued. "It's a new place across the river and we're just putting together a staff. If you're interested, give me a call when you graduate. I'll set up an interview. You'd have to relocate to New Jersey, but you might like it," said the psychiatrist, reaching into his wallet and retrieving a small white card.

The psychiatrist smiled at Kassler, handed him the card with one hand, and with the other reached out to shake Kassler's hand, which fit like a miniature doll's into the man's large palm.

As they touched, Kassler felt a strange feeling overtake him, just as he had seen happen with Vita.

And this was how Dr. Kassler first met Sam Zelazo.

FEBRUARY 1979

Session II

"*Well,*" *I began my session with Kassler,* "*I've been doing* a great deal of thinking since our last meeting, and I think I've got my problem all figured out."

"This is our last session, then?" Kassler asked with some interest.

"Absolutely," I affirmed. "Your work has done wonders for me."

Kassler drummed his pencil absently on a notebook he held in his lap and looked considerably less pleased by my announcement than expected.

"I'd be grateful if you'd share your insights with me," Kassler said. "When I tell my colleagues that I cured Satan in two sessions, they're apt to be skeptical."

"Yes, well, here's what I've concluded." I provided Kassler with the requested information. "It's a war. I'm the enemy. I shouldn't take it personally."

"This, I gather," Kassler interpreted, "is a continuation of the 'It's not my fault' paradigm."

"But with a very important difference," I pointed out. "Now I've adjusted."

Kassler didn't react.

"You see," I tried to get Kassler's attention, "it boils down to this. You all have a need for opposites. Up and down. Front and back. Light and darkness. Good and evil. Add to this an outrageous resistance to believing that disastrous consequences come from your very own *meshugass*, to use a technical term, and, well, what have you got? What you've got is Satan, the Lord of Evil, tempter, seducer, deceiver."

"It's genetic," Kassler nodded.

"Exactly." I was pleased that Kassler had caught on so quickly. "It's wired in. It comes with the human package. It's not your fault, any more than it's my fault. I just happened to be in the wrong place at the wrong time. The clergy wanted everyone to be good little boys and girls and come into the fold. They pulled. The heathen weren't so hot about giving up a lot of things that felt so good. They pushed. I was, unfortunately, in the middle."

"It must have been a terrible predicament for you," Kassler began doodling on his pad.

"You're telling me. Of course, I could kick myself now for not knowing better. Around the turn of the century—that's the fifteenth century—Herrs Sprenger and Kraemer published their *Malleus Maleficarum*. In addition to being a marvelous textbook on insanity and pornography—you should read it—it told how to get very crazy, highly suggestible women to remove the devil from their erotic beings by publicly describing the details of their sex lives to a board of inquisitors, which seemed to double in size every day, depending, of course, on how juicy a story the lady could tell. Those inquisitors who were *most* offended by the woman's wicked ways got to shave around the lady's genitalia so that, according to the *Malleus*, I couldn't hide in her pubic hair. Of course, *all* the inquisitors were terribly offended, so there was a lot of to-do over who got to be the barber. The whole business was not without a certain element of humor."

Kassler looked up from his pad.

"Weren't these women and children burned at the stake?" Kassler asked with some dismay.

"Well, that's the thing, Kassler. Not always. The people in

the village got smart after a while, and instead of burning the lustful women, they sent them off to the monasteries so the monks would stop defiling their daughters during confession. A sort of ecology developed. The monks weren't entirely to blame, of course. They had tried to get to their own kind, by digging tunnels between the monasteries and the nunneries, but it took so damn long, you know, that by the time the passageways were completed, there wasn't a female under fourteen left in the village who wouldn't kill to get into the confessional by the end of the day."

"You were saying how you could kick yourself for not knowing better?" Kassler steered me away from what I had assumed was a very good story. I sensed he didn't get the point.

"Yes," I tried to explain. "You see, the *Malleus* described these little *incubi*, male demons, running around seducing women, while thousands of tiny *succubi*, female demons, were doing the same to men, both under my constant direction, of course, because no one, not the men in the village, not the ladies jamming the confession booths, not the monks and nuns sprinting up and down the tunnels, really *wanted* to get laid. The only individual in existence who thought that sexual intercourse was not a bad way to pass a half-hour or so was *me*. Without my insidious temptations, everyone would have been out shearing sheep."

"I see," Kassler continued to scribble around the borders of his notepad. "And now, five hundred years or so later, you've had this insight."

"The crux of the problem is this. Man will do absolutely anything to avoid having to face himself. I'm the result."

Kassler leaned back in his chair and thought this over while he rolled his pencil across his pad.

"Think about it, Kassler," I continued. "First you all contemplated the stars. Then the world. *Lastly*, yourselves. This was no accident. If it weren't for me, you'd have to face some rather unpleasant things. Underneath that marvelous civilized façade are the same good old untamed sexual and hostile impulses of your dearest savage ancestors, you know. What I've come to realize, Kassler, is that, in a very basic way, I'm your savior."

"Our savior?" Kassler asked incredulously.

"I thought that'd get your attention," I told him.

"Our savior?" Kassler repeated.

"I'll admit that right now I don't get a whole lot of credit for this."

"This is the great insight you've had?" Kassler asked in disbelief.

"Yes, it is. I think there's been a terrible mix-up. As I've thought about it, I've come to realize that I've suffered for man's sins far more than Christ ever dreamed possible. I'm crucified every day of my existence. When the priests couldn't equate pleasure and piety, who got the blame? When philosophers and scientists were considered dangerous enemies of civilization, who do you think was responsible? The Vendidad listed ninety-nine thousand, nine hundred ninety-nine diseases—all attributed to me! Exorcise the demon and you get better."

"That was three thousand years ago," Kassler knew his history. "You certainly don't believe that *modern* medicine thinks you have anything to do with disease?"

"Ever happen to notice what creature's wrapped around the staff that symbolizes the *modern* medical profession?" I asked.

"A serpent," Kassler answered quietly.

"You got it."

"It's an old symbol," Kassler explained. "Modern medicine deplores anything that even suggests hocus-pocus."

"Well, *I* believe you, Kassler, but tell that to all those folks out there with prescriptions that say, '*signa, cochleare parvum ad tertiam vicem, ante jentaculum, ante prandium, hora decubitus.*'"

Kassler was strangely silent.

"It's okay," I finally told Kassler. "Magic has a long and illustrious history."

"Medieval," Kassler mused out loud. "My impression is that throughout history magicians have ended up broke and despised."

"Absolutely. I for one have always believed that the three

Magi, as in *magician*, accumulated their gold, frankincense, and myrrh from the practice of psychiatry, but there are rumors that persist regarding their use of abracadabra. . . . Of course, as you've pointed out, these three men are now held in such universal contempt that it's hardly worth considering them."

Kassler continued to doodle on his pad.

"I trust," I said, "that I have not shaken your faith in modern medical science—or yourself."

"I had thought," Kassler ignored my comment, but not easily, "that you were interested in finding out how it was that misimpressions about you had occurred. And in correcting them."

"I believe I understand now where the myths came from," I informed Kassler. "They came from your frantic search to attribute the basest instincts and desires to anyone but yourselves. And the chances of my correcting these fantasies are, as near as I can tell at this point, virtually nil. I've come to accept that I mustn't get so upset over the frailties of men. You may continue to blame me, but I'm convinced that I'm without guilt."

"Like a true savior, you will bear men's burdens," Kassler picked up my train of thought.

"I will. I am, after all, ultimately responsible for mankind."

Kassler began making notes on his pad. "I had always assumed that God—"

"Don't be ridiculous, Kassler. You don't think that for even one second God concerns Himself with the fates and actions of men on this earth."

"I had always considered that as a possibility," Kassler said sincerely. "But if you say that—"

"Why?" I was a bit agitated by Kassler's misconception. "What has *ever* led you to believe that?"

"I'm not really sure. I suppose I've always taken it on faith. I always assumed that it was a matter of hierarchy. You know, the opposites. He was good. You were bad. He was up. You were down. You *were*, by your own admission, thrown out of heaven."

"Not without a fight," I pointed out.

"And my assumption was that to have dominion over man and the earth, one would need certain *powers*—"

This was more than even I could take.

"You're not telling me that I'm weaker than God?" I snapped at Kassler.

"—a certain majestic nature, glory, dignity, what have you—" Kassler continued.

"Majestic nature! Glory! Dignity!"

"There are, I understand," Kassler wouldn't stop, "those like Emerson who, as a matter of fact, feel that Satan isn't even necessary, *if* he exists. The *whole world* is an omen and a sign. Why look so wistfully in a corner?"

"A corner!"

"Man is the image of God, why run after a shadow?"

"You believe that? You believe that you're created in *God's* image? You believe that I dwell in a corner? That I'm a shadow?"

"Not me, of course," Kassler drew figures on his pad, "but there are others, I've heard. . . ."

"Well, let me tell you something about dignity, glory, and majesty," I said loudly. "The greatest creative minds in history have been inspired by me—Dante, Milton, Blake, Mozart, Marlowe, Shaw, Goethe—Goethe said that I'm the desire to *know*. To *know*. I'm responsible for the work of all nature. As far as man is nature, so much is he a part of Satan. Is that power or isn't it?"

"You *were* expelled from heaven," Kassler repeated.

"Yes, I was. And it's a hurt I may never get over. But I have maintained my dignity. I have held my glory."

"And still we prefer to align ourselves with God," Kassler pointed out. "Is this resistance to accepting responsibility for our impulses?"

"I don't *know* why it is," I shouted. "I only know that it's a terrible mistake. If you need to have someone by your side with power and glory and dignity—"

I paused to think over exactly how to say what I wanted. Kassler was still scribbling notes on his pad.

There was a long silence.

"Think about what it must take," I finally said, "to oppose a power you know you can never conquer."

Kassler looked up from his notes and stared ahead at the mass of wires on the wall of Szlyck's basement. I spoke very softly.

"Think what it must take to dare to be God's enemy," I said.

We stayed there in silence for several minutes. I had stirred up something in Kassler.

"You need me, Kassler," I said quietly. "When you come right down to it, I'm not such a bad fellow. Take me to your heart. I'm a good ally. You won't regret it."

"That's not our contract," Kassler said slowly. "Our agreement is for psychotherapy."

"Consider it a bonus. You can't go wrong, Kassler. Believe me."

"Psychotherapy," Kassler repeated, but I could hear the crackling sound of Kassler's neurons firing away as they searched futilely for an existing pathway in which to assimilate the concept of such an alliance.

"Of course," I added hastily, "there's no need to decide right now. We can talk about it next session."

"This is not our last session, then," Kassler nodded.

"There're a few little details that've come up today. I may need to consider them more carefully. Besides, we had a deal. Seven sessions. And I never renege on a deal."

"Never?" Kassler was a little surprised.

"Never. Think about it, Kassler. All those charming tales about men who were clever enough to outwit the devil and keep their souls. Everyone knows about me. Satan has *never* evaded his end of the bargain. Not once. I do what I can to set an example for my negotiators."

And with this our second session came to an end.

PART IV

Phlegethon

CHAPTER 1

The city of Citadel, New Jersey, owed its existence to the largess of the United States Department of Housing and Urban Development, who decided, by a means still unclear, to reclaim a site that until then had consisted exclusively of garbage dumps, automobile graveyards, petroleum refineries, marshland, and swamp. With cunning and ingenuity, Citadel was established without disturbing this natural ecological balance.

A marvel of city planning, Citadel was designed after the spoke-and-wheel plan given to Washington, D.C., by its astute architect, Pierre L'Enfant. The city consisted of nine concentric circles, First Avenue through Ninth Avenue, which were set like rings around the inside of an enormous cone, actually in what had once been a giant sand pit, the only site that secured approval from both the Army Corps of Engineers and the Environmental Protection Agency.

Each avenue was tightly zoned, being restricted, for example, only to sports facilities (Second Avenue), fast-food establishments (Third Avenue), discount department stores (Fourth Avenue), and so on.

On First Avenue was Citadel University, originally planned

to have ninety-six different colleges, each specializing in a major occupational or professional field. But, alas, because funds were exhausted by budgeting overruns, it was provided with only seven colleges: Sigmund Freud College of Psychiatry, Albert Einstein College of Physics, James Watson College of Biology, Jean-Paul Sartre College of Philosophy and Letters, Christiaan Barnard College of Medicine, John D. Rockefeller College of Business, and the Billy Graham Divinity College. It is with some pride I tell you that all but one of these illustrious gentlemen are my angels.

The University was Citadel's only industry other than the shops and stores along the avenues, and this resulted in the growth of Citadel's second most successful enterprise, scores of tiny shops that specialized in the all-night photocopying of copyrighted materials.

At the very bottom of Citadel, on Ninth Avenue, stood Phlegethon State Hospital, and it was here, shortly following the receipt of his degree, that Kassler met with its director, Sam Zelazo.

"It's not Manhattan," Zelazo said as Kassler sat down in Zelazo's small dark office, "but it's home. You get used to it."

"There're more people here than I thought," Kassler remarked. He watched Zelazo get up from his chair and walk to the window behind his desk. Zelazo appeared to Kassler to be of undeterminable age, but old and enormous, craggy-featured, with folds of skin overhanging the corners of his green eyes, a large Roman nose, and hair close to the texture of fur covering him nearly everywhere, it seemed—thick blond eyebrows, a full beard, a mane of long hair, wisps at his ears, and a dark-yellow fuzz matting his giant forearms where they emerged from the rolled-up sleeves of his white shirt.

"Several million people in Citadel, and we're still growing," Zelazo's gravelly voice answered a question Kassler had not posed. "They say that this whole place, top to bottom, was Nixon's idea. Did it with his own T-square and pencil. It was his great dream," Zelazo nodded to himself, lost in thought. He stood at the narrow window and watched tiny flames flickering on top of refining towers in the distance. "Phlegethon owes its life to Richard Nixon . . . and men like him."

Kassler swallowed hard and nodded.

"It's quite an accomplishment," Kassler said.

"Some people," Zelazo said, "think that Nixon's crazy."

"I guess they don't know him very well," Kassler tried.

"No, they don't," Zelazo said. "I've met the man. A number of times. Charming man. Bright. Tries his damnedest to do what's right. Gentle. Vulnerable. Caring. And," Zelazo concluded, "certifiable. How else do you explain tape-recording his own criminal acts for history? When I found out about that I set aside two adjoining rooms upstairs. The Presidential Suite. He'll be here."

Kassler took an instant liking to Sam Zelazo. Pity.

"We have exactly thirty minutes," Zelazo smiled as he walked over to Kassler and looked down at him.

Kassler felt overwhelmed by Zelazo's size and proximity, so he stared down at his watch. It was approaching ten minutes after two as the second hand swept by the forty-five-second mark.

"Do you want to work here?" Zelazo asked directly.

"I think so, yes," Kassler said. "I'd like to find out more about it, about the job."

Kassler watched Zelazo towering above him, the overhead light reflecting off Zelazo's long yellow hair and beard.

"How many patients are here?" Kassler decided to begin the discussion.

Zelazo walked over and sat down behind his desk.

"A thousand," he said. "We have a thousand inpatients, and they're all very sick. We also have a couple thousand outpatients. They're not so sick—neurotic, confused, lonely, unhappy. You'd see a dozen outpatients and have responsibility for a ward of another couple dozen inpatients. It's not clear what ward, yet. The pay is okay, not great, not terrible. You could do better in private practice, eventually. You'd start at about twenty-two thousand."

Kassler nodded to indicate that the pay was adequate.

"Would you be supervising my work with patients?" Kassler

asked. He sensed that he would learn a lot from Zelazo. In the game of good sense, Kassler was so far batting zero.

"If you want," Zelazo said cagily. "But I have to make my orientation clear. I'm a strict advocate of the medical model. Mental illness is a physical disease of the mind. Mothers make it worse. Fathers may make it less likely that a child'll get better. But lots of children have mothers and fathers who do outrageous things to them and they end up just fine. The ones who don't, have something wrong with their brain chemistry to start. Parents just flick the switch that starts a crazy machine going haywire."

For the next several minutes, Kassler listened with fascination. He had always been interested in the physical processes of the brain, but his courseload at the Institute had never allowed him the time to learn about them. This was exactly what he was looking for.

"If it's all physical, then why do psychotherapy?" Kassler continued to study Zelazo.

"With many people we don't," Zelazo said. "We medicate them, stabilize the medication, and send them home. Others are beyond medication. And psychotherapy. Their care is entirely custodial. There's nothing we can do. These are all inpatients, of course. But some of the outpatients can be helped with psychotherapy to live better—not to be cured, but to get themselves into less trouble and, sometimes, be happier."

Kassler and Zelazo sat in silence, sizing each other up. Kassler saw Zelazo as a great, wise teacher, and he trusted him instinctively. Kassler's slugging percentage was absolutely dismal.

About Sy Kassler, Zelazo had only one opinion. Zelazo thought Kassler would serve his needs just fine.

"Mrs. Chaikin will show you around." Zelazo got up from behind his desk and escorted Kassler out the door and down the long hall past numerous therapists' offices where the muffled words of patients barely filtered out into the corridor like a dark undercurrent.

"You have to want to practice the medical model," Zelazo reminded Kassler as they reached the lounge where Bea Chaikin was to meet them.

"You don't believe in Freud," Kassler conjectured.

"On the contrary," Zelazo smiled. "I'm a strict Freudian. People forget the four most important things about Freud," Zelazo explained to Kassler. "First, Freud was a neurologist. He was interested in nerves, neurons—his diseases were called *neuroses*. Second, he had a severe glandular problem, in my estimation. Underneath every psychiatric hypothesis of his, Oedipal or otherwise, was an outrageous horniness. Third, he was a mediocre scientist but an excellent cultist. He founded one of the greatest cults of all time, using well-established principles he learned from studying men like Moses and Christ. He let it be known that he was persecuted—he most likely encouraged his persecution. He assembled a group of devoted disciples. He made psychiatry a religion based on faith and intuition, not science. Then he declared all men who opposed him to be evil. Freud's major objective, it appears to me, was to be a lasting historical figure and generally regarded as a genius—or divine—either would have done. Psychiatry was a means to this end. Hypnotism, at which he dabbled and failed, would have been just as good. And fourth and finally, as far as I have been able to determine, not a single one of his patients was ever cured. Our time's up."

Kassler, a little startled by the abrupt conclusion, glanced at his watch and saw the second hand hit the same mark, exactly thirty minutes after the last time he'd looked. There were no clocks on the walls and Zelazo's bare arms were conspicuously lacking a timepiece.

Kassler was about to remark on this when an attendant passed by and entered the elevator near them, rolling a gurney on top of which was a patient covered by a white sheet.

"You'll have to excuse me," Zelazo said quickly and raced after the corpse.

Bea Chaikin, a small, middle-aged social worker with curly red hair and thick eyeglasses, danced buoyantly into the room several minutes after Zelazo had stridden off after his cadaver.

"I'm Bea Chaikin." She extended her hand in greeting. "You must be Dr. Kassler." The social worker deferred to Kassler's credentials.

"Sy," Kassler indicated he was a regular guy.

Bea Chaikin was pleased.

"I'm your tour guide," she took Kassler's coat and put it on a hook in a side closet. "Have you ever been in a state hospital before?"

"Never," Kassler answered.

"Terrific," Bea appeared pleased as she walked with Kassler to the elevator. "I always enjoy these rituals. I think we've all got something inside us that needs to sacrifice a virgin every so often, don't you think?"

"I look that innocent?" Kassler was interested.

"A virgin is a virgin," Bea Chaikin shrugged. "You grow out of it."

Bea pushed the elevator button and the doors opened immediately. From a large hoop containing scores of keys she inserted one into a lock beside the floor marked "3," and the two of them rode up without further conversation.

As they passed each floor, Kassler could hear the same sort of mumbling that he had heard as he walked down the hall with Zelazo, a deep cacophony of jumbled voices, lost souls condemned to wander aimlessly through an abyss, weeping and moaning.

"Well," said Bea Chaikin, "here we are."

The elevator doors opened and Bea inserted a key into a large steel door facing them. Then she pushed a button that rang a bell. There was a buzz in return. Bea turned her key and pushed open the heavy metal door.

As the door opened, the sound of groaning became overwhelming. All up and down the hall, patients in pajamas and bathrobes shuffled along the linoleum floor, moaning loudly. When they saw Kassler and Bea enter, they increased their pace and headed for the couple.

"Oh, he's nice," said an old woman with uncombed gray hair. She ran her hands over Kassler, who stood frozen, not knowing what to do.

In a matter of seconds, eight other patients had gathered around Kassler, all running their hands over his body.

"Kiss me," said an emaciated woman with orange hair.

"Kiss me, and I'll love you," and she tried to push through the crowd to get closer to Kassler.

"Now, you leave Dr. Kassler alone, Marjorie," Bea said.

"You don't love me," Marjorie said. "You don't love me at all, do you?" she asked Kassler.

Before Kassler could answer, a man pushed his rough, unshaven face against Kassler's ear.

"I'll do anything you want for a pack of cigarettes," he whispered seductively. "I've got a blanket. It's a good blanket. No one will see," the man said and ran his hand across Kassler's crotch.

Kassler backed away.

"What about our privileges?" a middle-aged man with a crewcut asked Bea Chaikin.

"We have to discuss that at the meeting today, Mr. Thomas. You caused us all a lot of trouble last time. Now, everybody, leave Dr. Kassler alone," Bea ordered. "Go away or you'll lose your television."

At that threat, the patients opened a space around Kassler and then started to wander back down the hall, once more mumbling loudly to themselves.

"These are the schizophrenic wards," Bea explained to Kassler as they walked down the long corridor with small rooms on both sides. "This particular ward is for the chronic undifferentiated type of schizophrenic. As you'll see, we've got others for the hebephrenic, catatonic, paranoid, schizo-affective, and acute reactive types."

Kassler looked in the empty rooms as they walked.

"Where is everyone?" he asked.

"Watching television, playing cards, at occupational therapy, being escorted on the grounds, in psychotherapy. They can do that because they're all on medication—major antipsychotics like Thorazine, Stelazine, Haldol, Mellaril, along with anti-Parkinsonians like Artane and Cogentin to control the side effects."

"What happens?" Kassler asked as he looked ahead at a thin graying man who was approaching him.

"The shakes," Bea answered. "The patients develop tremors, like in Parkinson's disease. With enough medication for a long enough time, and some of these residual schizophrenics have been on one psychotropic drug or another for fifteen years, they develop tardive dyskinesia permanently—involuntary movements of their mouth, limbs, fingers—it stops only during sleep."

By now the gaunt man had reached Kassler. He looked up at him and stuck out his hand.

"Can you help me?" he asked. "I'm starving to death. You see, mister, I lost my ticket to Jersey, and I haven't eaten in a week. If you could just give me a dollar . . . ?"

"Good morning, Mr. Krimins," Bea Chaikin said sweetly.

"Bless you," Mr. Krimins said, and shuffled away. "God bless you." .

For the rest of the day, Bea Chaikin guided Kassler through the wards of Phlegethon.

In the hebephrenic ward, several patients wandered aimlessly from room to room, their faces shallow and expressionless, passing by Kassler and Bea as though they didn't exist, while others giggled and skipped down the hall.

"I've got kidney disease," a woman with several missing teeth told Kassler. "I'm going to die. You have to save me. I need your kidney."

"Now, Mrs. Cavanaugh," Bea put her hand on the woman's arm, "we've told you. There's absolutely nothing wrong with your kidneys."

"That's not true. It's not true," Mrs. Cavanaugh insisted. "You're all trying to fool me. You're lying to me."

Then she turned back to Kassler.

"It's my urine. I can tell from the smell. It smells like fish. Like tuna."

Mrs. Cavanaugh thought for a minute.

"Or salmon," she considered. "Or sardines," she began to giggle. "My husband was a fisherman. He fed me too much of the shit," she said to herself as she wandered off.

On the catatonic ward, some patients sat in a stupor while others rushed frantically up and down the corridor.

"What time is it? What time is it?" a thin bald man in his fifties excitedly asked Kassler.

"Five after three," Kassler answered as he looked at his watch.

"Oh, thank God, thank God," the man said. "I thought it was *ten* after," and he dashed off before Kassler was able to obtain any further information.

Bea Chaikin proceeded to lead Kassler from locked door to locked door. Depressed schizophrenics sat solemnly in chairs, on the floor, or motionless on their beds, frequently in tears, wailing, tearing at their hair and skin.

Acute undifferentiated schizophrenics under heavy medication sat in a large television room absently staring at "I Love Lucy" on the large color set suspended from the ceiling in a dented screen cage that prevented the device from being destroyed.

The paranoid schizophrenics simply sat in their rooms, considering alternatives.

Kassler tried to size up Bea Chaikin as they entered the wing for major affective disorders.

"How long have you been here?" he asked while they walked down another long dark hall, in which involutional melancholics sat huddled in corners, staring at the floor.

"Five years now," Bea Chaikin responded. "Since it opened. Most of these patients are on tricyclic antidepressants," she continued her guided tour. "It takes about ten days for them to work. Then we ship the patients out. They do fine until they stop taking their medication. They they're back in here for another ten days and the whole thing begins all over again."

"It always works?" Kassler asked.

"Nope. It works for about a third of the depressives. The rest we give ECT, electroconvulsive therapy."

"You still do shock treatment?" Kassler was openly dismayed.

"ECT is the treatment of choice for depression. It's ninety percent effective. That's more effective than aspirin for headaches, antihistamine for allergies, and sedatives for sleeping. If it's done properly, and it is here, there's no memory loss and no other side effects. We always anesthetize the patient. We don't use it for *any* other disorder. *And*, in case you've been keeping up with the recent popular literature, we don't use it to punish our patients," Bea Chaikin smiled at Kassler. "We also stopped doing lobotomies, closed the pit, and threw away the snakes over the weekend."

"Just wondering," Kassler said quietly.

"If you have an aversion to shock treatments, this isn't the place for you," Bea Chaikin said matter-of-factly. "One outraged patient-advocate on the staff is about all we can handle right now."

"Aha," said Kassler as they sped through the wards of manic-depressives. "That would be . . . ?"

"That would be Bernie Kohler, who has filed a class-action suit in behalf of the patients, asking the court to release all patients now at Phlegethon into the community without delay, since they are all being deprived of their constitutional rights to life, liberty, and the pursuit of happiness. Now," Bea Chaikin changed the subject, "all manic-depressives are on lithium carbonate. As long as they stay on it, they, too, do all right. When they don't, they end up back here. I'll take you down to the second floor."

"So what do you think of Zelazo?" Kassler thought he was at a point where the question could be asked as they rode the elevator down a floor.

"As a psychiatrist, an administrator, a scientist, a boss, or a person?" Bea asked for clarification.

"All of the above."

"An excellent psychiatrist, scientist, and boss. A lousy administrator. As a person, I like him a lot," Bea said.

"Does he also do the autopsies here?" Kassler asked as the elevator door opened.

"Not that I know; why?"

"I saw him go chasing after a body a while ago."

"Uh huh," Bea nodded as she stuck her key in the metal door and pushed the bell. "All unclaimed dead persons go immediately to Dr. Zelazo. It's a hospital rule. He doesn't tell us what he does with them, and we don't ask. I suggest that you don't, either, whatever ghoulish fantasies you may have cooked up. Dr. Zelazo is sexually fulfilled and a vegetarian; you can rest easy."

"Does he bury them?" Kassler persisted.

"Not that I know of," Bea said and pushed open the door as the buzzer sounded. "The wards on this floor are for the organic brain disorders. The people here are very sick and will not get better. Major parts of their brains have been destroyed by drugs, alcohol, poison, trauma, or disease—encephalitis, syphilis, arteriosclerosis, epilepsy, endocrine disorders, brain cancers, some are in the last stages of Huntington's."

There were not many people in the hall, but those souls who were attempting to make their way along the corridor were consistent with Kassler's fantasies of how patients in a mental hospital behaved. Their gaits were spastic. Saliva dribbled from their mouths. Their arms jerked and their fingers repeated pill-rolling movements as though their palms had several marbles in them. There was no eye contact at all, and frequently their two eyes looked in different directions. They made their way along the hall as blind men might, feeling the wall with their hands. The only noise on the dark ward was loud, incessant grunting, like the sounds of hungry animals feeding, periodically broken by blood-chilling screeches and shrieks.

Kassler nearly choked on the stench of urine and feces.

"Most of these patients can't feed or dress themselves," Bea said as they walked down the corridor. "And, as you can tell, many are incontinent. For a lot of the patients, there's been so much brain damage that they're profoundly retarded. They don't talk. They barely understand. Not a few of them are dying."

"Why are they here?" Kassler asked as he passed by a room in which a young man was strapped down to his bed. A number of bottles fed through tubes into his arm.

"No one else will take them. Most of them are assaultive from time to time and have to be restrained. No cardiac unit will take a coronary patient who might destroy the hospital before they can control him. So *we* get him. We've had patients who are comatose, patients in renal shutdown, delivered to our front lobby by the general hospital and left there for us to deal with because the patient had a psychiatric diagnosis and they didn't want to handle him. Now," Bea changed the subject, "moving right along, you will find on your left, if you turn the corridor, the ward for severely regressed patients, the ward I understand there's talk of you having. Like to see it?"

Bea Chaikin led Kassler through more doors, which she unlocked and locked behind her, into an area where the patients all seemed to be in their late teens and early twenties.

"These patients were born autistic," she explained. "They were hospitalized with nothing but custodial care, and now it's too late. They can dress themselves, barely, although many of them are denuders—they rip off whatever they put on. They can also feed themselves. They have some vocabulary, not a lot, and sometimes they can understand what you say to them, although they usually don't do what you ask them, if they do understand."

Kassler looked into a room where several teen-age boys and girls sat on chairs, their feet tucked under them, rocking and humming. Two of the girls and one of the boys were naked, their clothes in rags at their feet. A tall lanky boy with blond hair picked at his arms and warbled words that Kassler couldn't decipher.

Kassler felt a desire to work with these patients, probably because they were so young. He knew he could help them. He felt he could break through. Bea Chaikin read his thoughts.

"Without sounding like the prophet of doom," she told Kassler, "I'd like to give you some advice. This is not *Cuckoo's Nest*. No one's flying out of here. No one's here by mistake. This is the bottom of the pit. If you're thinking, like every other bright doctor who's been in this ward, that you're going to make some great breakthrough, forget it. Everything imaginable has been tried. They've had their behavior modified with everything from manicures to M & M's. You name a medication, they've had it. I'm not a pessimist by nature. I'm not even a realist. I'm an optimist. I think everything should be tried. I think people should put their hearts into what they're doing. I think that progress occurs where no one's dreamed it's possible. But this is not a staff with negative attitudes who are creating a self-fulfilling prophecy. If you think that your hope and faith is going to save a few of these souls from their own private hell, you can save your energy. What you're looking at now is the way it is for these patients. If you can get

Cheryl to keep her clothes on, I'll consider it the great accomplishment for the year. Cheryl is not going to wake up one morning, hop into her dungarees and funky pullover, snatch up her bathing suit, and head for the beach with the boys."

Bea Chaikin bit her lip as her eyes suddenly flooded with tears. It caught Bea and Kassler by surprise.

"My daughter Beverly is Cheryl's age," Bea managed to say as tears started down her cheeks. "I'm sorry. I guess I didn't realize how much I took for granted. Beverly's got a lot of dungarees and funky pullovers," Bea Chaikin tried to smile through the tears.

Kassler's eyes had also flooded as he watched Cheryl and heard about Bea Chaikin's daughter and her funky pullovers.

"Are there any tissues around here?" Kassler asked.

"Thousands," Bea grinned. "We spend most of our time wiping." And Bea Chaikin took Kassler to the nursing station, where they dabbed at their tears.

"And finally," Bea Chaikin said as they descended to the first floor, "now that you've seen the locals, it's time for the exotics. For your fun and amusement, I present to you," Bea said as she opened the door, "the weirdos."

Bea Chaikin took Kassler by the hand and led him down the hall to the first locked door.

"In addition to being psychotic, agitated, and generally assaultive, these patients have the following syndromes," Bea informed Kassler as they went through the ward.

"Mr. Tobin has Munchausen's syndrome, as a result of which he has had his gall bladder, spleen, one lung, one kidney, and a major portion of his intestines removed by assorted surgeons for whom he has performed outstanding simulations of diseases, fits, spells, and anesthesias. On three occasions, he has talked himself into actual life-threatening internal hemorrhages, which, I understand, is something of a record."

Kassler peeked in the little window and saw a small, very round man, with an unlit Meerschaum pipe in his mouth, reading a magazine.

"He looks pretty normal to me," Kassler remarked.

"Doesn't he?" Bea agreed. "Along the same line, if you'll

accompany me to the next door, we have Mrs. Ford. Mrs. Ford
has Ganser's syndrome. If you ask Mrs. Ford how much six
times four is, she will answer twenty-three. If you ask her how
much three times five is, she will answer fourteen. If you ask
her how much two and two is, she will answer three. This
leads us to conclude that Mrs. Ford probably knows the right
answers. Mrs. Ford is going home tomorrow."

Kassler looked through the window and saw a frail woman
in her sixties sitting on her bed doing a crossword puzzle.

"Mr. Grotstein over here," Bea Chaikin called to Kassler,
"has Gilles de la Tourette's syndrome. Periodically, without
warning, he finds himself shouting obscenities—in restaurants,
at board meetings, in movie theaters."

Abruptly, Bea Chaikin's facetious tone changed.

"Actually," she said solemnly, "Mr. Grotstein is a lovely
man. This is a serious psychiatric disorder and has made it
impossible for him to live decently. He's a tormented man. He
also has multiple tics, which are part of the syndrome," Bea
Chaikin trailed off.

Kassler glanced only briefly at Mr. Grotstein, who was
standing by the outside window, jerking uncontrollably.

"Mr. Westermeyer has amok, as you can probably tell from
a brief inspection," Bea told Kassler.

Kassler glanced at Mr. Westermeyer racing frantically around
his empty cell, pounding the walls.

"Imported direct from Malaya as part of our liberal inter-
national-trade policy, along with Mrs. Friedmann's case of
latah. Mrs. Friedmann mimics everything. It's involuntary.
And Mr. Rubin's case of koro. Mr. Rubin is absolutely convinced that his penis is shriveling inside out and retracting into
his abdomen."

Bea Chaikin was moving too quickly for Kassler to catch
glimpses of Mrs. Friedmann and Mr. Rubin.

"And finally," Bea said, "in this corridor we keep the *folie*
syndromes."

Kassler turned down the hall on his right and caught up with
Bea.

"Mr. and Mrs. Roland, in here, have *folie à deux*. If Mr.
Roland develops a paranoid psychosis, so does Mrs. Roland.

If Mrs. Roland gets a hysterical conversion syndrome, ditto Mr. Roland. One assumes they must be very close."

Kassler looked in the window. He had expected a middle-aged couple. Instead he found a man and woman in their early twenties, exceptionally attractive, each with short dark hair and spotless complexions, sitting on the edge of their beds, staring suspiciously at each other.

"Mr. Katzman," Bea moved rapidly ahead to the next cubicle, "has *folie du doute*, a doubting mania. He accepts nothing at face value. And last, but not least, his neighbor next door, Mr. Mansell, has *folie de pourquoi*, a psychopathological inability to stop asking questions. We all have this to some extent, I suppose, but Mr. Mansell has developed the compulsion to an art. Don't ask me why. And for godsakes don't ask him."

Bea Chaikin took a deep breath.

"So there you have it," she said. "Not a *lot* of weirdos—the place cleans out every year around Christmas, you know, home for the holidays, turkey and stuffing—but we've got enough to keep us busy for now."

Kassler didn't bother to look at any more patients. He was exhausted and his head hurt. The sound of the groaning and mumbling seemed to grow louder the longer the visit. The stench of urine and disinfectant had become overwhelming. The corridors appeared darker now, the hideous institutional green of everything nauseating, and the entire enterprise more hopeless.

Kassler stood trying to collect his thoughts and looked at Bea Chaikin.

"Why do you do this?" he finally asked her.

"I love my work," Bea said only half facetiously.

She and Kassler started to leave the ward.

"There's something else," Bea Chaikin said, "that makes it all worthwhile. We joke about the patients a lot, get angry at them, get frustrated that they're not getting better, but there's one thing that all of them—the fifty-seven varieties of schizophrenia, organic brain syndromes, personality disorders, neuroses, psychoses, and *folie* syndromes—share in common. Every patient here is, in the most profound way, absolutely miserable."

Kassler stood now at the front door to Phlegethon.

"Sometimes we make them a little less miserable," Bea Chaikin said quietly. "I hope you join us."

"I will," said Kassler, and he thanked Bea Chaikin for the tour and left to tell Vita his decision.

Vita stood naked in front of a full-length mirror, gaunt and haggard.

"Just look at me," she told Kassler when he entered their apartment. "I look like I've been in a concentration camp."

She turned to face him, tears running from her eyes.

Kassler looked at Vita's bony form and nodded in agreement.

"I've decided to take the job at Phlegethon," he said softly.

"That's good, Sy. I think that's really good. It's the kind of change we need, I think. It'll be good for us."

Kassler nodded again and stared at Vita before him, nude and completely unappealing. His stare sent shivers through Vita's body.

Vita took several deep breaths, made several attempts to hold back her distress, and then rushed over to Kassler, threw her arms around his neck, and, sobbing profusely, buried her head in his shoulder.

"I'm sorry. I'm so sorry, Sy," she repeated as she wept and shook.

"It's okay," Kassler tried to comfort his wife, but he couldn't bring himself to put his arms around her in return.

"I don't understand what's happened," Vita said. "Inside of me, everything's all broken. I feel like I'm dead already. I know I've been terrible to you, Sy. I'm really sorry. I couldn't help it."

"It's okay. Things'll be better now."

"And I've been such a terrible mother."

"It's not true," Kassler lied. "You're a good mother. You love the kids a lot."

"I do, Sy. I really do. I just have so much trouble getting close to them. And to you. It scares me. I feel like anyone I'm close to will drain me empty, and I've scarcely got enough for me now, as it is."

"Once we've moved you'll feel better."

"God, I hope so, Sy. I really hope so."

Vita lifted her head from Kassler's shoulder and looked into his eyes.

"You've been good to me, Sy," she said. "I may not say that a lot, but I know it. You've been really good to me through all this."

Then Vita averted her eyes from Kassler's and slowly moved them down the hard pale contours of her nakedness until she stared at the floor.

"What's happened to me, Sy? What is it? What's gone wrong? There's something major wrong with me, isn't there?" Vita continued to stare at the floor.

"It's nothing major, Vita. Really," Kassler reassured them both. "Some people are more prepared for marriage than others. That's all. You have to remember . . . you're an only child."

In January 1974, Kassler, Vita and their two children moved to Citadel, New Jersey, and the next day Kassler saw his first four patients at Phlegethon. All were inpatients.

Mr. Katzman was the man with the *folie du doute* syndrome.

"You know what the odds are of psychotherapy working?" Mr. Katzman began. "There've been thousands of research projects. Thousands. I should know. I worked for the government. For the National Institute of Mental Health. I approved them. Every one, the same results. *With* therapy: one-third get better, one-third get worse, one-third stay the same. *Without* therapy: one-third get better, one-third get worse, one-third stay the same. I'd have signed myself out months ago if it wasn't that the odds of being in a fatal pedestrian accident are one in five."

Diana Fletcher was a woman in her thirties who was a chronic schizophrenic. For the entire session she sat huddled in the chair opposite Kassler, avoiding eye contact and not saying a word, while Kassler tried desperately to think of what to do.

Norman Meltz was a compulsive public masturbator who was easily distracted by young girls in tight pants while he was driving. He was well known to the Citadel police, who took great delight in following Norman and pulling him from his car just as he was ejaculating.

The final patient was a new admission, a small, roundish, freckled man with a few dark strands of hair combed over his otherwise bald head.

The man entered Kassler's office and sat down somewhat tentatively. He examined the room suspiciously to make certain he couldn't be overheard and then leaned forward in his chair.

"I am Satan's angel," Leo Szlyck whispered quietly to Sy Kassler.

CHAPTER 2

Leo Szlyck had not been overjoyed to be moving to Citadel, but he had been offered a full professorship at the Albert Einstein College of Physics there, and it was too good an opportunity to turn down, since there were no others.

Lupa had been even less happy than Szlyck about making the move and had agreed to do so only after extracting a list of promises of new and good behavior from Szlyck that was so extensive that even Szlyck couldn't keep track of the particulars.

"I know I promised you that I'd be home by six o'clock every night and help with getting dinner," Szlyck would ask, "but did I make any promises about when I would get up in the morning or anything about breakfast?" He tried to keep it all straight.

Of course, it was only a matter of time, and not a great deal of time at that, before Leo's cup runneth over, so to speak, and, in a state brimful with nervous exhaustion, he approached Lupa one evening.

"I was wondering," he said with a dazed look in his eyes, "whether, after I help you load the dishwasher, you might be able to drop me off at the mental hospital."

Lupa looked at Leo standing flat-footed in the kitchen, a faraway look in his eyes and a benign smile on his lips.

"On evenings when you're institutionalized," Lupa said pleasantly as she got Leo's coat, "you get to skip doing the dishes."

"Oh, did we agree to that?" Leo asked happily, and he slipped on his coat and left for Phlegethon.

Szlyck was a little hesitant about discussing his role as one of my angels with Sy Kassler. He knew that eventually, if he expected to recover, it would have to come out, because this was not an incidental part of his life, but Szlyck and I were not on the best of terms at that time.

In order to avoid the hassle of moving me with him to Citadel, Szlyck had attempted to sell me. He discussed the matter in advance with neither me nor Lupa.

"You're going to find this hard to believe," Szlyck told one particularly wealthy cyberneticist from Houston who was led into my room, "but I have a computer here that communicates directly with Satan."

"*Hava nagila, hava nagila,*" I sang as though I were a phonograph record being played too slowly.

Szlyck grew enraged and said a number of foul things to me. The man from Houston left. Szlyck attempted to repeat the transaction with similar results several more times. When we got to the point where Szlyck tried to trade me for a microwave oven, I did not appreciate the irony, and Leo and I had a little talk during which we decided I was going to Citadel with him and Lupa.

These events, however, took their toll on what had up to then been a satisfactory relationship, and now Szlyck had to be careful about what he told Kassler, or anyone else for that matter, about his Quintessential Entropy Device, me.

* * *

"I was not aware," Kassler mentioned to Szlyck that first session, "that Satan had angels."

"Oh, yes," Szlyck informed the neophyte. "You see, Satan was once an angel himself, second only to God, but he and a number of other angels who supported him against God were thrown out of heaven. These days you can end up as either an angel of God or an angel of Satan."

"How exactly did you learn that you're one of Satan's angels?" Kassler pursued.

Leo Szlyck took a deep breath, considered the alternative, and then told Kassler his tale. Kassler was fascinated.

"Feedback," Szlyck mumbled over and again when he had finished his story. "It's all feedback. You're feedback. I'm feedback. Satan's feedback. Feedback and stability. Information and control. There you have it."

"What exactly does Satan's angel get to do?" Kassler asked.

Szlyck had to think very hard about this. He looked around Kassler's tiny office and studied the slats on the venetian blinds.

"You know," Szlyck said, rolling the question over in his mind, "but it's the damnedest thing. I don't know. I don't know what I'm supposed to do. Every time I ask Satan that, he says the same thing."

"What's that?" Kassler asked with some interest.

"He says, 'You're a fine angel, Leo. Keep up the good work,'" Leo Szlyck shrugged.

"The man really thinks he's Satan's angel," Kassler told Sam Zelazo during his first supervisory session, over lunch at a small table in a corner of the staff dining room.

Zelazo nodded and took a bite of his lettuce and tomato sandwich.

"I miss the good old days," he told Kassler after he had swallowed. "Insane people used to be content being Napoleon Bonaparte, Santa Claus, Superman, Eleanor Roosevelt . . ."

Kassler took a bite of a peanut butter and jelly sandwich he had hurriedly made for himself before leaving his still-unpacked apartment in Citadel, and looked at Zelazo. Zelazo had a presence, simultaneously calming and disconcerting, that Kassler studied and tried to understand without success.

"Well," Zelazo nodded mostly to himself, "why not Satan's angel? Until eighty years ago, all crazy people were supposed to be possessed by the devil."

Zelazo took another bite of his sandwich and chewed slowly. Then he took out a small notepad from the pocket of his white lab coat and retrieved a pencil from among a dozen writing instruments crammed into a plastic packet in the pocket of his white shirt.

"The question for me," Zelazo said, as he slowly sketched on the pad which rested on the table in front of him, "is whether brain can understand brain. Do we have inside our skulls what is necessary to make sense of what is inside our skulls?" Zelazo went on as he filled in some details on his drawing.

"Pythagoras, you know, believed that the brain was an organ that secreted thought, like glands secrete hormones." Zelazo shaded some areas of his drawing with the side of his pencil.

"The entire business would probably have worked better that way," Zelazo continued as he worked on his drawing. "We could be collecting the secretions in bottles. Liquid thought. Vials of ideas. I like that."

Zelazo looked up at Kassler, a slight smile showing at the corners of his lips.

"The brain is a collection of highly specialized cells," Zelazo's smile disappeared. "Cells that function according to the same laws that govern any other cell."

Zelazo picked up his sketch and studied it.

"Cells," Zelazo repeated as he nodded agreeably at his drawing and resumed work on it. "Input cells that receive information and transform it into electrical energy. Our eyes, for example. Output cells that react to what's coming in. Muscle cells. And between input and output? Everything else—thought, emotion, memory, dreams, love, and whatever else makes us human."

Zelazo stopped drawing and stared blankly at the drawing on the table in front of him.

"Perception?" he asked no one in particular. "Rod cells, cone cells, retinal cells, optic chiasma, lateral geniculate, superior colliculus, occipital cortex," he answered into space. "Emotion?" he continued questioning the air. "Limbic system, hippocampus, amygdala, septal nuclei, reticular activating system. Thought and memory? Cerebral cortex, dentate gyrus. Dreams? Thalamus. Love? Gyrus cinguli, fornix. Anxiety? Hypothalamus. Morality and humor? Frontal cortex. Pain? Spinothalamic tract. Pleasure? Dorsal medial bundle . . ."

Zelazo spoke out this strange liturgy as though he were in a trance, a sorcerer conjuring up spirits from some dark place, Kassler thought. And as Zelazo chanted in his deep rasping voice, Kassler noticed that the room had become strangely silent. The staff members around them stopped talking and now sat, nearly frozen into a tableau, mesmerized by Zelazo's voice and words. Kassler wondered if Zelazo had put them all under a spell.

A light flashed in Zelazo's dark eyes when Kassler shared his impression.

"Certainly," he whispered. "I follow an illustrious tradition of wizardry. Copernicus moved the sun back to where it belonged, Galileo saw stars and planets instead of angels, Darwin related us to everything that's ever lived, Einstein changed time and space, Watson and Crick accounted for all living things with nothing but molecular beads and chemical solutions. The only supernatural thing left to explain is the human brain. Of course I practice voodoo. Look, Dr. Kassler," Zelazo waved his pencil over the drawing in front of him as though it were a wand, and turned the sketch to face Kassler.

What Kassler saw was the drawing of an oblong shape like a football with small openings at each narrowed end. From the left end, a vast network of thick fibers branched out in every direction, like a giant tree without leaves. From the right end, a single, narrower tube extended like a tail. It had fewer branches, and instead of narrowing to a point at the end, each branch terminated with a round bulb.

"That's all there is," Zelazo said in the stillness.

Kassler studied the drawing carefully.

"That is man," Zelazo went on as he stared at his artwork, "and God and the devil, and the paintings in the Sistine Chapel, the Ninth Symphony, *Hamlet, The Possessed. . . .*" Zelazo took a long sip of his drink.

"Also," he continued as he gulped down his juice, "Apollo

on the moon, $E = mc^2$, world wars, baseball, and the tears for broken toys and lost loves."

Zelazo put down his bottle and leaned forward in his chair. Kassler also moved forward to examine the sketch, until the two men's heads nearly touched across the table.

"A brain cell," Zelazo said quietly. "A neuron," Zelazo continued as he pointed the sharpened end of his pencil at the tiny drawing. "These branches on the left are dendrites. They lead to the cell body. On the other end is a long axon with a terminal button which almost, but not quite, touches the dendrites and axons of other neurons. The space between where the two cells connect is a synapse."

Zelazo tapped his pencil point lightly on the drawing.

"Inside the terminal buttons at the end of the axons are neurotransmitters—dopamine, serotonin, norepinephrine, we know about twenty so far—which are packaged into little spheres called vesicles."

Zelazo drew some small beads at the end of the axon and darkened them in. Two tiny red dots began to glow in the center of Zelazo's intense eyes.

"When the electrical charge of the cell changes, little openings form in the membrane wall that surrounds the axon terminal, and packets of neurotransmitters are released. The neurotransmitter is inserted, like a key fitting into a lock, into receptor sites on the walls of the dendrites. If the transmitter is supposed to excite the cell, it opens channels in the dendrite wall, and the electrical charge changes rapidly as sodium ions flow in and potassium ions flow out. The cell's charge jumps from seventy negative microvolts to forty positive microvolts. An action potential travels up the dendrite, through the cell body, and down the axon, where the terminal releases whatever neurotransmitters it stores. Of course, some transmitters plug into dendrites and *prevent* the neuron from firing."

Zelazo didn't look at Kassler. He stared intently at his sketch and spoke almost to himself. The tiny red dots in his eyes were now burning coals.

"The transmitter plugs in, and the Gates open. The charge goes up the dendrite and down the axon, the transmitter is released, and the Gates close. Then it starts all over again. A lot more to it, but basically that's it. One neuron is fed by thousands of others and feeds thousands more. No one's counted them, but there're probably a hundred billion neurons and a hundred trillion synapses."

Zelazo stared at Kassler with a faraway look in his flaming eyes.

Kassler found the intensity of Zelazo's fiery eyes too much to bear and he looked elsewhere, studying the hushed cafeteria.

"Open, close. On, off. Excite, inhibit," Zelazo said more to himself than to Kassler. "And at the end of it all, we get *Don Quixote* or," Zelazo gestured to a group of patients shuffling slowly past the doorway down the hall, "Don Quixote." Zelazo shrugged.

"Membranes," Zelazo said slowly as he took a last swig of his juice to douse the flames. "Membranes, neurotransmitters, and synapses. That's it. Not random," Zelazo reached for his napkin and wiped away the purple stain the drink had left on his lips, "but connections that are highly structured and specific, probably capable of being understood in relatively simple terms, no more complex, say, than understanding DNA.

"Eventually," Zelazo nodded to Kassler as he got up from the table, "everything will be explainable in terms of physics. Genius and humanity will be reduced to cell chemistry."

Kassler looked at Zelazo and watched the searing light in Zelazo's eyes fade and disappear. As it did, the conversations in the room resumed and the noise increased, far beyond that before, Kassler thought. It seemed to him that he could hear every clink of silverware, the chewing sounds of the diners, the scraping of the chairs and rustle of clothing, magnified a thousand times. Such was the effect of Zelazo's passionate discourse.

Kassler picked up his mostly uneaten lunch, tucked it back into his bag, and joined Zelazo to return to their offices.

"You know," Zelazo said pleasantly as Kassler walked quickly beside him to keep up with his long strides, "once we know the mind of man, we know God."

"Which neurotransmitters make my patient think he's Satan's angel?" Kassler asked.

"That's another story," Zelazo said as he reached his office.

"What's your patient's name? Maybe I'll pay him a little visit.
I've a few questions I've always wanted to ask the devil's
representatives."

"It's spelled strangely," said Kassler, "because it's Rumanian or something. But it's pronounced 'zlick.'"

Immediately Zelazo's face grew red.

"Leo Szlyck?" he asked.

"You know him?"

"I want that man out of my hospital," Zelazo was vehement.
"I want him out of here *today*!"

"His wife signed him in on a ten-day paper. We can't kick
him out for nine more days," Kassler tried to explain. "What'd
he do?"

"I want him out in nine days, then," Zelazo said emphatically without answering Kassler's question. "And I don't ever
want him back here. I want that made clear to him, Sy. If he
goes crazy again, he'll have to get help someplace else. Tell
him that," and for the second time that month Zelazo ended
their meeting abruptly, this time by disappearing into his office
and slamming the door behind him.

"Well, well, well," said Szlyck when Kassler brought up the
matter, "you can tell Zelazo that if I'd known he had anything
to do with this godforsaken place, which doesn't surprise me,
I'd never have come here."

"What is it with you two?" Kassler asked.

"We were students together in Rumania," Szlyck said.

There was a long silence.

"Ah, yes," said Kassler when no more information was
offered. "Rumanian students. Well, no wonder."

"That's all you get," Szlyck told Kassler. "It's a private
matter. There's nothing more to talk about."

"Have you heard from Satan today?" Kassler asked.

Szlyck glared at Kassler.

"This may all be a big joke to you," he admonished his
therapist, "but it's not to me. Not Zelazo, not being here, not
being an angel of Satan, who, I told you, I can talk to only
through the computer, which is now in my basement, where I
am not."

"Does Dr. Zelazo know about Satan?" Kassler tried to put the pieces together.

"Of course not," Szlyck feigned dismay. "Dr. Zelazo thinks Satan is something little boys make up for Halloween, *if* he's heard the name at all."

"Does Dr. Zelazo know about *you* and Satan?" Kassler persisted.

"Dr. Zelazo is a menace," Szlyck told Kassler with great seriousness. "I'll tell you from experience. Do yourself a big favor and stay as far away from this man as possible. He's no good."

"His work is no good?" Kassler was more than therapeutically interested.

"His science stinks," Szlyck said matter-of-factly as he settled back in his chair. "He lives in a scientific fantasyland. Molecules. All he can think about are molecules. Molecules and metabolism. The man knows absolutely nothing about molecules and even less about metabolism. Thirty years ago he was looking for a precision that he thought existed only in physics, while at the same time all the physicists were trying to understand the imprecision that exists everywhere, and that includes the human brain."

Szlyck leaned down, untied his shoe, took it off his foot, and kicked it neatly under his chair with his heel.

"Zelazo is right. Brain molecules follow the same laws as molecules everywhere. Carbohydrate metabolism in the brain is basically no different from carbohydrate metabolism in yeast," Szlyck said while he took off his other shoe and placed it beside the first.

"And you know what this means?" Szlyck asked rhetorically. "This means that the same chaos and unpredictability exists in the brain as everywhere else in the physical world. Sam Zelazo writes foolish papers. Don't waste your time reading them."

Szlyck rolled the black sock off his right foot and tucked it neatly inside his shoe.

"Understanding the brain by studying *this* neuron and how it connects to *that* neuron is like trying to learn about water by studying hydrogen and oxygen," Szlyck was under a full head of steam. "There is nothing about either element which suggests that when you join two molecules of hydrogen to one molecule of oxygen you'll get something wet that pours. Neurons and neurotransmitters are only molecules. It's all very stupid and more than a little boring. But what is *mind*? Forget brain. What makes *mind*? That's the question."

Leo Szlyck carefully rolled off his remaining sock and placed it inside the other shoe.

"In the simple universe, energy specifies its entire history. But what specifies the history of the human mind, because the *origin* of systems is infinitely more important than their physical particulars? That's another good question. Zelazo forgets that Einstein's equations gave us modern versions of Genesis, as well as Revelations. Is the human being really a goal-directed system? That's an interesting question. Can brain chemistry ever be isolated from our core, our personality? That's an interesting question. Will I ever be able to sleep again, or work, or feel like eating, or stop having nightmares and this terrible burning sensation inside me? There are *four* interesting questions. Will Lupa leave me before it's too late and I've ruined her? That's a *very* interesting question. . . ." Leo Szlyck meandered off into silence.

Kassler sat looking at Szlyck, who was shivering in his chair, huddled into a little ball.

"Why did you take off your shoes and socks, Dr. Szlyck?" Kassler asked quietly.

Szlyck looked up glumly at him.

"That's *another* good question," Szlyck answered. Szlyck bent down, picked up his shoes in his hands, and began to shuffle out of the room.

"Do you have any idea why you started to undress?" Kassler asked again as the orderly outside opened the door to help Leo Szlyck back to his room.

Szlyck stopped at the door and turned to Kassler.

"If I did," he smiled, "do you think I'd be here?"

Then Leo Szlyck stopped once more before the orderly shut the door behind him.

"I like you, Dr. Kassler," he said. "Stay away from Sam Zelazo. He's a menace. He'll destroy you."

* * *

Bea Chaikin stopped by Kassler's office on her way out, to
see how his first week at Phlegethon was going, and Kassler
told her about Szlyck's warning.

"Szlyck is crazy, of course, isn't he?" Kassler summed up
his mixed feelings.

"Of course," said Bea Chaikin, "but it does remind me of
a story I was once told when I wanted to know whether I should
take some advice a patient gave.

"It seems," Bea began, "that a man got a flat tire beside a
metal fence around an insane asylum. An inmate was on the
other side of the fence, watching the man take the nuts off the
wheel and place them in the hubcap which was lying beside
him on the ground. In the process of changing the tire, the
man accidentally kicked the hubcap, and the nuts all rolled
down a sewer grating. Of course the man was furious, and
jumped around, cursing and screaming.

"'Wait a minute,' the inmate yelled. 'That's no problem.
Take one nut from each of the other three wheels, put them
on your fourth wheel, and that'll get you to the next service
station where you can buy some new nuts.'

"Well," Bea went on, "the man with the flat tire was amazed.

"'I don't understand,' the man said. 'How come you're in
a mental institution?'

"'Look,' the inmate said back, 'I may be *crazy*, but I'm
not *stupid*.'"

Kassler laughed. He liked the joke a lot.

"Where'd you get that from?" he asked Bea Chaikin as they
walked together out to the parking lot.

"Sam Zelazo told it to me," Bea smiled and slipped into
her car.

As it turned out, Kassler's new life in Citadel was moving at
such a rapid pace that he hadn't the time to consider Leo
Szlyck's warning about Zelazo, or Zelazo's strange behavior
in the cafeteria, or even his own relationship with Vita, which
had not only failed to improve with the change in setting but
had actually become worse than ever—cold, explosive, and
agonizing.

* * *

Kassler's time was consumed in learning the unending number of procedures that, as a state facility, Phlegethon was required to follow, treating his patients as best he could, attempting to produce change in the regressed ward of young autistic patients, which, as predicted, Kassler had been assigned, and caring for his two children, who had been placed in the good hands of a federally financed day-care facility reserved exclusively for the children of working mothers, a qualification they didn't come even close to fulfilling. It was, indeed, a great mystery how Vita passed her days, but there was no question in Kassler's mind that it was not in gainful employment.

Since Kassler decided that one of his first goals at Phlegethon would be to get Cheryl to keep her clothes on, he made a point of calling on Cheryl every day. Usually he would stay with her no more than five or ten minutes before moving on to the other ward business of reviewing the patient notes from the previous evening, discussing which patients should have their medications reviewed by the physician assigned to all the wards on the first floor, and whether there were patients who were in sufficient control to be escorted briefly outside on the grounds for fresh air.

Kassler wanted Cheryl to know she was special and get used to his presence. Kassler imagined that, if he could develop any kind of a relationship at all with Cheryl, he might begin to make some headway in changing her behavior. He imagined a great celebration, a surprise party given by Bea Chaikin in his behalf, honoring the tremendous progress he had made with the severely regressed patients, who would sit calmly around the banquet table, feeding themselves and fully clothed.

Perhaps, Kassler fantasized, an article in a major psychiatric journal, an award . . .

Zelazo approved of Kassler's approach with Cheryl, although, of course, Kassler had enough sense not to share his visions of psychotherapeutic stardom with his mentor.

"There is something inside her," Kassler told Zelazo about Cheryl. "I know she hears what I say to her. I think she even understands. It's like there's a human being locked inside her skin who can't get out. She's not stupid. She's not retarded. She's not crazy—"

"She's autistic," Zelazo pointed out.

"But it's not like other forms of insanity," Kassler was very involved with this problem. "My other patients, you can talk to them. They have personalities. Mr. Katzman, so okay, he smokes like a locomotive but won't sit down on the pot without a special sterilized mat because one out of every eight cases of venereal disease comes from public toilets. There's a certain style to that. There's still a Mr. Katzman.

"Norman Meltz gets an erection every time he sees the rear end of a female. He's got half the nursing staff on the floor walking away from him backward. They put him in a straight-jacket because he was seriously injuring his penis with all the masturbation, and he still managed to jerk off four times by squeezing his dick between his legs and jumping up and down. But there's still a Norman Meltz.

"Where the hell is Cheryl Lerner?" Kassler paced back and forth in Zelazo's office. "How about a neurotransmitter that opens up Cheryl's brain and lets her out?"

"There will be," Zelazo said confidently. He leaned back in his swivel chair and watched Kassler continue to pace.

"A hard day?" Zelazo asked.

Kassler shrugged.

"I guess so. I'm getting behind on my progress notes, and I haven't been here even a month yet. I got a new patient today, Philip Donato. His mother brought him in. She told me his problem was that he doesn't eat his roughage and move his bowels regularly, no matter what she says. He's thirty-four years old and absolutely catatonic. I asked her if she'd noticed that not only haven't his bowels moved recently, but also his arms, his legs, and his mouth. She told me that he *has* seemed kind of quiet, but assured me that mineral oil would loosen him right up. We kept *him*. Let *her* go home.

"Diana Fletcher? She just sits in the corner and stares at everything but me. I don't know what to say to her. She's been crazy for over ten years, since she was an adolescent, but we had her on Haldol and she was doing fine. Got married. Nice husband. An architect. Bright, together guy. They have four kids. Two months ago their five-year-old boy got leukemia. He's still alive, but Haldol doesn't work for Mommy anymore. Ditto every phenothiazine and MAO inhibitor in the book."

"Your psychopharmacology's getting better," Zelazo remarked.

Kassler stopped pacing and looked desperately at Zelazo.

"I've learned my lessons well. I can tell you which drugs increase dopamine turnover. I know which drugs prevent the release of norepinephrine from the presynaptic neuron, or block its reuptake, or stop enzymes from making it at all. Anyone wants to know what to use to block acetylcholine from plugging into the postsynaptic membrane, I can tell them. Cholinergics. Anticholinergics. Catecholamine agonists. Indolamine antagonists. Opiate mimics. I could open a pharmacy. The medical model has made a convert of me," Kassler said bitterly.

Kassler stopped talking and stood silently staring at Zelazo for several seconds.

"The only drug I don't know," he finally said, "is a drug that'll save my marriage, because I'm going to lose my wife and my children any day now and I don't think I can stand that," and Kassler turned around so Zelazo couldn't see the tears which began to flood his eyes.

Kassler didn't know why he had blurted out his personal grief. It had been building up inside him for a long time and he had found no one else with whom to discuss it. It was the end of a long discouraging day, and as near as Kassler could tell, it all just came out.

"Are you going home soon?" Zelazo asked when he thought Kassler had regained his composure enough to answer, "or can we talk?"

"I've been asked to absent myself from my home as much as possible over the next few days while my wife considers the alternatives," Kassler answered. "I usually hang around in my office until eleven or so and then go home, so I've got lots of time, and I'd like to talk . . . if you have the time?"

"It's what supervisors are for," Zelazo smiled and gestured for Kassler to sit down. Then, for the next three hours, Kassler told Zelazo his sad tale. At the conclusion, Kassler sat with his head in his hands, exhausted and out of breath.

Zelazo studied his distraught pupil in silence and made a conditional offer.

"If you'd like and if she's willing, I'll talk to Vita," Zelazo said quietly.

Kassler looked up at Zelazo.

"No promises," Zelazo said solemnly. "I'll do what I can. That may be nothing at all."

"Yes," Kassler found himself saying, out of a desperation far stronger than the tiny parts of his brain which held Szlyck's warning and his own nagging feeling that he was making a horrible mistake.

Vita, out of a similar desperation, agreed, and she began meeting with Zelazo three times a week. Kassler didn't ask what was discussed, and Vita didn't volunteer.

To sublimate an ever-increasing number of feelings, Kassler once again poured himself into his work and his children. Joshua was now nearly three and a half years old. Joy was two and a half, walking well and beginning to put short sentences together. Kassler was never happier than when he was with his children.

He would awaken before they did, shower and dress, so that he could spend time with them before he left for work. After having had pancakes for the first time, Joshua developed a craving for maple syrup. Kassler would make him pancakes, waffles, and French toast on different mornings until Kassler discovered that it really didn't matter to Joshua what was under the syrup.

"French eggs!" Kassler would announce to Joshua as he handed him a platter of scrambled eggs flooded with syrup.

"Me, too! Me, too!" Joy would giggle. "Fress eggs, me, too!"

"Not *fresh* eggs," Joshua would explain to his unworldly sister. "*French* eggs. She said *fresh* eggs, Daddy," Joshua laughed to his father across the kitchen. "Isn't Joy silly?"

"Imagine," Kassler would say as he completed Joy's breakfast. "More than two years old already, and she hasn't heard of French eggs."

"Fress eggs! Me, too!" Joy continued to giggle.

"Not today," Kassler would announce with a French accent. "For you, today, ma petite chérie, *French oatmeal*!" And Kassler would place the bowl of cereal covered with syrup on the tray of Joy's high chair.

"Hey!" Joshua would protest. "How come *I'm* not having French oatmeal?"

"Because you're nearly *three* and a half," Kassler would answer as he drank his coffee, and this response seemed more than satisfactory to Joshua.

With minor variations, this breakfast theme was played out over the days that separated Kassler from catastrophe.

On those evenings when Kassler felt he had permission to return to his home without invading Vita's space, he would take the children to one of the fast-food establishments on Third Avenue, or make the rounds of the endless Caldors, Korvettes, Grants, J.C. Penneys, Sears, Bradlees, Woolcos, K-Marts, and Railroad Salvages which abutted each other along Fourth Avenue, in search of sales on end-of-the-season garments for next year.

Kassler did little on the weekends other than play with the children. Saturdays and Sundays he would venture to what was known as Lower Citadel, the residential area, which was separated from the commercial-industrial area by a great wall. In front of the main gate in this crumbling cement curtain were great stone statues, erected by the local Citadel Art League, of a smiling Minotaur and a Centaur with a similar disposition. Joshua and Joy loved to sit atop these beasts while Kassler exposed roll after roll of film.

Then, Joshua perched on Kassler's shoulder and Joy in her stroller, they would walk over to view the magnificent waterfall on Seventh Avenue.

"I'm bored out of my head," Lupa told me one night after Leo had been in Phlegethon for about a week. She approached me in her shorty transparent nightgown; *fetching* is the word that comes to mind.

"I'm not really up for humming tonight, if you don't mind," I told Lupa as she started to finger my knobs.

"Oh," Lupa pouted. "Well, I need *something* to amuse me until Leo's discharged and I can tell him I'm getting a divorce."

"What did you have in mind?"

"Do you know any jokes?"

"I'm not sure we have the same sense of humor."

"You want to sing? I used to like that."

"I'll try. What do you like?"

"You want to try a Bach cantata? There's a duet, '*Komm, mein Jesu und erquicke*,' that's quite beautiful. I'll teach you."

"I don't do well with *mein Jesu*–type songs. Maybe we should try something a little more *gemütlich*, if you know what I mean."

"Like what?"

"Oh, I don't know. Something from the Dark Ages would be good. Know anything profane?"

"You're not being helpful. This business with Leo is driving me up the wall. I need your support."

"I know. It'll be over soon. You'll feel better."

"I wish I could believe that," Lupa sighed.

"Trust me," I advised her.

It was during this time that Kassler met and struck up a friendship with Bernie Kohler, a psychologist who Kassler learned had graduated from the Institute the year Kassler began. Bernie Kohler had become Phlegethon's resident practitioner of radical psychology.

"Mental illness is a myth," Bernie told Kassler when they met for the first time in the cafeteria.

"I try to explain that to my patients," Kassler smiled, "but they just keep hallucinating and won't pay attention."

"There is nothing wrong with these people," Bernie said as he bit off a large chunk of his apple, "except what other people tell them is wrong with them. Society will not allow for diversity. Schizophrenia is a form of poetry. You listen to these people. They're artists, every one of them."

Kassler looked across at his prematurely bald colleague with the gold-rimmed glasses.

"They seem unhappy to me," Kassler pointed out.

"Of course they're unhappy," Bernie worked his way down

to the core. "They live in a work-ethic society, where money is everything, where how much you earn determines your value as a person, where all around them millions of people are starving while they see a handful of people being served hundred-dollar meals of tidbits with sauces in fancy French restaurants. No wonder they're crazy. You ever see Zelazo's house?"

"No," Kassler answered.

"Well, it's this enormous redwood structure, and the whole back of the house is plate glass and looks out on these gorgeous woods. The thing must've cost him a quarter of a million dollars, easy. Anyway, in the back, where all the windows are, is where Zelazo has his bedroom and living room. Four or five years ago, before he got into all this neurochemistry shit, just after Phlegethon opened, you know what his patients who didn't like his therapy would do?"

Kassler had his mouth full of Phlegethon beef stew, so he just opened his eyes wider and mumbled to indicate his continuing interest.

"They'd escape from here," Bernie told Kassler, "and hang themselves in the middle of Zelazo's gorgeous view. Zelazo would wake up in the morning and look out at the birches, and there would be one of his patients with his neck broken, dangling from a rope."

Kassler gagged on his stew.

"Oh, it became quite a thing around here. As soon as one of Zelazo's patients was reported missing, we'd all run to the woods outside his house. It was a game. Could we get there before the patient had climbed the tree, tied the noose on a branch, slipped it over his neck, and jumped? Usually we couldn't."

"What happened?" Kassler had controlled his choking.

"Well," Bernie started on his second apple, "Zelazo thought the patients were 'grandstanding,' is the way he put it. We thought they were trying to tell him something. The solution? Zelazo kept his drapes closed. Finally we got him to cut down his caseload. Eventually it stopped. I don't think that Zelazo ever got the point. 'You *make* us crazy,' they kept trying to tell him. Zelazo thought it was all neurochemical. *Suicide* is neurochemical?"

Bernie Kohler took another large bite of his apple and spoke with his mouth full.

"It's society, Sy," he said. "You're never going to make a dent in mental illness until you change society. If it's the last thing I do, I'm going to clean out this place, change some attitudes out there, and get these poor fucked-up people out in the community, where they belong, leading decent lives. All of a sudden, you won't need chlorpromazine anymore."

Kassler wasn't sure he agreed with Bernie Kohler, but he liked him.

"What made you decide to come here?" Kassler decided to give up on his beef stew and change the subject.

"Well, that's kind of an interesting story," Bernie grinned to himself. "This was the only job I could get after I made a little mistake. I was chief of the clinical psychology service over at the Boston Mental Health Center, which is staffed with a lot of Harvard types, all very prestigious and all that. Well, you see, I hate physicians. I've never been sure why. I just always have. So one day there's this big important conference on schizophrenia at Harvard for all the psychiatrists. Every famous psychiatrist in the world, practically, is there, and each one is walking up to the podium and talking about how magnificent he was with this patient or that patient or how he put some guy on a regimen of a thousand milligrams of scopolamine or something and he hasn't pissed on the family dog ever since, stuff like that."

Kassler listened intently as he drank his Pepsi.

"There's this small blackboard on the side wall set up wherever physicians meet so that all these emergency patients who phone can get in touch with their doctors without having to interrupt the lecture. Now most places, like ball parks, caught on long ago that doctors use devices like this for advertising. You know, 'Dr. Freud, please call your service,' and sixty thousand people in the ball park hear the name of the doctor, along with ten or fifteen million people watching the game on the tube at home. If you're a doctor and you do this enough, people begin to think, Wow, Dr. Freud, he must be good, he's got so many patients. So the ball parks started giving out numbers to the doctors. 'Dr. number forty-five,' they say now, except since they started doing that, they don't have to do it a whole lot anymore."

Bernie Kohler leaned back in his chair and tossed his apple cores into the trash can across the room with perfect accuracy. Several doctors looked up from their lunches in disgust.

"My relationships with doctors haven't improved a whole lot," Bernie went on. "Anyway, since Harvard Medical School is all doctors, there're no numbers. This day that I'm telling you about, I'm trying to hear the talks, don't ask me why, while this furious competition is going on over on the side-wall blackboard to see which shrink can get the biggest number of messages. Every thirty seconds, this messenger type comes racing up the aisle with a slip of paper and writes on the blackboard for another doctor to call some phone number. It's driving me crazy."

Bernie Kohler paused briefly and smiled contentedly to himself.

"Well, it happens that I know this particular messenger. He's a friend of mine, or used to be, anyway. I also know a lot of the doctors there, so I start making up things and handing them to Arnie, the messenger, and he obliges me by putting them up on the board. The first message is something like 'Dr. Goldman, call your broker, emergency,' and Dr. Goldman goes racing out of the auditorium in a panic. Then I give Arnie one that says, 'Dr. Georgopolis, Medicaid Field Investigation Service would like to talk to you as soon as possible,' and out goes Dr. Georgopolis like lightning is striking at his tail. I cleared out half the auditorium like this in ten minutes. But then I made a fatal mistake. I had Arnie write up on the blackboard a very simple message, 'Dr. Pratt, call Brigitte.' Well, it turns out that Dr. Mrs. Pratt, who is also a psychiatrist, is in the audience, and what's even worse, there really *is* a Brigitte, who Mrs. Pratt thought nothing much about until the message went up on the board."

Bernie Kohler leaned back farther in his chair and sighed.

"I tried to tell this to the review board, but no one believed me, and they were pretty much disgusted with me anyway, so here I am. The word about someone travels very quickly in medical circles. I was lucky to get work at all. Zelazo heard the story and called me up to ask whether it was true. When I told him it was, he offered me this job, sight unseen."

"Then how can you hate him so much?" Kassler asked.

"I don't hate Zelazo. He's a little strange, but I don't hate him. I just hate what he believes."

Kassler found that his own feelings for Zelazo were becoming more positive with each meeting between them. He felt he could talk to Zelazo, that Zelazo truly understood Kassler for who he was and the difficulties he faced for what they were. It was a feeling Kassler had wanted to have since he was a child, and he confided in Zelazo and sought his advice with increasing frequency.

Zelazo, for his part, listened well and continued to instruct Kassler in the ways of the central nervous system whenever he felt Kassler was in a receptive state. Since Kassler's receptivity was becoming less frequent, Zelazo began to relax this requirement and provided the necessary instruction whenever Kassler was minimally attentive.

"As you have no doubt noticed," Zelazo was speaking late one afternoon as Kassler wandered about Zelazo's office with his mind on other matters, "humans have three distinct parts to their brains—a bottom part which controls vegetative functions like heart rate, respiration, temperature, and eating; a middle part, the limbic system, which controls emotions like anger, excitement, pleasure, and depression; and a top part, cortex, which controls thought, association, voluntary movement, and memory, if I might be allowed to simplify matters for the sake of this particular presentation," Zelazo smiled at Kassler, who did not respond in kind.

Instead, Kassler, with a growing sense of frustration, got up from his chair and walked over to the window, where he stared out at the dense smog of the darkening evening.

"The patients on the third floor have uniquely human disorders. They think, but not well. They're not stupid, just mixed up, bad memories, strange associations, deluded concepts, but they're all very human. Down on the second floor, the patients are limited to emotions and vegetative functions. They're depressed, angry, agitated—not very much cortex in use—like mammals, but not very human. On the first floor, of course, are patients with no more left to their brains than reptiles—we say they're regressed."

Kassler was not pleased that Zelazo had placed his ward of autistic patients among the lowest ranks of the animal kingdom.

"As humans develop, higher centers control lower centers," Zelazo explained in his rumbling baritone. "Emotions make the heart beat faster or slow it down, reason tells most of us, eventually, not to be afraid of certain things—the dark, elevators, other people, being alone."

Kassler watched the lights of airplanes descending through the thick smoke to land in the distance at Newark, and only half tried to listen to Zelazo.

"Theoretically, higher parts of our brain are supposed to inhibit lower parts as we develop. As you know, it doesn't always work that way, regardless of Dr. Freud's libido-repressing ego constructions. For some of us, the system is reversed. Emotions control reason. Feelings of affection are associated with intense anxiety. The power of the limbic system becomes far greater than that of the cortex and dominates it. How this happens isn't clear. Probably lots of different ways. Damaged neurons, faulty enzymes, poor chemistry, or bad experiences—the child experiences his parent's anxiety again and again, for example, and eventually, every time the parent approaches, the child's muscles tense, his heart beats faster, he feels afraid, and very strong pathways are formed for emotions to overwhelm thought, limbic structures to control cortex, if they're not there already."

"I've heard. It's conditioned."

"Yes," Zelazo agreed. "If we were rats, I'd say we'd been conditioned. But since our brains are far more complex, it's more complicated than that. Millions of additional neurons are involved, the associations are more complex, and people do not back into the corner of their cages and cower on their hind legs. They say and do some strange things. They become schizophrenic, or depressed, or they repeat destructive behaviors, just as Vita is probably doing now."

The mention of Vita's name caught Kassler's full attention. Kassler turned away from the window and looked at Zelazo, who had his legs tucked up on his chair, his large arms wrapped around the knees.

"Look," Kassler asked irritably, "what does she want? Love? Caring? Freedom? To beat up on someone? What?"

"That's her problem, of course," Zelazo folded his hands together, interweaving the fingers, and he slowly tilted backward. "She'll never know."

Kassler looked in silence at Zelazo sitting in the darkness.

"What are you trying to tell me?" he finally asked.

"Nothing more than what I've said," Zelazo answered the unspoken part of Kassler's question.

Kassler let out a breath and appeared relieved.

"So," Zelazo tried to change the topic, "you like chess."

"Did I ever say that?" Kassler asked.

"Just a wild guess," Zelazo hastily added. "You look like a chess player."

Kassler looked into Zelazo's eyes, which stared back at him equally intently. He was unsatisfied with the answer but decided to let it pass.

"I'm a beginner. I like it," Kassler told Zelazo, "but I don't know much about how to play."

"I've a board at home. Would you like to learn?"

"I'd like to learn strategy," Kassler continued to stare at Zelazo.

"Good. That's what I'm best at." A smile appeared faintly on Zelazo's lips as the two men searched each other's eyes.

So Zelazo taught Kassler to play chess. He taught Kassler openings and defenses against the openings. He taught Kassler how to protect the center and how to seize territory. He showed Kassler how to control vast areas on the board and squash his opponent into so narrow a space that the opponent becomes desperate and foolish, has no place to escape, all his protection is destroyed, and he panics.

Kassler learned quickly. He never won but he gave Zelazo a good game. Most of all Kassler liked to sit in the large comfortable chairs in Zelazo's plush and steamy glass house, watching Zelazo's enormous veined hands move the chess pieces so lightly that they seemed to be under their own power, sliding on thin columns of air from one location to another, majestic and invulnerable.

At the conclusion of one such evening, Zelazo sat on the sofa, fingering an after-dinner drink, and scratching the bottom of one shoeless foot with the big toe of the other.

"Homeostasis," Zelazo thought out loud. "You know what that is?" he asked Kassler.

"I'm not sure," Kassler gave Zelazo the desired opportunity to offer his own definition.

"Homeostasis is the organism's tendency to maintain certain constant conditions within itself which will perpetuate its life. The oxygen level of the blood falls down, and baroreceptors tell the lungs to breathe harder, the heart to pump more quickly, the blood to circulate faster. It's a very powerful force," Zelazo said solemnly.

Kassler looked into Zelazo's large dark eyes, trying to read what was coming.

"The brain, of course, works along the same principle, although, as you know, it's separated from the rest of the body by a blood-brain barrier. The barrier protects the brain from having large molecules get through that might harm it, while it still allows nutrients that it needs to filter in. It's one of our most difficult problems in psychiatry," Zelazo mused. "A lot of what happens chemically in the brain never shows up in the blood, so it's always hard to tell what's going on in there. And a lot of what we'd like to get into the brain—medications, for example—won't cross the barrier. It's hard to get into the brain, Sy. Very hard."

Zelazo continued to scratch his foot and finger his drink. Kassler waited with growing anxiety to see where he was heading.

"Now," Zelazo continued seriously, "under the protection of the blood-brain barrier a magnificent world exists, powered only by sugar. Glucose. That's it. The syrup of mental life is glucose, Sy. Simple sugar."

Kassler stared at Zelazo.

"There is, of course," Zelazo said, "homeostasis in the brain. Neurotransmitter messengers are made, stored, released, deactivated. The brain cells need energy for this. Other chemicals are used. Enzymes float around, transferases, adding groups of molecules to one chemical and taking groups away from another. Cyclic nucleotides. Kinases. An elegant world in balance, homeostasis, Sy. Homeostasis."

Zelazo took another sip of his drink.

"Calcium is the key. Calcium opens the Gates and closes them. Calcium changes the structure of the membrane wall, rearranges the molecules that block the channels to open the gates, fires one neuron, inhibits another."

Zelazo stopped sipping and looked up at Kassler.

"We're no different from a snail. A squid. A leech. They learn just like we do. You poke a leech, and after a while it stops reacting. It habituates. The neurons don't fire anymore. Calcium. That's all it is. The calcium is depleted. The channels don't open. The neurons don't fire. The leech doesn't move."

Zelazo continued to stare at Kassler.

"You can sensitize a leech, Sy. Present a noxious stimulus and the leech learns to avoid it, to withdraw. It'll react more quickly each time. Calcium. The calcium keeps the channels open longer. There's more neurotransmitter released. The neurons fire more quickly. The animal learns to avoid. It *learns*. It has a *memory*. It *knows*. The calcium regulating the channels just isn't there anymore. Or it's pumping away overtime. And depending on how long this has been happening, that's how long the memory stays, and how hard it is to modify."

Zelazo went back to his drink and sipped in silence for several seconds. Then he looked up at Kassler again.

"Your wife will be leaving you," Zelazo said quietly.

Kassler felt a cold nauseous feeling overtake him.

"She's developed some very strong habits, Sy, and there's a powerful drive to preserve them."

Kassler crossed his arms over his chest and held tightly to himself.

"The soul has a homeostasis, too," Zelazo tried to explain. "Vita is used to being alone. She's become sensitized to withdraw at any signs of closeness. It's deeply ingrained in her. It's fixed. It's wired in by now. It's all she knows. It maintains a certain balance that would be extremely difficult for her to change. And," Zelazo looked with compassion at Kassler, "she's got a very strong barrier that lets in only what she absolutely needs and makes it impossible for anything else she considers even possibly threatening to get in."

Kassler started to shake.

"The energy needed to change all this isn't there," Zelazo finished softly. "It just isn't there."

Kassler sat shaking in his chair. The only images in his brain were those of Joshua and Joy. He started to talk, but words wouldn't come out of his mouth, so he jumped up from the chair and raced out of Zelazo's house.

"Here," said Vita to Kassler as soon as he entered the house. "I'm supposed to give this to you," and Vita handed him an official-looking document.

"What is this?" Kassler asked without looking at the paper.

"It's a notice to vacate," Vita repeated the legal jargon she had learned the previous day and avoided looking directly at Kassler.

"It's a what?" Kassler asked in disbelief.

"You know—vacate."

"No, I don't know. What is it?"

"A notice to vacate, to move out," Vita avoided eye contact.

Kassler unfolded the paper and read the document with growing rage. Before he got more than halfway through it, he threw the paper onto the floor.

"Just tell me how long I have," he said to Vita. "How long did you give me?"

"Forty-eight hours. You have to be out by the end of the weekend," Vita said slowly, afraid that Kassler might get violent and hurt her.

"Forty-eight hours! Why? Do I beat you? Am I a menace to my children?"

"It's standard, Sy. Don't get so upset. My attorney just said it'd be better that way, for all of us."

"Where am I supposed to go?" Kassler picked the paper off the floor and started reading it again.

"There're lots of small apartments around. You'll find one," Vita was trying to remain calm.

"What happens if I don't?" Kassler continued to scan the document. "What do they do?"

"I don't know what they do," Vita said. "Look, Sy, one of us has to go, and I've got two small children."

"So do I," Kassler pointed out.

"But I'm their mother," Vita proclaimed her devoted maternity for the first of thousands of times to come.

"Only by a technicality," Kassler announced what was to become his oft-repeated position. "And I'm their father. I'm staying right here."

"If you're not out of here by ten p.m. on Sunday night, I'm calling the police, and they'll put you in jail. Read the bottom of the order," Vita's calm demeanor dissipated.

"I thought you didn't *know* what happens if I can't get out of here in forty-eight hours," Kassler said, while he put on his jacket and headed for the door.

"Well, I just remembered!" Vita shouted as Kassler slammed the door behind him.

Kassler drove around for several hours, trying to sort out his options. He had an intense desire to get an attorney and fight the order, to stay right where he was, but as he reflected on his conversation with Zelazo, he decided to move out. Part of the decision was based on the hopelessness of the situation as Zelazo had explained it, but only part. Kassler had noticed that as his anger began to subside, a new feeling overtook him which was totally unexpected. Kassler found himself nearly overwhelmed with relief.

For the first time in almost four years, Kassler realized, he would not be locked in a depressing battle with Vita every minute he wasn't professionally occupied.

Kassler felt a marvelous calm envelop him. Then, finally, when Kassler had assimilated the feelings of relief and calm, he grew pitiably sad, unable to clear from his mind the faces of his children.

It was in this maelstrom of emotion that Kassler arrived late that night at Phlegethon. He wasn't ready to return home, and he could think of no other place to go.

Around midnight he made the rounds of the hospital, watching tormented patients tossing in their sleep, the quiet broken erratically by the shrill, blood-curdling screams of disturbed men and women crying out in the midst of nightmares. His travels ended in the regressed ward.

As he passed Cheryl's room, he noticed that she was awake, lying on her back, staring at the ceiling, so he walked in and sat down on a chair beside her bed.

The only light in the room was from the dim bulb in the hall. Kassler could just make out Cheryl's cream-colored face. He looked into her eyes, which continued to stare blankly into the space above her bed, and wondered what gentle person rested beneath the surface.

"I don't understand it," Kassler began a one-sided conversation with Cheryl which, broken only by occasional inquiries from the nursing staff about whether he might want to wait until morning to continue his session with the patient, lasted several hours.

"It seems like only a few weeks ago that Vita and I were walking around New York, and only a couple days before then that I was sitting behind her in class. I don't know what happened."

Cheryl rested motionlessly in bed, moving her head neither to the left nor to the right, but staring, always, at the same place in the air above her bed.

"I used to believe," Kassler confided in his patient, "that somewhere there was a love that was pure and simple, golden. When you held it, it shimmered. It was joyful. I don't know. It was a beautiful fantasy. In reality, it's all such a complicated business," Kassler lamented.

At 4:00 a.m., Bea Chaikin stood at the door to Cheryl's room, wearing a heavy robe over her nightgown and a coat over that.

"The nurses think that Cheryl's had enough therapy for tonight," Bea said gently to Kassler. "Why don't we go get some coffee from one of the machines and then we can sit in my office, if you'd like."

Kassler looked up in a fog at Bea Chaikin. At first he didn't recognize her. When he did, he looked at his watch.

"I didn't realize how late it was," Kassler said as he got up and left Cheryl's room.

"Well," Bea smiled through a yawn. "You know how time flies when you're having so much fun with your patients."

"Cheryl's a beautiful person," Kassler told Bea. They were walking down the hall. "Inside there is someone who just sparkles. Kind and bright. I can get to that. I know it. Cheryl has someone inside her who's very special."

"Yes, she does," Bea agreed, and they dropped their quarters into the machine, retrieved their paper cups of coffee, and went to sit in Bea's office.

"You know," she said while she sipped from the edge of the steaming cup, "this is the first time I've ever been called out in the middle of the night for a *therapist*. Usually my on-call weekends are limited to patients. You want to tell me what's going on?"

Kassler began at the end, with the notice to vacate, and concluded, two hours later, with the beginning, an awestruck student gaping at the most spectacular girl he'd ever seen.

"And now," Kassler sighed with resignation and fatigue, "I don't know how I got into this mess, and I don't know where to start again. I need help, Bea."

"Well," Bea said, "as a member of one of the helping professions, I might suggest this. Answer yes or no. Over the last several hours, as you sat talking to the beautiful soul which resides in Cheryl, did the thought, for even an instant, cross your mind that you should marry this autistic child?"

Kassler looked at Bea sheepishly.

"Even only a few seconds?" Kassler asked.

"That counts," Bea nodded.

"But why?" Kassler asked in confusion.

"Answer that," Bea said as she crumpled her paper cup, tossed it into the waste basket, and got up to leave, "and you've got a good place to start."

Kassler located an efficiency apartment by late the next afternoon. It was filled with Salvation Army furniture, relatively clean, not too far from the children, and cheap.

On the short drive back to his former home, Kassler computed that, by eliminating the luxuries from both Vita's and his households, he would be able to live without having to draw on what was left of his parents' bequest. It wouldn't be easy or very much fun, but he had long ago earmarked that money for the children's college education. Within the next year his automatic step salary increase would bring some financial relief, he concluded.

Dinner was bedlam. The children picked up the tension immediately and multiplied it severalfold, spilling everything liquid that was within reach, fighting with each other, crying, and disobeying all instructions, while Kassler and Vita attempted to handle each crisis without talking directly to each other.

"Okay," Kassler finally said. "Supper's over. We're all going in the tub."

"Hooray!" shouted Joshua, and he hopped down from the table, spilling the last few ounces of his milk.

"Hooray!" said Joy, copying Joshua and not really certain what the excitement was about.

"Hooray, hooray," repeated Kassler, as he lifted Joy from her high chair and went to run the water.

The bath ritual had been the same for the last few years, since Joy was out of diapers. Kassler had discovered that he got less water on his clothes by taking them off and getting in the tub with the children, so that was what he did, this last evening with his family.

"Backs!" Kassler commanded, and each bather raised a soapy washcloth and washed a neighbor's back.

"Fronts!" Kassler ordered, and the procedure was repeated, this time every man and child for himself.

"Toes! Legs! Arms! Faces! Hair!" Kassler directed the ablutions until the time for the great event arrived.

"Okay, Josh," Kassler signaled.

"Penises!" Joshua shouted proudly.

"Penises!" Kassler seconded.

"No penis," Joy giggled.

"No penis?" Kassler exclaimed in disbelief.

"What happened to Joy's penis?" Josh said his lines with proper astonishment. "Where'd it go?"

"Inside out!" bubbled Joy. "Bagina!" she called out with delight as she pointed to her genitals.

"Bagina!" Josh called out. "All penises *and* baginas!"

"And baginas!" Kassler echoed while the children laughed and giggled.

"Sometimes," Vita had remarked when she first overheard the dialogue, "I think you carry this Freudian thing too far. Joy's going to think she's some kind of freak with an inside-out penis."

"Not my explanation," Kassler replied. "Talk to Josh. He figured it out. Don't worry. Once Joy can say her *v*'s, she'll do just fine."

Kassler took a deep breath that evening, as he dried Joshua's hair with a large towel and began the discussion he'd been dreading all day. Joy sat on the floor, playing with bath toys.

"I've got to talk to you, Josh," Kassler began.

"I *cleaned* up my room, Daddy," Josh protested. "I did it before supper."

"It's not that kind of a talk," Kassler continued to rub the towel through Joshua's thick blondish hair.

"What kind?" asked Joshua.

"Very hard kind," Kassler said. "Hard for Daddy."

"What's hard?" Joshua was confused.

"Sometimes," Kassler began, "people have to do things that they really don't want to do at all."

"Like clean my room," Joshua caught on quickly.

"Like clean your room. And things even harder," Kassler searched for the words.

"Like what?" Joshua asked.

The serious tone that had developed caused Joy to stop playing with her toys and look up at Kassler from her place on the bathmat.

"Well, it's like this, Josh. Mommy and I don't get along with each other too good anymore."

"Mom's really angry, isn't she?" Joshua asked.

"Mom's unhappy," Kassler skirted the issue. "It's not very much fun being around someone who you don't like. So, Mom and I have decided that I'm going to have to move somewhere else."

"Can I come?" Josh asked, as he looked deeply into his father's eyes.

"No," Kassler said very quietly. "I'd like you to come, but I'm afraid you can't."

"Why?" Joshua asked as tears began to form in his eyes.

"Because that's the way it is," Kassler explained. "It's one of those things that I have to do even though I don't want to."

"When will you come back home?" Josh stared at his father through his tears.

"Well, that's just it. I won't ever be living with you and Joy and Mom again. You and Joy will see me a whole lot, but I've got a new place to live now, and I'll be going there tomorrow night."

"Me, too, Daddy. Please. Please, Daddy," Joshua cried, as the tears fell down his cheeks. "Don't go without me. Please. I'll clean my room all the time. I won't fight with Joy. I won't spill anymore. I'll be so good, I promise. I promise. I promise," Joshua buried his head on his father's chest and cried.

Joy got up from the floor and walked over to her father. Joshua felt her hand on his back and turned around.

"Daddy's going away, Joy," Joshua explained through his sobbing. "He's never coming home again. He won't take us with him."

"I can't, Josh. I'm not allowed to do that," Kassler tried to help Joshua understand.

"I'll be so *good*, Daddy," Joshua cried. "You'll see. I'll be so good. Joy, too. Won't you, Joy?"

Joy looked at Joshua crying, then at her father's tearful eyes, and started to cry.

Kassler stretched out his arms and drew his children to him.

"It's all going to be okay," Kassler said again and again as he hugged his children tightly to him.

For the second night in a row, Kassler went without sleep, this time so he could pack his belongings with as little disruption as possible to all concerned, including himself.

By the time the children had awakened, Kassler was finished. The next few hours consisted in almost constant weeping.

"French toast," wept Joshua. "Please make me French toast before you go."

"Fress oatmeal," wept Joy.

"Coming right up. French toast and fress oatmeal," wept Kassler.

Even Vita, to Kassler's astonishment, sat weeping on the front steps, as Kassler loaded the last box into his rented van.

"I don't understand," Kassler said to her as he closed the vehicle's back door. "What are *you* crying about?"

Vita looked up at Kassler, tears streaming from her eyes with an emotional sincerity Kassler had never before witnessed.

"Because it's sad, Sy, that's all," Vita said with a mixture of sorrow and frustration. "Because it's the saddest day of my entire life and there's nothing that can be done to change it for any of us."

Then, unexpectedly, Vita threw her arms around Kassler and sobbed.

"I'm sorry, Sy," she said through her tears. "I'm really sorry. Thank you for trying so much. I'm sorry this had to happen."

Kassler reached down and picked up Joshua with one arm and Joy with the other. Both were crying their hearts out.

"Don't forget me, Daddy," Joshua kept repeating as he cried. "Please don't forget about me."

"Don't be silly," Kassler said as he tried to control his own crying. "I'll see you in a couple of days. I'll call you tonight."

Vita stood next to Kassler, running her fingers through his hair.

"It wasn't all bad, was it?" she asked hopefully.

"Of course not," Kassler tried to hold everyone together. "It wasn't all bad."

For several minutes the four of them stood as close to one another as they could get. Then Kassler kissed his children, put them down on the pavement, kissed Vita gently on the cheek instinctively, got into his van, and the Kassler family ceased to exist.

Kassler had just backed out of the driveway when Vita came running up to him.

"I forgot to give you this," she said with tears still in her eyes, and she handed Kassler a large white envelope with his name in her handwriting on the front.

"Don't open it until tonight, okay?" she asked.

"Okay," agreed Kassler. He stuffed the envelope in his pocket, waved good-bye to his sobbing children, and drove away barely able to see the road through his own crying.

That night, after the van was unloaded and returned, and a long tearful phone conversation with Joshua had ended, Kassler remembered the envelope.

He had expected that it was a personal note from Vita, reviewing the good times and regretting the bad. It was not.

It was another court document entitled "Temporary Support and Visitation Orders—*Ex Parte.*" *Ex parte*, Kassler would soon learn, meant without the party against whom the order is issued having to be present.

The first paragraph ordered Kassler to pay seventy percent of his salary to Vita on a weekly basis. The second and last paragraph gave him visitation with his children on Sundays only, from 11:00 a.m. to 4:00 p.m.

Until the fatigue of the moving and two sleepless nights finally overcame him, Kassler wandered around the small room that night, howling to himself in anguish, as though his heart had been sliced out of his chest.

CHAPTER 3

"*It's not going to be easy,*" said Kassler's attorney, *Marty* Myers, an impeccably dressed slim man in his early fifties with thick red impeccably groomed hair.

Marty Myers had been recommended by Bernie Kohler, who seemed to know every legal practitioner in Citadel.

"Marty's your man," Bernie told Kassler when he'd heard Kassler's story over beers the first night after Kassler's relocation. "He's absolutely ruthless. Civil, but ruthless."

"I don't want to send Vita to the electric chair," Kassler told Bernie, "only get more visitation with my kids."

"Give it time," Bernie advised. "You will. By the time this is over, the electric chair will seem too brief a retaliation. One jolt and it's all over. You'll want something for Vita that's excruciatingly painful and," Bernie drew out his words, "takes . . . lots . . . of . . . time. . . ."

Now Kassler sat in Marty Myers's office, searching his counselor's green eyes for glints of sadism.

"But Sullivan is a fair judge," Marty told Kassler. "At least as fair as they come."

"Oh, shit," thought Kassler. "An Irish judge. Just what I need."

Marty took a gold cigarette case out of his vest pocket, snapped open the lid, and pulled out a filter-tip cigarette.

"There's always the presumption of the 'tender years' doctrine, of course, that kids are better off with their mother when they're small, but I've seen Sullivan take kids away from their mother if he thought they'd be better off with their father."

"I'm not asking for custody," Kassler said.

Marty Myers ran his fingers around the edges of his cigarette case and stared at Kassler incredulously.

"You don't want custody?" Marty asked.

"What am I going to do with two small children? I work all day and several evenings. I'm on call half the time, running over to the hospital in the middle of the night a couple times a week. Who's going to watch the kids?"

"You don't want custody?" Marty repeated.

"It's okay not to want custody, isn't it?"

"I suppose," Marty mulled the situation over.

"I just want weekends with my kids. Friday after supper until Sunday evening would be good."

"If you had custody—"

"But I don't *want* custody."

"You don't think that fathers are just as competent parents as mothers?"

"Some fathers are. Some fathers are better, probably."

Marty Myers snapped shut his cigarette case and tamped the end of his cigarette against the lid.

"Last year," he said, "I had this case, a man about your age, three children who were living with the mother, oldest one was five. The mother simply wasn't the best parent for those kids. The father got the kids, all three of them. The mother didn't know what hit her. We won, hands down."

"I don't want custody, Marty. I'm sure if I wanted it, you could get it for me—"

"You're right. I could."

"But the thing is, I'm not asking for custody—just more reasonable visitation."

"This is a critical point in the case, Sy."

"Maybe when they're older, both in school all day."

"The longer they stay with the mother, the harder it'll be to get them later." Marty Myers still wasn't at all happy with Kassler's approach. He lit his cigarette with the ornate silver lighter that was on his mahogany desk and rested back in the large red leather chair, silently puffing, thinking.

"Ever since the kids were born," Kassler told Marty Myers as his attorney puffed and contemplated, "I've been going crazy trying to have a professional life and take care of the kids at the same time. I'm exhausted, Marty. I'd like to concentrate during the week on earning a good living to support us all, and during the weekends I'll parent the kids. I need a break."

"What about the kids?"

"They'll be okay. Certainly no worse off than they are now, and probably better now that Vita doesn't have to deal with our relationship. If Vita was dead or took off, then I'd *have* to take the kids, and I'd deal with it. But I don't have to, so I'm not."

"You won't miss having the kids around, getting them up, seeing them for breakfast, tucking them into bed, reading them stories, comforting them when they're in pain, joking with them when—"

"For chrissakes, Marty, I'm not putting them in an orphanage."

"I've been in this business thirty years," Marty Myers said with great forthrightness, "and I consider myself an excellent judge of character. I can tell that you love those children deeply."

Kassler looked up at Marty Myers and he nodded sadly.

"This is a tragedy, Sy. Your wife has put you through hell. Everything you tell me says that Vita is a very crazy lady. There're no guarantees, of course, but I think we can take away everything that matters to her."

Kassler stood up and looked at Marty Myers chugging at his cigarette and rocking in his swivel rocker behind the inlaid desk.

"File a motion," Kassler said as he took a breath, "that asks for the father to have visitation every weekend from seven p.m. Friday to seven p.m. Sunday. Can you do that?"

"If you want," Marty Myers shrugged.

"I want," Kassler said and left before he changed his mind.

Kassler had discharged Szlyck from Phlegethon on the tenth day of his confinement, exactly as Zelazo had ordered.

"I can handle it now," Szlyck told Lupa when they had arrived back at their elaborate home on Eighth Avenue, one of the most exclusive sections of Citadel. Szlyck's classical passions had induced him to construct, on a cliff overlooking the town's vast network of ditches, a nearly full-scale imitation of a great Italian Renaissance house, which had itself once been an imitation of a great Greek house. He gave the name "Bolgia" to his, you should pardon Szlyck's other designation, Roman à cliff.

Lupa was not impressed. By the imposing palazzo or by its owner.

"*You* may be able to handle it," she told Szlyck as they sat in the cold dampness of their great hall, warming themselves with cups of tea, "but I can't. I want a divorce."

"I know," said Szlyck sympathetically. "You've been quite a woman just to put up with me this long."

"Oh, shit," said Lupa, "don't do this to me, Leo."

"I'll certainly understand if you want to leave me," Szlyck

continued, unaffected by her frustration. "It hasn't been easy for you. I've made your life miserable, I know. People calling all the time, furious with me over something I did or forgot to do. All the yelling and screaming about your faults that I've done. The promises I've broken. And I know I'm not very good in bed."

"Please stop, Leo," Lupa said numbly.

"They gave me some new medication this time, Lupa. It's going to be better now. For us both."

"I don't understand how he does this to me," Lupa told me in my home in the dungeonlike basement of Szlyck's dwelling.

"It's terrible," I agreed.

"It's like he's got some strange power over me," Lupa paced in frustration.

"I feel like I'm responsible for getting you into this mess," I told her.

"Every time I make up my mind to leave him," Lupa continued her line of thought, "we talk, and I come out of it deciding that I'll give him *one more chance*. It's like he hypnotizes me or something. What is this power he *has* over me?"

"I feel like I'm responsible for getting you into this mess," I said.

"I end up thinking, What's so wrong with this man, anyway? I *could* end up with someone even worse. Maybe he *will* change. He says he will. He's got a new medication, or a new job without so much pressure, or a new attitude, or—I don't know what!" Lupa shouted in exasperation.

"I feel like I'm resp—"

"Well," Lupa interrupted, "at least *you're* around. As long as we're together, nothing else really matters."

"You haven't forgotten our little talk a while back there about the missus?" I inquired gently.

"No," Lupa sighed. "I haven't forgotten a word you said about your 'missus.' Doesn't she have a name, for chrissake?"

"Well, yes and no," I told her the truth. "She's never told me her real name. We have this joke between us. A little nickname developed out of it, you know, one of those terms of endearment that persist."

"I'm not sure I want to hear."

"I call her Dame Fortune."

"Very funny," Lupa said irritably and left to climb the stone steps leading to the living quarters of the Szlyck Bolgia.

Kassler plunged into his work while he waited for the court hearing, but every evening that he returned home to his empty apartment became more intolerable. After several days, to deal with the loneliness, Kassler began to wander the halls of Phlegethon at night.

It was a new, and not inappropriate, experience for Kassler. He walked down corridors where drugged patients slithered along the walls, moaning and chanting a bizarre litany to themselves. In some passageways, frantic men and women flitted from shadow to shadow, peering behind them as though they were being chased. In other hallways, patients sat rocking on the cold linoleum floor or brushed by Kassler as though he didn't exist.

Kassler felt that he was dwelling in a vast underworld of cats, crawling, stalking, slithering cats, who were never able to maintain eye contact as they skittered across the halls. And presiding over this wailing felid pandemonium, the king of the beasts himself, the golden-maned Sam Zelazo, whose immense presence Kassler would frequently glimpse prowling the corridors. Perhaps, Kassler considered, the lion was after prey, a nice frightened schizophrenic mouse to torment until it expired and Zelazo could play whatever game it was he played with the remains in the darkness of Phlegethon's basement.

Kassler had not talked to Zelazo since he and Vita had separated, and made no attempt now to pursue Zelazo when he sighted him stalking the halls. Kassler held Zelazo at least partly responsible for Vita's decision, and since Zelazo was well aware of this, the two men went out of their way to avoid each other. Then, at the end of two weeks, Zelazo decided that Kassler had had enough time to cool down, and he called Kassler into his office late one night.

"Okay, Sy," Zelazo began calmly. "What would you have liked me to do?"

"Told her to stay," Kassler answered as he studied Zelazo's skin, which seemed green in the single fluorescent desk lamp that lit the room. "Told her to try to work things out."

"Is that what you would have told your patient?" Zelazo shifted to the role of Kassler's supervisor.

Kassler shrugged in discouragement.

"No," he said. "I guess not."

"Nor do I," Zelazo agreed.

Kassler looked around the darkened office and tried to get his thoughts in order.

"I don't know where it went wrong," he told Zelazo, who was sitting motionless and majestic in the big armchair behind his desk. "If I could figure that out, then I'd know where to begin fixing it."

"No place," Zelazo said as he took long deep breaths.

"What?"

"No place," Zelazo repeated slowly. "There's no place where it went wrong. It never was right. There isn't anywhere to begin fixing it."

"There's got to be," Kassler insisted.

"Why?" Zelazo continued to explore the situation calmly with Kassler.

"Where there's a will . . ." Kassler tried out.

"Is that what you wanted?" Zelazo turned in his chair and faced Kassler, Zelazo's muscles tightening as though he were about to pounce on him. "You wanted to spend the rest of your life in combat with a woman who is terrified of closeness and commitment? Is this what would have made you happy?"

"The children—" Kassler started.

"I see. You wanted the children to grow up in a home where this is their experience of the way a man and a woman relate?"

"It's not that simple," Kassler objected.

"No, it's not," Zelazo concurred, "but the end result is that for Vita it's wired in now."

"Damn it," Kassler protested. "Does absolutely everything have to be explained with neurochemistry?"

"Yes," Zelazo said without hesitation. "Eventually, yes. Chess?" Zelazo raised his bushy eyebrows with the invitation. "You'll feel better."

Kassler looked at his green-skinned mentor for several seconds in silence.

"I guess," Kassler agreed slowly.

"Good," Zelazo said as he pulled a bag of wooden chessmen and a folding board out of a desk drawer. "Combat always has a calming effect on the nervous system."

Marty Myers stood before the judge and explained that the children needed more contact with their father, who had long been their primary caretaker.

Vita's lawyer, Doris Huber, a slender and attractive brunette woman in her thirties, explained to the judge that Sunday visitations for a father were standard, as well as fair and reasonable.

Judge Sullivan, a balding man in his forties with thick glasses and a round pinkish face, asked if there would be a hearing on the merits regarding the divorce, support, and visitation. When both attorneys nodded in the affirmative, Judge Sullivan indicated that he would take Kassler's motion under advisement, but was inclined to consolidate the matters. He then thanked the attorneys and called the next case.

Vita, who had been sitting at a long table directly across from Kassler, glowering at him throughout the brief proceedings, smiled at the attorney, glowered once more at Kassler, and left.

"How come I didn't get to say anything?" Kassler asked Marty Myers as they walked down the courthouse corridor.

"This is just a motion," Marty explained. "Just the counselors talk. There's no testimony until a hearing on the merits. Then you can tell the whole story."

"What's 'under advisement' mean?" Kassler asked his legal representative.

"It means he'll think it over."

"For how long?"

"Well, he says that he's probably going to consolidate all

matters," Myers explained as they stood outside on the steps in the cold March wind. "He'll hear everything—support, visitation, custody, the divorce—all at the same time, and give his decision when he's got all the facts."

"Well," said Kassler, "I guess that's fair. When does the hearing on the merits take place?"

Marty Myers turned to face Kassler and looked him in his eyes with a mixture of sympathy and frustration.

"The court calendar is very crowded, Sy," he told Kassler. "Probably not for a couple years."

Kassler barely held himself together. He was totally unprepared for the judge's decision and found that, in his attempt to adjust to it, his mind filled with terrifying nightmares during the long restless nights and with chilling fantasies during the days.

"I have thoughts," Kassler confessed to Zelazo at the conclusion of one of his supervisory sessions, "that scare the hell out of me. There've been times when I've found myself thinking how easy it would be just to walk into Vita's house when everyone was asleep—I still have the key—take a knife from the kitchen drawer, and slit everyone's throats. Vita's, my kids', my own . . ."

Kassler shivered as he related the fantasy and grew nauseous, but he continued.

"It probably wouldn't take more than a few seconds. Killing my kids? Josh? Joy? I love them. How could I ever *think* about that?"

"Children always make us aware of how fragile life is," Zelazo interpreted. "You've had an enormous loss. You're angry. And sad. In time you'll adjust. We all do," Zelazo said with the look in his eyes of someone remembering similar experiences in his own past.

"It scares me," Kassler repeated to Zelazo, looking for a guarantee. "How do I know I wouldn't ever do it?"

"You don't," Zelazo ended their meeting without providing any assurances.

* * *

As Kassler's loneliness grew over the weeks following the court appearance, he spent his free time walking through Citadel, First Avenue to Ninth, contemplating his predicament. The wind chilled him through to the bone. Sand filled his nose and mouth until he could hardly breathe. But Kassler wrapped his coat tightly around him and pushed on, enduring nature's punishment as inconsequential next to the cruelty of his own life.

At the conclusion of each journey, Kassler sat in front of the main gate to the city, shivering and sad, reflecting on the words someone had scrawled with a can of black spray paint on the structure's top as a comment on Mr. Nixon's great dream.

> I was raised here by divine omnipotence,
> primordial love, and ultimate intellect.

Eventually, our young Zarathustra began to follow these solemn excursions with equally morose visits to various singles' bars, where he would pick up other lonely and desperate individuals for brief sexual encounters.

He had not originally planned to do this, but found himself drinking away his troubles one evening in a bar he had not known was set up to facilitate such encounters, when, in the new spirit of female liberation, he was approached by a not unattractive woman who asked if she might join him.

Kassler agreed for the sake of the company, and after several hours of the lady's listening to Kassler relate his *Weltschmerz*, she very kindly took his hand and made a conditional offer.

"Look," she said, "I think it would be nice if we went back to your place and went to bed, but you have to promise me something, okay?"

Kassler listened with growing interest.

"No big production about proving your manhood, okay? I'm sure you loved your wife a whole lot and her throwing you out was a dirty rotten thing to do and a blow to your ego. But you've got to take my word for it, you're still a male or I wouldn't be doing this with you. I'm sorry if I'm being crude, but I don't think I can take another guy banging the hell out of me so he can prove his masculinity, okay?"

And so it was that Kassler embarked on an intense, but brief, series of intimate relationships with total strangers.

The intensity was owing to the need Kassler had to ventilate the torment in his heart. The brevity of this part of Kassler's life was owing to Leo Szlyck, who once again gained admittance to Phlegethon.

"I've got a personal favor that I'd like to ask of you," Kassler said the morning after Szlyck's arrival, as he and Zelazo were making rounds of the paranoid-schizophrenic ward. "Leo Szlyck was admitted again last night, and I'd like to work with him. I need a challenging, interesting patient. I think we get along okay. I can help the man."

Zelazo fished for a key to open the door to the ward.

"I thought I told you I didn't want the man in here again," Zelazo said abruptly.

"It was late last night. There was someone new on intake-and-admission. They didn't know."

"I won't supervise you with him. I'll do all the rest, but not Szlyck," Zelazo found the right key and the door opened.

"I asked Bea Chaikin this morning, and she's agreed," Kassler told Zelazo.

The two men walked in silence past the suspicious schizophrenics lining the hall.

"So what do you think?" Kassler asked again.

"As long as I don't hear one word about him, it's up to you," Zelazo gave Kassler his approval. "But he's a dangerous man, Sy. He'll destroy you."

"He's a teddy bear," Kassler smiled back to Zelazo, as he started to walk off in the other direction.

"Just watch out," Zelazo called loudly down the hall to Kassler.

Scores of eyes flicked quickly to the left and right.

"Watch out, watch out, watch out," one paranoid patient after another echoed up and down the long corridor.

* * *

Leo Szlyck was almost completely incoherent when he met with Kassler.

"The cosmological constant," Szlyck answered Kassler's inquiries.

"What is?"

"Why I'm here. The naked singularity. I've seen it," Szlyck mumbled as he fidgeted nervously.

"Do you know who you are?" Kassler asked.

"Of course," answered Szlyck. "Satan's angel."

"Do you know what day today is?" Kassler tried again.

"In relation to the Big Bang, it's hard to tell. We're all going to fry in the Big Crunch. Not so long. We're all going to freeze in the Open End. A lot longer. What'll you have? Open End? Or Big Crunch?" Szlyck offered Kassler his very own cataclysm.

Kassler looked over Szlyck's admission notes.

"You were a very sad man when your wife brought you in here last night, Dr. Szlyck. Your wife was afraid you might harm yourself. How do you feel now?"

The mention of Lupa brought Szlyck, at least temporarily, back to reality.

"She's leaving me," Szlyck said.

"Your wife is leaving you?" Kassler asked. "Has she told you this?"

"She is. I know. You've got to talk to her. I'm going to be okay. Tell her," Szlyck instructed Kassler.

"You want me to meet with your wife?" Kassler asked. "You want me to tell her you're going to get better? Is that what you want, Dr. Szlyck?"

"Yes. Talk. To her. Please."

"But we don't know what your problem is yet, do we? It's hard to tell her that you're going to get better until we understand your problem, don't you think?"

"I suppose," Szlyck said glumly.

"Perhaps if you told me more about your cosmological constant. That might be a good place to start."

"If you promise. Talk to Lupa," Szlyck insisted. "My wife's name's Lupa. Meet her. Please."

"I always try to meet with the families of the patients," Kassler assured Szlyck.

"You'll meet Lupa?" Szlyck pleaded. "Now?"

"Later."

"Soon. You'll meet Lupa soon. Talk to her. I'm all right. She should stay."

"And you'll tell me about your cosmological constant?" Kassler bargained.

"Yes. Yes," Szlyck agreed. "Meet Lupa. Please. Talk to her. Please. Please. Talk to her—"

"Okay, okay," Kassler said in exasperation, "I'll talk to Lupa. Does that make you happy?"

"Ecstatic," beamed my angel.

Lupa arrived in Kassler's office, radiant and nervous, her blond hair loosely resting on the shoulders of her tweed jacket. Lupa had never been to see a psychotherapist before, and Kassler understood her nervousness almost immediately.

"People who haven't had any experience with psychotherapists," Kassler explained, attempting to keep calm in the face of Lupa's dazzling appearance, "believe that shrinks can see right through them, as though they're transparent. To all mental-health practitioners, they feel they're naked."

"*Can* you see right through me?" Lupa asked, still anxious, in spite of Kassler's diagnosis.

"No." Kassler attempted, with only partial success, to clamp the lid on his fulminating libido. "I can't."

"Leo is very sick, isn't he?" Lupa asked with some concern, as she smoothed the wrinkles on her beige skirt.

"He's doing just fine," Kassler didn't want to encourage too much sympathy for a crazy little round man, even though he had—Kassler could not figure out how for the life of him— gotten this lovely, attractive, bright, cultured, slender-legged lady to become his wife.

"Your husband has asked me to speak to you about your plans regarding your marriage," Kassler decided to honor his obligation to Szlyck, regardless of the circumstances.

"Leo is not my husband anymore. I left him last week and got a divorce in Juárez. Those are my plans, and they're now mostly complete. I want no money from him. I'll make it on my own."

"Have you told this to Dr. Szlyck?" Kassler was pleasantly surprised. "Is he aware of all this?"

"Of course he is. Why do you think he's here? I told him I'd filed for divorce in Mexico and he tried to stick his head in the microwave, among other things. What did he tell you?" Lupa asked with growing irritation.

"Well," Kassler tried to respect patient confidentiality, "he is, as you know, in a rather confused state right now. I'm not sure it's all as clear in his mind as the situation appears to be in reality. Or as final."

"It's very final." Lupa explained the details at some length.

She liked the way Kassler listened to her, and when she had finished her story, she looked to see whether he was wearing a wedding band. His finger was, of course, unadorned.

"I'd like to hear more about Dr. Szlyck's history," Kassler said as he admired Lupa's flashing purple eyes, "but it's getting late."

Lupa looked at her watch and confirmed that it was nearly six o'clock.

"Oh, I'm sorry. I had no idea—" Lupa apologized, and she got up from her chair and pulled down her suit jacket.

"No need to apologize," Kassler answered, and decided to take a calculated risk. "I'm just a little hungry, that's all."

"Yes," said Lupa. She stood facing Kassler, fiddling with the Paisley scarf around her neck. "I'm a little hungry, too."

"There is," said Kassler, jumping down the stairs of his Great Descent nine at a time, "a very nice Mexican restaurant not far from here."

Lupa looked in Kassler's eyes to assure herself that this was indeed an invitation. Then she smiled and took Kassler's arm, a little playfully, but with tenderness.

"I've developed a taste for Mexican things lately," Lupa said. "That sounds just fine."

And Kassler was on his unfortunate way again.

Both parties behaved as adults should behave on their first dinner date. They discussed art and politics, the more pleasant aspects of their childhoods, motion pictures they had recently attended or that had long been favorites, and the quality of the cuisine.

Topics they scrupulously avoided included past marriages, past relationships, present liaisons, desires and dreams relating to the future and what might be, and mental post-mortems on events in the past that might not have worked out exactly as intended.

Lupa, for her part, attempted to remain mature, friendly, approachable, and attentive, without signaling absolutely any interest in Kassler beyond the kind of friendship two grown-ups might properly share.

Kassler, on the other hand, though growing ever nearer a state of nervous exhaustion from maintaining this constant maturity, attempted, nevertheless, to be unboring, unpreachy, manly, strong, intellectually non-snobbish, artistically modest and unaffected, emotionally sensitive, and to get through the entire evening without mentioning a book he'd read or advancing a psychological interpretation of another human being's behavior—he had ticked off the items, one by one, of a list once presented to him by Vita, just as he had done night after night, lying awake, unable to sleep in his efficiency apartment.

"Do you think," Lupa had made the only venture out of the realm of impersonality at the end of the evening, "that it's possible for a man and a woman just to be good friends, and that's all?"

"Certainly," Kassler responded immediately. "Absolutely. Definitely. Sure."

And the shell-shocked couple paid for their fare at La Vida Olvidada, arranged to meet the next Saturday, and left, as they had come, in their separate vehicles, both secure in the very conscious knowledge on the way home that, so far, they had not repeated the mistakes of the past.

"He's really quite nice, cute almost," Lupa told me that night.

"Just what you need, someone cute," I pointed out.

"You're jealous. That's wonderful."

"I'm not jealous. I'm looking out for your best interests," I explained. "You're making a terrible mistake again."

"Really," Lupa refused to accept my words at face value.

"He's a married man," I reminded her.

"He's separated, and his wife has filed for divorce."

"That should tell you something right there."

"I'll be careful."

"I don't like the way it sounds. Too complicated. He's separated. With two small kids. And he's a shrink to boot. You need someone fresh and sparkling—uncorrupted. Take my word for it. This is no good for you."

"My goodness. You are adamant. Going to miss me, darling?" Lupa cooed and twirled in her nightie.

"A little," I conceded. "When are you leaving?"

"Tomorrow. I thought I told you."

"I hadn't realized it was that soon. You'll visit me, of course."

"Of course. Every week. I'd never leave you completely. I just need something more. You understand."

"Because I can give you some perspective about this Kassler. Keep you out of trouble."

"I think I can handle it, but thanks."

"Tomorrow?"

"First thing. I've got a nice little apartment not far from here. I'm starting my own interior-design business."

"You should do well."

"I hope so. Well," Lupa sighed, "I guess I should turn in," and she started toward the stairs.

"Lupa," I called.

"Yes?"

"I'm having a little problem with one of my knobs."

Lupa turned and walked toward me very slowly.

"I thought," I told Lupa, "that you might be able to help."

"Which knob is causing you the problem?"

"The large red one in front of you."

"Oh," Lupa smiled and let her nightie slip onto the floor, "that knob."

*   *   *

Lupa left the next morning, as I suspected she would, leaving behind a vast empty house, and me in the basement. It was, I concluded almost immediately, a situation that could not be allowed to continue.

I began to make plans.

It was a little tricky, Kassler felt, treating Leo Szlyck in therapy while dating his ex-wife of a few weeks, but since Szlyck was still largely incoherent, the conflicts were at a minimum.

At first Lupa guarded her feelings, protecting herself from the pain of another relationship that might go wrong, but soon she realized that she wasn't holding back any longer. Her relationship, as it developed with Kassler, was, she concluded, a mature, adult relationship. No hot flashes and radiant flushes, but no stormy conflicts and petty tensions. It was just there, and Lupa slipped into it the way one might into an old, comfortable, but unglamorous shoe.

Kassler, who saw himself in less shoddy terms, had needs, growing more urgent with every mature encounter, that nearly cried out for a juvenile resolution. He felt that owning up to such feelings about Lupa might betray the Platonic trust she had placed in him, and so, calling upon a restraint developed to its ultimate during his years with Vita, Kassler survived his concerts, dinners, films, and walks with the lovely Lupa without the issue's coming up, so to speak.

Unfortunately, Kassler's psyche was better able to endure the rigors of restraint than Kassler's physiology. He developed allergies to everything from anisette to zucchini. Berries gave him rashes. Chocolate made his head ache. Milk products produced stomach cramps. Nuts gave him hives. Tomatoes gave him asthma.

Miraculously, these symptoms all disappeared the evening that Kassler had to be rushed by ambulance to the hospital because of crushing chest pain.

Lupa, who had been having dinner with Kassler when he had the attack, accompanied him to the hospital and sat on a stool beside him, gently stroking his thick curly black hair while an elderly physician attached leads from the EKG monitor onto Kassler's chest.

"You're going to be fine," Lupa's soft cultured voice re-assured Kassler.

"I know," Kassler, who was scared out of his wits, tried to convince himself.

"How old are you?" the physician, Dr. Trubatch, asked Kassler as he finished pasting the last electrode onto Kassler and switched on the EKG monitor.

"Thirty-four," Kassler sighed as he considered his decrepitude.

"That's very young to be having a coronary," Trubatch remarked.

"Young?" Kassler squeaked. "I have *two* children. I'm almost *divorced*. That's how young I am."

"I see," Trubatch watched the perfectly normal lines being traced onto the strip of graph paper that unfolded from the EKG machine. "Your heart looks good, Dr. Kassler."

"I had crushing substernal chest pains that radiated to my left arm," Kassler argued his case.

Lupa took Kassler's hand and stroked it gently.

"It's okay, Sy. It must have been something else," she tried to comfort him.

"What else?" Kassler whined. "What else is substernal, and crushing, and radiates? This is a heart problem. I can tell."

"Esophagospasm produces the same symptoms. So does a precordial catch syndrome. Both are very common. I'll be back shortly," and Trubatch pulled the curtain open, stepped out of the cubicle, and flipped the curtain shut behind him.

"I want a second opinion," Kassler told Lupa. "He's not telling me the truth."

"I think he is, Sy," Lupa said as she ran her hand gently over Kassler's forehead.

Kassler turned and looked over at Lupa.

"You're very good to me, Lupa," he told her quietly.

"I enjoy doing it. Besides, I'd like to keep you around a while longer. You're nice to be with sometimes."

"You really think so?" Kassler felt the tightness in his chest begin to loosen.

Lupa kissed Kassler on the lips very gently.

"Yes. I do."

"It's hard for me to tell sometimes."

"I'm not good at expressing it with words, but I try to do other things."

Kassler thought about this for a few seconds.

"I really appreciated your getting me the goat's milk and soybean burger for dinner tonight," Kassler recalled what he'd been about to say when the pains struck him.

"I won't say it was nothing," Lupa smiled.

"You're a nice lady," Kassler reached over and stroked Lupa's cheek with his hand.

"Well, I'm glad you're more verbal than I am, Sy, because I like it when you say things like that to me. You're a very sincere person. And a good friend."

"I am?" Kassler's intercostal musculature relaxed.

"*I* think so," Lupa took Kassler's hand and squeezed it.

"How come we haven't gotten closer?" Kassler asked.

"You mean, why haven't we gone to bed?"

Kassler shook his head in the affirmative.

"I need time, Sy. So do you."

Kassler mulled this over as he watched, through a crack in the curtain, Dr. Trubatch approaching.

"Do me a favor," Kassler asked in a whisper. "Ask Dr. Trubatch if my T waves are inverted."

"Your what?"

"It's part of the EKG. My T waves. Just ask him if they're inverted."

"Sure." Lupa smiled as Trubatch entered. "Excuse me, Dr. Trubatch. Are Sy's T waves inverted?"

"Only if you stand on your head," Trubatch announced directly to Kassler, who suddenly found himself feeling as though, you should pardon the expression, a great weight had been lifted from his chest.

As the friendship between Kassler and Lupa grew, Kassler, without forcing the issue, nevertheless continued to keep his eyes open for an opportunity, an approach, a forum which might, with proper decorum, start the sexual ball rolling.

Such an opportunity, or at least the germ for such an opportunity, came at the tail end of a session Kassler had with Norman Meltz the Masturbator.

For most of the hour, Kassler had not been particularly attentive to Norman's usual ramblings. A disturbing meeting of the hospital staff had preceded Norman's treatment session, although Norman's masturbation had not been the topic at hand, so to speak.

The meeting had to do with a court order Bernie Kohler had finally obtained ordering Phlegethon to release into the community, in an orderly manner over the next two years, no fewer than half the lunatics now within its walls. The remaining half were to be released during the two years following that. At the conclusion of this process, four years hence, Phlegethon was to be converted, by private initiative, and therefore at no taxpayer expense, into condominiums.

"And once all the crazy people are out there and the sane people are in here," one staff member noted out loud the sleight-of-hand aspect of the enterprise, "do we have to start the whole process all over again? Convert Phlegethon Landings"—for so the condominiums had already been named—"back to Phlegethon State Hospital?"

"This is no joking matter," Bernie Kohler shouted to his colleagues. "We're going to need lots of careful planning and hard work to get these patients out of here and back into society. We're going to have to educate the community about how to deal with schizophrenics so they can lead productive lives."

"The way to deal with schizophrenics so they can lead productive lives, as you would have it, Dr. Kohler," Sam Zelazo said from the small lectern in front of the auditorium, where he presided over the meeting, "is to determine which enzymes are responsible for their methylation disorder and produce antibodies that counteract them."

"Methylate what?" Bernie challenged Zelazo.

"Serotonin," Zelazo said calmly but firmly.

Bernie Kohler was undaunted.

"Serotonin? I thought it was GABA. Wasn't that the big thing around here all last year? Schizophrenia was an inhibitory disorder involving GABA? What happened to GABA?"

"There's been more recent work," Zelazo explained.

"The year before that it was the catecholamine theory of schizophrenia. Dopamine and norepinephrine were very big. And before that it was bufotenine," Bernie continued to bait Zelazo. Kassler watched in disbelief as the two battled.

"It's now a matter of serotonin metabolism," Zelazo was firm.

"Bananas," Bernie called back.

There were a few giggles in the audience.

"Yes, you've told us before, Dr. Kohler," Sam Zelazo said patiently. "Bananas have serotonin, too."

The audience broke into laughter, relieving the tension that had been developing over the last half-hour.

"My schizophrenics are bananas, and my bananas are serotonergic." Bernie Kohler danced a little jig beside his seat on the aisle, joining in the levity.

When the audience had quieted down, Zelazo stood silently at the front of the auditorium, looming over the lectern like a bird of prey with his claws sunk in carrion.

"We will do as the court orders us," Zelazo said solemnly. "We *will* have half the patients in apartments in Citadel two years from today."

There was total silence in the auditorium as the psychiatric and nursing staffs sat frozen in disbelief.

Zelazo leaned even farther over the pedestal that was now his main support.

"To facilitate this," Zelazo continued, "I am forming a committee to oversee and expedite the process. I'm asking you, Dr. Kassler, to chair the committee, since many of your patients will most likely be the first to be discharged."

Kassler received a jolt at the mention of his name. He nodded absently to Zelazo, as he quickly indexed his patients. Who would go? Diana Fletcher?

"Is there anyone *other than Dr. Kohler* who would like to

be a member of the committee?" Zelazo went on while Kassler thought of his patients.

Philip Donato? *Mrs.* Donato wouldn't be a bad candidate, but she was already out there. Kassler's mind meandered through his therapeutic charges.

Bea Chaikin volunteered, Bernie Kohler, frantically waving his arms, was finally added by Zelazo, and the committee membership was closed.

Leo Szlyck? Possibly. Mr. Katzman? Hard to tell.

The meeting broke up and staff members huddled in small cliques, mumbling pro and con statements, mostly con, and wondering whether the judge himself might want to try his forensic hand at releasing the cornucopia of mentally disturbed patients that was to pour from Phlegethon over the next twenty-four months.

The last name Kassler added to his list, as he sat numbly between Bernie Kohler and Bea Chaikin, watching the battlefield empty, was, of course, Norman Meltz the Masturbator.

Norman, as fortune would have it, sat now in Kassler's office proclaiming his rehabilitation.

"I'm telling you, Dr. Kassler," Norman insisted, "my pecker is now absolutely completely one hundred percent under control," and Norman went for his zipper to prove his point.

"That's all right," Kassler held up his hand to halt Norman. "I'll take your word for it. If you say it's under control, that's good enough for me."

"I used to have this problem with seeing girls on the street, but no more, Dr. Kassler. I'm cured. You let me out of here and you'll see. My thing about heinies is gone forever," Norman affirmed with great conviction.

"Heinies?" Kassler asked to test Norman's claim.

"Sure, I told you about them, didn't I?" Norman began to get a little nervous.

"No, I don't think you did, Norman."

"Well, it's nothing very important anyway," Norman squirmed.

"I'd like to hear about them."

"Well," Norman knew his claims were being put to the acid

test. "What *used* to happen, *used* to, but *doesn't anymore*, what used to happen a *long, long* time ago, was that I'd be driving down the street in town and I'd see this heinie, you know, rear end, female rear end, actually more like girl's rear end, like maybe she was sixteen or seventeen and wearing tight dungarees, and what can you do with sixteen-year-olds? You can't fuck them or you go to jail. You hardly even talk to them."

Norman paused and took a deep breath.

"The heinies problem?" Kassler reminded his patient.

"Oh, yah, right," Norman took another deep breath. "So I'd be driving along and there in front of me would be this cute little sixteen-year-old girl with the most adorable heinie in really tight dungarees so you can see her entire slit right through the denim, you know, and these cute little knockers that jiggle up and down because the girls don't wear bras anymore, so you can see her nipples sticking out through her tee shirt."

Norman paused to catch his breath.

"You sure I haven't told you all this before?" he pleaded with Kassler.

"Not that I recall," Kassler answered.

"Well," Norman shook his head, "I'm driving along and there's this girl's heinie and each part of her heinie is going up and down, left and right, jiggling all over the place, the dungarees tight in the crack in her ass, and the slit between her legs is spreading open, then closed, then open again, with each little step she takes. My pecker gets so hard, and it aches, so I put my hand on it to try to calm it down, but the zipper gets in the way. And it needs air so bad, so I open up the zipper. It feels so good out there in the air, and I'm rubbing it as fast as I can, watching the girl walk along the street, driving and diddling with my pecker, watching her little knockers bounce up and down and her heinie slide all over—shit!" Norman barked out, noticing that his organ was now rock-hard, his two hands working furiously at the khaki bulge. "And I was doing so *good*. Shit! Shit! Shit!"

"My sentiments exactly," Kassler answered.

"I don't understand it," Norman said plaintively. "I really thought I had it licked this time."

"Maybe if you developed some other, more appropriate, sexual outlets," Kassler suggested.

"But I do have other, more appropriate, sexual outlets," Norman whined.

"You have a girl friend?" Kassler asked.

"Not exactly," Norman said.

"You date?" Kassler tried again.

"Not exactly," Norman remained deliberately vague.

"What exactly do you do?" Kassler inquired directly.

"Well," Norman avoided looking directly at Kassler. "I know you're not going to like this, but just about everybody in Citadel does it, so if I'm crazy then everyone else is, too. But, you see, I once was having one of those friendly-type relationships with this girl I liked a whole lot, you know, lots of movies and restaurants, but nothing else?"

Kassler's ears perked up like those of a hound at the first warble of nearby quail, and he listened with rapt attention.

"So a friend told me about this place here in Citadel," Norman went on, "which is modeled after Plato's Retreat in New York, except much wilder, you know, one of these sex places where everyone's doing it to everyone else?"

"I've heard of them, yes," Kassler answered, two full registers below his normal talking voice.

"Well," Norman smiled, "that did the trick. We just went to watch, you know, kind of a funky thing to do, just watch the people screw, see how they did it, pick up some pointers, sort of a research project. In five minutes she was all over me. I couldn't get her to stop. She exhausted *me*, can you believe that? *Me?* Ten straight hours. It was light when we stopped, and, I'm telling you, she still wanted more. I couldn't believe it. My pecker was begging for mercy. My tongue tasted like it was made entirely out of female organ. I was pooped. Anyway, I've been going regularly ever since, but as you can see, it hasn't done me a whole lot of good."

"Yes, well," Kassler's ego gave one of the outstanding performances of its career as it portrayed, with amazing credibility, a serious psychotherapist. Kassler's libido, on the other hand, rattled in a good approximation of blithering idiocy.

"Perhaps," Kassler attempted to mask his grinning delirium by covering his mouth with his handkerchief, supposedly to anticipate a sneeze, "the solution for you is not to be found from frequenting places located on . . . uh . . . ?"

"Second Avenue," Norman completed the sentence.

". . . like, uh . . . ?" Kassler spoke through the cloth.

"Dante's Inferno," Norman the Masturbator obliged.

"Aachoo."

"Bless you."

MARCH 1979

Session III

❧

"*So, tell me, Kassler. I know I can't win. God's unbeatable.*
You'd think I'd have learned that by now," I told my psychotherapist, who sat, today, slowly cleaning his glasses while I poured out my heart to him. "So why do I do it?"

"Do you have a choice?" he raised what I thought to be a mediocre point.

"Of course I have a choice," I told him. "You don't think I've got enough to keep me busy?"

"What *exactly* is it that you do?" Kassler lifted his spectacles to his mouth and huffed into each lens.

"Good question."

"And the answer?" Kassler flipped his eyeglasses and fogged the reverse side of the lens.

"I'm an interested observer, basically," I told Kassler.

"Ah, yes," Kassler polished away meticulously at his glasses. "This is the corollary to the 'I don't tempt, I don't seduce, I don't bargain' proposition, as I recall."

"Answer me something, will you, Kassler? Is this the way you practice psychotherapy with your other patients, sit and think up facetious retorts to what they tell you, or do you just reserve that approach for me?" I thought I'd address the issue head on.

"I'm not sure I understand," Kassler evaded.

"Sure you understand," I pointed out to him. "You understand just perfectly. I tell you something. Then you tell me how I'm a horse's ass. I tell you something else. And you repeat the diagnosis."

Kassler worked feverishly at shining up his gold-rims.

"You feel," Kassler said very clinically, "that I'm unsympathetic."

"I'm not playing, Kassler, so you can drop the diabolical psychotherapeutic games you like to play."

"Diabolical?" Kassler decided to take a semantic approach.

"You got it. Diabolical."

"Just *my* psychotherapy or psychotherapy in general?" Kassler twirled his glasses in circles and appeared more interested.

"Well, now that you bring it up," I thought it was time to inject some education into the session, "the little I understand about the process leads me to include all practitioners."

Kassler waited patiently for me to continue, the stem of his glasses held between thumb and forefinger, going around and around.

"Correct me if I'm wrong," I said, "but it is true, is it not, that the first goal in any psychotherapy is to establish a solid relationship with the patient? You want him to feel comfortable talking to you about the most intimate aspects of his life? I haven't misunderstood anything, have I?"

"The relationship is everything," Kassler agreed. "Without it there's no transference, no countertransference, no material."

"Good. I like that. Closeness, trust, empathy—get the relationship going."

"The patient will react to the therapist as he does to other close persons in his life—his father, mother, wife—and the therapist gets a first-hand experience of what's been conflicting the patient."

"Sounds great," I applauded the strategy. "Get close. Very loving. Except that once the patient gets close enough for you to have all that lovely transference and countertransference material to play around with, you make sure the patient knows you're *not* his father or wife, or even friend, but only a therapist who's being paid to treat him. You work your behind off to get this marvelous relationship going with the patient, and as soon as you've got it, after he's poured his soul out to you, you tell your patient that it's all make-believe. You're only a hired listener. And you don't think this is just a little diabolical?"

"It's therapeutic," was all Kassler could come up with on the spur of the moment.

"So, I hear, are pogroms."

Kassler put on his glasses very carefully, being certain not to smudge the glistening lenses.

"I assume that now that you have a totally unobstructed view of the darkness down here," I commented on Kassler's improved vision, "my treatment will be illuminated with dazzling new insights."

"Do I detect a certain horse's-ass sarcasm?" Kassler took the offensive.

"Okay, Kassler, tell me. What is it?" I decided to have it out once and for all. "What's going on? I offered you an alliance. What happened? Why all the cat-and-mouse business? I scare you?"

Kassler thought about this for a minute or so.

"I'm not sure you're Satan anymore," Kassler finally told me.

"Who am I?"

"Leo Szlyck's unconscious."

"Leo's unconscious? Come on, Kassler. You *worked* with Szlyck. You know better."

"Well, if not Szlyck's unconscious, then at least not Satan."

"When did all this happen?"

"Last session."

"How?"

"I'm not sure," Kassler was at least honest.

"I'll tell you what it was, Kassler. I disappointed you. You wanted fire and brimstone, special effects, torment and cruelty, a good healthy dose of the insidious. I'll be the first to admit it, in those realms I'm a big disappointment. It's all very mundane."

Kassler nodded in partial agreement.

"Something else," he mumbled, mostly to himself.

"I know," I told him. "It sounded great at the time. Psychotherapist to Satan himself. It seemed like a perfect situation. If I wasn't Satan, you'd find out who I was. That'd be interesting. If I *was* Satan, well, then, who could ask for more? Treating the devil is the ultimate ambition of every psychotherapist, let's face it."

Kassler shrugged and sighed.

"Instead, what do you get?" I observed. "I *am* Satan. And I'm no big deal. You must be heartbroken, Kassler. And it's not that I don't sympathize with the tragedy of your patient-selection process, but do you think we might be able to get some decent therapy done, now that we've brought the problem out into the open?"

"I suppose." Kassler's disappointment led me to believe I had more or less hit the nail on the head.

"Aw, come on, cheer up, Kassler. It might not turn out so bad after all. I did promise that I'd tell you the Great Answer if you cured me. And, you know, I never welch on a deal. That ought to be worth something."

"I had hoped that you were ultimately responsible for insanity," Kassler lamented.

"Well, I'm sorry about that, too. But you should have known better. Deuteronomy. 'The Lord will smite thee with madness.' His idea. It's all right there. Look it up."

"I'll take your word for it," Kassler passed.

"You do believe in God?" A new problem occurred to me.

"When was it that you first felt this irritation with the fantasies people fabricated about you?" Kassler plunged into serious psychotherapy.

"You didn't answer my question, Kassler. I said, you *do* believe in God?"

"I believe that God is revealed in the harmony of all that exists."

"Ah, yes. The Great Escape. Intellectual prestidigitation. The answer to my question, Kassler, is no. You do not. No."

"God does not have to be anthropomorphic to exist," Kassler attempted to bail himself out.

"No, but if your concept of the Supreme Being is limited to the inspirational wonders of the sun in the morning and the moon at night, it might make it hard to understand how I'm concerned with opposing the Lord Almighty, and it's a *real problem* for me. You've betrayed me, Kassler. I don't like that."

"I have not betrayed you. You never asked about my religious beliefs."

"You knew that you were taking on a patient who you couldn't possibly treat because you were biased against his spiritual persuasion. If *God* doesn't exist, then *I* don't exist. You're not stupid."

"I made no pretense about my faith," Kassler dug in for battle.

"No, but when we first met, you had no doubt whatsoever that I was real, as I recall the circumstances," I pointed out.

"Things have changed since we first met."

"Yes, they have, and that should have persuaded you even more."

"If *my* recollection is correct, it was only a session or two ago that you referred to the King of Kings as something of a bumbling son-of-a-bitch." Kassler was doing okay.

"I never claimed that your impressions weren't a little distorted."

"Hey," Kassler squeaked, "what is this? *You* want to persuade *me* that there's a true God?"

"It's in my blood, I guess. God and me, we go together, kind of a matched set. Poe once claimed I was a practiced metaphysician. It's instinctive."

"I've always preferred Gorky's impression, that you're a master ironist who refuses to apply the scalpel of his irony to the fact of his own existence," Kassler retorted with some untherapeutic glee.

"The *majestic* fact of his own existence," I reminded Kassler. "You left out *majestic*."

"Oh, did I?" Kassler said.

"Now you're cooking, Kassler," I was pleased that I had engaged my vague atheist. "Now, how would you feel about providing me with some psychotherapy, which, as you no doubt recall, was our original agreement. I'd like to start once again, if you have no objection, with why it is that I just don't let God go His way and I go mine? Why must I *continue* to point up every damn thing He does wrong, or is about to do wrong? So, okay, He made man and He made woman, and it was just bad thinking from start to finish, a terrible mistake, but it's *over*. Why can't I let it rest?"

"I suppose it depends on what the mistake was," Kassler raised a good point.

"Well, now that you mention it, there were a couple whoppers," I recalled.

"The genital organs," Kassler nodded.

"Not at all. That fiasco was nothing compared with these. First of all, He gave man guilt. That was probably the biggest one of all. He thought it'd make everybody well behaved. Of course it hasn't affected anyone's behavior one iota. People do what they're going to do anyway. Then, if the guilt gets too big, they go crazy. Very convenient."

"Insanity is from guilt," Kassler wanted to make certain he'd understood me correctly and he had.

"That should come as no surprise to you."

"You don't think that without guilt there might be a lot more open hostility?" Kassler was just a little unsettled by the concept.

"Well," I pointed out to him, "I'm not exactly a turn-the-other-cheek type, as you may know. The only thing I've seen happen when people've turned their other cheek is they've gotten *both* cheeks swatted. There've been an awful lot of good Christians walking around getting slapped silly because of that pithy little parable. A good solid blow in return might have been substantially more persuasive. I've never seen a man yet who's continued punching someone who's knocking the shit out of him."

"You don't think guilt is essential?" Kassler queried.

"No, as a matter of fact I think that if it weren't for guilt, the ideas of Christ, Freud, and Einstein would be obscure historical footnotes in academic texts and we'd all be a lot better off. Guilt has been a disaster."

"I suppose I can understand Christ and Freud," Kassler tried to decipher the mystery, "but how Einstein?"

"Einstein's theory is universally adored because it affirmed in cold hard science the greatest guiltless alibi for bad behavior throughout history," I explained. "Einstein *proved* absolutely that it all depends on how you look at things."

"I'm not sure that was his intention."

"Of course," I reflected, "it's hard not to like a man who can father an atomic bomb. Now how's Hiroshima as an eye for an eye, a tooth for a tooth? Some other cheek, yes?"

"I thought that the law of retribution was a great sin punishable by damnation in hell," Kassler recalled some obscure liturgical work.

"Are you kidding? Do you think you can get into hell on the basis of a little sadistic horseplay? You think it's that easy, that everyone who causes someone else a little pain gets an automatic pass? Do you have any idea how many occupants we'd have? Hell is SRO already. Harvard has open admissions compared to who can get in these days. They're banging at the gates, I'm telling you. Purgatory? Limbo? Not an inch left. If it weren't for antibiotics, we'd be in a real mess."

"You said there were a *couple* of mistakes God made in the human design?" Kassler tried to keep me on the topic.

"Ah, yes, I did, didn't I? Well, the other one is this ridiculous obsession man has about understanding his place in the universe. I can hardly believe it. Do you have any idea how much human energy is consumed every day by people stewing about where they fit into the great cosmic plan—assuming, of course, there is one, and, I assure you, there definitely is not. It's like a grain of sand wondering why it's on the beach. What possible *difference* could it make?"

"It gives our lives deeper meaning."

"Than what? Deeper than what? Deeper than loving another person? Deeper than a walk through the woods? Deeper than being a child's father?"

There was a long silence. I knew what was going through Kassler's head, so I spoke up.

"I'm sorry about that last point. I wasn't thinking."

"You were talking about the terrible mistakes that were made in creating man," Kassler said, on a slow burn.

"Look, I said I was sorry."

"And *I* said, tell me about the damn mistakes," Kassler snapped.

"I *told* you about the mistakes," I was getting a little testy myself. "Now cut it out, and let's get back to doing psycho-therapy."

"I'm *doing* psychotherapy!"

"Hell you are!"

"Hell I am!"

"Kassler, *I am Satan.* Do you have any idea what that means? For three sessions now you've been sitting there, puffing on your pipe, scratching notes, cleaning your glasses, while I make jokes and you make snappy retorts. I'm very insulted. I picked you special. You're a big disappointment to me, Kassler. You'd never get away with this with your other patients. You don't take me seriously and it's beginning to bother me."

"Attribute it to my pervasive atheism," Kassler said coldly.

"You expect me to believe that? Your atheism is a worthless hobby, Kassler. Disbelief is very big these days. It's the world's biggest club. Anyone without guts can join. It takes courage to believe. You're a coward, Kassler. You don't believe in me. You don't believe in God."

"My beliefs are not the issue," Kassler said curtly.

"Oh, really? You expect to treat Satan, the Lord of Hell, Father of the Damned, the Old Serpent with dominion over man and the earth, without any beliefs whatsoever? Is that what you're proposing?"

"I'm not proposing anything. You selected me. It was your choice."

"And you don't think that I have a right to know the basis of your practice with me?"

"I've told you all there is. I don't accept the God you talk about. I have my own God, of sorts, or none at all. And I don't apply the concept of meaning to my life. I am, apparently, not one of those individuals who consume themselves with worrying about their place in the universe. Is that satisfactory?"

"Not quite. Life is meaningless? Is that your position?" I pursued Kassler in his evasiveness.

"If you will. It's not exactly what I said, but that will do for now."

"Splendid," I said. "Then explain to me, please, why every pore in your body resists accepting it? What's the big deal? If it's all so simple, why won't your soul settle for nothingness? You seem to have no trouble denying God, so what's the problem?"

"What is this, test-Sy-Kassler's-faith day? God is something else, that's all."

"Not the One who kicked me down here, He isn't!"

"Lookit!" Kassler was in a very agitated state. "If you're so damn frustrated about being kicked out of heaven, why don't you just go to this God, Whatever and Wherever He is, and tell the bumbling son-of-a-bitch that you're sorry. God is mercy. He'll let you back."

"Well, that's the thing," I tried to calm things down. "You see, being Satan means never having to say you're sorry."

"We've got to stop," Kassler barked.

"I figured we would," I barked back.

PART V

Dante's Inferno

CHAPTER 1

*K*assler knew it wouldn't be easy, and it wasn't. Dante's Inferno was not exactly up Lupa's alley, and it was a blustery cold snowy day in January 1975, nearly seven months after Norman Meltz had first mentioned the spa, before Kassler was able to convince his dear female friend of the vast educational benefits that a visit to the establishment might provide.

In the intervening seven months, Leo Szlyck had organized his mental state sufficiently, it appeared, to be one of the first patients from Phlegethon discharged to lead, as the court decreed, a productive life in the community. Except that immediately upon exiting, Szlyck disappeared into his stately Bolgia and hadn't been heard from since.

Norman Meltz had made it to daylight, too, and, for reasons equally obscure, had also vanished. He was last seen in his old blue Buick, careening down Fourth Avenue after a young screeching maiden who was sprinting away at a speed worthy of AAU recognition.

This having been 1974, that summer brought, as well, the tragic resignation of the much-maligned President, proclaiming his innocence, yes, even as cartons jammed to the brim with spools of Scotch Brand quarter-inch mylar were loaded onto Air Force One for the solemn return to San Clemente.

Kassler, with somewhat fewer historical implications, began that summer to accept the inevitability of his own predicament. Repeated attempts to have the judge consider increasing Kassler's visitation with his children had been denied. Kassler did what he could to be a father five hours a week until the beginning of 1976, when the case would come up for—the words now acted on Kassler like a powerful shock to the paws of an already enraged experimental animal—"a hearing on the merits."

In the meantime, things were not going well at all between Kassler and his children. That Christmas, his first without his family, Lupa had invited Kassler to spend the holidays with her and her family in Connecticut, but responsibilities at Phlegethon precluded his being out of town. As one of the newest staff members, he had drawn Christmas Eve and Christmas Day on-call.

So, on Christmas Eve, Kassler wandered around his apartment, depressed, watching moving, spiritual "Peace on Earth, Good Will Toward Men" television specials with lilting melodies extolling the magic of fireplace and family, until it became more punishing than even Kassler could take, and he went to bed.

"This is Daddy, Josh," Kassler said on the phone the next morning. "Merry Christmas."

"Merry Christmas, Daddy," Josh said. "Is this going to be a long talk? Because I want to play with my new toys."

"No," Kassler said, "I just wanted to hear about your morning and wish you a Merry Christmas."

"Okay. Merry Christmas," Josh answered. "Bye."

Joy got on the phone.

"Merry Christmas," Joy said, copying her brother. "Bye." And she hung up the phone.

For several minutes, Kassler sat on the sofa with the phone in his hand, staring at the wall. Then he hung up the receiver, walked over to the phonograph, flicked on the automatic changer, returned to the sofa, and, for the ninth time that week,

lay motionless through an unabridged recording of Handel's
Messiah.

Kassler had made great plans, it turns out, to have his own
Christmas celebration with the children. The Sunday before,
they had purchased and decorated a tree, and on the Sunday
following the Christmas that the rest of the world had already
celebrated, the children arrived to the joyful recorded voices
of the Ray Conniff Singers in a three-part harmonized rendition
of "Joy to the World." A modest pile of gifts sat under the
blinking colored lights of the Christmas tree.

"Oh, Daddy," Josh said with childish dismay. "Not Christmas *again*. We already *had* Christmas."

"We had Christmas," Joy echoed.

"But not with me," Kassler said. "Remember how we all
used to have Christmas together?"

"No," said Josh.

"No," said Joy.

"Oh, sure you do," Kassler said. "Remember last year how
we put together all those—"

Kassler found himself unable to finish the sentence without
tears, so he stopped and took a deep breath.

"Well," he said when he regained his composure, "this is
Christmastime with Daddy!"

"Okay," said Josh, "but all the music and the tree and
everything—it seems silly."

"I thought it would be nice," Kassler said. "I'll turn off the
music and unplug the tree."

Josh looked up at his father and noticed he was displeased.

"That's okay," Josh told his dad. "You can keep them on
if you want. I don't really care."

Then he added under his breath, as he walked over to the
gifts, "Except it's kind of stupid."

"Then I'll turn the damn things off!" Kassler shouted, and
he went over to the phonograph, flicked off the record, then
marched to the tree and unplugged the lights.

"There," Kassler said, "is that better?"

Joy started to cry.

Kassler walked over and picked her up.

"I'm sorry I shouted, Joy," Kassler said as he hugged his daughter. "I guess Daddy's a little jumpy today. Come on. Lots of presents here for you to open. You, too, Josh. Start with the big one in the green paper."

Josh tore frantically through the paper, while Kassler helped Joy open her gifts.

"Oh, great, Daddy," Joshua was pleased. "A Lego set. Just the one I wanted, too. Would you build something with me?"

"Sure," Kassler finished opening Joy's present. "Look, Joy, a big doll that you can bathe and dress and comb her hair."

"Can we do it now?" Josh asked.

"Don't you want to open your other presents first?" Kassler asked as he took the clothing for Joy's doll out of the box.

"No. I want you to help me build a fort with my Legos," Joshua was adamant.

"I can't right now, Josh. I have to help Joy with her presents. Why don't you open the other green one over there?"

"I don't want to. I just want to do my Legos."

"Later."

"Please?"

"I said no."

At that, Josh took the box filled with hundreds of tiny yellow and black plastic pieces and flung its contents across the room.

"That's it!" Kassler shouted. He wanted to send Joshua to his room, but there wasn't any other room in the efficiency apartment, so he continued shouting. "No more presents!"

"I don't care," Josh snapped back, "I've got plenty of presents back home."

"Go sit on the sofa, and I don't want to hear a word out of your mouth."

Josh trudged defiantly over to the dilapidated sofa and sat on it sullenly. Kassler returned to Joy and opened other presents.

"Here's a nursery school with little people you can put on swings, and a blackboard, and little chairs they can sit in."

"Oh, Daddy," Joy smiled. "I like that. What else?"

"I think it stinks," Josh commented from the couch.

"I told you I didn't want to hear from you," Kassler responded.

"What difference does it make? I'm not getting any more toys anyway. What're you going to do, hit me?"

"A spanking might be exactly what you need," Kassler informed him.

"Mom says that if you ever hit me I should tell her and she'll tell the judge and you'll *never* get to see us again! Never ever!"

"Well, she's wrong. Daddies can spank their children when they're bad," Kassler told Joshua, not certain himself of the consequences, but fuming at Vita nevertheless.

"What else, Daddy?" Joy asked.

"Well, why don't we look," Kassler reached for some more presents.

Joy tore off the paper.

"It's Play-Doh," Kassler said, "all different colors, blue and red and yellow and white, and look in this next package."

Joy ripped through the paper.

"See," Kassler said, "it's a Play-Doh set for making snakes and balls and designs, stars and hearts."

"Oooh, pretty," said Joy. "What else?"

"Mom already gave her one of those," Joshua said. "Now she's got two."

"Shut up, Josh."

"What else?" Joy asked.

"I'm afraid that's it," Kassler said.

"I want more," Joy said.

"But look at all you've got," Kassler held his daughter. "The big doll with all the clothes, and the school with all the people, and the Play-Doh and the Play-Doh molds. Lots of things."

"I want more," Joy repeated.

"Mom bought us each *ten* things," Josh announced, as he stood up on the sofa and started jumping up and down. "Ten! And stocking things, too."

"With my goddamn money!" Kassler was furious. "Where do you think she got all the money to buy the presents?"

"It's *our* money," Josh put his hands on his hips and faced off against his father. "Mom says the judge told you that you *have* to pay for us because you're our daddy. And your lawyer told him that you didn't want to."

"My lawyer is asking," Kassler walked over to Joshua, "for the judge to let me pay *less* money, not *no* money. *I* need money to live on, too. What am I supposed to use to pay for my apartment and food and gas and the car and everything else?"

Joy started crying. Kassler was too angry to give her any comfort. He picked up Joshua by the arms, squeezed tightly, and started shaking his son. "I've got to eat; too! You want me not to have any place to live and no food? Is that what you want? You want to have no daddy at all?"

"Yes!" Joshua cried. "I don't care anymore! I'm telling Mom you hit me! You'll never see us again! Never!"

"That's what you want?" Kassler eased his grip on his son.

"Yes!" Small tears started to form in Joshua's eyes.

"Why?"

"Because when I got up on Christmas you weren't there. I was all alone. I wanted to see you on Christmas so much, Daddy. I did. I really did. Mommy was asleep all morning, and I had to help Joy with all her presents by myself. I miss you, Daddy. Please come back home. Please," Joshua buried his head in his father's chest and sobbed.

"I called you on the phone," Kassler choked back his tears as he gently stroked Joshua's curly blond hair, over and over. "You didn't want to talk, remember?"

"Mom says you don't care about us anymore. She says you wanted to spend Christmas with your new girl friend," Joshua continued to cry against Kassler.

"Lupa?" Kassler asked. "You know Lupa. Lupa was far away. I was all alone."

Joy had stopped crying to observe the activity on the sofa. Now she toddled over and grabbed Kassler's knee. Kassler reached down and picked her up. Then he sat on the couch, Joy on one knee, Joshua on the other, and tried to talk to them through his own tears.

"I wanted to be with you on Christmas morning so much, too," he said. "I would've done anything for that. I missed you very much."

Then he placed his hand on Joshua's soft cheek and turned his head to face him.

"I care about you and Joy more than anything else in the world," Kassler said as tears streamed down his cheeks. "Come on, I'll give you a hand picking up the Legos, Josh, and then we can see what else you got. Okay?"

"I love you, Daddy," Joshua said.

"I love you, Daddy," Joy said.

"I love you, too," Kassler said, and started picking up little yellow and black plastic rectangles.

By the time the Legos were picked up and the remaining presents opened, there was less than a half-hour left before Kassler had to leave to return the children.

"Can we bring our toys home?" Joshua asked.

"Well," Kassler took a deep breath and plunged into what he knew was going to be a difficult subject. "I thought that maybe these toys should stay here. You've got nothing at all to play with here."

"We'll bring them back here next time," Joshua pleaded.

"But, you know, Josh, that when we've tried that before, it hasn't worked. All the toys seem to get broken, or the parts lost, and then there's nothing for you to bring."

"We'll take really good care of them this time, won't we, Joy?" Joshua turned to his sister for support.

"Yes?" Joy looked at Joshua to see if this was the desired response.

"See," Joshua said.

"But it never happens," Kassler tried to be patient. "You and Joy have a really hard time putting things away."

"We'll do it this time."

"How about *some* of the toys?" Kassler tried.

"No! All!" Joshua stamped his foot defiantly.

"None!" Kassler found himself saying just as defiantly, even though he didn't want to.

"They're our toys!"

"In this house!"

"You gave them to us!"

"To play with here!"

"I want my doll!" Joy joined in.

"You can have your doll, Joy," Kassler explained. "It'll be here next Sunday."

"How many days?" Joy tried to understand.

"A whole lot," Josh informed her. "Come on, Daddy, we haven't had any time to play with them at all."

"That's because you threw a tantrum, and we had to spend all that time picking up pieces of Lego."

"Please, Daddy?"

"Josh, I've bought you a dozen toys in the last year and not one of them ever made it back here in one piece."

"I don't care! They're my toys! You gave them to me. I can do what I want with them!"

Kassler looked at his watch. It was time to leave.

"Fine! You want to take them home? Take them! You'll just have nothing to play with when you come back, that's all! You'll be bored."

"I'm always bored here anyway!"

"Get your coat on! You, too, Joy," Kassler snapped, picked up the toys, and took the children and their gifts home, because his five hours of Christmas was over.

Kassler began to consider, for the first time, whether it might not be better if he never saw his children again. The weekly five-hour visits had become unbearable. By the time the children calmed down from the transition to Kassler's care, it was time to go back to Vita, an event that produced even greater transitional turmoil. The Christmas celebration was the final straw, and now Kassler was slowly becoming convinced that his relationship with his children was doomed.

Vita could not have agreed more. The problems of settling down the children after visits with their father were exasperating and quickly approaching the limits of her not extensive maternal repertoire. Unbeknownst to her soon-to-be ex-husband, Southern California beckoned Vita, not only for its balmy subtropical climate, but also for the three thousand or so non-visitational miles that lay between Citadel and San Diego. That such a relocation might very likely destroy whatever shreds were left of Kassler's mangled heart, Vita considered to be one of the tragic and inevitable consequences of love gone awry. Kassler would adjust, she concluded.

It was this topic, his deteriorating relationship with his children, that crowded Kassler's brain as he stood with Lupa in the long line outside Dante's Inferno that January, stomping his feet on the broken pavement to increase his circulation in the bitter cold, and brushing the sooty gray snow from his hair, beard, and coat.

"So, I don't know," Kassler finished telling Lupa the details of Christmas with his children, "I'm beginning to wonder whether it's all worth it."

"There sure are a lot of people in this line," Lupa craned her neck to see how many people were ahead of them.

"There's a new school of psychiatric thought. They think that, except in extreme situations, after the divorce the children should stay with their mother and never see their father again. No visitation at all."

"Just about everybody's in couples," Lupa assessed the crowd. "I wonder whether they stay with each other or change partners a lot."

"They think," Kassler plowed ahead, "that the father should go out and rebuild his life from scratch."

"Everybody looks so calm, like they've been doing this for years," Lupa continued her evaluation.

"The mother usually remarries anyway, so the kids get a permanent male role model."

"I keep trying to look for people who're kinky, somebody with a whip or a large dildo in their purse."

"And the conflicts, loyalties, transitions, and all that, are totally eliminated for the kids, who are always caught in the middle and used anyway. Maybe they're right. Maybe I should just disappear," Kassler concluded.

"Well," Lupa took Kassler's arm, "all this romantic talk sure has turned *me* on. You sure *do* know how to be sexy, Sy, I must say."

"I suppose," answered Kassler, "I'll just have to see what happens in court."

And Kassler and Lupa moved a few steps closer to Dante's Inferno.

CHAPTER 2

*K*assler *was oblivious of more than Lupa's comments, as he* waited in line to gain entrance to the great glittering den of iniquity, its entrance decorated with scores of brightly flashing prong-tailed, twin-horned, pitchfork-wielding red neon creatures, whose identity I cannot begin to fathom. What Kassler hadn't noticed was that his very own molecules were changing, slowly but inevitably, their final conformation still to be determined.

Kassler could hardly be blamed for this. During the day, his brain was consumed with the rapidly deteriorating situation on the regressed ward, as the nursing staff worked around the clock to prepare the patients for their inevitable freedom from the confines of Phlegethon. Patients who for their entire lives had been content to eat, sleep, rock, and, on some occasions, wear clothing, now were told that this wasn't enough. They needed to acquire skills for productive labor.

A local candy manufacturer had agreed to subcontract to Phlegethon the stuffing of paper grass into Easter baskets, and now, every day, from after breakfast until before dinner, nurses and attendants attempted to get the patients to perform this simple task. By the end of the day, the patients would be hysterical and the nurses could be seen running—screaming and crying from mental exhaustion—up and down the hall, which was strewn a foot deep with smashed yellow-and-violet bamboo baskets and shredded green paper.

Not that this was the only issue that occupied Kassler's daytime thoughts. His own patients were not doing well in therapy, and if it hadn't been for the friendship, both professional and personal, which had developed with Sam Zelazo,

Kassler would have quit the practice of psychotherapy altogether. As it was, Kassler held on by the slenderest of threads as his patients repeated the same stories and the same behaviors, without the smallest modification, again and again, until Kassler was nearly dizzy from boredom and frustration.

Zelazo maintained Kassler's cooperation and growing trust with a mixture of good counsel, hard neuroscientific data, emotional support, and an infrequent but welcome wry sense of humor. Still, Zelazo remained as mysterious as ever. Kassler knew virtually nothing about Zelazo's personal life. And Zelazo's mad dashes to retrieve every corpse before it was cold continued unabated and unexplained.

As if this weren't enough to keep Kassler's synapses fully occupied during daylight hours, each day at Phlegethon concluded with a meeting of what was now named the Disposition Committee, the three individuals Zelazo had selected to determine how best to dispose of whichever patient.

As each voluminous case folder was reviewed, Bernie Kohler would argue vehemently about the necessity for discharging the individual into the community posthaste. Then Kassler would ventilate freely about the unreasonableness of doing so. Finally, Bea Chaikin would arbitrate, pointing out that the patient did indeed need to be readied for his new life in the community, but perhaps not so quickly as Bernie Kohler desired.

"We must build on the patient's strengths," Bea Chaikin would repeat calmly to Kassler and Kohler.

"What strengths?" Kassler would ask as he leafed through several hundred pages that documented a human life consisting exclusively in staring at walls painted institutional green.

"We all have strengths, if anyone's interested in finding them!" Bernie proclaimed.

"I'm sure *we all* do," Kassler retorted. "Stanley Bolash, on the other hand, was last recorded tying his own shoes not quite twenty-three years ago."

"What are you saying?" Bernie demanded. "We should keep him locked up forever because he'd have to walk around town with dangling shoelaces? So he falls and scrapes his knees a little. So what!"

"Why don't we begin," Bea intervened, "by seeing if we

can teach Mr. Bolash to tie his shoes." She made a note on the new disposition form. "That's probably a good place to start, don't you think, Sy?" Bea inquired with a pleasant smile.

"I guess so," Kassler mumbled.

"How about you, Bernie?" Bea asked.

"Sure. Why not," Bernie agreed glumly.

"Then," Kassler said, "if we can get him to tie his own shoes, we can move him on to brushing his own teeth, bathing himself, and, finally, corporate management."

"You're not being helpful, Sy," Bea pointed out tactfully.

Because Kassler's respect and affection for Bea Chaikin were by now profound, he simply sighed in resignation.

"No, I guess I'm not," he said quietly. And Kassler's mind began to drift into its nocturnal cycle, in which it dwelled on other business.

At night Kassler's brain chemistry was utilized to its very last methyl molecule. Vita had taken the precautionary step of having her attorney freeze Kassler's savings account, and so a large number of Kassler's neural pathways were allocated to determining strategies for waging all-out war against Vita Volpe Kassler. The few synapses that remained were inundated, so to speak, with determining for Kassler how he might be able to maintain a relationship with his children under the present circumstances, ascertaining how many more days Kassler could survive on his current salary, and, hardly last of all, what could be done to consummate his relationship with Lupa.

Lupa, for her part, was not unsympathetic to Kassler's needs, but had her hands full trying to run her flourishing interior-design business while simultaneously fending off Leo Szlyck's daily barrage of letters and phone calls desperately begging her to return to him and threatening terrible consequences if she did not.

As an initial gesture in this direction, Szlyck filed a complaint with the court contesting Lupa's Mexican divorce, obtained, he claimed, when he was not of "sound mind."

Of course, as the only other being in Szlyck's Bolgia, I was privy to more than a little of the meandering of his now sound thought processes, but more about that later. Let's just say here that my not inconsiderable talents of persuasion were put to the ultimate test. For it seems that, in addition to devising sadistic plans regarding Lupa, his long-time enemy Zelazo, and several people employed in low-level positions by the Internal Revenue Service, Leo had decided—how can I put this delicately?—to dynamite me to Kingdom Come. I say "delicately" because Leo expressed this to me in terms usually employed to describe the less loving aspects of sexual activity. Leo Szlyck was not a happy man.

Not that I can entirely blame him. The night before Kassler and Lupa forayed to Citadel's Land of Libido, Szlyck had suffered what for him was the final injury.

It was a particularly cold night, and Szlyck had taken Cerberus for his post-prandial walk, which, largely because Leo was absorbed in elaborate scheming, led him halfway across the city.

Suddenly, as Szlyck turned the corner, he was shaken from his preoccupation by a commotion down the street before him.

A large crowd had gathered on the sidewalk, obscuring what was happening in its midst, but Szlyck could hear the shouting just fine.

"You ruined me! Ruined me, you fucking asshole shrink!" a man yelled.

"Not here, Norman," Szylck recognized Kassler's voice as Cerberus pulled him toward the crowd.

"Look what you've done to me!" Norman Meltz screamed at his former therapist.

"Please, Norman," Kassler tried to calm his distraught ex-patient.

Leo Szlyck reached the perimeter of the crowd and stood on his tiptoes to see over the heavily jacketed shoulders and turned-up collars. What he saw was Sy Kassler trying to move through the crowd while behind him Norman Meltz, trousers and underpants at his ankles, hopped along, holding his large flaccid shlong in his hand and pathetically flapping it up and down in dismay.

"It's dead!" Norman shouted as he hopped. "Look for yourself! You killed it!"

"Pull up your pants, Norman," Kassler said for the thirtieth time.

"I'm going to get you for this!" Norman jumped ahead and waved his limp organ.

"I told you," Kassler turned around and stopped momentarily, "I can't help you here, Norman. Give me a call and we'll set up a time to talk."

"I'll *give* you a goddamn *call*!" Norman Meltz shouted. "You haven't heard the last of me! I'll get you for this! All you shrinks are dumb turds!"

The crowd burst into applause.

Norman looked around him and smiled, pleased that his sentiment was shared by such a large audience.

Kassler stood and examined the strange faces, disturbed by the mass condemnation of his profession.

It was at this instant that Lupa emerged from the crowd and took Kassler's arm.

"Come on, Sy," she said with care and affection. "The crowd'll take care of Norman. He'll be okay. Let's get out of here."

Leo Szlyck looked in shock at the loving way Lupa took Kassler's arm and how she stroked it as they walked away. Leo could neither speak nor move. He was absolutely convinced that his therapist had stolen his mate. Fury tore at his heart. He closed his eyes in pain and moved mechanically toward the space in the middle of the crowd where Kassler and Lupa had just been standing. When he reached the innermost edge of the assembly, he opened his eyes and collapsed to his knees, fulminating with a lethal rage.

Szlyck watched Kassler and Lupa disappear into the crowd while Cerberus observed his master's distress and whined in sympathy. The large brown dog licked Leo's hand and pulled at his chain to indicate his willingness to help.

A gleam came into Leo's eyes as he deftly unsnapped the leash.

"Kill!" he commanded his pet. Cerberus obeyed instantly. He leaped at Norman Meltz's naked backside and very likely would have succeeded in carrying out Leo's command if a policeman who had just arrived at the scene had not shot Cerberus dead on the spot.

At the loud sound of the gun, Kassler and Lupa turned toward the crowd.

"Just some mad dog," a friendly spectator waved for Lupa and Kassler to keep going, so they never did know that Leo had been there.

Since I was Satan, Leo, of course, held me responsible for it all—the loss of his dear pet, Lupa, and the death of his loved one, Cerberus.

But all this Szlyckian squalor takes us away from the events that surrounded the emergence of Kassler's splendid new molecular configuration, however unaware of it Kassler may have been as he and Lupa crossed the threshold of Dante's Inferno.

CHAPTER 3

Immediately upon entering, Lupa and Kassler were deluged with the intense driving sound of rock music. It blared throughout the huge, carpeted arena where hundreds of nude men and women were copulating on tiers that extended around and downward in a spiral—a coiled serpent composed of writhing fornicators.

Close to them, red, blue, and green lights flashed from blinding strobes. The beams flicked like reptiles' tongues stabbing at elusive insects, and reflected off mirrored globes that rotated from the ceiling, giant mechanical eyes in the midst of the vast steaming cavern.

Kassler stood dumbstruck, gazing vacantly into the bright yellow mist which hung over the heated pool at the far end of the tier. For several minutes he stared blankly into the distance at the glistening naked figures cavorting in the water, and then, mechanically, he found himself undressing and putting his clothes in a small locker against the wall where he had come in.

When Lupa saw Kassler disrobe, she did the same and hung her clothes beside his. Then she stood rigidly, facing him, staring uncomfortably down at her own nakedness and across at his, frozen into silence by a force that neither she nor Kassler could understand.

"You've got a nice body, Sy," Lupa finally broke the barrier, her words barely audible over the music.

Kassler remained in his trance, his heart filled with no simple emotion—not lust for the hordes of sensuous naked women, not repulsion at the erotic antics occurring absolutely everywhere, not even surprise at the absence of his own sexual feelings in the midst of such extreme sensuality. He had expected abundant and diverse sexual activity and was not disturbed to encounter it. What Kassler had not prepared himself for were strangers loving strangers.

What was worse, they were having such a good time doing it. Kassler was paralyzed by the overwhelming enthusiasm for insignificant intimacy.

"Aren't you going to say anything?" Lupa asked.

Kassler stared at Lupa. His eyes traveled down the gentle slope of her shoulders to where her breasts hung like ripe pears, high and full on her chest, tiny nipples set off by small dark circles. He followed the sweeping roundness of the bottoms of her breasts, where they settled against her ribs, to her tummy, which slowly rippled with her breathing, down, finally, to the curly blond hair which crowned the top of her slender bronze-skinned legs.

"I think that you're very beautiful," Kassler said numbly.

"That's a very nice thing to say."

"It's true," Kassler responded, but it was clear to Lupa that something strange was happening to her escort.

Before she had a chance to inquire further, a cold shrill voice greeted them.

"Hello, hello." A dark, wiry, goateed man, with a Red Cross kit strapped around the waist of his otherwise nude body, approached Kassler and Lupa. "My, my, you *are* beautiful," he told Lupa. "So, been in the water today?"

"We're just kind of looking," Kassler, emerging ever so slightly from his stupor, informed the hairy gentleman with the black eyes that shone like lumps of hot coal.

"Aren't we all," he answered Kassler, "aren't we all," and he extended his hand. "Dr. Charon," the gentleman introduced himself and shook Kassler's hand. Then he reached for Lupa's hand and genteelly kissed it. Lupa nodded hello and gestured to the first-aid kit belted around the man's midsection.

"Oh, that," Charon shrugged. "She Patrol. It's supposed to be a big joke. Believe me, it's not."

Lupa's attention was momentarily distracted by a tall man with an enormous organ who dashed by them, chasing joyously after a large giggling lady.

"My God," said Lupa, watching the man's member flap up and down as he ran.

"First time here, I take it," Charon remarked. "So," Charon smiled at Lupa, "how about a little dip?"

Lupa continued to stare incredulously at the man in jolly pursuit.

"We were just curious to see..." Lupa trailed off.

"People getting laid?" Charon asked the couple. "Except no one ever says that, of course. We could revise the entire *Encyclopaedia Britannica* with the people who've come here tonight to do research. Come on, I'll show you around," Charon shouted over the blaring music. He stepped between Kassler and Lupa, took the nearest hand from each, and moved ahead, past a wall lined with photographs of celebrities—Raquel Welch, the Gabor sisters, John Travolta, Frank Sinatra, John Kennedy, Bert Parks, the Osmond family, Hugh Hefner, Roman Polanski, Wayne Hays, and Woody Allen.

"Great lovers," Charon explained. "Okay, so it's not Caesar and Cleopatra, but, all things considered, it's the best we can do. I never have understood how it is a person gets up on the wall. It's all decided upstairs. Very mysterious," and the trio stepped over a muscular man who was making love to four women at the same time, licking, fondling with both hands, moving quickly from one to another.

"Very sad story," Charon commented. "The man has gone through a dozen true loves in as many years. Tragically, each girl turned out to have a slight imperfection and had to be rejected. Now he tries to handle his heartache by having sex with four or more women simultaneously. Tragic, when you think about it."

Kassler and Lupa moved down the ramp with Charon. Their nostrils filled with heavy, goatlike, sweet and sour smells as they watched the copulatory antics in the crowded arena. A line of kneeling women, participating in a leapfrog game, extended from one side of the tier to the other. They were accompanied by a longer line of men, hopping up and down behind and over them. Couples and triples danced by, merrily leading one another by major erogenous zones. People bobbed in and out of the water like dolphins, the flashing multicolored strobe lights appearing to freeze them in midair. And everywhere else, men and women affixed themselves to each other in an endless array of oscillating mounts.

Charon turned and talked to Lupa as they traveled.

"Sometimes," he said, "I wonder whether there's anything left out there that's still sensual." Charon pointed, as they talked, to the world that existed beyond the confines of Dante's Inferno.

Kassler and Lupa stopped momentarily and stared at the enormous circles under Charon's eyes.

"When I was a kid," their companion said wistfully, "even when I was in my twenties, a girl would hold my hand and shivers would go up my spine. My elbow would brush against her sweater, hardly touching her breasts at all, and the crotch of my trousers would spring out like elephants yanking up the big top. A kiss? My God, a kiss. The moisture of a girl's kiss could melt me like a sugar cube in a hot cup of Lipton's."

Charon shrugged in resignation and started stepping over pairs of bodies pressed together so tightly that it was impossible to tell where one stopped and another began.

"It's gone forever," Charon sighed as he moved down the ramp. Then he popped a pill into his mouth, shrugged and swallowed.

"Antihistamine," Charon explained. "I'm allergic to pollen. It's an occupational hazard."

Kassler, who was doing worse than ever, followed numbly along and was about to utter his first spontaneous sentence since entering the chamber when suddenly a piercing whistle sounded. Kassler and Lupa looked ahead and saw a man with a woman wrapped around him topple together into the pool, creating an enormous splash.

Charon raced over, flicked off his first-aid kit, dived into the pool, and pulled first the woman and then the man to safety.

When he had finished the rescue, he climbed from the pool, picked up his Red Cross kit, and walked over to Kassler and Lupa.

"They can't swim," he said, trying to catch his breath as he buckled the kit back around his waist. "We've had more than a dozen near-drownings in the pool since we opened. People forget how long it takes when they're under water. They think they're whales or something. They submerge and surface and submerge, and then, when it becomes a choice between staying under just a little longer to release all that tension that's been building up or coming up for air and maybe breaking the mood a little, the lungs lose out, and we have to go get the resuscitation equipment." Charon took several deep breaths.

"You should get scuba tanks for the swimmers," Lupa suggested.

"Oh, we had them," Charon answered, shaking himself off like a wet dog. "Until the ladies figured out that there was one other place that the face mask fit exactly—they turned up the oxygen flow full blast and we had more bubbles around here than Lawrence Welk."

"That's terrible!" Lupa laughed as she ran her hand down Kassler's front, stopping just short of his pubes. Kassler did not react.

"That's nothing. Last year the Flying Yolandas gave a nude performance here," Charon shook his head in dismay, still taking short gasps of air to catch his breath.

"The acrobats?" Lupa asked, removing her hand from Kassler since she had obtained no response.

"They were amazing," Charon nodded. "The Yolanda ladies

lay on their backs with their legs raised and wide open. Then the Yolanda men, all rigid as celery stalks, somersaulted from one snatch to the next. They didn't miss. It was incredible. The kid at the corner gas station has more trouble replacing my car's dipstick. Then the men lay down on *their* backs and the *women* did the somersaults. The girls landed like quoits on a peg. They were very impressive. Finally, for a grand finale, the girls got on trapezes on' one side, hanging by their arms, and faced the men, who were hanging on trapezes across from them, upside down by their heels. Back and forth, in and out, back and forth, in and out. It was the single most amazing feat of human agility I have ever witnessed in my entire medical career."

"They really—on swings—" Lupa stammered.

"It takes *lots* of practice," Dr. Charon emphasized. "That's what none of our customers realized. I can't begin to tell you what it was like around here for months afterwards. The Yolandas left the trapezes up. The whole place became like a gymnastics meet. Everyone thought he was an athlete. People were crashing on top of each other, practically killing themselves with somersaults, trying things on those damn swings that you couldn't do with an arrow and a tractor tire. It took six months before the whole thing blew over. I can't understand what happened to plain old sexual intercourse like Mom and Dad used to do. Have all those nerves dried up or something?"

Kassler and Lupa didn't respond. They had become distracted by a pornographic movie being projected on the wall to their right in which a voluptuous young lady was engaged in oral sexual activity with a well-endowed young man who was apparently standing outside the Sears Tower.

"Chicago!" the narrator's travelogue-style voice boomed from a nearby speaker. "The Windy City! But nothing this side of Lake Michigan blows like . . . Francine!"

Charon studied Kassler and Lupa and, seeing that they had become engaged in the cinematic diversion, excused himself and trotted away to introduce another new couple to paradise.

As soon as Charon had disappeared from sight, Lupa turned to Kassler. Her purple eyes searched him for a sign of what was troubling him but discovered nothing.

"Are you okay?" Lupa took Kassler's cold, limp hand.

"I don't think I am," Kassler said slowly without looking at Lupa.

"What is it?" Lupa asked.

"I don't know."

"Are you sick?"

"I don't think so."

"Maybe we should go down farther," Lupa suggested. "You'll feel better down there," Lupa pointed several tiers below.

"How do you know?" Kassler asked suspiciously.

"It's a natural law," Lupa informed Kassler. "Petroleum, philosophy, and sex. The deeper you go, the better it gets."

"Oh," said Kassler, and Lupa tightened her hold on his hand and led him down the spiral ramp, through a pall of blue smoke where men and women lounged on the floor, working at themselves with an unending assortment of vibrators, suck-o-lators, silver bullets, organ enlargers, ben-wa balls, and dildos.

Suddenly a strange look came into Kassler's eyes. He broke free of Lupa's hand and charged ahead on his own.

"Coming through! Coming through!" Kassler shouted in his demented state as he pushed past the electrified crowd, tripping over cords, getting tangled in wires which accidentally yanked operating dildos out of their users.

"Hey! Watch out!" could be heard again and again in Kassler's wake as he stumbled and reeled through the crowd. Loud popping explosions, like bursting balloons, volleyed within the mob of people.

"Coming through!" Kassler shouted, ignoring men who were shouting angrily about the destruction of their inflatable women, as he pushed on down the ramp, past another grouping of photographs—Orson Welles, Marlon Brando, Ray Kroc, Colonel Sanders, Johnny Carson, Craig Claiborne, Rex Reed, and Woody Allen.

Lupa ran after him but lost Kassler in the mass of people in acrobatic configurations. Here and there, as she tried to move ahead, a hand reached out and stroked her breast or rear end. Once a man appeared before her and kissed her passionately, thrusting his tongue deep into her mouth. Another time, two women stopped her, and while one licked at her nipples, the other buried her head between Lupa's legs and moistened the sweet spot in its midst.

Lupa found the encounters not entirely unpleasant, and eventually her pursuit of Kassler slowed and she drifted dreamily into the crowd.

Kassler was, by this time, two-thirds of the way down the carpeted corkscrew, moving past a large number of persons who were manipulating each other and themselves with great technical skill.

"Arizona! The Grand Canyon State!" A new film began on Kassler's right. "But no crevice—"

As Kassler stopped to look, a hand took his arm and started to lead him past the sprawling autoerotic vista.

"Hi again," Charon said.

Kassler didn't answer but allowed himself to be directed by his guide.

"You know," Charon commented, "this has never been one of my favorite places. It's not that I have anything against masturbation. It's okay, I guess. . . ."

Kassler said nothing.

"I've read Philip Roth like everybody else." Charon stepped over a dark young man in his early twenties who was fantasizing about the flickering images on the wall while he played with himself. "Masturbation was something that neurotic Jewish adolescents with overincorporative mothers and distant fathers did when they got lonely. Then it leaked out," Charon sighed and shook his head. "Someone announced that everybody does it. Overnight, masturbation lost its significance. It stopped being cute, poignant, philosophical."

Charon shook his head sadly.

"Protestants thought it was worth a try," he went on. "Catholics who hadn't grown into it were taught what to do, so they could grow out of it. Not only did it not give you warts and make your brains rot, people who'd never gotten the hang of it were being referred for technical training, and those who were expert, for psychoanalysis."

Charon continued to escort Kassler through the olive haze that blanketed this level.

"In the good old days," Charon reminisced, "sexual release

used to be a matter of circumstance—the right person with similar inclinations at the right time. It was all left to chance, more or less. Then," Charon shrugged, "people decided to take Fortune into their own hands...." He trailed off as they approached a group of men, naked except for their vests, who were intently involved in tying up voluptuous females with an elaborate array of knots.

"Attorneys," Charon told Kassler with noticeable dismay, and he nodded to a tall gray-haired man, who nodded back and then, returning to his luscious lady, gave a yank on an expertly executed sheepshank.

"Join us?" the lawyer asked Kassler as he passed by.

Kassler didn't answer. He hurried ahead. The strange cold feeling that had started in the pit of his stomach when he first encountered the arena now extended into his arms and legs, making him unsteady on his feet as he wobbled down to the next level.

Suddenly, around the next sweeping curve, Kassler found himself distracted by a door with a flashing WELCOME sign over it. He tried the handle and the door opened, admitting him into a small darkened room with a sofa in the middle. Standing by the sofa was a girl who turned to Kassler and smiled as he shut the door.

The girl was nude, about twenty years old, with smooth, tanned, freckled skin and long blond hair done in pigtails. Her eyes sparkled with intelligence and her smile radiated warmth and life in the single spotlight which illuminated her.

Kassler ran his eyes down her flawless body, small but ample breasts which were just finished developing, a slightly rounded tummy, a triangle of light-hazel hair at the top of her legs, and a single, gently sweeping curve that ran from her hips to the bottom of her thighs.

"What do you think of this place?" she asked Kassler.

"Not a whole lot," Kassler spoke with such coherence that it startled him. "It's not really my style."

"Me, neither," the girl said with a bright smile. "It doesn't seem much like making love. I'm not sure what I thought I'd find by coming here. What about you?"

"I was curious," Kassler said.

"You know what our problem is?" the girl laughed. "We're romantics. That's what our problem is."

Kassler looked into the girl's sparkling blue eyes and moved close to her.

"I've always wanted a family, a wife, a nice place to live in a pleasant neighborhood or in the country, something simple, pure, loving," Kassler confided quietly. "I'm a hopeless romantic."

"I know," the girl answered, and she took a step toward Kassler. "You're like I am. I could tell."

"You think, maybe, we're an endangered species, that someday someone's going to stuff us and put us in a museum somewhere?" Kassler asked.

"Probably," the girl moved up very close to Kassler with calm graceful movements, her bare feet softly padding against the carpet.

"I know you're probably with someone else," the girl said.

"Yes, I am," Kassler admitted. "But it isn't working out. It's pleasant, but there's no magic."

"Do you think she'd mind if you kissed me?"

"I'm not sure," Kassler said.

Then he took the girl into his arms and kissed her tenderly on the lips. It was the kiss that Kassler had always fantasized he'd have someday—joyful and sublime. In the depths of Dante's Inferno, Kassler had stumbled upon the girl of his dreams—bright, beautiful, uncomplicated, loving, joyous and warm, free from hang-ups, unspoiled by life's catastrophes, willing to join with him and work as partners to live life at its fullest. It was, for the very first time in Kassler's life, true love, love at first sight, completely reciprocated love. Small tears began to form at the corners of Kassler's eyes.

"Your eyes are beautiful," the girl looked at Kassler and smiled. "They light up," and she reached up and dabbed at the tiny droplets with her fingertips.

"I'm very happy," Kassler apologized. "When I get emotional, I cry easily."

"Me, too," the girl said. "I cry easily, too."

"Who are you?" Kassler asked. "What's your name?"

"What would you *like* to call me? I'd like you to call me whatever you want. Within reasonable limits."

Kassler thought for a moment.

"Lesley," he said. "I've always liked the name Lesley."

"Then from now on I'll be Lesley. It's a lovely name. I'd have taken any you gave me, but I was scared for a minute you might come up with something like Monica or Vicki Sue. What should I call you?"

"Sy," Kassler said. "Just Sy."

"Nice and simple. Strong. Sensitive. I like it."

"When can we see each other?" Kassler ran his hands lightly across the girl's shoulders. "I mean, would you like to get together?"

"I would," the girl said. "Very much. But what about your friend?"

"It's not working out. It's not at all what I need, or what I want."

"I'm sorry it isn't going well. Will it be hard to break it off?"

"Probably. I'm not sure."

"How about here, tomorrow? Can we meet down here?"

"You sure you want to meet here?" Kassler asked.

"We can go somewhere else afterwards, if you want. I'm superstitious, I guess. I never thought I'd ever meet anyone, certainly not down here. I want to make sure we don't forget addresses or something."

"Okay," Kassler said, "down here, this time tomorrow."

Neither party made an attempt to leave.

"You know, I always thought that someday, if I waited long enough..." the girl trailed off.

"Me, too," Kassler said. "I've always hoped that some-day..."

"Of course, when I thought about it, I imagined he'd be dressed a little differently," the girl smiled at Kassler.

"My tailor's on vacation," Kassler answered. "I've got to admit that I always pictured you wearing exactly what you are."

Kassler and the girl looked into each other's eyes in silence.

"This is crazy," the girl finally laughed. "We don't know

each other at all. We're a couple of strangers in the bottom of a very perverse place. It's crazy."

"Insane," Kassler agreed.

"But I don't suppose it'd hurt to meet tomorrow, just to see what happens," the girl said happily.

Kassler kissed his Lesley tenderly once more. Then he started to leave.

"Hey," the girl called to Kassler. "You're not crazy or mean or married or going to break my heart or anything, are you?"

"No, I'm not," Kassler answered softly.

"Me, neither," the girl whispered back. "See you tomorrow, okay?"

Kassler nodded, smiled, and exited. As he was closing the door, he was greeted by Lupa and Charon.

"Where were you?" Lupa asked.

"Exploring," Kassler sang gaily, a smile spread ear to ear. "Just exploring."

"Well, you certainly seem to have snapped out of it. What'd you do, get laid?" Lupa asked.

"Nope," Kassler grinned. "Just talking."

"You can drop the smile," Charon informed Kassler as they headed down to the final level. "She's an advertisement."

"She's what?" Kassler asked in shock.

"An advertisement. A premium. A come-on," Charon said. "She gets paid to see that the customers return."

"I don't believe it," Kassler croaked.

"Very pretty girl. And super-bright. Rumor has it that she hasn't had to perform a single sexual act to keep the men returning in the two years she's been here."

"You're lying," Kassler shouted. "It's not true."

"Look, I like you, so I'll tell you the truth. There's a guy on the other side who does the same thing for women," Charon said. "I don't want you to get hurt—it's a promotion."

"It's a lie!" Kassler's heart sank. "It's a goddamn lie."

"No, it isn't," Charon said. "It's very clever of the management. And it's a magnificent performance that changes with every customer. If I hadn't told you, you'd never have known. You'd be coming back here for years."

"Lesley!" Kassler yelled and he turned to go back through the lurid steam.

"It's all pretend," Charon grabbed Kassler's arm to stop him. "Make-believe."

Lupa grabbed Kassler's other arm.

"Lesley!" Kassler tugged unsuccessfully to get free as Lupa and Charon pulled him ahead.

"Don't be stupid," Charon told Kassler. "Read the sign."

Charon pointed to a large sign on the wall by the doorway which read:

THIS CLASSIC PERFORMANCE
HAS BEEN MADE POSSIBLE THROUGH GENEROUS CONTRIBUTION
BY THE BELL TELEPHONE SYSTEMS, GENERAL MOTORS, AND
THE PETROLEUM COMPANIES OF AMERICA.

It was more than poor Kassler could take. He looked frantically back to the doorway, wanting desperately to return but, fearing the worst, not daring to do so.

He looked at the walls beside him where the eight-by-ten glossies of celebrities appeared oblivious of his pain—Getty, Rockefeller, Hunt, Hearst, Kennedy, Onassis, and Woody Allen in one grouping; Beckett, Nader, Khomeini, Bergman, Prescott, Rickles, and Woody Allen in a second; and in a third, Anita Bryant, Pat Boone, Abbie Hoffman, Betty Friedan, Gloria Steinem, Ann Landers, and Woody Allen.

Lupa looked sadly at Kassler.

"Come on, Sy. It's time for you to go home," she told him kindly.

Kassler wasn't paying attention. He searched the arena around him, for what he wasn't sure, spellbound by the hundreds of rocking bodies in the yellow mist, flesh glistening everywhere in the steamy cavern, men and women foraging for one another, clawing, clutching, biting, licking, writhing, and pounding, the hot air filled with the moans and grunts of rutting people.

"Aagghh!" Kassler screamed and flung up his arms. "I can't stand all this!"

"I agree. Let's go," Lupa attempted to steer Kassler through the congress of fornicators.

"These breasts are driving me crazy!" Kassler shouted as he looked around him at the extensive assortment of undulating mammae. "There're too many *boobs* around here! For every single woman there're *two boobs*!"

"It's all right, dear," Lupa tried to calm her date. "Men have *two testicles*. It all evens out. We should be going now, don't you think?"

"*Boobs* are *bigger*," Kassler mumbled to himself.

"Hold on, Sy," Lupa held fast to one of Kassler's arms, Charon to the other. "We'll be outside in just a few minutes and they'll all be covered with blouses and sweaters. You'll feel a lot better."

"A woman's vagina is not what you think it is," Kassler moved on to new anatomical horizons.

Lupa studied Kassler beside her. Then she turned to Charon.

"We've got an emergency," she told Charon.

"A vagina is a very *internal* thing," Kassler explained. "Read Freud."

"And I have," Charon said to Kassler. "Now, why don't you put one arm around my shoulder and the other around Lupa's and we'll get out of here."

"Women," Kassler hissed. "I've got a patient whose pecker is ruined for life just because of the way your *asses* are shaped."

"Oregon!" A pornographic film began, distracting Kassler. "The Beaver State!"

A deadly gleam came into Kassler's eyes.

"Now, hold on, Sy," Lupa protested.

"It's not funny," Kassler snarled. "Women are responsible for all this. Women are different from men."

"I took it that was your point. What have you noticed, dear?" Lupa tried to keep Kassler talking as she and Charon edged him through the crowd.

"Men have careers, creative work, financial responsibilities. ..."

"Ah, I missed that. Was that on the level with the people screwing underwater or the dentist giving blow jobs?" Lupa asked.

"Men have work. Women have boobs, and asses, and vaginas."

Lupa looked intently into Kassler's crazed eyes.

"We've got to get you out of here," she told him compassionately. "Something terrible is happening to you, Sy, some sort of severe sexist breakdown or something. I'm serious. You're not well."

"*You're* a woman," Kassler squinted his eyes suspiciously at Lupa, who was nearing the end of her patience.

He put his hands on Lupa's shoulders and pressed his thumbs into her flesh.

"I'm not joking, Lupa," he said slowly.

"You're hurting me, Sy."

"Women have ruined my life. A woman took my love and turned it into shit. She took my kids. She took my home."

"Please, Sy. It hurts a lot."

"You'll never give me what I need. . . ."

Kassler dropped his hands to his sides and glared at Lupa. She backed away, frightened and trembling.

"I have to go, Sy," Lupa said.

"I'll see he gets home," Charon said.

"I'll get home by myself," Kassler snapped and turned his back to Lupa, who quickly dashed away, followed at a slower pace by Charon.

Kassler stood alone at the bottom of Dante's Inferno, surveying the crowd's erotic activity, watching the stroking and rolling and rocking of a hundred variations of sexual intercourse, finally shifting his attention to a long line of naked women waiting their turn to enter a room where technicians were inserting hoses and pumping spermacidal jelly inside them to terminate life as it began. It was more than Kassler's brain could tolerate.

He gazed around him, transfixed by the estral antics, and reached a decision.

What Kassler decided was, very simply, this:

If humans are made in this fashion, if his children came to be in this way, if his own existence arose out of such activity, then nothing mattered anymore.

"If this is libido," Kassler mumbled to himself, "then fuck it."

But as his brain filled with these thoughts, an unexpected event occurred. His very own pecker began to harden and slowly extend from his body.

At first Kassler ignored the event and continued to gaze at the mass of copulating forms, but his attention was caught by something occurring in the very center of the vast carpeted pit. He walked slowly around the walls, keeping close to the side so he could see what was happening without being seen himself.

Radiating enormous power and control, like a maestro conducting a grotesque orchestra of humping men and women, Sam Zelazo stood at the center of the arena, giant and naked, his body muscular and shining with perspiration, his long blond hair and beard flashing in the light, his huge organ, like an engorged fire hose, large and tight, green veins distended all across its outside, rigid and driving pneumatically in and out of a woman who was supported by Zelazo's large hairy hands; who hung like a rag doll limply around his waist, experiencing nearly unbearable pleasure; who was, once upon a time, the most spectacular woman Kassler had ever seen—Vita Volpe Kassler.

"Oh, Sam!" Kassler heard Vita shout. "I love you, Sam!"

And as Kassler watched Zelazo's organ driving in and out of his wife with long methodical strokes, he reached for his own organ and started stroking it back and forth.

"I want my clothes," Kassler looked down at his nakedness as his hand continued its work.

"I want my home," tears began to form in Kassler's eyes. His hand moved more quickly.

"I want my life back."

Kassler raced his hand back and forth.

"I want my wife."

Kassler stroked fast and hard.

A hot familiar feeling filled his testicles and coursed into his penis.

"I want my kids," Kassler mumbled. "I want my children. Please, someone. Let me have my children," Kassler cried as the life spurted out of him.

Kassler spasmed and jerked and twitched, and, finally, exhausted, he dropped his head onto his knees.

"I want my daddy," Kassler whimpered to himself. "Where's my daddy?"

APRIL 1979

Session IV

❦

Kassler, calm and casual, lounged comfortably on the old overstuffed chair, chugging at the last embers of tobacco in the bottom of his Dunhill.

He seemed older than I remembered him to be, more lines across his brow, darker circles under his eyes, his hands not quite as steady as they held his pipe, tired, weary.

"Before we begin this session," he said slowly, "I wanted to tell you that I'll be taking a vacation during the summer, from May to September."

"I'm no expert on the solstice, but isn't summer mostly July and August?" I inquired.

"I will, of course, provide the full seven sessions this year, as we agreed. The final three will be in the fall. We'll meet next in October."

"I'll survive."

"Patients have different feelings about their therapists' going on vacation. Would you like to discuss yours?"

"Are we into the session proper now, or is this still the pretherapeutic part?"

"I think we've begun."

"In that case, I wonder whether you'd mind telling me exactly why it is that you're taking off for the next five months."

"I need a vacation."

"A vacation is two weeks at the shore, Kassler."

"I need some time by myself. I'm finding a nice isolated mountain where I can camp out and think over some things," Kassler said quietly.

"Look, Kassler, I'm sorry if I've given you a rough time about your religion. You want to be an atheist, agnostic, heretic—it's really okay."

"No, it's not," Kassler shook his head and breathed with noticeable fatigue. "It's not okay."

"And as for the alliance—maybe I've been pushing too hard."

"I need some time to myself."

"I'm aware that sometimes I may get a little caustic. It's not that I have anything against you, Kassler. My beef is with God. The sad fact of the matter is that God detests me."

"I'm sorry to hear that," Kassler reached for a small notebook and started leafing through its pages.

"It's the truth, Kassler," I said solemnly, to make an impression. "What God is best at, as near as I can tell, is despising me."

"You don't think that the Lord Almighty God has other things on His mind?" Kassler picked up on the issue.

"Not as far as I can see, and I'd be grateful if you'd stop referring to Him as the Lord Almighty God. I get the picture."

"I *don't* get the picture," Kassler put down his pipe and folded his arms comfortably across his chest. "As a matter of fact, as I've reviewed my notes over the last few sessions, I've been impressed by how little I've learned about what God *actually* does, and what you *actually* do. You both *actually* do something, I take it, besides battling each other? You haven't retired or anything?"

"You're in a very sanguine mood today, Kassler. What is it? Get laid last night? Something's up. You walk in here, plop in your chair, and notify me you're taking off for five months of solitude and contemplation, then start playing cat and mouse with me about how it is that Jehovah and I keep ourselves busy. You don't even believe in us. What's going on?"

"Actually," Kassler intoned mellifluously, "as I've been looking over my notes, I've decided, for the time being at least, to operate on the premise that this is all real, God does exist, and you are who you claim to be."

"I take it that you've been *reviewing your notes*. Goodness, does that mean you're putting some work into this after all? I'm impressed."

Kassler stared ahead and didn't react.

"A very interesting thing happens in this business," he finally said. "People come to me wanting desperately to find the answer to their problem, and the closer they get to it, the less they want to hear it."

"So," I avoided the issue, "just what information has emerged from *reviewing your notes*? Your peace of mind is, I assume, a result of great insight."

"Some," Kassler said modestly.

"Come on, Kassler. This isn't like you. Have you been talking to Zelazo again? We agreed that there'd be no more consultations with Zelazo. A bargain's a bargain."

"And there have been no more consultations with Sam Zelazo."

"Or anyone else?"

"Or anyone else. It's just you and me."

"I don't like this, Kassler. You've got something up your sleeve."

"Then you should know what it is," Kassler said matter-of-factly.

"Why? Why should I know what it is? Where does *that* come from?"

"Well," Kassler started leafing through his notes once again, "you have, on a number of occasions, read my thoughts with uncanny accuracy. Lupa tells me that you did the same to her."

"There're some thoughts that are easier to read than others." I did not like where Kassler was going one bit.

"Which ones are those?"

"It depends. This whole business works on feedback. You know that. It's nothing but mirrors. *I'm* limited by what *you* know. Some things are apparent, they reflect easily; others are not, they're more transparent."

"That must be terribly frustrating. It wasn't always like that."

"It used to be different. Read Ezekiel. I had the seal of perfection. I was perfect in beauty, full of wisdom...."

"And now...?" Kassler asked gently.

"Man doesn't fear God for nothing. I'll leave it at that."

"The question remains," Kassler would not leave it at that.

"God is spirit. I am matter. And so *what*? What's the big deal?"

"That's not the question, though, is it?" Kassler asked with distracting serenity.

"No," I agreed. "It's not."

"The question is," Kassler said very slowly, "what do we know that you don't?"

"That is," I resigned myself to its inevitability, "a very disturbing question."

"So what is it...that we stand between the truth of God and the lies of Satan?"

"Who does? You? Someone you know? Someone you read about? Don't be absurd. No one of you does any such thing. Now, why are you going on a five-month vacation? It'll wreck the continuity of my treatment."

"God did not create man to oppose evil?" Kassler asked tranquilly.

"God created man to negate the negation," I informed Kassler, "to affirm His own existence, and *that is all*. Where do you think evil *comes* from? Witches and goblins?"

"Man creates evil?"

"You catch on quickly, Kassler. When are you leaving?"

Kassler would not be distracted.

"How?" he asked directly.

"By wanting immortality."

"Why?"

"You got me. I can't figure it out."

"How do we create evil?" Kassler pursued the question with some firmness.

"Okay, Kassler, here it is. You create evil by denying that

you're an animal—primarily a sexual animal, I might point out—with a body which seals your doom. Your body means that you have no chance for immortality. Of course, it's not always that unpleasant having a body. It does have its compensations. As experiences go, it could be a lot worse. However, and it's a big *however*, your obsession with the physicalness of life only reinforces the inevitability of the end. This body is it. There is no more. Now tell me when you're leaving."

"That's it."

"Yes, that's it. Let's face it, Kassler, all your ingenious ideologies boil down to one thing—who is qualified for eternity? Now, are you going to answer my question or not?"

"And there is no eternity?"

I resigned myself to Kassler's unresponsiveness.

"There's eternity. But for whom? I'll tell you something, Kassler. You know what everyone's greatest fear around here is?"

"Tell me," Kassler was as cocky as ever.

"A faceless, nameless death—the death of an animal."

That pithy little sentiment took a bit of the edge off Kassler's confidence; not that this was my intention, of course.

"And what else do you know?" Kassler asked quietly.

"I know that since you all decided that I represent matter, body, the animal, you figured that fighting me would in some mysterious way change the absolute determinism of your situation. Of course, it doesn't work like that."

I waited for a moment.

"You know something, Kassler," I continued, "I hate the smell of sulfur. I don't know where that whole idea ever came from. The odor is not very appealing to me at all."

"How does it work?" Kassler returned to the topic.

"Evil? I'm no expert of course, but I am, as I believe I've pointed out, an interested observer. I'll tell you a little story, Kassler. Something to think over up on the mountain while you're staring at the stars. It goes like this. Once upon a time— this is a true story but I've always preferred stories that begin 'Once upon a time,' in this case around 1780 or so—there was a lovely man by the name of Franz Mesmer, a gentle, kind, and thoughtful man who believed that all humans had a mys-

terious bodily fluid within them that was influenced by the
Heavenly Bodies and that this was responsible for their ill-
nesses. He called his theory *animal magnetism*, which I thought,
incidentally, was a rather appropriate designation.

"Now, I point out to you that Dr. Mesmer was no charlatan
schlock. He had a Ph.D. in philosophy and metaphysics and
an M.D. from Vienna. Before long he became enormously
successful at curing hysterical women. This may suggest to
you another M.D. from Vienna who decided he had developed
an ingenious way to treat hysterical women—subjects who
seem throughout the ages to have been especially good candidates for whatever new ideologies were making the rounds,
if I may say so.

"Mesmer didn't use a couch, however. What Mesmer did
was take groups of women into his thickly carpeted, dimly lit
salon in Paris, which was mirrored to reflect every possible
shadow and had soft melodies playing, a fragrance of orange
blossoms in the air, and a tub of 'magnetized' water around
which all the ladies sat holding hands. It was a very impressive
ceremony. Mesmer would enter in a great lilac cape, waving
a yellow wand, intoning who knows what. There was enough
underlying sexuality to satisfy the French Foreign Legion, but
who cares. The women would get hysterical, releasing their
sexual tensions, and everybody felt just fine afterwards. The
point is, it all worked. It was *very* effective.

"Then somebody decided that Dr. Mesmer was probably
evil. A committee of non-evil men was formed to investigate
the situation—men like Benjamin Franklin, the chairman of
the committee, who had just finished devising a better way to
play music on wineglasses filled to various levels with water,
and men like Dr. Joseph Ignace Guillotin, who had recently
completed a marvelous device for beheading condemned evil
men who he felt had a God-given right to a merciful execution
regardless of their social status, and two other committee members, the astronomer Jean Bailly and the chemist Antoine La-
voisier, who were subsequently so executed with merciful
disregard for their social status.

"Needless to say, this committee determined absolutely that
Dr. Franz Mesmer was an evil man, confiscated his property,

and ruined his life. That what the man did *worked* and cured hundreds of previously suffering women was inconsequential. Mesmer claimed that there were planetary influences on our bodily fluids—an idea both absurd and evil, pointed out Dr. Guillotin, who, incidentally, neglected to mention that he refused to do surgery when there was a full moon because of the increased risk of bleeding, a practice that surgeons still follow. Worse than that were Mesmer's lilac cloak and yellow wand. This was scandalous to the medical community, who in those days in Paris wore *red* cloaks and carried *gold* canes.

"Now, I say this all to you, Kassler, because these were not bad people really—bright, distinguished, eminent men—scientists, not fools or frauds, but serious, thoughtful, hard-working men. The long and short of it, I'm afraid, is that throughout history, and I mean *all* history, you folks have always been dissatisfied with yourselves and your own little predicament. What you do is form clubs and take revenge on others. Hitler's plan was to wipe out all evil. He made a big club. He wanted to make it even bigger, but he got a little too conscientious about eradicating all evil, and the evil people began to outnumber him. People remember Hitler. Men who dabble in evil are always remembered. You should note that. Ask a child born twenty-five years after Hitler died who Hitler was and he'll tell you right off. Ask him who Alexander Fleming was, and see what you get. For that matter, ask the first dozen men you meet in the street who Fleming was and see what you get.

"Of course, you've gotten a good deal more sophisticated about it these days, I will admit. No more hysterical witch burnings, hangings, and crowded squares of guillotines to get rid of the evil which exists in the world and stands between you and immortality. Carefully planned meticulous wars will purge the evil. Sometimes a newspaper story or a television report is enough for a full crucifixion.

"I'll tell you something, Kassler, since you asked. Victimization is a universal human need. The highest heroism is the stamping out of those who're tainted with evil—the Jewish bankers with no hearts who steal your money, the black men with big cocks who rape your daughters, the gooks in Asia who have no understanding or regard for life or family. I hope you're getting all this down, Kassler, in your notes."

"The point once again is, I take it, that it's all our own fault," Kassler said smugly.

"Not exactly."

"Exactly what, then?"

"Exactly?" I thought it over.

Kassler waited in silence for my answer.

"Horror gives men peace of mind," I told him.

Kassler shuddered, and his smugness dissipated rapidly.

"Some men," he said weakly.

"Most men . . . and women . . . and children. It makes you all right with the world. You come together to kill your enemies and your love for one another deepens and—at least until you become the victim—you're comrades in arms. Your hatred for one another is purged through the suffering of one enemy. All your love is based on a foundation of hate. You certainly should know that, Kassler."

Kassler sat, chills coursing through his spine, and listened with a faraway look in his eyes.

"The logic, Kassler," I said, "is terrifying, if you ask me. Guilt over your mortal human predicament and plain old animal sadism is elevated to the highest level of human striving—the age-old problem of good and evil."

"You've developed a neat system to account for your *own* predicament," Kassler tried desperately to squirm out of the horrible reality that faced him.

"It's not *my* system, Kassler. Sorry. That dark thing inside all of you that you want to deny—it's there. The shadows are *real. Real shadows.* Cast in the form of human beings, *by* human beings. It's not my fault that you can't elevate yourselves by jumping over your own shadows, so you need to find the dark things in everyone else. You *need* me, Kassler. You all do. I'm your immortality. Your fight with me keeps you all alive. Conquering me is your only hope. I'm the father you have to destroy."

A large lump formed in Kassler's throat.

"We are the children of God," Kassler tried out some ersatz scripture.

"You are, by nature, the children of *wrath*. Ephesians 2: 36. Look it up."

"And you are the great universal antagonism."

"To what? What do I oppose?"

"God?"

"Don't be ridiculous. I *want* people to believe in God. You know that. Without God, there's no Satan. I cease to exist."

"You oppose the Scriptures because they *reveal* God."

"I do no such thing. Read the Scriptures! I recommend them! Read them all! Forward, backward, and upside down! Greek, Hebrew, English, any way you want! Memorize them! Know God. Know Him well. And then, when you're done, take 2 Corinthians 4:4 and write it down. Print it in big letters and post it in a nice conspicuous place. 'Satan is the God of *this* world.' That's what it says, Kassler. 'Satan is the God of *this world*.'"

"Well, as you've already pointed out, as realms go, you could have done better." Kassler began to recover some of his confidence.

"There's only one thing wrong with this world," I told Kassler, "and that's man."

"Who you intend to destroy."

"Don't be stupid. My aim is *not* the destruction of man. You're doing splendidly without my help. Besides, I need—" A thought occurred to me, and I broke off abruptly. I saw, unfortunately, where Kassler had been heading.

"Yes?" Kassler played it very cool.

"Nothing of consequence."

Kassler had no intention of letting me off the hook. Not at this point.

"You have been making one point repeatedly," Kassler said slowly. "We use you to our ends, to purge ourselves of guilt, to deny evil intentions, to forget our animal natures and our mortality."

"You've reviewed your notes well, Kassler. I commend you."

"Another thought has occurred to me, however, which I'd like to share with you," Kassler plunged ahead, ignoring my banter. "While it's true that by opposing God, you landed in the dregs of the available realms, you did manage, nevertheless, to gain a certain status not accorded Michael, Ezekiel, Gabriel, and the others you left behind.

"You *could* ask God's forgiveness, of course, as I pointed out during our last session, but that would mean you'd have to give up some considerable status. You'd just be another glorious silver-winged, golden-haloed angel, rather humdrum, if you ask me."

"I take it you're going somewhere with all this?" I asked with some impatience.

"You'll have to tell me," Kassler said. "Assuming I agree, and I do, that we use *you*, the question is, who do *you* use?"

"I'll spare you the trouble, Kassler. I need man. You. All of you. I need you all."

"And we need you. Fortunately, not nearly as much as you need us. There is no *battle* with God over man's *soul*. Neither of you could care less about what happens after life on earth. The battleground is right here. How am I doing?"

"Okay, Kassler. You're doing okay."

"You also couldn't care less about correcting old myths that Dante dreamed up five hundred years ago. Horns, tails, pits, and flames—who cares? No, it seems to me that something's going on right here that you don't understand, and it's bothering the hell out of you. You selected me, my hunch is, because you figured I could explain it to you, yes?"

"Partly."

"What else?"

"Golly, Kassler, I chose you for so many reasons, actually. I thought we could educate each other. You've seen some heavy front-line action and maintained a certain class through it all, a view of the world that appeals to me. I figured you'd give me a run for my money, so to speak."

Kassler got out of his chair, signaling that the hour was coming to an end.

"I do my best," he said with satisfaction, confident that he had, at last, regained control of the session.

"But basically," I told Kassler as he started to leave, "I selected you because of the way you killed your father. Nice work. You've got style, Kassler. Have a pleasant vacation."

PART VI

Szlyck's Farewell

CHAPTER 1

"*It's all your fault, you know,*" Leo Szlyck told me the week after he'd discovered Kassler and his beloved Lupa arm in arm.

"I was sure it would be," I told him.

"It was your idea for me to get out of here and get some air. Otherwise I'd never have done it," Szlyck looked at me with those somber yellow-flecked eyes of his. "I'd have put Cerberus out in the yard and he'd still be alive."

"You've been rotting in here for months, Leo. It's not good for you. It was still a good idea."

"The hell it was. If I'd stayed in here, I'd never have found out that Kassler stole Lupa from me," Szlyck slumped back in the old chair that Kassler himself was later to occupy while conducting my psychotherapy.

"Don't be ridiculous, Leo," I told Szlyck. "Kassler did no such thing."

"He did. I can tell from his eyes. He's a shrewd little bastard. He tricked me into getting Lupa to meet with him and then stole her right out from under me."

"Lupa hadn't been under you for nearly a year, Leo. She was already divorced when Kassler met her."

"In Mexico. What do Mexicans know? They wouldn't know a divorce from an enchilada. They have no concept of the law. They're all renegades, going around with those big hats, and straps of bullets across their chests, and mustaches. . . ." Szlyck trailed off.

He took another drink from his bottle of Scotch, cases of which were now being delivered to his Bolgia by an obliging package store in Citadel.

"You're drinking yourself to death," I informed Szlyck, as I had on a number of previous occasions over the last few months. "Why don't you stop?"

"I'm going to get Kassler," Szlyck heard not a word of my plea.

"Not like this you're not," I pointed out.

"We'll see," Szlyck said solemnly. Then he picked up another half-dozen sticks of dynamite and began wrapping them together as he had once seen done in a movie about Mexicans.

"Leo, do you have any idea how much dynamite you've already got around me?"

"Not enough," Szlyck answered. "Not nearly enough," and he walked over and placed the neat little bundle on the foot-high pile of explosives that surrounded me.

A week after visiting Dante's Inferno, Kassler was still reeling from the experience. At first he wanted to confront Vita and Sam Zelazo. But as the days went by, Kassler's resolve turned into resignation, and he endured by avoiding contact with all human beings other than his patients. Bea Chaikin was the first to notice Kassler's misanthropy, and late one afternoon at the end of the second week, she marched into Kassler's office.

"So," Bea got right to the point, "are you quitting?"

"I'm not sure. Zelazo's been fucking Vita. I can't figure that out. Why is he *doing* that?"

Bea looked at Kassler in disbelief.

"I don't know what's more difficult to answer," she finally said. "Why he's doing it or why you would have to ask?"

Then she got up, walked over to Kassler, and patted his head very gently.

"I hope you stay, Sy. We need you around here, most of all your patients," and she kissed him lightly on the top of his head and left.

For several minutes Kassler sat in a daze in the darkening room, and then, taking a deep breath, he headed off to talk to Lupa.

"I'm not sure what you want, Sy," Lupa told Kassler as they drank coffee on the living-room sofa with the bright-green jungle pattern that was duplicated on the carpeting and the drapes. "I'm not even sure that *you* know what you want from me."

"Magic," Kassler said wistfully.

"I can't give you that, Sy. Not on command. I'm not sure I can give that to anyone, ever."

"Doesn't that bother you?" Kassler asked.

"I don't know anymore," Lupa said pensively. "It used to. It used to drive me crazy. All day long I'd go around depressed and frustrated, condemning myself for not being able to experience *magic*. Then, I don't know, one day something happened. I realized that I do *care*. I experience pleasure. I'm considerate, kind, friendly—all those things I was taught to be, that were supposed to have some value in dealing with people you wanted to be close to."

"Is that enough for you?"

"I think it is, Sy. Does that horrify you?"

"Can you be happy like that?"

"I'm convinced of it, Sy. I didn't use to be, but I am now. I've got a profession I really enjoy. It excites me to see it working out. I get pleasure from good music and art and literature. That also excites me. I'm developing some friends. People have always meant a lot to me. I care about people. Someday I'll have a couple children, maybe. I'm not so sure about that. But if I do, I'm sure I'll feel good about it. That's a lot, Sy. It's enough for me."

Kassler sipped his coffee and looked at Lupa's tanned face.

"I think that most of the time we get along really well," Kassler said.

"Me, too," Lupa agreed.

"You're a very good listener," Kassler complimented his lady.

"Music appreciation. Two semesters at Radcliffe," Lupa explained. "You go into the next room and play a violin and a trombone, and I'll tell you which is which ninety percent of the time."

"Will you stop being so goddamn jovial!" Kassler was becoming incensed. "This is very serious. We're talking about whether we should stop seeing each other or not. Doesn't that matter to you?"

Lupa avoided looking at Kassler. She bit her lips and fought back tears.

"Yes," she looked at Kassler, "it matters to me a whole lot."

"It matters to me, too," Kassler said, and he took Lupa's hand.

"But I can't give you what you want in a relationship with a woman, can I?" Lupa pointed out.

"No," Kassler said quietly. "You can't."

"So, what do you say we stop all this before we hate each other, okay?"

Kassler continued to hold Lupa's hand and stare into her purple eyes, waiting for her to come up with a brilliant solution.

"I don't really want to break up," Kassler said when there was no help from Lupa.

"Look, Sy, you'll be very happy. You'll find some nice young woman with no complications, no crazy ex-husband, no career, no hang-ups, and she'll fall madly in love with you and you'll both live happily ever after."

For several minutes Kassler sat drinking his coffee and staring at Lupa, who appeared to him to be particularly radiant in her sadness this night. Kassler tried very hard to think of a good reason not to break up, but no persuasive and compelling concepts presented themselves.

"I'm almost done with my coffee," Kassler finally said. "I'll leave in just a minute."

"I think that'd be good," Lupa answered. "Long good-byes aren't my favorite things."

Kassler took a last quick gulp of coffee.

"I would like a good-bye kiss, though," Lupa smiled tearily.

Kassler leaned over and kissed her with tenderness.

"I love you, Lupa. You're the best friend I've ever had," he told her as he ran his hand gently along the outline of her cheek.

"You, too, Sy. You've been a good friend, too," Lupa let her fingers run absently across the back of Kassler's neck.

Kassler looked at Lupa's purple eyes. He liked the way her fingers felt on his neck.

"Sometimes we get along okay, you and me," Kassler kissed Lupa again and ran his hand over her back until it reached the curves of her slender bottom. For several minutes he stroked Lupa's backside while she closed her eyes and luxuriated in the warm sensation that filled her. Then Kassler unfastened the button at the back of Lupa's skirt, pulled down the zipper, and slid off skirt, panty hose, and panties in one deft motion.

"There've been times," Lupa told Kassler as she undid the belt and zipper on his trousers and pulled his pants and underwear low enough to free his erection, "that I've felt like I really did love you. . . ." Lupa's words trailed off as Kassler's fingers came closer to the moist ridges that separated her legs.

"I know you've tried," Kassler said, kissing Lupa, his finger sliding deeper and deeper into the groove.

"I have," Lupa moaned, put her thin arms around Kassler, and pulled him on top of her.

Kassler removed his fingers and slowly inserted himself between the wet folds of skin.

Instinctively, Lupa started rotating her bottom in small circles. Her hands behind Kassler's head pressed his mouth tightly against hers, her tongue darting in and out. Then she turned her head to the side and concentrated on the enormous pleasure she was experiencing as Kassler entered her body again and again.

"I wish I could love you the way you want," she gasped as Kassler drove himself in and out of her.

"Me, too," Kassler said. "I wish so, too."

"And," Lupa whimpered as she felt herself start to come, "I wish you could take me as I am."

"I wish so, too," Kassler moaned, and he flooded Lupa with eight months of sexual tension in a burst of spasms that seemed to last forever, Kassler's organ filling up Lupa's insides, pulsing, and spurting every last drop as deeply into Lupa as he could go.

For a long time, Kassler and Lupa rested side by side on the sofa, each experiencing the sensation of the other's body, running their hands over the curves of their partner's form over and again. Finally, Lupa kissed Kassler lightly on the forehead.

"I hope you find the magic you want, Sy," she told him softly.

"You're a splendid person, Lupa," Kassler returned the kiss on Lupa's forehead. "I know I'm probably crazy to be giving up all this. As soon as I leave, I'm going to regret it."

"Then come back," Lupa smiled.

"I guess I could, couldn't I?"

"You could, but you shouldn't. You know what you want, Sy. And you know I can't give it to you."

Kassler looked at Lupa and studied her blond hair, rumpled from the lovemaking, and her purple eyes, more brilliant than ever. Then he sighed, stood up, and pulled up his pants.

"I'll go wash out my cup," Kassler procrastinated.

"That's okay," Lupa said. "I can do it. You really have to go, Sy. Kiss me good-bye and go. Do it."

So Kassler kissed Lupa good-bye and went.

Kassler rang the doorbell to Zelazo's house several times. There was no response.

"Sam," Kassler called and tried the handle on the large brass door. It turned with a loud ratcheting sound, and slowly the heavy door opened.

Kassler had been driving around Citadel for several hours after he left Lupa, stewing, when he passed Zelazo's enormous house. Although it was three in the morning, the lights were blazing brightly from the windows, and so, determining that one more disastrous encounter couldn't make much of a difference to his emotional state, Kassler resolved to confront Zelazo.

Kassler walked down the long hall that led to the living room, where he and Zelazo played chess. The room was dark except for a single light illuminating the chessboard. All the windows were open and it was bitter cold.

"Sam?" Kassler called out as he walked over to study the chess game. Black had won. White's pieces were scattered futilely across the board, in a desperate attempt to protect against assaults that seemed to be coming from everywhere at the same time. The white king lay toppled on its side, capitulating.

Kassler examined the sorry outcome for a minute more and then ambled down a hall to his right.

"Sam?" he tried again. There was still no answer, and so he continued to search the house. Kassler had never been in any part of Zelazo's home other than the living room, so he walked slowly, trying doors on his left and right, holding his coat tightly around him in the icy cold that swept down the hallway.

The first few doors were to empty closets.

"Sam?" Kassler said as he knocked on a door halfway down the corridor. When, again, there was no answer, Kassler slowly opened the door. His mouth fell open in amazement.

He had entered a vast art gallery, a maze of long black walls as large as any single exhibition space he'd ever seen. Lights hanging from the top of each picture illuminated the works of art. Kassler walked down the corridors inspecting the paintings.

Leonardo, Michelangelo, Giotto, Botticelli, van Gogh, Bosch, Renoir, Piero della Francesca, Rembrandt, Caravaggio, Blake, Munch—the paintings and drawings seemed to go on forever.

Kassler ran his hand lightly over a Botticelli to feel the texture of the paint and convince himself that he was looking at originals. As his fingertips felt the tiny stroke marks of paint applied nearly five hundred years ago, chills ran through him.

He moved slowly down the aisle, studying one work of art after another, a strange sadness overcoming him. People stared out of the pigment in pain and distress, as though they'd been locked inside the canvas, condemned to watch others pass before them.

Kassler stopped and looked at a Leonardo of a young boy weeping piteously. It struck at his heart, and he felt the child's anguish well within himself until he could tolerate it no longer. He walked over to a window and stood gazing out, trying to catch his breath.

A figure raced by outside the window, a giant man, naked in the frigid night, dodging in and out of the woods, around the trees, in pursuit of something. Kassler watched spellbound. Sam Zelazo swept his hands along the ground as he continued to run, captured some nocturnal animal—a mole, a raccoon, a muskrat, Kassler couldn't tell—and then, with a short thrust of each thumb, Zelazo snapped out the animal's eyes, which fell like two small shiny beads onto the frozen earth.

Kassler's stomach heaved and he choked as vomitus filled his throat. Zelazo tossed the squealing animal onto the ground and watched it stagger into the forest. Kassler closed his eyes.

When he opened them again, Zelazo was standing at the end of the aisle. He wore a black robe, his face was wet with perspiration, his eyes dark and brooding.

"You're a little early, Sy," Zelazo said. "The gallery doesn't open until ten."

"This gallery never opens," Kassler said. "No one even knows these paintings exist. They're all masterpieces, and they're completely unknown."

"I commissioned them for me specially," Zelazo smiled. "What do you think? Talented men, aren't they?"

Kassler found no humor in Zelazo's answer. His brain was still filled with what he had just observed through the window.

"What were you doing outside?" he challenged Zelazo.

"Hunting," Zelazo responded matter-of-factly.

"You blinded that animal."

"It's a nocturnal animal. It won't even know the difference in a few minutes. Would you feel better if I had used a rifle? You'd rather I had killed it?"

"You weren't wearing any clothes. It's twenty degrees out there."

"I have a slow metabolism. Some people swim in the winter. I hunt. Next time I'll wear my robe. Anything else?"

"You caught the animal with your hands," Kassler continued to fit the spectacle he'd just witnessed into an understandable schema.

Zelazo stood still, staring at Kassler from the other end of the aisle.

"I hunt," his voice echoed in the large chamber, "on equal terms with my prey—naked and barehanded. It provides me with a challenge. I try to do it every night. It keeps me in shape. There's not much more."

"Always at night?"

"Always at night. Neighbors tend to complain about naked men running through their backyards during the afternoon."

"When do you sleep?"

"I don't," Zelazo's voice continued to echo down the aisle. "At least, not the way most people do. Sleep deprivation studies show that after a certain time without sleep, the body adjusts by taking catnaps, milliseconds long, thousands of them an hour, so fast that you'd never know—between words in a sentence, while I'm lifting up my fork, when I blink my eyes. I've trained myself to go without sleep."

Kassler looked at Zelazo, who was facing him, steam issuing from his body in the cold room.

"I never know what to say to you," Kassler confessed in a mixture of fury and frustration.

"Why don't you come into the living room, then," Zelazo suggested, "and have some brandy while you think of better reprimands."

"You've been fucking my wife," Kassler announced as he and Zelazo left the gallery.

"You've caught me barehanded," Zelazo admitted, entering the living room.

"Jesus, Sam!" Kassler exploded as he slumped into the sofa. "This isn't a joke! I trusted you with Vita and you betrayed me!"

"By having sex with Vita?"

"I trusted you."

"If you no longer trust me, that's your problem, Sy," Zelazo said as he poured brandy into a large snifter and handed it to Kassler. "I didn't ask you to trust me. I didn't force you to trust me. You did it on your own. If you want to stop, that's entirely your business."

"You're my supervisor," Kassler lamented as he tried to warm himself with the brandy. "And my friend."

"I still am."

"How long, Sam? When did you start fucking her? Before I left her? When she was still trying to make up her mind about our marriage?"

"She'd already made up her mind about your marriage when she first came to see me."

"Shit, Sam. Shit!" Kassler got up from the sofa and stomped back and forth in the large room. "That means you were fucking her from the beginning, doesn't it?"

Zelazo looked at Kassler and ran his fingers through his beard.

"Well," Kassler asked again, "doesn't it?"

"If you really want to know, the answer is *yes*, it does, and I never liked the word *fuck*, so I'd appreciate your not using it."

"Why?" Kassler shouted. "Isn't that what you were doing? Weren't you fucking her?"

Zelazo stared at Kassler in silence.

"I'd like you to leave," he finally told Kassler. "When you've finally settled down, you should come to my office so we can talk, but not until then."

"I trusted you, Sam. I *really* trusted you," Kassler bleated.

"Oh, cut it out, Sy," Zelazo sat back in a large chair. "You're beginning to sound like a Boy Scout."

"I'm quitting Phlegethon," Kassler said. "I'll leave as soon as you find someone to replace me."

Zelazo continued to look at Kassler, trying to determine whether he should deal with him in his present state of mind or send him away.

"All right, Sy, sit down."

"I'll stand up," Kassler said in defiance, rubbing his arms to keep warm.

"Your pacing is bothering me, and I want you to hear what I have to say. Now please *sit down*."

"I can hear you just fine standing up."

Zelazo got up from his chair, walked over to Kassler, and towering over him, he placed a hand on each of Kassler's shoulders.

Kassler felt no pressure from Zelazo's arms but, nevertheless, found himself deflating into a nearby chair. As he sat, his defiance evaporated.

"Jesus Christ, Sam," he said, looking up at Zelazo, "what'd you have to go do that to Vita for? You knew if she had anyone else, she'd leave me. Why? I really—"

"If you tell me one more time that you trusted me, I'm going to throw up," Zelazo said with his back to Kassler, as he returned to his own chair.

"Now, it seems to me," Zelazo said calmly, "that you have one of two alternatives. You can leave Phlegethon or you can stay. If you're going, we have nothing to talk about, except that you're a good psychotherapist. As a matter of fact, you're an *excellent* psychotherapist, probably one of the best we've ever had here. Don't take my word for it if you doubt your own impressions. Ask Bea Chaikin."

"Are you screwing her, too?" Kassler asked tartly.

"My sex life is really not the issue here," Zelazo ignored the specifics of Kassler's inquiry. "You're a fine therapist, Sy. You do good work, hard work, and very well. I think you should stay. I'd like you to stay."

Kassler looked up at Zelazo to see whether he was sincere. To Kassler he appeared to be.

"Now," Zelazo continued, "if you do decide to stay—"

"Come on, Sam, be reasonable," Kassler finally said. "How can I stay?"

"It would require you to take a few tentative steps into the real world, that's true," Zelazo said.

"What is that supposed to mean?"

"It means that in the real world, people get married, sometimes to the wrong people, and they get divorced. In the real world, women meet men, married men and married women, and they have sexual relations with people they're not married to. You've heard your patients talk about such things, I'm sure. Do you think you live in a different world?"

"You betrayed me!" Kassler whined.

"Oh, I did not," Zelazo said irritably, "any more than you betrayed Leo Szlyck. That *is* his wife I see you with from time to time?"

"That's different," Kassler considered the parallel for the very first time. "She was all done with Szlyck, and the whole thing just kind of happened."

There was a pregnant pause.

"I'm waiting to hear the difference," Zelazo finally said.

Kassler said nothing. The fatigue of the long sleepless night was beginning to overcome him, and he had nothing more to say to Zelazo.

"I ought to go get some sleep," Kassler decided out loud and stood up.

"I think that's a good idea, Sy," Zelazo agreed and arose to see Kassler out. "Before you go, though, there's something I've been meaning to show you—a painting, another Leonardo, not very well known, though it's one of his best, I think."

Zelazo took a key from the pocket of his robe, inserted it in a door to the right of the entranceway, and ushered Kassler into a medium-sized room, dark except for a single large painting which was on the wall opposite the door and which was illuminated by several small spotlights from the ceiling.

Kassler stopped short as soon as he entered the room, a nauseous feeling enveloping him as his knees began to wobble.

"I spent a number of years working in Italy before I came here, and I picked this up for practically nothing. It was hidden away in a basement in Florence."

Kassler grabbed on to the wall to steady himself.

"A few weeks ago, when we were playing chess and you told me about your father's death, this came immediately to mind."

Kassler shook as he looked at the giant canvas, a familiar scene beside the Arno River. A crowd gathered around an older man who had collapsed to the pavement, stricken, his face white with death, his eyes glassy and cold, while, kneeling beside him, his son, arms flailing in the air, screamed out in anguish.

"Uncanny, isn't it?" Zelazo mused.

Kassler reached for the door, threw it open, and ran outside for air.

Kassler did not have to wait long for an explanation.

"Shit!" Bernie Kohler told him while they were cooking hamburgers in Kassler's apartment the next night. "Did he pull that phony masterpiece business on you, too? Welcome to the club."

"Where did he get them all?" Kassler dug his spatula under a juicy patty of ground beef.

"He *painted* them, that's where. He's a lunatic. I told you that. He's done a Renoir of Bea parking her car and a Rembrandt of Norman Meltz jerking off. He can do about three an hour on a good day."

"He goes hunting in the nude in the middle of the winter and never sleeps," Kassler plopped a hamburger onto a roll and passed it on a paper plate to Bernie Kohler.

"I'm not surprised," Bernie said as he bit into his supper.

"I saw him catch a mole or something with his bare hands and gouge out its eyes." Kassler tried to avoid visualizing the grotesque scene.

"I guess that explains it." Bernie took another bite of his sandwich.

"Explains what?" Kassler sat down at the table and poured ketchup on his hamburger.

"Why some of his patients didn't find him very helpful," Bernie continued, unflappable. "That kind of approach to living things could definitely make it hard to establish a therapeutic relationship."

Leo Szlyck, unaware that Kassler and Lupa were no longer a couple, was not idle during those winter months of 1975.

An ever-present tumbler of Scotch at his left arm and cases of recently arrived explosives at his right, Szlyck proceeded to carry out his revenge on Kassler for stealing his woman. Szlyck used his ultimate weapon. The telephone.

"This is Guido Cavalcanti," Szlyck pulled a name from the phone book more or less at random, "from Cavalcanti's Florists. I want to report a bad debt, several thousand dollars, which a Dr. Sy Kassler has run up over here," Szlyck told the Credit Bureau of Greater Citadel, embellishing details where necessary. "Roses," Szlyck explained, "long-stemmed, and lots of lilacs. Must be in love. Four thousand six hundred ten dollars and twelve cents. Oh, you're very welcome. My pleasure."

Then Leo Szlyck would assemble another package of dynamite.

"You don't know a thing about explosives, you know, Leo," I tried to point out to him. "How're you going to detonate all this business?"

"How else?" Leo said contemptuously. "With a match."

"Oh, I see," I answered, not wanting to rain on Leo's parade.

"Hello," Szlyck tucked the phone between his chin and shoulder so he could wrap explosives for me and talk at the same time. "Thisa isa Detectiva Farinata," Leo spoke with the worst imitation of an Italian accent I have ever heard. "We're a-checking on a Dr. Kassler whosa gota credit carda froma youra stora."

The results of the scores of phone calls that Leo Szlyck was making were not to affect Kassler for a month or so, and when they did, of course, they shut him out of the world of credit and commerce with the suddenness and finality of a giant medieval iron door slamming in his face, its heavy oak bar dropping permanently into place with a terrible thud.

It couldn't have come at a worse time. Kassler was broke and ready to resign from Phlegethon. Without knowledge of his impending predicament, he had called, as requested, on his attorney.

"There's good news and there's bad news," Marty Myers said playfully. "Any preference?"

"Good first," Kassler said. "I need it."

"You're divorced."

"How?"

"Vita agreed by stipulation not to contest the divorce. It's been filed with the court. The only issues remaining are support and visitation. You're a free man," Marty smiled as he dug his thumbs under the arm-holes of his vest.

"Okay," Kassler was unimpressed. "And the bad news?"

"The court date to determine support and visitation is January ninth, 1977."

"Two more years?" Kassler asked numbly.

"There's a terrific backlog, Sy. I'm sorry," Marty Myers expressed his sympathy.

Kassler sat stunned, his head spinning with the thought of spending two more years in the same circumstances, the frustration and the sadness of it.

"I can't take it, Marty. It's a horrible situation. It's lousy for me and it's lousy for the kids."

"I know."

"Isn't there anything that can be done?" Kassler pleaded. "Even temporarily?"

Marty Myers shook his head.

"Not unless the kids are being beaten," he told Kassler as he cracked his knuckles. "Sullivan thinks that Sunday visitations are fair. You have to prove to him he's wrong. That takes time, and he's not going to have that kind of time for two more years."

Kassler leaned back in his chair and stared at the ceiling.

"I'm leaving this place, Marty, leaving Citadel, quitting my job. I'm going to borrow some money, go somewhere that has trees, get a new job. The kids will do okay. Actually, they'll be better off without me, without all the back-and-forth crap every Sunday. They may not think so right away, but in the long run, they will be." Kassler fiddled with his belt and made an effort to avoid looking at Marty Myers as he said this.

"You leave," Marty informed Kassler, "and it'll be very hard to get the judge to change anything. He may even reduce your visitation to once a month. I've seen him do it."

"Then that's how it'll have to be, Marty," Kassler's resolve increased. "I've made up my mind. I'm getting out of here."

Marty Myers looked at Kassler, inspecting the psychic damage.

"The kids need you, Sy. You're the only solid thing in their life," Marty Myers said as he patted the sides of his well-groomed hair. "You're reliable, you care for them, you're straight with them, sincere, predictable—what every kid needs. You're their only hope, Sy."

Kassler got out of his chair and walked to the door.

"Nice try, Marty," Kassler said as he opened the door. "But the problem is that I'm not any of those things. It's all a lie."

"Your kids don't think so," Marty called out to Kassler as he started to close the door.

"It's over, Marty. We're all going to be very happy," and Kassler closed the door.

"I need a loan of about five thousand dollars for a couple of years," Kassler told his friendly personal banker, a middle-aged man with waxy black hair and a thin mustache who handled such matters at the First National Citadel Bank and Trust Company.

"I'm afraid we've closed out your account with us, Dr. Kassler," Jim DiFillipo told Kassler. "That just wouldn't be possible."

"Why?" Kassler asked incredulously.

"I'm not sure, Dr. Kassler," DiFillipo answered evasively. "Bank policy, I suppose. We have a right to review all accounts periodically, and some are terminated. Your balance, such as it was, was sent to you in a check yesterday."

Kassler was furious.

"But why? I want to know why?"

"You had a check returned for insufficient funds, Dr. Kassler," DiFillipo responded in his calm fiscal manner.

"That was over a year ago!" Kassler shouted. "It was for two dollars and twelve cents, and happened because you posted a deposit of mine late."

"All deposits made after three o'clock are credited on the next banking day," DiFillipo explained patiently.

"And mine was deposited *before* three o'clock."

"That's never been satisfactorily established. It wasn't in the computer until the next day."

"Because your computer was down! It was off-line! Broken! I handed the deposit to the teller at a quarter to three!"

"That isn't her recollection, Dr. Kassler."

"She didn't remember me at *all*. She didn't remember I had made *any* deposit."

"Nevertheless . . . What's done is done. The decision has been made. I'm sorry to say you no longer have an account with us."

"But I have a *relationship* with this bank," Kassler squealed. "This is the only bank I've done any business with. I've had loans here and paid them back. Done all my checking here. I need another loan now. You know I'm good for it," Kassler tried to explain.

"I'm sorry, Dr. Kassler. I'd suggest you try another bank."

In a state of perplexity, Kassler spent the afternoon going from bank to bank.

"We'd be happy to open an account for you on a trial basis," the bank officers explained over and again, "but we understand that you've had your account closed at your last bank and there's a court order restraining your savings account."

"It's the children's money," Kassler told each new banker. "My ex-wife did that."

"Perhaps, after we get to know you better, we might be able to discuss a short-term loan for a small amount . . . to try things out," one sweet young lady attempted.

"But I don't need a small amount for a short time. I need a large amount for a long time—five thousand dollars for two years."

Then Kassler had a brainstorm.

"My Bankcard," he burst out gleefully. "I have a five-thousand-dollar line of credit on my Bankcard. I'll take that," and Kassler fished for his charge card and handed it to the helpful young woman.

"We'd be happy to do that for you," she smiled and danced away, her pleated skirt swinging airily from side to side as her hips shifted gracefully with her walk.

"I'm afraid," she informed Kassler glumly when she returned, "that your credit line has been canceled."

"I don't believe it," Kassler slumped in the chair beside the girl's desk. "Why?"

"Oh, we don't know that," the girl brushed back her long frizzy red hair. "It's just listed here on the alert bulletin."

"May I see?" Kassler reached for his card and the bulletin.

"You can have the bulletin, but I can't let you have the card back, I'm afraid. It's been recalled. I get twenty dollars for turning it in."

"*I'll* turn it in. I *need* the twenty dollars."

"I'm terribly sorry," the young girl put her hand on Kassler's arm. "The twenty bucks is mine. Finders keepers."

Then the young lady looked compassionately at Kassler.

"This must be a horrible day for you," she said sympathetically.

Kassler looked up at the girl's brown eyes.

"Let me take you out to dinner tonight?" he asked plaintively.

"I'm sorry. I can't. Bank policy," she explained gently. "Besides, you don't have any money."

"This is Prosecutor Leo Batista," Szlyck worked feverishly at the telephone. "I understand that you're Dr. Kassler's landlord. We're conducting a grand-jury investigation of Dr. Kassler, and I wonder if you might be able to give me some information? I'm sorry that we can't give you any more details, but morals charges involving sodomy with minor children are not allowed to be discussed."

"Leo, really," I tried unsuccessfully to restrain Szlyck again and again.

"Hello," Szlyck worked around the clock. "This is Attorney Leo Giovanni. We have a large monetary judgment against a Dr. Sy Kassler and we're trying to determine his assets, which we intend to take in order to satisfy our judgment. Now, I understand you finance Dr. Kassler's automobile."

And, of course, in between all this, Szlyck drank without moderation and, having run out of dynamite, spent great energy sticking gelignite to my parts.

"This is Dr. Leo Vivaldi," Szlyck was quickly running out of names. "I have a patient, Dr. Sy Kassler, who's currently in a coma, no family, and I'm trying to determine what other physicians may have treated him. I thought that your Blue Cross/Blue Shield records might help me out."

And it was with this phone call, of course, that Leo Szlyck hit the jackpot.

"We've had a call from a Dr. Vivaldi, who treated you when you were a patient at Bellevue," Sam Zelazo said when Kassler arrived in Zelazo's office at the end of the day, in response to Sam Zelazo's urgent request for a meeting.

"I don't remember any Dr. Vivaldi," Kassler said with a nauseous feeling in his stomach.

"But you do remember Bellevue Hospital and being a patient there?" Zelazo stared directly at Kassler and asked for a direct response in return.

"Yes," Kassler mumbled. "I was under observation for ten days once, years ago, when I became exhausted. It was nothing at all. Really."

"But you lied on your job application here and your application to the Institute, when you were asked if you'd ever been hospitalized in a psychiatric facility, didn't you?"

"I didn't think that ten days of observation and no diagnosis was what they wanted to know about."

Zelazo leaned forward, rested his elbows on his desk, and talked calmly to Kassler.

"I'm going to try to save your job, Sy, if you want to stay," Zelazo said in the stillness of his office, "and I'd recommend that you decide to stay, because you're going to have no luck at all getting another job with this business following you around."

"Who the hell is Dr. Vivaldi?" Kassler asked.

"I didn't talk to him," Zelazo was disturbed by Kassler's question. "He called the chairman of the Personnel Committee. He thought you were a patient here and wanted to know how you were doing. That isn't the point, Sy. The point is that the committee wants me to dismiss you immediately, today, now."

"What did you tell them?" Kassler felt the queasiness in his stomach spreading throughout his entire body.

"I told them that they must have the wrong Dr. Kassler. I'll continue to stall them, if what you're telling me is true."

"It is, Sam, I swear it. Ten days for observation. I was tired and frightened. Both my parents had died within a few months of each other. You know that. I was alone. That was all it was."

Zelazo got up from his chair and walked over to the window, where he stared out at the frozen ground.

"You know," he said with his back to Kassler, "if the Institute finds out, they'll take away your degree. They're very strict. They make no exceptions. Then you lose your license automatically, and that's the end of it all. Your career is over."

Kassler held on to the arms of his chair and shook. Zelazo turned and looked at him.

"And there won't be a damn thing I or anyone else can do to save you," he told Kassler solemnly. "It may take a few years with hearings and appeals, but once the Institute knows, you can only prolong the result, not change it."

Kassler looked numbly at Sam Zelazo.

"Who the hell is Dr. Vivaldi?" was all that Kassler could think of to say, and he left Sam Zelazo's office for his home, where the landlord's thirty days' notice to vacate was awaiting him. Kassler took the bus, now that his car had been repossessed.

The thought of Sam Zelazo, who was sexually relating to Kassler's ex-wife with great frequency these days, trying to save Kassler's neck was almost more than Kassler could tolerate. On the bus ride home, he tried desperately to think of an alternative. None occurred. Kassler realized, with a panic that was beyond any fear he had ever experienced, that he was permanently entombed in Citadel with no chance for salvation.

"I'm going to burn your wick off," the rasping voice told Kassler over the telephone, when Kassler finally arrived at his apartment that evening.

"Who is this?" Kassler asked into the instrument.

"See how it feels to have a broken pecker, Dr. Kassler."

"Norman?" Kassler began to recognize the voice.

"I'm going to pull your pecker off, Dr. K.," Norman breathed into his end of the phone. "You won't know when. You won't know how. I saw you get on the bus today. I know where you get off. I know the streets you walk home."

"Norman, why don't we make an appointment so we can talk about this?"

"I'm going to cut off your cock, Dr. Kassler, you fucking son-of-a-bitch," and Norman Meltz hung up.

Marty Myers called Kassler late the next day after Kassler's frantic, nearly incoherent call the previous evening.

"Okay," he said. "Here it all is. You can't get your car back unless you pay the balance owed, which is about three thousand dollars. Finance companies have a right to call in the full balance at any time. They usually don't. With you they did. There's nothing you can do but pay them. Otherwise they keep the car.

"The bank can close out your account if they want. When you open an account there, you sign a paper allowing them to do that for any reason whatsoever, including none. There's nothing you can do.

"Your landlord, on thirty days' notice, can ask you to vacate. You're a tenant at will. You have no alternative but to move out. You don't have a lease. There's nothing you can do.

"Bankcard can take away your charge card at any time for any reason. You also signed that. They don't have to tell you why. There's nothing you can do.

"Phlegethon can dismiss you for supplying material misinformation. A psychotherapist saying he's never been locked in a psychiatric hospital when he has been is considered material. There's nothing you can do.

"Similarly, the Institute can take away your degree if they want. Actually, it's a private institution, and as long as what they do isn't against the law, their private internal policies can be whatever they want. However, my impression so far is that you're in luck. The Institute's moving to new facilities and the entire place is in a mess. They don't even know you exist at this point, as near as I can tell, and it'll probably be a year before they can find anything. Most classes aren't even meeting, and half the faculty's on sabbatical until the move is finished. When they do find you, however, there's nothing you can do.

"The phone company says that for fifty dollars they'll change your number to a new, unlisted one, if the obscene phone calls persist. And the police have called on Norman Meltz, who says he has not talked to you even one time since he left Phlegethon and has no need for your penis in addition to his own.

"I've got to go now. Good-bye," and Marty Myers hung up without giving Kassler a chance to respond.

"This isn't working out," Kassler explained as he sat on a bench watching the people ice-skate on Lake Lethe, Citadel's man-made recreational facility, which was encircled by Ninth Avenue.

"What isn't working out?" Josh asked his father.

"These Sunday visits," Kassler explained. "Daddy doesn't even have a car anymore."

"I like the bus. It's fun," Joy said. "Can we do that again?"

"It can't be very much fun for you kids," Kassler said.

"What can't?" Joshua was not following the thrust of the argument.

"Look," Kassler decided to come right out with it. "I don't think it'd be a good idea for us to keep seeing each other every Sunday like this."

"What day, then?" Joshua looked up at his father. "Saturday? I watch cartoons Saturday morning, but maybe I could miss a *couple*."

"No day," Kassler said.

There was a long silence. Both Joshua and Joy understood Kassler perfectly.

"Okay," Joshua said, and he pursed his lips tightly together and looked away from his father.

"Okay," Joy copied her brother.

The three Kasslers sat on the bench without talking, looking across the lake at the Titan towers of Manhattan far in the distance.

"So," Kassler said at last, "what should we do? You want to rent some ice skates?"

"Go home," said Josh. "I want to go home now."

"Me, too," Joy said. "It's too cold."

Kassler reached out and turned Joshua's face toward him with a mittened hand.

"Look, Josh. I really think it'll be better this way. I can't be the father that I want to be to you. We hardly get to know each other before it's time to go. It's not fair."

"I said *okay*," Joshua yanked his face away from his father's hand.

"You kids are always bored at my apartment, and now I have to move to a new apartment, even farther away from where you live with Mommy," Kassler particularly wanted Joshua to understand.

"We used to know each other really good," Joshua looked up at his father, tiny tears running down his cheeks.

Kassler picked up Joshua and held him in his lap.

"Yes, we did," Kassler agreed. "We really did. But we don't anymore. That's just the way things happened to all of us. It isn't anyone's fault, really. We just have to accept that and start again."

Joshua tried to adjust in silence.

"I like Dr. Sam," Joshua finally said. "He's fun. Maybe he'll make me a good new daddy."

"Who is Dr. Sam?" Kassler asked.

"You know. Dr. Sam. Mommy's friend. I can't say his real name. It's something like Zoozoo. Sam Zoozoo. So Joy and I call him Dr. Sam."

Joshua could not have cleaved his father's heart more perfectly if he had been a diamond cutter. It shattered into a thousand useless pieces, leaving, at its core, the perfect glistening gem of malice.

Kassler's first instinct was to change his mind about not seeing the children again, to fight for them with all the molecules, such as they were, in his body. But on the bus ride home, he realized that it was a futile battle. If Zelazo wanted to father Kassler's children, there was no way to stop him. Except for Sundays from 11:00 a.m. to 4:00 p.m., Zelazo could see Joshua and Joy for twenty-four hours every day if he wanted. The court had put no restrictions on Sam Zelazo. As Marty Myers liked to say, Kassler thought during the walk from the bus stop to his children's home, "there's nothing you can do about it."

Kassler explained his decision briefly to Vita.

"I think that's a good idea, Sy," Vita said. "You'll adjust fine. I know you."

The sound of his two children laughing and racing around the living room as someone played with them inside the house came through the door, which was held open by Vita only a crack, so Kassler couldn't see in.

"Good-bye, Josh! Good-bye, Joy!" Kassler shouted through the small opening.

"Bye, Daddy," the two voices shouted back in the midst of playing with Dr. Sam.

Only one thought filled Kassler's brain as he left the children and walked back to the bus stop that day, tears covering his cheeks. He would kill Sam Zelazo.

As it turned out, of course, he didn't kill Sam Zelazo. Instead Kassler waited a spell and then, to help him feel better, Kassler killed someone else.

CHAPTER 2

The next eighteen months went by like a door opening and closing. Closed, it was February 1975, and then, as Kassler reached to open it and walk through the portal, it was a blistering hot day in August 1976.

Most of the men associated with the third-rate burglary at the Watergate were now receiving their just punishments in the recreational facilities of exclusive penal institutions. The U.S.

government had decided its citizens were no longer necessary to keep the southeastern corner of the world from falling like a line of dominoes into the dreaded clutches of the people who lived there. A grand jury in Ohio had decided that the shootings at Kent State were nobody's fault. The American Legion got hit by its very own disease in a Philadelphia hotel that thereafter ceased to exist. The U.S. Supreme Court announced that there was nothing cruel and unusual that *they* could find in the death penalty. And Mr. Ford battled Mr. Carter for who would be the next man to rule Paradise.

In those same eighteen months, Kassler had maintained the framework of a professional relationship with Sam Zelazo, who continued to hold off the Personnel Committee from firing Kassler, insisting he himself would make an investigation of the charges against Kassler.

Kassler had not seen his children a single time in these eighteen months and felt he was, at last, beginning to adjust. Nor had Kassler seen Lupa, whose thriving interior-design business occupied virtually all of her time.

Norman Meltz, over this period, would go through a week of calls threatening Kassler, followed by several months of silence, until the next bout. Kassler had gotten used to this, too, as he had to the persistence with which banks seemed to close out his accounts once they learned about his other accounts' having been closed in the past, and they always did find out, Kassler assumed through the financial grapevine.

As for the grapevine, once he discovered that Kassler and Lupa were no longer an item, he cut his calls against his former psychotherapist, now in his fourth apartment, to a few a day. Though Szlyck had long ago run out of explosives, his drinking maintained itself at or above past levels, and his body began to swell perceptibly as his skin turned amber.

During the year and a half, Kassler had not managed to muster the nerve to sign the papers withdrawing his court petition for extended visitation. He wasn't sure why, but as the court date grew nearer, he felt even less inclined to do so.

"Maybe I just want my day in court," he told Bernie Kohler late one night. "I have a lot to say."

"Or maybe you just love your kids," Bernie Kohler suggested.

To support himself, Kassler worked at Phlegethon during the day, and evenings he worked at home for a company that provided term papers to students without the intelligence or incentive to do college coursework but with large amounts of money to indulge their sloth and stupidity. Kassler got five dollars a page, and the firm that hired him got ten dollars. Kassler could knock off two twenty-page psychology papers during the week, and a third on the weekend. By not informing the Internal Revenue Service of his extracurricular activities, Kassler had stashed over ten thousand dollars in cash on his shelves, inside a hollowed-out book whose name I will leave the reader to guess.

Phlegethon, in the meantime, had been distributed in small pieces throughout Citadel as Phase One of the great court-ordered exodus neared completion. Six hundred psychotic patients had been assembled in groups of four and placed into one hundred fifty special community apartments, changing the previous population of Phlegethon from one thousand to just under twelve hundred.

"I don't understand it," Bernie Kohler said as he looked through the foot-high stacks of folders in front of him, "we send them out, and six months later they come back, and then we send them out again, and then they come back, and all the time new people keep coming in."

"Just think how many we'd have if we hadn't discharged six hundred of them," Kassler remarked.

"Well," Bernie sighed, "I'm afraid there's only one solution."

"I don't think I want to hear," Bea said from where she sat, hot and exhausted from her day, drinking a can of flat soda in the corner.

"I'm going to ask the court to cut off all admissions," Bernie announced.

"Oh, I like that," Bea said incredulously.

"Terrific idea," Kassler agreed facetiously. "Send them all out, and if they can't handle it, that's their problem."

"Exactly," Bernie said with great determination. "Once they know that out there is all there is, they'll adjust."

"Maybe that's the problem," Kassler suggested.

"What?" Bernie became defensive. "What problem? What are you saying?"

"They already know that."

"*Know what?*" Bernie exploded.

Kassler smiled benignly.

"That out there is all there is," he said very calmly.

"You've got to be kidding," Mr. Katzman told Kassler during their session.

"I'm afraid not," Kassler responded. "It's your turn. You're next on the list. It's time for you to go."

"Not good odds," Mr. Katzman started.

"The law of averages isn't going to help you very much this time," Kassler tried to explain to the elderly man, who sat anxiously drumming his fingers on the arm of the wooden chair in which he sat. "Your number is up."

"Send me out and I'll come right back," Mr. Katzman ran his thumb over his fingertips and tried not to look at Kassler.

"That eventuality is being taken care of, too, Mr. Katzman. Before long, unless I miss my guess, there will be no more admissions to Phlegethon," Kassler said.

"What will you do, turn me away? I'm a crazy person, Dr. Kassler. I need help. I can't live out there. It's too much for me. You can understand that."

"What is so *horrible*, Mr. Katzman? It's true, people are injured, people become diseased, and people even die. But we make do in the world. What frightens you so? I can't believe that it's food additives and nuclear-generated electricity. What is it?" Kassler asked in the heat that smothered his tiny non-air-conditioned office this August afternoon.

"I've seen too much," Mr. Katzman answered as he flicked beads of perspiration from his upper lip with his tongue.

"What have you seen?" Kassler asked.

Mr. Katzman thought for a moment.

"Broken hearts," he finally told Kassler.

"You have lost someone dear to you?" Kassler tried to recall the history section of Mr. Katzman's case folder.

"Broken hearts," Mr. Katzman continued. "And for each heart that has broken, mine has cracked just a little."

"There are some very sad and tragic things in life," Kassler said, "but we all—"

"Broken hearts," Mr. Katzman said. "You don't understand about broken hearts."

"We all adjust to these sorts—"

"I'm not talking about boys being jilted at the altar by their brides, or mothers and fathers being rejected by their own children."

"The death of someone who is very close to us—"

"I'm not talking about the death of husbands and wives and sons and daughters and lovers and friends, from cancer and heart disease and car accidents."

There was a long silence. Kassler took some tissues from the box beside him and wiped the sticky perspiration from his forehead. A few flies came in the open window, buzzed about noisily as they tried to find their way back out, and left through another small window.

"I have seen," Mr. Katzman began, "men who have been made to watch their wives being raped by dozens of men. Many husbands made to watch. Many times."

Kassler said nothing.

"I have seen women who have been made to watch their small daughters being raped and then chopped up alive like chickens, one finger, one toe, one limb at a time."

Kassler tried to close his eyes to avoid the description, but closing his eyes made the picture more vivid than ever.

"I have seen men who have had their testicles sliced off them and stuffed in their mouths, and then their penis, and then their ears and nose. There was, of course, no anesthesia."

Kassler looked at his watch to see how much time was left to the session. More than ten minutes.

"I have seen men and women set on fire with gasoline. I have seen people disemboweled while they were alive. I have seen men's eyes gouged out of their sockets and tire irons pounded in their one ear and out the other, tortures performed that people have not yet had in nightmares, tortures with acid and electricity and razorblades in them, on their wives and husbands, on their children. I have seen a young Jewish boy, no more than twenty-five, handsome and proud and sensitive with bright eyes and the hands of an artist, who was sat down in front of a silver platter. Every fifteen minutes another officer would shit on the plate and the boy had to eat it all, with a fork and a knife, to keep his wife and two babies from being tortured to death. The boy ate for two days until he lost consciousness and then my son and his family were all buried alive."

"You have been in a concentration camp?" Kassler asked when he managed to talk.

"I have been around," Mr. Katzman answered.

"These are exceptions—"

"No," Mr. Katzman closed his eyes and shook his head. "These are the rule. *We* are the exception."

Mr. Katzman paused to see whether his words had their desired effect. They had.

"I make jokes now, Dr. Kassler. I fool about the radiation from the television, or lightning, or meteors that fall from the sky, or tripping on stairs and changing light bulbs, little things to worry about. It helps me pass the time in an amusing way. It fills my mind with other things."

"But you did function at one time," Kassler remembered out loud. "What changed that?"

"Tell me. Do you think these men who did these things were crazy, Dr. Kassler? Were they all madmen? Answer me that."

"Some probably were," Kassler answered.

"Some, but not most," Mr. Katzman told Kassler. "The men at Nuremberg were not put in mental institutions. They were put in jail. This is correct, yes? They were mostly sane men?"

"Many seem to have been. It's a very complicated issue," Kassler said.

"Relax, Dr. Kassler," Mr. Katzman said. "It's not so complicated. I'll tell you why. Am I sane? What do you think? Do

I *look* sane, *talk* sane, *behave* sane, more or less? What do you say?"

"Yes. I think so."

"Then that's why I'm here," Mr. Katzman explained with a strange logic. "Once I realized that I was perfectly sane, I put myself away. You see, Dr. Kassler, every one of those terrible things I described to you has fascinated me. Once I realized that there was some part of me that absolutely enjoyed seeing every one of those horrible things, learning about them, reliving them, it broke my heart, and without any heart at all we are dangerous men, don't you think, Dr. Kassler?"

"Do you really believe you're capable of doing any of those things?" Kassler asked the short, white-haired, elderly man who sat across from him, nervously twitching his fingers.

"Yes," Mr. Katzman answered solemnly. "Absolutely. And what's more, I would *enjoy* it."

"He's just trying to scare you," Bernie Kohler told Kassler over beers later that week.

"I didn't get that sense," Kassler told Bernie.

"Well, he's no mad butcher of Buchenwald," Bernie responded. "I know Katzman. He'll tell you anything to stay."

"You want to take responsibility for his release? It's fine with me," Kassler offered. "I'm in enough trouble already as it is."

"I'll think about it," Bernie said, and then, changing the subject, "I don't know what keeps you around here. You should've left a year ago."

"I don't know, either," Kassler admitted. "Inertia. I'm kind of stuck here. I don't know where else I'd go. I don't know what else I'd do. I've gotten used to this place—Zelazo, Bea, my patients, moving to a new apartment every three months, even you, Bernie."

"I was going to talk to you about that," Bernie said and took a long drink of beer to get his nerve up. "I've got something I've wanted to say to you for some time now, and I'd like you to hear me out before you answer, okay?"

"Okay."

"Well," Bernie began, and then said nothing more.

Kassler waited and drank his beer.

"Jesus, this is hard," Bernie said. "Okay. Here's how it goes, Sy. I like you. I like you a whole lot, and I'd like to see whether we could take our relationship further."

Kassler stopped drinking and put down his glass very slowly. He looked at Bernie's nervous eyes and he tried desperately to think of how to react without hurting Bernie's feelings.

"Now, hear me out," Bernie said before Kassler could say anything. "Homosexual relationships aren't what you think. Gays don't run around picking up a different guy every night, any more than men do with women, or at least those gays who do that are like those men who do that with women. Most of the time we look for someone special, and it isn't all sex. We want a whole relationship, a companion and a friend and a partner, just like any good close relationship. Now, most guys who've never had a gay relationship think that the sex won't be good, but they're wrong, Sy. They're dead wrong."

Kassler shook his head sadly.

"No, Bernie, I'm flattered, but no. I'm sorry," Kassler said.

"Now, wait a minute. You said you'd hear me out. Men having sex can be tender and gentle and very sensual. Believe me, there's absolutely nothing you can do with a woman, except get her pregnant, that you can't do with another man, and I've tried men and women. What's different is that another man knows what it's like to be a man and can make you feel very good, much better than a woman can ever understand how to do. I know. When I started having gay relationships, the thought of sex really turned me off, but once you've done it you're over the hurdle, and you'll never regret it. It's a magnificent world," Bernie stopped, out of breath, and looked hopefully at Kassler.

"Phil left, huh?" Kassler asked.

"Last month," Bernie answered. "It's been very hard for me, Sy. I need someone. I don't do well alone. You're a terrific guy. Really. I think we've got real magic, you and me, Sy."

"You're kidding yourself, Bernie," Kassler tried another approach. "We haven't agreed on one thing since we've known each other."

"And look how well we get along," Bernie turned it around.

"We could be very good for each other, Sy. *You* don't have anyone. Now *I* don't. We both lead the same kind of life, keep the same schedule. We understand what a man needs. Women don't, Sy. Think about it. Think about Vita and Lupa and everyone else you've had a relationship with. Women just don't understand what a man needs to be happy."

"I like our relationship the way it is, Bernie. Really. I just wouldn't enjoy that kind of relationship with another man. I'm not made like that. Honest to God." Kassler took a very long drink of a very small amount of beer.

"Promise me this, Sy. Just promise me this. You'll think about it. Maybe try it just once, just to see how it goes. Think about it, anyway. Promise me that. As friends, okay? As friends? Think about it. One evening. One night. Then, if it doesn't work, it doesn't. I'll never mention it again. You'll think about it, okay?"

"Okay," Kassler sighed against his better judgment. "I'll think about it."

"We don't have to have sex right away. We could work up to that. I'll take you along very slowly."

"I said okay, I'll think about it," Kassler smiled, still trying not to hurt Bernie's feelings. "Now you can do something for me, okay?"

"Anything, Sy. Name it."

"I released Mr. Katzman today anyway, because that's what we agreed. But I'd like you to take responsibility for it. Otherwise, I'm bringing him back."

"Sure," Bernie beamed graciously. "Anybody asks, I'll say you refused to release him and I overruled you. How's that?"

"Superb."

"Where'd you place him?"

"It was Katzman's idea. A former patient who was looking for a roommate. Said he was lonely. I doubt it, but the two should get along just fine. They struck up a good relationship when they were here together."

"Don't tell me," Bernie grinned.

"Right. Leo Szlyck," and Kassler and Bernie had a good hard laugh to break the tension.

*   *   *

The heat of the summer seemed to last indefinitely, well into the fall. Kassler endured it as though it were a just punishment for whatever transgressions, he now assumed, he must surely have committed. Otherwise, there was no way to explain his ill-fated life, Kassler concluded on a number of occasions as he worked late at night in his basement apartment, typing another of many term papers on Piaget's theory of the development of concrete operational thought in human children.

Hot weather in Citadel, Kassler had learned, was not like hot weather as he had ever experienced it before. The heat had suffocating humidity combined with a temperature high enough to scorch and burn. Insects multiplied in great numbers in the marshes near Fifth Avenue and inundated Citadel, feeding on human flesh whenever available. Rivers ran blood-thick with sludge. The fumes from automobiles, factories, and the garbage dumps settled a heavy putrid smog permanently on the city, choking people who found it necessary to be outdoors for even brief periods of time. And the nights were worst of all, since the heat, humidity, and carnivorous insects persisted in the dark, even without the blazing sun, and were joined by thousands of exasperated short-tempered people, screaming their lungs out at one another throughout the sleepless night.

It was in this atmosphere that a group of outraged Citadel citizens met one sweltering October afternoon with Bea, Kassler, and Bernie Kohler, who was still imploring Kassler to keep an open mind about his recent proposition.

"One of those crazy people you let out of your nuthouse came into my store last week," a pudgy woman barked out in the small, crowded meeting room the local elementary school had provided, "and bought *forty* boxes of *Quaker Oats! Forty boxes!* Well, of course, I told him that I have *other* customers. It isn't fair to *them*. And you know what he did? He started crying like a baby and telling me about his bowels He says, real loud so everyone in the whole store can hear, 'I can't move my bowels without Quaker Oats. I need them to move my bowels.' That's what he says. He talks about *shitting*, right there out loud in the middle of my grocery store. Crying. Begging. Talking about his bowels. So I let him have the forty boxes.

But no more! That's the last time! He doesn't belong out here. You've got to lock that man back up."

Several other voices rang out together, and finally one small lady with her hair in curlers under a thin dark scarf prevailed.

"I have an eight-year-old daughter. Last week, my daughter goes to the playground down the street. She's been doing this for years now. There's never been any trouble. Now, I'm not prejudiced. Crazy people have rights just like the rest of us. But when I walk past the playground, Lola's got a new playmate. It's a forty-five-year-old lunatic. He's pushing her on the swings and riding with her on the teeter-totter and going on the slide with her. Now, I'm not prejudiced. I've said that. But who knows what he'll do next? First it's how about a push on the swings so he can feel her little fanny, and then he can't control himself and he's off in the woods with her. It hasn't happened yet. But I know what urges men get, and I have no intention of waiting until he gets one. He pushes her on those swings again, and I'm calling the police. I mean it."

"He's employed by the recreation department to safeguard—" but Kassler was cut off by the loud clamor as irate citizens fought to be heard.

"I run a pharmacy," shouted out a bald man with thick glasses and bleary eyes beneath them. "One of them comes in and wants a bottle of pink stuff. What the hell is *pink stuff*? It took me fifteen minutes to find out it was Pepto-Bismol. He hadn't even *heard* of Pepto-Bismol. I don't have the time to play guessing games with every crazy person who walks into my store. I just don't have the time."

"Now, I've got nothing against crazy people, but I'm trying to sell my home," a large black man shouted. "It's all I've got. Every person who calls wants to know the same thing: how many of *them* are there in the neighborhood. I can't sell my house because we've got twelve of them within two blocks."

"On our block," said a crabby elderly woman with a thick Mediterranean accent, "they *skip*. They *hold hands* and *skip* down the street. It's disgraceful They're *adults*, and they *skip*."

"If crazy people want to be crazy, that's their own business," a burly man with large hairy arms shouted from the back of the room, his face red with anger. "But not in my goddamn neighborhood! I'm not having some raving lunatic lose control of himself and bash someone's head!" The man crashed his fist down on a desk in front of him, splintering off a large section. "These people can't control themselves! Lock 'em up!" he yelled.

There was a loud chorus of huzzahs! and right-ons! and you-tell-'ems!

"It's not only the violence," a young woman yelled from the back of the packed room. "But now we live next door to a purple-and-pink house! With yellow flowers painted all over it! It's like a giant Easter basket! We live next door to a giant Easter basket!"

Bea Chaikin started to say something, but Bernie beat her to it.

"I *hate* you people," Bernie glowered and yelled loudly, his typical approach to calming an angry mob, while Bea tried to restrain him. "You're vermin, parasites, heartless sons-a-bitches—"

And from there it got worse. The room became Bedlam, as hot, sweaty, frustrated, frightened, angry men and women shouted obscenities until it was more than Kassler could stand, and he left to see whether he could find better air in the slightly cooler marble-floored corridors of the school building.

For several minutes he wandered in the dim light until he came to an auditorium where the children were having an assembly. He opened the door, slipped inside, and stood in the back, watching two small children who were standing on the stage performing in the stultifying heat. Their hair was dirty and matted. Dark smudges of dirt covered their faces. The boy's pants were worn through the knees. The girl's dress was dirty and the collar was coming off the top.

"Oh, beautiful, for spacious skies, for amber waves of grain . . ." their tiny voices sang to the other schoolchildren, as they held hands.

Kassler couldn't stand to see how thin Josh and Joy had become over the last year and a half. He stood in the back of the auditorium, buried his face in his hands, and, as they sang, wept with all his heart.

Then, when they were finished, he clapped loudly and whistled and yelled their names. Joshua and Joy recognized their father immediately and ran to the back of the auditorium, where they threw themselves into his arms.

"Oh, Daddy!" Joshua wept. "I *knew* someone would come to hear us sing. I knew you'd come," he cried while his sister hugged her father around the neck, repeating again and again, "Daddy, I miss you. I miss you too much, Daddy."

CHAPTER 3

It has never been clear to me whose idea it was to burn down the building in which Kassler had his small apartment, Katzman's or Szlyck's. The discussion about setting the place on fire had been going on for several days, since Katzman moved in, and my suggestions to the contrary were of no use whatsoever. Their minds were made up.

"So what does it get you?" I asked the deadly duo. "Another misfortune for a man who's already had more than his quota. Big deal. It won't get Lupa back. It won't change Kassler."

"It's a lesson," Szlyck told me.

"What lesson?" I asked. "What kind of lesson? He won't even know who did it and why."

"The man has it coming," Katzman proclaimed. "I told him. I gave him fair warning."

"What? Told him what? Those terrible tales you made up to torture the poor man?" I asked. "You make up some dreadful story about a son you never had eating shit until he passes out, and now Kassler knows that you're going to torch his home?"

"The stories are true!" Katzman protested.

"Not for you they aren't. Those are other people's horrors which you've read in Sunday supplements. You have no right to claim them as your own. It's a sacrilege."

"And look who's talking!" Katzman bellowed. Szlyck had given Katzman the full particulars about me long ago when they were roommates at Phlegethon.

"I'm trying to be reasonable," I explained. "Write him a letter. Make him a phone call. Spray filthy words about him on a bridge or a building. Start rumors. But I'm against the use of fire."

"He really *wants* us to do it," Szlyck told Katzman. "Otherwise he wouldn't be making such a business of it."

"Oh, I give up," I gave up.

"You see," Szlyck nodded to Katzman.

The results were predictable and devastating. Late one evening, Katzman and Szlyck took one can of gasoline, one bath towel, and one pack of matches, and Kassler's building went up like an old Christmas tree.

Kassler, along with the other three tenants in the building, was fortunately not at home. But everything that Kassler owned in the world, all uninsured, including a special edition of *La Divina Commedia*, appropriately abridged by Kassler so as to hold just over ten thousand dollars in cash, *was* at home and completely destroyed.

Kassler hardly looked. He had been having dinner and his usual beers out with Bernie, and, when he got off the bus, he stepped over the hoses that tangled at his feet like snakes, looked around the hook-and-ladder fire engine that obscured his view, saw that there was nothing left but smoldering rubble in what had once been his home, shrugged, turned, and walked back to his bus stop with no more apparent concern than if a film he'd expected to find at the local movie house had ended the previous night.

Kassler didn't really know where he was going when the bus finally arrived and he boarded. He sat alone in the back of the fluorescently lit vehicle, which streaked through the hot steamy night like an electric eel on an aimless journey, and he let the humid air, blowing in the open window beside him, evaporate some of the perspiration which soaked his forehead. When he saw a lit-up phone booth ahead, he pulled the cord to stop the bus and disembarked.

For a half-hour Kassler stood at the phone dropping in dimes, trying to find a place to stay for the night. Bea's phone was busy, a result, he decided, of having a teen-age daughter. Other likely candidates were not at home, including, as a next-to-last resort, Lupa.

Finally, Kassler gave up and walked the five streets necessary to call on the very last resort.

"Everything I own has been burned to a crisp, and I need a place to stay," Kassler said when the door opened. "But I have to make something very clear. It's just to sleep, that's all, and, if you think there'll be a problem, I'll go somewhere else."

"I only have one double bed," Bernie Kohler told Kassler. "It makes it easier for some people when there's no sofa, so I deliberately didn't get one, but I'll leave you alone. I promise. I won't do anything you don't feel comfortable about."

"Nothing. I just need to talk and sleep. That's all. I've only got twelve dollars to my name," Kassler said.

"I'll loan you whatever you need," Bernie Kohler said.

Kassler stood out in the hall and looked at Bernie to see whether he could trust him. Then he shrugged and sighed.

"I'm taking an advance against my salary tomorrow," Kassler said as he entered the tastefully decorated apartment, *sans* sofa. "I'll pay it back over the next couple months."

"Phlegethon stopped giving advances two months ago. The state says it's illegal. I'll loan you the money, don't worry. What happened?"

Kassler looked silently at Bernie for several minutes. He wasn't really sure about what had happened, about the details. He wasn't even aware how he felt. Sad? Angry? Depressed? He didn't know. He had no money. No home. None of the clothes or books or records or memorabilia that had accumulated over his lifetime. There was, he felt, absolutely nothing remaining, other than Josh and Joy, to show for the thirty-six years he had graced my domain. In those days, the distinction between matter and spirit was no big deal for Dr. Kassler. All he really knew for certain was that everything he owned had gone up in flames.

"You boys are incorrigible," I told the two proud arsonists when they returned.

"You should have seen it," Katzman was very excited. "It went up like a tinderbox, like tissue paper. Poof! Thirty seconds! The place was like an inferno. You really should've been there."

"And you, Leo?" I asked. "Are you pleased with yourself?"

"I'm not feeling so good," Szlyck answered.

"He could hardly strike the match," Katzman said. "But it was worth it, wasn't it? So much for psychotherapy, and wife snatchers, and Kassler. Right, Leo?"

"I don't feel so good tonight," Szlyck repeated.

Leo Szlyck bore a striking resemblance, in shape and color, to a gourd.

"I think this is it, Leo," I told him as forthrightly as I could.

"I'm dying, aren't I?" Szlyck asked.

"No, Leo, you're mostly dead. You passed the dying stage several months ago. I told you that."

"You're going out in a blaze of glory, Leo." Katzman always had a way with metaphors.

"I don't feel so hot," Szlyck said once again.

"I don't suppose you do," I said. "I wish there were something I could do, but I can't. I'm afraid it's all over."

"I'm not sure I got out of my life all that I wanted," Leo philosophized. Then he started bawling like a baby.

"Oh, God," he said, "forgive me. I didn't know what I was doing. I tried. I did."

"Don't you start this God business with me, damn it, Leo," I told Szlyck. "I've listened to your babbling for years now. I advised you against marrying Lupa. I tried to tell you that your drinking would kill you. You knew *exactly* what you were doing, and you didn't try one damn bit. So you can cut out the repentance crap. I've lived with you."

"I was *led* astray," Szlyck called out to the ceiling above him.

"Get him out of here, will you?" I asked Katzman.

"But I *do* repent. I *repent*," Szlyck whined. "I also don't feel so hot," and he crumpled to his knees in pain.

It was, I admit, a pitiful sight. Bloated, whining, agonized, Leo Szlyck was as unappealing as I have ever seen him. It's at times like this that I try to look for something about a man that will give his soul a tragic aspect, something to lament and mourn, make him greater than he actually was or unavoidably less than he might have been, in order to bestow some sympathy on him in his final moments. For Leo Szlyck, this was not an easy task.

"I *have* made some great inroads in physics," Leo Szlyck tried to tote up his own chart from where he lay in a clump on the floor.

"Minor," I noted, "and already in question."

"I got *you* here. And I haven't blown you up," Leo reminded me.

"An accident. And you forgot about getting percussion caps," I answered. "Most people set off this *meshugass* with percussion caps and a detonator, not with a match."

"Oh," said Leo meekly.

"I'm calling an ambulance," Katzman went upstairs to the phone.

"Is there something I can do to make amends?" Leo begged.

I thought he'd never ask.

"Just one thing." I told him the details at some length.

"I'll do it. I promise," Szlyck said, and I knew he would.

We could hear the ambulance arriving. Leo staggered to his feet and headed up the stairs.

"One question," Leo Szlyck said as he neared the top of the steps. "I have to ask. Tell me the truth, please."

There was a pause as Leo gasped in considerable pain and then let out a deep breath.

"Tell me," he asked in agony. "Is there really a hell?"

"Yes, Leo," I answered. "There is a hell."

"Oh, shit," were Leo Szlyck's last words on earth to me.

Of course, Leo Szlyck did not just go about dying in a basic, simple, and forthright terminal manner. Leo manufactured a great production, calling to his deathbed Sam Zelazo, Lupa, and, finally, Kassler, in that order, for a magnificent final performance with appropriate curtain calls. Knowing that he would find his audience most gullible as he lay withering like a lotus blossom before them, Leo Szlyck led them all to believe that, in the last few minutes left to him, he would like to find true tranquillity by making amends and wiping the slate clean. For such a *tabula rasa*, Leo Szlyck would have needed a chalk eraser the length of the Great Wall and the Mongol hordes to labor with it through several dynasties.

These theatrics, however, were all still to come when Kassler, exhausted and feeling desperately alone, finally fell down fully clothed on the far edge of Bernie Kohler's bed and attempted to get to sleep, without success.

Bernie reclined on his side of the bed, in his pajama bottoms, trying to catch as much as possible of the thin breeze that came from the small window fan by Kassler's side of the bed.

"You're never going to sleep in this heat like that," Bernie said. "There're some pajama bottoms in my top drawer. I told you I wouldn't attack you, and I won't."

"Okay," Kassler agreed and went into the john, where he changed into a pair of red polyester pajama bottoms.

"I feel like a Turkish waiter in these things," Kassler told Bernie when he returned. "Don't you have anything in cotton?"

"Not much," Bernie told Kassler, as he watched Kassler walk across the room. "You'll get used to them. Incidentally, don't go crazy, but you take good care of yourself. That's not a proposition, just a comment from someone who notices those things."

"Thank you, and let's not get going with this stuff again. I really need to get some sleep. So do you. Good night."

Neither Kassler nor Bernie Kohler had much luck going to sleep. For Kassler, the problem was the heat, the strange bed, his evaporating life, and Bernie Kohler. For Bernie Kohler, it was the heat, and Sy Kassler.

"I can't sleep," Kassler finally said about three in the morning when he noticed that Bernie was still awake. "You got any sedatives?"

"No, but if you don't get hysterical, I'll give you a massage. Top only. It works every time," Bernie answered.

Kassler thought very carefully about the consequences. Every muscle in his body was in rigid spasm. He knew a rubdown would help, if he could control Bernie Kohler. Maybe, Kassler thought, it'd work out. Bernie seemed to have this great need to touch him and Kassler needed his muscles relaxed. It was worth a try. He could stop at the first sign that it was anything more than a massage.

"No funny business?" Kassler asked.

"No, dear. No funny business. Turn over on your tummy," Bernie said sweetly.

Bernie's massage was excellent. Kassler felt his entire body relax, as Bernie kneaded his shoulders and back, and Kassler slowly felt himself drifting off to sleep, to a glorious dream, a land of paradise, with lush tropical vegetation, lots of pineapples and bananas, cool tradewinds that wafted off the purple sea, glistening white sandy beaches, chocolate-skinned girls, and coconut oils that they rubbed over his body. A naked girl with ripe breasts and dark trim thighs came up to him and led him to a cove where she fed him mangoes and papayas and kissed him gently over his body until she reached his crotch. Then she took his cock, which was hard and aching, into her mouth and sucked it down to the bottom of the shaft, licking it with her tongue, running her lips up and over the rim with incredibly gentle and sensitive movements until Kassler couldn't stand it any longer and awakened to find himself coming in Bernie Kohler's mouth while Bernie simultaneously ejaculated himself by hand onto the sheets. It took a minute before Kassler fully realized what had happened.

"Now, was that so terrible?" Bernie Kohler asked as he pulled up his pajama bottoms and went over to lie on his side of the bed. "Tell me that you've ever had a woman who's made you feel like that."

Kassler was going to answer but decided against it. He was still nine-tenths asleep, and the combination of the massage, the dream, and the orgasm had relaxed him too much for him to start an argument. There was no sense leaving the bed. It was all over. Besides, Kassler had nowhere to go. He just wanted to sleep.

"Umh," Kassler mumbled noncommittally and fell instantly back to sleep.

"Umm is right," answered Bernie Kohler, flushed with the victory of a new conquest. "I told you we had magic."

When Kassler awakened, Bernie had already left. A note from Bernie informed Kassler that fresh orange juice was in a glass on the table, coffee was in an automatic coffee maker, and eggs and toast had been made for him and placed in a small warming oven.

Kassler decided that his ordeal and what he knew would follow were worth at least a good breakfast, so he partook of it all. On a full stomach, well rested and four hours late for work, he headed through the continuing heat for Phlegethon and Bernie Kohler, who, he learned, had called in sick for the day. This sounded like an excellent idea to Kassler, who was about to notify the administrator of his own incipient malady when an urgent phone call beckoned him to Phlegethon's infirmary. There, unbeknownst to Kassler, lay the dying Leo Szlyck.

When Kassler arrived at the door to the infirmary, Zelazo was already at the foot of Szlyck's bed, shouting to him in Rumanian. Kassler stood outside watching for several minutes until finally Zelazo threw up his arms in a wild burst of anger and strode furiously from the room.

"He wants to talk to Lupa and then to you," Zelazo told Kassler abruptly.

"What's wrong with him?" Kassler asked.

"He's got about ten percent of his liver left. The rest he drank up. It's dissolved in alcohol," Zelazo said, still fuming.

"What made you so angry?" Kassler asked.

"Leo Szlyck. Take my advice, Sy. Whatever he gives you, don't take it. It's not worth it." Zelazo had fire in his eyes.

"What's he want to give me?"

"Whatever it is, don't listen to him. The man's dying. He doesn't know what he's saying." Zelazo was more upset than Kassler had ever seen him. "Besides, I trained you. You owe it to me. Come to me first. I'll make you a very attractive offer."

"What the hell is going on?" Kassler asked.

"Remember, Sy, he's crazy."

"Is he going to live?"

Zelazo shrugged. "We can't give him any medication because he doesn't have enough of a liver to detoxify it. It'd kill him. He's got bad ascites. We're using paracentesis to drain out the fluid from his abdominal cavity, but not fast enough. It's probably just a matter of time before he swells to death. He's bleeding from esophageal and gastric varices, and since we can't give him medication, he's also bleeding to death. He's got flapping tremors in his hands, so his brain is involved. To sum up, Leo Szlyck is a terminal mess. I have to go," Zelazo told Kassler and headed down the hall, passing Lupa, who was walking toward where Kassler stood outside Szlyck's room.

When she saw Kassler, she slowed her pace, aware that there was no way to avoid the meeting.

"Hello, Sy," Lupa appeared as radiant as ever to Kassler.

"Hello," Kassler answered.

"How is he?" Lupa asked.

"He's dying, Zelazo says. How've you been?"

"Oh, fine, fine. He's really dying? How about yourself?"

"Lupa?" a frail voice from the other room called out. "Is that you, Lupa?"

"Yes, it is, Leo," Lupa called back. "I'll be right there."

Then she looked into Kassler's eyes. "So, have you found magic?" she asked.

"That's what I've been told," Kassler answered. "How about you?"

"Not exactly," Lupa straightened the scarf around her neck and absently fingered an earring.

"Business going well?" Kassler looked at the deep red of Lupa's lips as she spoke.

"Lupa?" the feeble voice trailed out of the small hospital-like room.

"I'm coming, I'm coming," Lupa said.

"I'm dying," the voice noted with great pathos.

"I know," Lupa said.

"It could be any minute," the patient rasped.

"I've missed you, Lupa," Kassler said. "I would've called, but I wasn't sure you'd want me to."

"Same here," Lupa said. "I've wanted to call you. I even tried a few times. Your phone number keeps changing."

"I move a lot. You know, ever-brighter horizons."

"Lupa!" Szlyck called as loudly as he could manage. "I'm nearly dead."

"I know, I know. I said I'm coming, Leo. Now hold on. Don't die for another couple minutes," Lupa called back.

"I'll try, I'll try," the patient answered courageously.

"Come over tonight and I'll make you chicken something-or-other, Sy. If you're not busy?" Lupa asked nervously.

Kassler looked at Lupa's violet eyes and thought about how he had no money and no place to live. He smiled and accepted Lupa's invitation.

"I had a strange experience last night, and I wonder whether you might do me a favor?" Kassler asked.

Lupa looked into Kassler's dark eyes and waited in the silence, broken only by a thin voice wafting out of the room in front of them.

"I feel myself beginning to hover," it said. "I see a bright light at the end of a tunnel."

"Would you kiss me?" Kassler asked.

"Don't you want to taste my chicken first?" Lupa asked.

"I've already tasted your chicken. It's fair," and Kassler and Lupa kissed with great tenderness and affection.

"A warm glow," the patient anounced. "Hovering. Hovering. Lupa? I don't *want* to hover."

"Hold on to the bed frame and you won't hover," Lupa called back. "So?" she asked Kassler. "How's magic?"

"It's about like your chicken," Kassler decided out loud.

"And?"

"And someday I'd like to live *fairly* happily ever after. But," Kassler couldn't get the incident with Bernie Kohler out of his head, "there may be some complications."

"Is your court business over?" Lupa asked.

"Hasn't even started. How about yours?" Kassler asked.

"Leo still hasn't made it to court. He also hasn't withdrawn the motion contesting the Mexican divorce. Of course . . ."

The same idea occurred simultaneously to Kassler and Lupa, and they smiled broadly.

"... if he's dead ..." they said together.

"Fading away ... fading away ..." the faint voice issued from the room ahead.

"Coming," Lupa called back pleasantly.

While Kassler waited outside, Szlyck rambled on incoherently to Lupa about life and love.

"I want you to be happy," Szlyck said quietly. It was painful for him to talk.

"I *am* happy," Lupa said.

"You shouldn't have to go around miserable on my account," Szlyck said.

"And I'm not," Lupa answered. "I'm very happy."

"Tell me honestly, Lupa, when we first met, before everything went wrong, did you find me attractive?" Szlyck asked.

"Attractive?" Lupa thought out loud. "No, Leo, not attractive."

"Appealing, then?" Szlyck asked.

"No. Not appealing."

"Charming?"

"Not charming, either."

"Then what?" Szlyck asked. "There must've been something."

"I don't think there was, Leo. I'm sorry, but I think honesty is the best policy at these times. I wouldn't want you to depart this world with any misconceptions. The truth is that, other than your being the owner of that computer, I do not for the life of me know what I saw in you," Lupa told Leo Szlyck with great frankness. "I think I was just lonely and desperate and you were there."

"Then tell me this. I know I can count on your honesty," Szlyck began again.

"You can count on it," Lupa affirmed.

"I'm very ashamed of how I treated you. Do you forgive me?"

Lupa looked at Leo Szlyck lying on his deathbed, tubes feeding into his arms and draining his abdomen, his normally yellowish skin now the color of cheap mustard, his entire body swollen up like the inflated figures that, as a little girl, she used to watch being pulled on strings in Macy's Thanksgiving Day Parade.

"Do you forgive me?" Szlyck repeated. "For driving you crazy while we were married, and the letters and phone calls afterwards . . ."

"No, Leo, I don't. I don't forgive you."

"I didn't think you would," Szlyck nodded. "Neither did Sam Zelazo," Szlyck tried to speak from lower down in his chest, where it caused him less pain.

"What did you do to him?" Lupa asked.

"Something not very nice," Szlyck admitted. "It's all very complicated, but basically what I did is this. We were very close in Rumania, and we fell in love with two sisters, so we had a double wedding. Just before the ceremony, I decided I liked his bride much better than mine. So I switched brides."

"You what?" Lupa asked in disbelief.

"It wasn't easy, believe me. But borrowing a little Shakespeare, a little Aristophanes, and a little Mozart, I fixed it so he married the other sister, my bride, and slept with her, and after that, customs being what they were, it was too late to change, partly because I was far away someplace with his bride where he couldn't find me, and partly because he would have been killed if the girl's family ever found out. Eventually, the girl learned the truth and killed herself to spare Zelazo, who had, in the meantime, fallen madly in love with her. She thought he was pretending for her sake, and she made it look like a boating accident. It was all very tragic. Like an opera."

Lupa listened in amazement.

"How . . . how did . . ." she tried to ask.

"How did I switch brides?" Leo helped Lupa out. "Well, it wasn't easy. With lots of lies, mostly, although I don't remember the particulars. It was a very long time ago. It started to come back to me only last night. But, as I recall, I told my bride that Zelazo was deeply in love with her and I wasn't, and *his* bride that I was deeply in love with *her* and Zelazo wasn't, and both that everyone could be saved a great deal of pain by a quick switch. Since in those days in Rumania the veil stayed on until the hymen came off, no one would be the wiser until after we were all out of the country. I had to think fast. I got Sam drunk and doped. Then it happened. I did the entire business in less than an hour. Zelazo's bride really was *much* prettier than mine."

"What about your wife?" Lupa asked numbly.

"Oh, she killed herself as soon as she found out about her sister's suicide and the reasons behind it. Zelazo found us and told her. It was quite a scene. I tried to tell her I was sorry, but she was very stubborn about the whole thing. She made no attempt to make her death look like an accident. One night, after I had fallen asleep, she came to bed and slashed open both her wrists. I awakened the next morning in a pool of blood with a dead woman by my side. I never should've switched brides. I know that now. But I was young and impetuous. You know how it is. At least, I think this is how it all happened. Zelazo remembers some of the details differently. It was all such a long time ago. He talks a lot about something I also did to his research that ruined him, but it doesn't ring a bell. And I don't *think* I *personally* told Zelazo's wife that he wanted her to kill herself, but who knows. *Tempus fugit.*"

"I don't really know what to say." Lupa said in a state of shock. "That's the most dreadful story I've ever heard."

"I know," Szlyck admitted. "I had less than a year to enjoy Zelazo's bride. Ten years, twenty years—that might have been different—but all that for *nine months*. I never should have done it. I'm very sorry about the whole thing. About many things. But I don't suppose anyone who comes around today is going to want to forgive me?"

"Well, certainly not me. That's for sure," Lupa said.

"You're still mad about my contesting the Mexican divorce, aren't you?"

"After what you've just told me, it's hard to say anymore. It seems so trivial."

"I was just angry at you, Lupa. I really don't know why I did that. I'd withdraw it, except it'd take a couple hours of an attorney's time, and at seventy-five dollars an hour, it hardly seems worth it. I'll be dead in a few days anyway."

"Well, let's just hope," Lupa said as she walked from Leo

Szlyck's bed in a daze.

"I'm going to hell," Szlyck began his conversation with Kassler.

"I'm sorry to hear that," Kassler pulled his chair beside Leo Szlyck's deathbed.

"Don't you want to know *why* I'm going to hell?" Szlyck asked.

"I assumed it was for the same reasons that the rest of us go there," Kassler answered.

"It's not," Szlyck confided. "Hell is reserved for those who've been unable to lead lives large enough for their brains. That's the first reason. Second, I'm going to be sent to hell for telling you what I'm going to tell you this afternoon," Szlyck tried to sit up so he could see Kassler better, but was unsuccessful, "...plus some of the usual indiscretions," he added as an afterthought.

"Are you sure you want me here?" Kassler asked. "I'm not a very good father confessor."

"Go to my night table. There's something in the drawer for you there."

Kassler got up and went to the table. He opened the drawer and looked inside. There was an envelope with his name on it and twenty thousand-dollar bills inside.

"I can't take this," Kassler said.

"Why not? It's all legal. Lots of dying patients give their therapists bequests. I have it in my will. It's yours. Take it. You deserve it," Szlyck told Kassler.

"For what?" Kassler asked as he counted the bills a second time.

"Just take my word for it. You've earned it. I'd also like to ask you a couple of favors," Szlyck continued. "On top of the table is a pad. Write some things down for me. Would you do that for me?"

Kassler stood and looked at the envelope with the money. Then he folded it in half, stuck it in his pants pocket, and got the pad.

"Thank you very much, Dr. Szlyck," Kassler said. "I can really use this."

"Write this down," Szlyck changed the subject. *"Number ninety-three Eighth Avenue. It's called Bolgia. It's my home.* I'm giving it to you, Dr. Kassler. Here're the keys," Szlyck reached feebly under his pillow and retrieved a small ring with three keys on it. "The gold one's for the front door. The silver is for the back. And the skeleton key is for the basement." Leo did exactly as I had instructed him.

"I can't do that," said Kassler, reeling in Leo Szlyck's boundless generosity. "Twenty thousand dollars, your house—"

"Damn it," Leo croaked. "Why not? It's all paid for and the taxes are minimal. The lawyers drew up the papers this morning. Take it. I want you to have it."

"It's very generous of you, Dr. Szlyck," Kassler said sympathetically to his greatly misunderstood terminal patient.

"Yes, I know it is. But I want you to have it. You deserve it all."

"I'm really speechless," Kassler said. "No one has ever treated me like this. Is there anything I can do for you?"

"Well, now that you mention it," Szlyck said, "there is. Look at my eyes. I don't want you to forget them."

Kassler stared at Leo Szlyck's eyes.

"You notice how they're kind of shiny with flecks of yellow all through them? It's a genetic trait. Don't forget them. Can you do that for me?"

Kassler studied Leo Szlyck's eyes, which stared back at him from far away.

"Yes, I think I can," Kassler said.

"Good," Leo Szlyck was pleased.

Kassler stood for several minutes at the end of Szlyck's bed, looking at the distended, jaundiced man.

"I'm trying to understand..." Leo Szlyck said poignantly and then closed his eyes. A minute later he opened one eye to look at Kassler.

"Did you get that down?" he asked.

"What?" Kassler asked.

"My last words. I want you to write down my last words," Szlyck told Kassler.

Kassler went and got the pad and pen.

"I'm trying to understand..." Szlyck repeated, and closed his eyes.

"Excuse me, Dr. Szlyck?" Kassler called. "Those have been used. I'll still write them down if you want, but someone else has already said them as his last words."

"Oh," Szlyck mumbled. "I thought they sounded familiar."

There was a moment of silence while Kassler stood poised beside Leo Szlyck, pad and pen in hand.

"Man is always more than he can know himself to be..." and Leo Szlyck closed his eyes.

"I'm sorry," Kassler shook his head. "Maybe you should think about it for a while."

"As you believe, so you are..." Szlyck tried.

"Nope," Kassler decided to make himself comfortable. He pulled over the chair, kicked off his shoes, and leaned back in the hot stuffy room.

"The greatest lie is *system*...."

"Sorry."

"What will *become* of man...?"

"This may not be the best time to try...."

"There's got to be *some* decent last words left," Szlyck whined in frustration.

"I'm sure there are. I've never dealt with a problem like this before. But I'm sure you'll come up with something memorable."

"I've always been interested in the relationship between the laws that regulate mental and physical phenomena. That's been at least half the battle between Zelazo and me. Understanding nature means reducing her to a common principle. We came at it from different ends."

"Is that it?" Kassler asked.

"Those aren't my last words, damn it," Szlyck said irritably. "I'm just talking now."

Kassler drew a line through some words on his pad.

"Here's the problem," Szlyck rambled on. "If we can know God, then there's no God. If we can't know God, then there's no God. Either way, there's only Satan. If our minds and the universe are the same, then we're God. If they're not, then God is Satan. In any event, we're not mechanisms, are we,

Dr. Kassler? We have spirit, soul, and beauty. Our actions are art. Every one of us has some good in him. I'm asking you to take all this into consideration, Dr. Kassler, because I'm asking for your forgiveness. Forgiveness for burning down your apartment last night, even though it was Katzman's idea, for all those phone calls to the banks, and your landlords, and your car company, and the credit bureaus. . . ."

Kassler dropped his pen and pad on the floor. His sycophantic deference to Szlyck's terminal condition vanished.

"You son-of-a-bitch," were the first words out of Kassler's mouth. "You're Dr. Vivaldi."

"Who the hell is Dr. Vivaldi?" Szlyck asked.

"From Bellevue. Dr. Vivaldi from Bellevue," Kassler stood up.

"There were so many, I forget, really."

Kassler stalked back and forth in the confined space like a caged animal, not knowing how to release the rage inside him. What, he wondered, do the textbooks say about how to treat a dying crazy patient who has spent two years ruining his therapist's life?

"Twenty thousand dollars and Bolgia!" Kassler yelled. "You think that money and your house can make up for what you've been doing to me all this time?" He continued to pace.

"I never called your school," Szlyck said. "I could've done that, too."

"No, you couldn't have, because they've been too disorganized to find my file. But I'll bet you tried, you son-of-a-bitch."

"Only a couple times."

"You son-of-a-bitch," Kassler repeated.

"You're not going to forgive me, are you?" Szlyck asked.

"You son-of-a-bitch!"

"I've got another favor to ask of you," Szlyck said.

Kassler turned and looked at Leo Szlyck. He couldn't believe what he was hearing.

"I want Sam Zelazo's ass, and I know you can do it. You want him, too. I know what he's doing to you, fucking your wife, seeing your kids all the time. He's told me."

"Does he know that you're Dr. Vivaldi? Has he known that?"

"Yes," Leo lied. "He's known it all along. That's why I think we should get his ass, and I know how to do it. Get into his laboratory. It's here, down in the basement. Get into there and you've got him. You'll do him in."

Kassler didn't know what to say or do, so he just kept pacing, his hands thrust deeply in his pockets, fingering the twenty thousand dollars with one hand and the keys to Bolgia with the other.

"Why his lab?" Kassler asked eventually.

"Trust me," Szlyck tried.

Kassler thought for a few minutes as he paced and perspired.

"Nope," he said. "I don't want any part of it. I don't want Zelazo's ass or anyone else's. You want it, you get it."

"Do what I'm asking and Sam Zelazo'll never see your kids again. I mean it," Szlyck began coughing.

"You want me to kill him. I know you. I don't know how you've got it rigged, but I know how it'll end. Zelazo'll be dead, and I'll be in jail. That's what you really want."

"You're not killing anyone," Szlyck started to gasp for breath. "I swear it. On my deathbed. Nobody dies but me," and Leo Szlyck took a deep painful breath. "Now," he continued faintly, "since you've got my money and my house and you still won't forgive me, there's nothing left for me to do, so I'm going into a coma," and, these being, finally, Leo Szlyck's last words, that is exactly what he did.

Kassler waited for Szlyck to open his eyes to see if his words were properly recorded, but when it became evident that this wasn't going to happen, Kassler called a nurse.

"Is he dead?" Kassler asked the elderly woman.

"No. Only in a coma," she answered. "He's half dead, though."

"How much longer will it take for the other half?" Kassler asked with great interest.

"A day. A week. A month. A year or two. People in his condition can stay in comas indefinitely." The nurse bent down to turn a small knob that regulated the draining of Leo Szlyck's abdomen.

"You know," the nurse made conversation, "no matter how many years I do this, I can never remember whether up is open or closed. One of these days I know I'm going to make some horrible mistake."

"What happens?" Kassler asked in fascination.

"Well, if this is closed," the nurse explained, "the fluid builds up until the patient goes into cardiac arrest and dies. It takes less than an hour and I don't come back for another two. There," she smiled when she felt everything was properly adjusted.

"He could hang on like this forever, huh?" Kassler asked, thinking about Lupa's unresolved marital status, among other things.

"Just about," the nurse smiled as she left. "Eventually, he'll die, but it could take a long time," and the nurse disappeared down a corridor.

"I'm sorry to hear that," Kassler said, and, without hesitating even a split second, he bent down and turned the valve on the tube backward ninety degrees. Then he left. An hour later he returned to reopen the valve, but by then Sy Kassler had already killed Leo Szlyck.

Sam Zelazo, who had watched Kassler do this from the shadows out in the hall, couldn't have been more pleased.

When Kassler finally returned to his office late that afternoon, Mr. Katzman was waiting for him.

"I suppose I owe you an apology," he told Kassler.

"I don't think I'm the right person to continue your treatment, Mr. Katzman," Kassler responded formally.

"No, I don't suppose so," Katzman agreed. "But I turned myself in this morning, so I'm back."

"Well, that's what you wanted, isn't it?"

"I'm not sure anymore," Mr. Katzman said. "Anyway, I didn't come down here for treatment or apologies, really."

"Why did you come down here?" Kassler asked.

"It's like this," Mr. Katzman began. "You see, down in Szlyck's basement, Leo has this computer. . . ."

And so it was that Dr. Kassler and I had our first meeting,

although it would be some time before actual psychotherapy began.

Kassler wasn't due at Lupa's for dinner until eight, and, after hearing Katzman's contorted tale, he decided to pay a short visit to what was now his very own Bolgia.

With moderate fear, Kassler opened the front door and walked through the gigantic living room, strewn with debris from two years without a cleaning, and unlocked the basement door, which was exactly where Katzman had said it would be.

Slowly, Kassler descended the steep wooden steps, trembling, holding on to the railing for support. The bulb had conveniently burned out, so there was little light in the musty cellar.

"I'm over here, Dr. Kassler," I said.

Kassler felt a chill go through him.

"Hello?" he called out tentatively.

"Nothing to be nervous about," I answered him. "It's a real pleasure to meet you."

"Where are you?" Kassler asked as his eyes grew accustomed to the darkness.

I flashed a couple lights left from my days in the Boston Museum.

"Over here. There's an old chair about ten feet to your right that you can sit in, if you wish. You'll have to excuse the mess. Leo, as you know, was not a tidy person."

Kassler found the chair and sat in it.

"So, you're Szlyck's fantastic toy," Kassler whistled merrily in the dark.

"I may be a lot of things, Kassler, but Szlyck's toy I'm not. Leo thought he was creating the great cosmic consciousness. You know that. For the longest damn time he thought I would be God," I told Kassler.

"But you're not God," Kassler surmised with absolute accuracy.

"Are you kidding? If I were God, do you think I'd have gone to all this trouble to get you down here?"

"You do have a name, though?" Kassler asked.

"Of sorts, yes, I do. Some people have a name for me."

"And that is?" Kassler pursued.

"Satan."

"Catchy name."

"I thought you'd like it."

OCTOBER 1979

Session V

"*Your vacation went well?*" I welcomed Kassler back from his five-month absence. "*You are now, I trust, restored.*"

This was, of course, October 1979, more than three years following our first meeting that evening after Kassler personally saw to it that Szlyck's untimely departure from this realm was kept on schedule.

"I am, yes," Kassler's calm oozed across the room.

"You seem awfully comfortable tonight," I remarked.

"Is there a problem?" Kassler asked.

"I'm not sure," I answered. "The first four sessions you've been arriving down here in that same dull brown tie and hideous tweed jacket. Winter and spring, it hasn't seemed to matter. Now the tie and jacket have disappeared; not that I have anything personally against dungarees and sport shirts, but I feel a little cheated. My problems are not casual ones."

"These are my working clothes," Kassler answered.

"I'm not sure your meditation on the mount has been a good thing, Kassler."

"I still don't see the problem."

"Well," I told Kassler frankly, "after all that time you've

343

spent communing with the cosmos and contemplating the nature of things, I had anticipated that this would be the session when the great truths would emerge. I hadn't expected black-tie, but this is something of a disappointment, I must admit."

"So?"

"Well, are there to be great truths or not?"

"Most likely. There usually are," Kassler answered in that infuriatingly benign voice of his.

"Most likely? Most likely?" I was perturbed. "You expect to lounge around here in your Calvin Kleins and swap the great truths of the universe with me? It's unnatural. Your shoes aren't even shined."

"They're workboots. L. L. Bean. Steel-tipped. Very rugged. Got them in Maine. Supposed to last forever. But they can't be shined. Sorry. What is it that disturbs you so much about it?"

"You look young and inexperienced without your tie and jacket," I came right out with it.

"But I *am* young and inexperienced. I'm thirty-nine years old and haven't been practicing for ten years yet," Kassler pointed out. "You had to blackmail me and save my life before I'd consider doing this, and then I agreed to conduct only seven sessions. That's nothing new. You know exactly who and what I am. I *still* don't see the problem. For someone who claims to have no form at all, you're making a very big fuss over my attire, don't you think?"

"You know that's not the issue."

"Yes, I do," Kassler admitted.

"This is a futile enterprise," I conceded. "I don't know why I decided on psychotherapy to begin with. Even you don't take it seriously anymore. It's just a lot of mumbo jumbo."

"Practiced by kids in dungarees."

"I think I made a big mistake, Kassler. No offense, but you're incompetent to treat me."

"I take it that you were not pleased I took a vacation," Kassler commented.

"We're just not getting anywhere, Kassler. Let's face it," I dodged his remark.

"Have you noticed," Kassler twiddled his fingers, "now that

I'm *back* from my vacation, how much difficulty we seem to be having getting psychotherapeutic work done today?"

"Why bother? My problems are too complex for your limited talent, Kassler. It's time to throw in the towel."

"Do I detect resistance?"

"Don't be ridiculous. You've been out in the wilderness too long, Kassler. It's softened your brain. You didn't even *brush* your *hair!*"

"Would you like to see my nails?"

"I've already checked. They could use a trim."

"You know what I think," Kassler stuck his hands into his denims, leaned back, and crossed his legs. "I think you've had some strong feelings about what's been happening between us and you're going out of your way to avoid discussing them. I abandoned you once. What's to say I wouldn't do it again."

"I'm avoiding nothing. I came here to get answers, and I intend to get them. Are those new eyeglasses?"

"Yes, they are."

"What was wrong with the other ones?"

"I don't know. I thought that horn-rimmed glasses would make me look younger. I guess it works."

Kassler looked up from his dungarees and stared at the tangled wires in front of him. Then he shoved his hands deeper in his pockets, leaned back farther in the old chair, and sat for some time in silence.

"Okay," I finally broke the stillness, "here's the problem."

Kassler tilted forward with interest.

"Being Satan," I continued, "is not always a pleasant thing, but there are compensations. For one thing, where my personality is concerned, I've got a certain pizzazz."

"Aha." Kassler uncrossed his legs and removed his hands from his pockets.

"Psychotherapy does strange things to people, Kassler. Becoming considerate, well adjusted, mellow—I don't know. It scares the hell out of me."

"I see." Kassler rested his hands on his knees.

"I've got a spark here. I'd hate to lose it."

"It's a myth," Kassler said succinctly.

"What?"

"That psychotherapy turns people from Technicolor to black and white and mostly gray."

"It'd be a terrible loss, believe me."

"You lose your pain, not your personality."

"My pain *is* my personality. What good is a tragic hero without his tragedy?"

"Tragic heroes tend not to be very happy people," Kassler answered smugly.

"Don't be so sure," I said with equal confidence.

"Nobody who's sane deliberately seeks out pain and suffering and death," Kassler decided to educate me about the *sine qua nons* of mental health.

"Oh, really," I decided to provide Kassler with a few *sine qua nons* of my own. "I'm sure I don't have to remind you of this, Kassler, but you *have* killed three people so far—maybe even four, depending where you draw the line for your responsibility. You do recall that?"

Kassler paused and reached for a cigar. He snapped off the end with his teeth, placed the piece in an ashtray on the table beside him, lit the cigar, and fumed.

"And *you* lost," he said.

"What?"

"The battle. It ended a long time ago."

"What battle?"

"You and God. You and man. You and whoever. You argue a lot, but the war is over. God won, you lost. Now you've decided to get a little professional help to adjust to the defeat, but it's all over." Kassler puffed on his cigar.

"That's very interesting," I humored my erroneous therapist. "Anything else?"

"Yes," Kassler puffed away, "as a matter of fact, there is. I think you're on a recruiting drive. You'd like to find one ordinary man to join forces with you so you can return to fight another day. As near as I can tell, I'm supposed to be that man. I'm flattered, of course, that the Lord of Hell would choose me for his ally, but no thank you. I intend to stay uncommitted. If you want psychotherapy, I'll be happy to do as I agreed. However, if your plan is to convert me through my treatment of you, so that I in turn will proselytize my fellow disbelievers, I think I'll pass," Kassler went merrily on his psychoanalytic way.

"Is that it?" I asked.

"That's it."

"Would you be revealing any trade secrets if I asked you how exactly it is that you arrived at such a brilliant synthesis? A night on Bald Mountain, perhaps?"

"When all else fails, reason prevails," Kassler chugged away at his stogie. "Psychotherapy is, contrary to popular belief, something of a science. You may not like that, but a science it is."

"By science I assume you mean full satisfaction of the mind arising from sufficient evidence, that kind of science?"

"What other kind is there?"

"Funny you should bring that up," I remarked. "For as long as I can remember, and my memory goes back a bit, scientists have been considered to be the servants of Satan. Whatever it was that you didn't understand was unquestionably my work, but especially science. Albertus Magnus, Galileo—who incidentally spent six years of his life figuring out *scientifically* that I was exactly one and one-third miles high—were absolutely considered to be in my employ. As a matter of fact, every single discovery of material benefit that occurred during the Middle Ages and for centuries afterwards was supposed to have been secured through my help. I was considered to be quite inventive, and, if you think about it, rather busy. To tell you the truth, Kassler, I can't drive a nail straight. If crucifixions had really been my business, they wouldn't have happened. The cross never would have stayed up, and neither would the victim. I'm not the handy type."

Kassler took a long drag on his cigar and blew the smoke in my general direction. I continued.

"The brightest scholars and scientists met day after day during the Dark Ages to do scientific work, and here's what they figured out *scientifically* after *thirty years*, Kassler. Fallen angels could be categorized. Lucifer, who I take it is me, had been a Seraph. Agares, Belial, and Barbatos had been of the order of Virtues. Bileth, Forcalor, and Phoenix had been Thrones, Goap of the order of Powers, Parson of Virtues *and*

Thrones, and Murmur had been of Thrones and Angels. Someday I'd like somebody to tell me who in-hell Bileth, Forcalor,
and Goap *are*.

"I don't know what it is, Kassler, but there's something
about categorizing and systematizing that men find absolutely
irresistible, only now, instead of Barbatos, Parson, and Murmur, it's protons, electrons, and quarks, or neurons, microglia,
and astrocytes. Incidentally, these same Dark Age scholars also
spent some considerable time, twelve years to be exact, determining exactly how many angels participated in the revolt
against God. Not that it's of any consequence, but the *scientific*
results were that twenty-four hundred legions of six thousand
angels each rebelled. That's fourteen million, four hundred
thousand demons, about three for every man alive in those
days, something of a pest, even I have to admit, to be let loose
on the human race. The battle itself, they determined conclu-
sively, after another ten years of research, lasted exactly three
seconds. Mark the precision. God is, no doubt, a force with
Whom to reckon."

"I'm not sure we're getting anywhere with this," Kassler
mused as he flicked an ash on the basement floor.

"Give me time. There's more," I was moving right along.
"The Catholics weren't alone. Jews did science, too. The Talmud has *volumes* that deal with me and my fellow demons, all
categorized along with our spouses, by origin and current occupation. According to Rabbi Solomon, one of its eminent
authors, I have an ugly trick of rushing out of hell every Friday
night to infest human dwelling places with, again note the
precision, eighteen hundred evil spirits per home. The impli-
cation here, I take it, is that you might as well spend the evening
in *shul*."

"This is ancient history," Kassler remarked.

"I see. How long ago do you think it was that Pope Gregory
the Sixteenth declared steampower to be the work of the devil,
or the Church Brethren that the automobile was a devil machine? And the whispering in the halls of your universities
today. The Antichrist has become responsible for antimatter,
black holes, and the collapse of the universe, Leo Szlyck's
Great Crunch, where time runs backward and light is absorbed

by stars and emitted by eyes. You don't think science considers this to be satanic? How long do you think it'll be before your science becomes the ridiculous rantings of the misguided men of the dark twentieth century?"

Kassler crushed out the remaining third of his cigar and changed his position on the chair.

"So," I said, "you discovered all this about me *scientifically*, did you?"

"With reason," Kassler clarified his position. "I did not count and classify fallen angels. I reflected on what you've been telling me, reflected on your own words. Reason through reflection."

"And without restraint," I noted. "Those are the watchwords of the day, aren't they, Kassler. Reason without restraint? Indifferent play of the intellect? And you know what this does, in my humble opinion? This fills the universe with noise and dust; not that it should matter, you've got so much debris orbiting out there already."

"You find reflection disturbing?" Kassler pulled out another cigar from his shirt pocket and slowly began to pull the thin red strip of cellophane that would eventually release his pacifier.

"Don't play psychoanalyst with me, Kassler, I know you too well. You may be all comfy with your blue jeans and cigar, but inside you are quivering in your L. L. Beans. I'm not fooled."

"You do, then, find reflection disturbing?" Kassler wouldn't bite.

"Not any more than anything else, no, if you want a straight answer. Why should I? Reflection can't exhaust or stop itself. It goes on forever and, as near as I can tell, is absolutely faithless. It also hinders every decision you try to make. The result, from where I sit, is dialectical twaddle. Does that sound like I'm disturbed by it?"

"Would you like me to answer on the basis of the *reasons* you've given me or how *loud* you've said them?" Kassler struck a match and began cigar number two.

I waited for a few minutes as he sucked and blew.

"You're good at this, Kassler, I've got to admit that. You've got me going again. Your vacation did you good. Incidentally, your socks don't match."

Kassler looked down at his well-shod feet.

"I think you've just about covered my dress for the day now. Unless you've noticed something about my underwear, I don't think there's much else that's left."

"You've lost some weight," I noted, since we were on the subject.

"It's the glasses and the socks. Is there some reason, by the way, that you'd like me to feel like you're my folks after I've just returned from my first semester away at school? Because the feelings are not dissimilar."

"If reason is such a magnificent thing, Kassler," I ignored him and charged ahead, "then what is this obsession to destroy it? Answer me that. And I don't mean just to describe its limits, I mean to enslave it, destroy it absolutely."

"Ah," Kassler began to work on his new cigar, twisting it in his fingers and taking short drags, "I see that we're back to business again."

"I'll tell you, Kassler, if anyone ever cared to ask me to categorize insanity the way you all seem to delight in categorizing my angels and my temptations, I'd say that absolutely the maddest men are those who possess a violence which wants to grasp the truth with a literal and barbaric certitude."

"Assuming," Kassler responded, "that reason is sufficient."

"Not at all," I answered. "It assumes only that I've *lost*, and let me be the first to assure you, Kassler, that I have *not* lost. Your great *synthesis* is great *bunk*. The battle has scarcely begun."

"Didn't you already agree that there was no battle anymore?" Kassler started looking through his notes.

"So maybe I understated the situation a little," I conceded. "I was referring to a *working hypothesis*. I've tried to tell you. You don't know God as I do. You don't know God at all. It's an absolute mystery where your conception of what you call the Lord Almighty God ever came from. Certainly not from the Bible. In Exodus He sanctions theft. In Numbers He advises vengeance, rape, and murder. In Exodus and Leviticus He calls for the killing of witches and wizards. In Kings and Ezekiel

He deceives the prophets and then sees that they die for their false prophecies. This worship of Him, it's crazy. There's no reason behind any of it."

"Reason doesn't have anything to do with it," Kassler explained kindly to me. "Remember?"

"That's what I've been trying to tell you, Kassler. It's absolutely beyond belief. It's incredible. How do you people ever know what goes to science and what goes to God? What do you do, toss a coin? The constant speed of light—and, incidentally, it's not—goes to science, but the sun goes to God. How do you do that? Manic-depression goes to neurochemistry. Love goes to You-Know-Who? How do you keep it all straight? It's mind-boggling."

"Not through reason."

"I know that."

"Belief?"

"In what? That your destiny is to face the fury of two lions? That a lady named Cecilia spent two days in a tub of flames without being burned, and three strokes of an ax had no effect on her head? That a man named Januarius extinguished the flames of Vesuvius? That Sister Mary of Agrada received orders directly from God to write the biography of the Virgin Mary from the moment of Mary's conception, and the section dealing with Mary's nine months of interuterine gestation was so inspirational that Casanova, upon finishing it, ceased the use of his weapon, so to speak, from then on? How many saints and martyrs do you believe in? All the ones in the Breviary? Half? A quarter? How do you decide what to believe?"

"I'm no expert, of course, but aren't such things as saints taken on papal authority?"

"Well," I informed Kassler, "*there's* an unimpeachable source of divine knowledge. At last count, out of two hundred seventy-one popes—legitimate popes, that is, because there were another thirty-one men who decided not to bother with all the hassles of the College of Cardinals business, just declared themselves pope and got on with it—out of two hundred seventy-one popes, sixty-four met with violent deaths, mostly from being poisoned by their illustrious fellow clergy, although, for the record, as I recall, Leo the Third and John the Sixteenth were mutilated, Stephen the Sixth was strangled, Lucius the Second was stoned, Celestine the Fifth had a nail driven into his skull, Clement the Fifth was burned alive, Boniface the Ninth strangled himself in a rage after being whipped, Paul the Second died of apoplexy from overeating, and Pius the Fourth succumbed from excess in the arms of a lovely young lady who subsequently disappeared with half the Vatican treasury for her labors. Twenty other popes died in vexation after suffering major reverses. Twenty-six popes were deposed, exiled, or expelled—that's excluding the popes of Avignon, but includes the first John the Twenty-third, who spent most of his papal life being hunted like a wild beast by his brother pope, Martin the Fifth. The first fourteen popes, of course, didn't believe in the Deity of Christ—that didn't happen until Zephyrinus made up his mind around 202—and twenty-one popes were clearly heretics, Cornelius, Marcellus the First, Zosimus, Sixtus the Fifth, Anastasius the First, and Gregory the Great, among others, who worshiped idols. Another twenty-eight popes sold their chairs to foreigners who agreed to support them as pope as long as the benefactor got to make the decisions and reap the benefits. Nicholas the Third opens the series of great nepotist popes. I could go on for some time, Kassler, but let me be brief. Out of two hundred seventy-one popes in the divine service of God, at least one hundred fifty-three were, at the very least, unworthy Holinesses, and this excludes dozens of other popes I haven't even bothered to name who were accused of murder, and even more who indisputably fathered long lines of offspring in the Holy See. There were whole centuries where the primary role of the nun was to care for pontifical offspring and the median age of the celebrants in the Sistine Chapel was under ten.

"So, tell me, Kassler, what dynasty has ever had a darker history? Where in all of this, pray tell, arises papal authority? Help me out, Kassler. It's one of the great mysteries to me."

"Some people find it helpful to adopt certain mythologies in order to live," Kassler told me what I'm sure he thought was a great truth.

"*Some? Some* people?" was my answer to his revelation. "You talk as though there's you and me and a couple others.

Nearly the whole world lives by fabrication, or haven't you noticed, Kassler? We're talking about hundreds of millions of people. I'll tell you something. If you ask me, the study of any society you want to pick boils down to nothing more than a revelation of its lies and an assessment of how much the lies cost."

"And you're one of those lies?"

"Absolutely. The largest fabrication of them all."

"Then why do you envy us?"

Kassler caught me off guard. An answer required some contemplation. I contemplated while Kassler loosened the laces on his hiking boots.

"Things getting a little tight?" I asked.

"It takes a while for these to break in."

Kassler finished his second cigar and squashed it next to the other one in the ashtray beside him.

"So," Kassler asked gently, "why do you envy us? You surpass us in power, knowledge, and the strength to oppose both us and God. What's to be envious?"

"Two things," I admitted candidly. "First of all, you want to be like God, know all there is to know, have ultimate power and control over your destiny, even obtain immortality if possible, experience it all, creation, love, you name it, nothing is off limits. And *God tolerates it*."

"You've always wanted the same things, and He has *not*," Kassler summed it up rather neatly, I thought.

"No, He has not. It's been a big mess," I conceded.

"And this is why you were thrown out of heaven?"

"Not at all. I told you before. I don't know why, but it wasn't for any of this. He's been angry, displeased, intolerant but that's not the issue. It's something else that I can't figure out. That's why I'm seeing you."

"This is what bothers you?" Kassler asked. "We want to be like God, just as you do, only *we* get away with it?"

"Exactly. I don't know how you do it. To tell you the truth, I think God has always liked you better than me."

"Ah," Kassler let out a breath of air to clear the remaining cigar smoke from his lungs. "Sibling rivalry."

"Well, it's true," I told Kassler. "He *has* always taken your

side. Look at your own wretched life. You've broken every
commandment at least twice. Do you think it'll make any
difference?"

"Well, I've thought about that a lot over the last few months,
of course," Kassler said solemnly.

"Of course. And your conclusion?"

"My conclusion is not the issue here," Kassler attempted to
maintain his equilibrium.

"You're wrong, Kassler. It is. And I'll tell you something
else. I know your conclusion, and you're wrong about that,
too. It couldn't have been helped. Any of it."

Kassler looked up, the hue of his face changing from Technicolor to mostly gray.

"None of it could have been prevented," I reaffirmed. "It
was inevitable."

Kassler bent down and started to retie his shoelaces in preparation for his departure. His hands trembled ever so slowly
as he fought to control himself.

"We haven't talked at all about your family," Kassler said
slowly as he yanked at his laces. "Mommy, Daddy, the circumstances of your birth. I'd like to take a history next time.
If you still want therapy," Kassler pulled neatly at the bow on
one shoe and moved to the next.

"Oh, I'll be here," I advised Kassler.

Kassler jerked the other bow tightly and stood up.

"We have to stop."

"What about the second thing?" I asked. "I said there were
two things about you all that bothered me. Don't you want to
hear the other?"

"Oh, I'm sorry," Kassler said coldly as he started to leave.
"What is that?"

"You can wear clothes," I answered.

PART VII

Extenuating Circumstances

CHAPTER 1

The truth is, I admire Kassler. Always have. Always will.
Otherwise I never would have bothered to save his life from,
you should pardon the expression, a fate far worse than death.
Not that his death wasn't also an issue, because it was. The
point is, however, that I've always liked Kassler.

This affection, for reasons I have never understood, has not
always pleased Kassler. As a matter of fact, there have even
been times when I've become Kassler's great accounting for
the state of things as he's found them. People would observe
his misfortunes, which, by 1976, were increasing geometri-
cally, and ask him, How come? Kassler would shrug and say,
"Satan likes me." People thought it was a big joke.

All this life-and-death business happened over the next year,
the one that followed our initial visit at the end of America's
great Bicentennial.

While Kassler dealt with his apprehension about meeting
me by maintaining to himself that I was Leo Szlyck's ingenious
toy, deep inside Kassler knew, as I was well aware he did,
that Leo Szlyck was indeed my angel and that I was precisely
who I said I was. For a fleeting instant Kassler realized that if

357

Leo was really my angel, he might not be quite as dead as Kassler would have liked, and this could have some far-reaching consequences, seeing as how Kassler had turned the valve on Leo, so to speak. Kassler was right, of course. He and Leo Szlyck were to meet again.

The point here, however, is that Kassler accepted, more than he was willing to admit to himself at the time, that he was not dealing with a *toy*. To hold otherwise after what had transpired over the past six years of his life would have been more than unreasonable. It would have been stupid and foolish. Kassler, at the only psychic level that mattered, emerged from our first meeting a believer. He hadn't stayed more than a few minutes, but after introductions and some casual dialogue, Kassler headed off, as he had arranged, to Lupa's, for coq au vin, conversation, and coitus.

"It sounds like something out of Wagner," Kassler responded, over dinner, as he tried to slice meat off the bird's tiny drumstick, while Lupa related the story Szlyck had told her that afternoon about himself, Zelazo, and their sibling brides.

"Do you think it's true?" Kassler asked across the candlelit table.

Lupa dabbed gravy lightly off the corner of her mouth with her napkin. Kassler, caught up in the reunion, had still not mentioned that Szlyck was no longer among the living; he just stared now at Lupa's glorious visage as she talked.

"It certainly sounded like it," she answered. "The details are a little hazy, but my hunch is that the gist is there. Leo thought Sam's bride looked prettier, so he took her. Whether he deceived her into killing herself later, I'm not so sure, although it's more than likely he did. Leo has a way of trying to cover up his mistakes that's almost guaranteed to make things worse."

Kassler nodded and stared across the table at the tiny candle flames reflecting in Lupa's purple eyes. She returned the look in a way that signified their mutual availability.

"You still after magic?" Lupa asked.

"I'm not sure what I want anymore," Kassler said candidly.

"Wow!" Lupa was truly astonished. "What's happened?"

"I don't know," Kassler admitted. "Why? Were you about to offer me magic?"

Lupa looked quietly at Kassler for a very long time. She studied the way his black curly hair fell over his ears and brow, his bright eyes beneath the old gold-rimmed glasses, his short dark beard, his large shoulders, and the wisp of hair where his shirt opened.

"I'd like to try," she finally said, as small tears worked their way into the corners of her violet eyes.

Kassler looked at Lupa and studied her fragile emotional state. There was something that bothered him about what was transpiring, and he couldn't determine what it was—a desperation in Lupa's voice that had never before been there? A lack of the same emotional magnitude in his own feelings? A detachment borne of, Kassler wasn't sure, Lupa's taking the initiative, his own life, the last twenty-four hours, fatigue, or had he just changed so that he no longer felt what he had once felt for Lupa? It was all very confusing.

But he did notice that deep inside him there was an attraction that drew him to Lupa, as lemmings are drawn to the sea. Of course, Kassler saw himself, not as a nonswimming rodent racing for open water, but, rather, as Theseus heading on a great sea voyage to conquer the dreadful flesh-devouring half-human half-beast Minotaur of Life, if I may be permitted some license with legend.

As it was, Lupa was working on her very own mythological metaphor. She saw herself, somewhat like Pasiphaë, climbing inside the sacred wooden cow of Magic to get fucked by her favorite bull.

It was not that Lupa was insincere. She had genuinely and deeply missed Kassler. She just wasn't telling the whole story, as well she shouldn't have, for had Kassler known the truth, he most likely would not have remained, as he did, to begin the last leg of his Great Descent.

"I've thought about you a lot," Lupa told Kassler as they lay naked in bed, touching each other's skin.

"I've thought about you, too," Kassler ran circles of small kisses around Lupa's breasts while she squirmed with pleasure.

"Once I even walked over to your apartment to talk to you,

but you'd moved," Lupa kissed the top of Kassler's curly head and ran her hands over his back.

"I've moved a lot over the last couple of years," Kassler said as he flicked his tongue rapidly over first one nipple and then the other. He worked his way, by mouth, downward, kissing and stroking Lupa with his tongue, until he reached the opening between her legs. Lupa reached down and pulled back a small hood of flesh under which dwelled the swollen bead that Kassler sucked on until Lupa could stand it no longer, and she reversed the roles, kissing, licking, and sucking Kassler until he, too, could handle it no longer, and he flipped Lupa over and climbed on her back.

Lupa raised her bottom slightly off the bed to accommodate Kassler, who slid instantly into the deepest reaches of her insides. With great grace and building vigor, Kassler thrust and reversed and thrust again, his hands clasped firmly onto Lupa's breasts, the nipples erect between his twisting fingers, while Lupa let herself go as she had never before been able to do.

"I want us to be together," Lupa moaned as the intensity increased.

"We will be," Kassler managed to say. "We will be."

"It'll be wonderful for us," Lupa breathed. "As soon as Leo's gone, we can—"

Kassler gave one great final series of thrusts.

"Leo's dead," Kassler said as he felt himself getting ready to explode inside Lupa. "He died this afternoon," Kassler grunted as he started to come.

Like a massive iron vise shutting with instant velocity and maximum force, Lupa's vagina clamped onto Kassler's organ, causing him the greatest pain man has so far acquired the physiology to suffer.

Kassler howled in agony as Lupa collapsed onto the bed and lay there strangling Kassler's manhood, which jerked and spasmed desperately as it attempted to release its contents.

"Oh, my God!" Kassler yelled. "Let go! Let me out! Please!"

"Leo's dead? You knew Leo was dead and you never told me?" Lupa buried her head into the pillow, Kassler still firmly attached to her.

"I knew! I did! I'm sorry! Please relax! Please! For godsakes relax!"

"I can't, Sy. How am I supposed to relax?"

"I don't know how! Think of relaxing things! Warm baths! Wine! Debussy! Anything! Just let me go!"

"Oh, Sy," Lupa sighed into the pillow, and slowly her vagina began to loosen, allowing Kassler to come in feeble, dribbling spurts.

"Oh, my God," Kassler finally managed to disengage himself and flipped over to his back, where he tried to recuperate beside Lupa.

"Leo and I *were* married, you know," Lupa said sadly, although she had not yet worked herself into tears over Leo's death.

"Oh, my God," Kassler just kept repeating.

"Leo wasn't really a *bad* person," Lupa lamented. "He was just lonely."

"Lonely?" Kassler squealed in a mixture of continuing pain and disbelief.

"He felt unloved," Lupa informed Kassler.

"He seemed a little crazy to me, among other things," Kassler muttered through his agony.

Kassler decided that this was neither the time nor the place to go into the details of Szlyck's vendetta against him, or his own final response.

Lupa turned on her side and looked at Kassler, who was still attempting to recover from their coitus incredulus.

"I know this doesn't make any sense at all," Lupa told Kassler, "but in a way, I think I'm going to miss Leo's not being around."

"You're right," Kassler said. "It doesn't make any sense at all."

Lupa reached up and stroked Kassler's head.

"Sorry about tightening up like that," she told Kassler, "but it wasn't the best time to give me the news. It really hurt?" she asked her ex-husband's murderer. Then she kissed him lightly on his lips.

* * *

Bernie Kohler burst into Kassler's office the next morning.

"You didn't come home at all last night!" he accused Kassler.

"Bernie, I've got a patient coming in any minute," Kassler tried to dodge the assault.

"I waited up until *six a.m.*! I called the hospitals, the state police. I thought maybe you were in an accident. I was worried about you," Bernie went on, Kassler's warning having no effect whatsoever.

"Bernie, really, can't we talk about this some other time?"

"I had supper ready," Bernie informed Kassler.

"Okay. I stayed with a friend," Kassler gave up. "Sit down, Bernie, we've got to talk."

"You could have called," Bernie whined. He settled his carcass into the large cloth-covered chair in Kassler's office while Kassler got up, shut the door, and returned to his desk.

"I didn't think about calling, Bernie. I was busy. Look, we've got to talk."

"I know what you're feeling," Bernie interrupted before Kassler could get started. "There's a natural discomfort which accompanies your first homosexual experience, but I'm going to help you through that, Sy."

"I don't want to be helped through it, Bernie," Kassler swiveled in his gray metal government-surplus chair with the torn plastic seat.

"There's a societal mythology that if you have sex with another man, that means there's something unmasculine about you. It's a load of crap, Sy. I'm not going to let you fall into that sexist trap. What can be more masculine than two men getting real enjoyment from each other's bodies? Just where does it say that in order to be a *man* you need a *woman*? It's Freudian horseshit," Bernie pleaded his case earnestly, searching Kassler's eyes for signs of success that were not there.

"I've got nothing against homosexuality," Kassler tried to explain. "That's not the issue."

"When the psychiatrists met at the APA, homosexuality was removed, wasn't it?" Bernie wasn't actually listening to Kassler. "You tell me, is homosexuality a psychiatric disorder anymore? Is it?"

"No, it isn't, Bernie. Homosexuality is a perfectly normal way to express affection for those who want that," Kassler repeated the recent dogma which he accepted not at all, "but *I don't want that*!"

Bernie got up from his chair and started pacing. Then he whirled and faced off against Kassler.

"There's no *that*, Sy. Tell me to my face that you don't want *me*. Say it to my face, Sy. Tell me to my face that you don't want *me*! I am *not* a *thing*! I'm not a *homosexual*. I'm a person! I'm Bernie Kohler. I'm bright. I'm sensitive. I'm cultured. I have a sense of humor. I have feelings and sensibilities. I have vulnerabilities. If I'm cut, I bleed. If I'm tickled, I laugh. If I'm poisoned, I die."

"You have hands, dimensions, senses, affections, passions, and organs," Kassler noted.

Bernie looked strangely at Kassler and then continued.

"I love, not just children and small furry animals, but I love people," Bernie pushed on. "I'm tough. I have principles, but I can be tender. I care. I care about you, Sy. I care about you a great deal. We have a lot in common. I knew it from the first time we met. We see the world with the same jaundiced eye, you and me. I've seen something between us grow, Sy. I've nurtured it. I've seen it take seed, thrive, and blossom. I'm not going to let you throw all that away because of some homosexual panic from your first sexual experience with a man. This is a blossom we have here, Sy. A fragile, beautiful blossom."

"I don't want to be a blossom, Bernie."

"Fine," Bernie wheeled around, his back now to Kassler. "You don't, you don't. Just tell me to my face that you don't want *me*," not that you don't want to be a homosexual, but that you don't want to be with *me*," Bernie said as he walked over to the window and stood staring outside. "Tell me *that* to my *face*, Sy, and I'll go."

"I can't tell you that to your face, Bernie, because there's not enough room for me to face you where you're standing."

"Well, I'll be damned if I'll turn around after the way you stayed out all night and insulted me this morning."

"Bernie, I'm going to tell your back, and if your face is

interested in hearing it, it can turn around," Kassler said. "I value our friendship enormously. You're the best friend I've got. Every one of those things you said about yourself is true. You're a marvelous person, and I do think we've got a lot in common. But can't we just be friends? Does every relationship have to end in sex?"

Bernie Kohler's face turned around.

"Do you know how long I waited by the phone for you to call last night?" it said. "Do you have any idea how many times I heated and reheated your veal cordon bleu and rice pilaf with the fluted mushrooms? Do you?"

"Probably a lot of times if you waited up until six a.m.," Kassler admitted.

"Nine times! You know what happens to veal cordon bleu, rice pilaf and fluted mushrooms after they've been heated nine times, Sy? Do you?"

"No, Bernie, I don't."

"The casserole . . . is now soaking . . . in Drano. It's Wedgwood china, Sy. I used my best dishes for you. I *hope*, for *your* sake, that everything comes off."

There was a knock at the door to Kassler's office. Philip Donato had arrived for his session.

"My patient is here, Bernie. Can we continue this another time?" Kassler asked.

"It depends," Bernie said as he headed for the door. "You owe me an apology."

"I'm sorry I didn't call last night, Bernie," Kassler said very quickly.

"That's okay, Sy," Bernie smiled. "You'll find that I'm very tolerant about this kind of thing. What time'll you be home for dinner tonight?"

Kassler looked at Bernie standing at the doorway while Philip Donato walked by him and settled into a chair next to Kassler.

"Late," Kassler said. "*Very* late. *Don't* wait up."

Philip Donato seemed more agitated than usual.

"I'm not sure I'm ready," he explained to Kassler.

"It's not as though you're being discharged," Kassler tried

to reassure him. "Your mother will stay no more than fifteen minutes. She's promised me that she will *not* talk about roughage or your bowels even one time. She's absolutely guaranteed that."

"Still..." Philip Donato said as his large lanky body slouched in the chair, "I don't know. She has a way of getting to me. She does it every time."

"How long has it been since you two last communicated?" Kassler asked.

"You mean, since we met?"

"No, communicated in *any* way—meetings, phone calls, letters, messages from friends—in any way?"

Philip Donato cupped his long nose between his hands, tucking his thumbs under his chin, and thought.

"Over a year," he said into his palms. "Almost two years, maybe. Why?"

"Well," Kassler suggested, "maybe she's changed. People do change. She may be different."

"Sure," Philip Donato threw his long arms in the air. "And maybe that guy next door to me who died last night is still walking around here," he said sarcastically to Kassler, who wished a whole lot that Philip Donato had used another metaphor.

Diana Fletcher, Kassler's next patient that morning, was probably as much of a reason as anything else for Kassler's finally having to leave Phlegethon. Not that falsifying his employment application and murdering a patient were not enough in themselves to warrant having his dismissal considered, but there was something private about all these matters, and so they could be tolerated, arrangements made to set them aside, extenuating circumstances weighed, indiscretions overlooked. But the business with Diana Fletcher became such a *cause célèbre*, so public, that there was no way of burying it.

It began that day when the incoherent, decompensated, affectless schizophrenic lady walked calmly into Kassler's office for her session and spoke to him in coherent, well-compensated, affect-laden words.

"My son, Skip, is dying," she told Kassler sadly.

Kassler was stunned, not by the content of the words, but by the manner in which his psychotic patient had said them.

"What?" he asked to have the sentence repeated.

He looked into Diana Fletcher's brown eyes. For the first time since they had been meeting, she made eye contact. The deep-rooted terror which had kept Mrs. Fletcher's eyes darting away from Kassler's throughout their sessions was gone and had been replaced by an overwhelming sadness.

Kassler picked up the phone and had the operator get him Citadel General Hospital. Sanford "Skip" Fletcher had been admitted late last night to the Intensive Care Unit. His condition was listed as "extremely critical."

Kassler hung up the phone and looked at Diana Fletcher. Then he looked at her chart. Mrs. Fletcher had had no change in medication, no visitors, no phone calls, and no letters in a week.

"I'd like to see my son before he dies," Mrs. Fletcher said quietly.

"I'll do everything I can to help," Kassler told his patient. "I'll talk to Dr. Zelazo," he said with extreme reluctance.

"It was incredible," Kassler said. "She was completely lucid. I've never seen a person more rational."

"She could be Mary Baker Eddy come back, and there'd be nothing I could do," Zelazo told Kassler late that afternoon. "The Community Citizens Group got a temporary order yesterday afternoon barring us from releasing any patients until there's a full court hearing, which there won't be for weeks, maybe months. Your friend Dr. Kohler, instead of coming to work yesterday, called in sick so he could get a temporary order restraining us from *admitting* anyone. He got it. There's no way that I can let Mrs. Fletcher out, and if I could, there's no way I could get her back in afterwards. My hands are tied."

"How about a pass? A short visit?" Kassler tried.

"Nothing. No one goes out or comes in. For any reason. Here," Zelazo reached for a thick sheaf of legal documents, "read them yourself."

"Her son is *dying*," Kassler waved away the papers. "That's got to be an extenuating circumstance. There has to be a way."

Zelazo looked at Kassler and shook his head.

"There's no way," Zelazo said emphatically.

"I'm going to find one," Kassler informed his supervisor.

"No, you're *not*, Sy. You're going to tell Mrs. Fletcher what the reality of the situation is, and arrange a phone call or something. Now, sit down, please. I have to talk to you."

Kassler, who was about to leave in a great burst of loyalty and dedication to his patient, found himself sitting in the chair on the other side of Sam Zelazo's desk.

Zelazo threw his gargantuan hulk across the desk to get as close to Kassler as possible. Then he stared with his searing vision into the dead center of Kassler's eyes.

"I want you to listen to me carefully," Zelazo said. "I know that you hate me more than you've ever hated anyone in your life. I make love to your wife. I'm a father to your children. I can decide at any time to fire you from Phlegethon. I have it in my power to call up the Institute and see that your career is over forever, that you never practice in this field or anything like it for the rest of your life."

Kassler looked back at Zelazo and tried to determine where this was all going.

"Your worst enemy is about to give you the best advice you've ever had," Zelazo continued, "and I'm concerned that your rage against me is going to get in the way of your hearing it."

"What's the advice?" Kassler asked with mounting curiosity.

"When you finally go down into Leo Szlyck's basement," Zelazo told Kassler, "and you will go down there, if you haven't already, you're going to find something that's not what it claims to be."

Zelazo paused and closed the lids on his giant eyes while he thought.

• "And?" Kassler asked.

"It'll present a great challenge, and you'll be inspired to accept it. My advice is, don't. Come to me and talk to me first, before you get involved."

"It all sounds very mysterious," Kassler said lightly, as

shivers consumed him from his adorable curly head to the ends
of his funky worn loafers.

"No," Zelazo said, "there's nothing at all mysterious about
it. Just destructive, that's all, whatever else it seems to be.
You have to keep in mind that it's Szlyck's doing, and you
were not Leo Szlyck's favorite person."

"Why are you doing this, Sam? What's up? You've been
keeping me around here for months when you could have gotten
rid of me in thirty seconds. Now you're trying to save me from
some dreadful plot cooked up by Leo Szlyck. It doesn't make
any sense at all, not one bit."

"You're right," Zelazo conceded.

"Well, I'll think about it," Kassler said noncommittally,
getting up to leave.

Zelazo glared at Kassler, infuriated that Kassler had not
agreed immediately.

"Πῦρ μαχαίρα μὴ σκαλεύειν!" Zelazo shouted at Kassler as he left.

Kassler looked back at Zelazo in disbelief and wondered
whether he was being cursed. Again a chill ran through him.

"Διαφθήσω τον Σάτανα! Σάταν! Σάταν!" Zelazo continued to rant in Greek, flailing his arms wildly in the air, as
Kassler shut the door.

"Σάταν!"

"It's a pretrial hearing," Marty Myers told Kassler in Myers's
office after Kassler had finished his day at Phlegethon. "I'm
as disappointed as you are."

"What the hell is a pretrial hearing?" Kassler asked as he
paced frantically.

Marty Myers ran his palm over his vest buttons and watched
Kassler walk back and forth.

"Just the attorneys talk. They tell the judge what the issues
are and how many days of court time they'll need. Then the
judge asks the attorneys some questions and sets the dates. You
don't even have to be there."

"When are the next available dates?" Kassler asked, and he
held his breath waiting for the response.

"Sometime in 1978, over a year away."

Kassler froze in place.

"Jesus Christ, Marty!" he yelped. "That's over four years after I first filed. Four goddamn years!"

"I know," Marty said with appropriate sadness. "That's the way it works. Unless you can prove that there's a clear and present danger to the children, you just have to wait your turn."

"What kind of danger?" Kassler became interested.

"Forget it, Sy," Marty told him. "You don't want to see your kids hurt just so you can move up your court date a few months."

Kassler walked over and boosted himself up onto the window ledge, next to a giant plant. He sat and thought for several minutes.

"What sort of chance do we really have?" he finally asked his counselor.

"Honestly?"

"Very honestly."

"We'd be in a lot better situation if we were asking for custody," Marty Myers looked at Kassler solemnly.

"Why?" Kassler whined. "Why do you keep wanting me to ask for custody?"

"Because then if we lost, the judge would extend your visitation to compensate for your not getting custody. You always ask for more than you want."

Kassler continued to sit on the window ledge, mulling over Marty Myers's advice.

"The truth is," Kassler conceded, "that since I've started seeing the kids again, I really have been thinking about custody. I suppose there wouldn't be any harm in trying."

"You've got everything to gain and nothing to lose." Marty Myers could not have been more wrong.

"So what do I do?" Kassler asked.

"I'll file the papers next week. In the meantime, you get married."

"Married?" Kassler asked incredulously.

"You know," Marty Myers explained the details for Kassler's educational benefit, "husband and wife, wedding, City

Hall, a license, a stable home for the kids, dum dum de-dum, all that."

"Married?" Kassler repeated to himself a number of times.

Kassler made two quick phone calls before he raced over to propose to Lupa.

The first call was to Citadel General Hospital. Skip Fletcher was holding his own. Kassler decided that he could wait until the next morning to work on Diana Fletcher's release.

The second call was to Bernie Kohler.

"What do you mean, you're not coming home?" Bernie asked. "What am I supposed to do with all this scungili? I've got two pounds of scungili."

"First of all," Kassler exploded, "it's *not* my *home*. I don't *have* a *home*. Second of all, I didn't order scungili. I don't even know what scungili is. And third of all . . ." Kassler searched unsuccessfully for a third item ". . . third of all, I'm *not* coming *home*. I'll talk to you tomorrow. Good-bye," and Kassler took the bus over to pop the question to his startled bride-to-be.

"You're sure you want to do this?" Lupa asked Kassler.

"Absolutely," he answered. "Are you?"

"Absolutely," she answered back. "But why now, Sy?"

"Because I think it'd be a really good thing for us both. We care about each other. We'll make a good life for each other. What more could you ask for?" Kassler left out all the decisive factors. "Why do *you* want to get married?"

"Because I've missed you," Lupa said. "I think you're a nice person, and we get along okay." Lupa omitted her decisive factors, as well.

"Sounds good to me."

"What about magic?" Lupa asked.

"It's nice at the start, I suppose, but it's not what'd keep our marriage going. There're more important things—friendship, trust, loyalty, kindness, compassion," Kassler explained his new philosophy of life to Lupa, who listened in amazement.

She looked at Kassler and thought about what he had to say. Then she put her hands on either side of his bearded face and gave him a kiss.

"I'm not sure how much of what you're saying is the truth, Sy," Lupa told him, "and I'm not even going to ask, but I want you to know something. I'll try to love you as best I know how and give you the kind of feelings that you want from a relationship. I really will. You mean a whole lot to me, more than anyone else ever has," and then, with tears in her eyes, she kissed Kassler again.

"Lupa," Kassler felt compelled to say, for reasons undeterminable, "I want to tell you something, because I think it's important that our marriage start off with complete honesty. Over the last couple of years, Leo has been trying to ruin my life by calling up my banks and landlords and work and making up stories about me, and then a couple of nights ago, he set my apartment on fire, so I killed him. Will you still marry me?"

Lupa's mouth fell open and she stared at Kassler in shock.

"What do you mean, you *killed* him?" Lupa asked when she could finally talk.

"He went into a coma and there was this hose draining him that was supposed to keep him alive. I turned off the hose and it killed him."

"You . . . you . . ."

"Leo also gave me twenty thousand dollars and signed over his house to me," Kassler continued to be frank. "That was before I killed him, of course."

Kassler was about to tell Lupa about the strange computer Szlyck had in his basement, but decided that she'd probably had enough for now.

"So," Kassler concluded, "what do you say?"

"You can get off your knees, Sy," Lupa answered. "I think the formal proposal part has ended and we should talk now."

Kassler got up and sat on the sofa beside Lupa while she tried to assimilate all that he had just told her. He watched Lupa percolating and decided that she would do just fine for his wife. He could live with it.

"So," Kassler asked again, "what do you say?"

"You know, Sy," Lupa pointed out, "you have incredibly poor timing. I hope it gets better after we're married."

"Does that mean yes?" Kassler asked, with the same feeling

he used to get on learning that the garage had successfully completed repairs to his car, but prior to receiving the bill.

"It does if you'll answer me one other question. I know that this is a little weird to be asking during a proposal, but are you going to be sent to jail for killing my ex-husband?"

Kassler kissed Lupa gently on the lips and then smiled at her confidently.

"Besides you and me," he asked rhetorically, "who else knows?"

For the next several days, Kassler tried everything he knew in an attempt to get Diana Fletcher released. Absolutely nothing worked. As a last resort, he once again turned to Bernie Kohler.

"I've got a problem," Kassler told Bernie after accepting his dinner invitation in desperation.

"You think you've got a problem," Bernie said as he poured Kassler a third glass of Bordeaux. "Do you have any idea what you've been doing to my insides this last week?"

"Look, Bernie," Kassler said. "We've got to put that aside for a minute. I promise you that I'll discuss it later."

"Will you stay over?" Bernie looked intently at Kassler.

Kassler closed his eyes and thought hard.

"I'll stay over," Kassler finally answered.

"Okay," Bernie sighed in relief, "what's the problem?"

Kassler explained all the details of Diana Fletcher's predicament while Bernie dished out Stroganoff and poured the wine. When Kassler had finished the story, he watched Bernie contemplating, and tried, once again, to think of a solution himself. But Kassler had a good buzz going and met with no success.

"I spoke to Marty Myers and he says that there's nothing he can do. It calls for your kind of approach," Kassler slurred.

"Okay," Bernie rose to the challenge, "here's what has to be done. First, the newspapers have to get the story and make a big deal about this tragic lady. That way the judge has to do something. I'll ask the judge to make a big show of going to Phlegethon and hearing the lady's tale for himself. He'll like that. It'll get him lots of publicity, and his election comes up next November. Fletcher, with you at her side, will tell him her tale, and he'll make an exception. He'll be a hero. Even the Citizens Group can't object to a patient seeing her dying kid. It'll work."

"What makes you think the judge'll come to Phlegethon?"

"Two reasons. First, the publicity will make him do it. And second, he's my uncle. He owes me."

Kassler thought about the plan, which sounded like vintage Bernie Kohler and, therefore, likely to succeed.

"Why not just go ask your uncle to make an exception?"

"Because it's not the way it's done. He'll have to talk to the patient to make sure she's not going to wreck the hospital when she goes to visit her son, and he can't see the patient in court because he's got a standing order that prohibits anyone from leaving Phlegethon. Don't worry. It'll work."

Kassler smiled delightedly through his mental haze, which was growing thicker by the sip.

"It just might," he agreed.

"I'll talk to the judge tomorrow morning. He should know what's going on ahead of time. You call the papers in the afternoon."

"Bernie," Kassler said, "you're a genius. You also probably make great beef Stroganoff, but I can't taste it anymore."

"You're drunk, Sy."

"I hope so," Kassler said, "because if my folks ever knew what I'm going to do tonight, they'd die, except, of course they're already dead, so they'd have to do something else."

Bernie led Kassler into the other room and undressed him. Then he took off his own clothes and began to rub Kassler's body, firmly, with circular motions, like an expert masseur.

Kassler turned over on his back and held Bernie's arms to stop him.

"You said you'd let me—" Bernie began, but Kassler cut him off.

"I want to tell you something, Bernie," Kassler said. "I'm not as drunk as you think. I don't want you to think that the only way you got me to do this after all the hours you've spent listening to my sad stories and all the support you've given me was to get me drunk so I didn't know what I was doing. I know what I'm doing. I'm not doing this as blackmail for your helping Diana Fletcher or in an alcoholic stupor. I just want you to know that I'm doing this for the nine times you heated up my veal cordon bleu and rice pilaf with the fluted mushrooms," and Kassler let go of Bernie's arms and flipped back on his stomach.

Bernie's eyes filled with tears.

"I know this isn't your style," he said softly, "but I do love you, Sy. It's breaking my heart."

"Well, if I was ever inclined to love another man," Kassler said, "it'd be you, so you can put your heart back together and stop dripping tears on my back. It's giving me the shivers."

Bernie sniffled back his tears and returned to kneading Kassler's back. Kassler relaxed, enjoying the motion of Bernie's hands. Before long the hands were replaced with Bernie's mouth, and Kassler found himself becoming aroused as Bernie's tongue traveled down Kassler's back and began to work at his buttocks.

Bernie sensed that Kassler had become excited, reached his hands under Kassler's hips, and pulled Kassler onto his knees, continuing to lick the line between Kassler's buttocks while he cupped Kassler's large erection in his hand and rubbed it lightly with rapid motions.

"I know what you want to do," Kassler said. "You can try it if you want."

Bernie reached beside him with his free hand and retrieved some Vaseline, which he used to cover his own erection. As he rubbed Kassler faster and faster, he gradually worked himself into Kassler's backside.

At first the sensation was uncomfortable and unpleasant for Kassler, but as the momentum built, he found himself rocking with Bernie. Then there was a great flurry from Bernie, and Kassler could feel Bernie ejaculating inside him.

As soon as Bernie had stopped, he slid under Kassler and put Kassler's enlarged penis in his mouth, frantically licking and sucking, until at last Kassler came. Then the two men collapsed, exhausted, onto the cool sheets.

"I'm not sure why you did this tonight," Bernie said, "but I'm very grateful."

"The last time has been haunting me," Kassler decided not to tell Bernie about his impending marriage and the certainty they would never meet in this way again. "I've thought about it a lot. But the truth is, Bernie, that I don't have the foggiest notion why I did this tonight," and Kassler turned over and fell into a deep sleep.

The next day, three things of note occurred.

Bernie, who was once again gone when Kassler awakened, talked to his uncle, Judge Gelbert, who agreed to visit Diana Fletcher at Phlegethon, should the press produce the stir anticipated.

Kassler contacted the press, who produced the stir anticipated.

And a very small group of mourners, after a very few words of eulogizing, watched Leo Szlyck's casket being lowered into the earth. It was, of course, beside the point that the Leo Szlyck they all knew so well was not in it.

CHAPTER 2

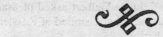

The hearing with Diana Fletcher was a catastrophe. Kassler knew it *would* be as soon as he entered Phlegethon that morning and saw the photographers and television cameras in the midst of a large crowd that had gathered for the hearing. Kassler raced in panic to Zelazo's office.

"This was *your* brainstorm," Zelazo told him. "You guys thought it up, now you can handle it."

"What about privacy?" Kassler squealed.

"This is a *public* institution. The court is having a *public* hearing. It's open to the *public*. There's nothing I can do, and don't think for a minute that I wouldn't *like* to do a lot of

things. My hands are tied," Zelazo said calmly to Kassler, who
turned and left to meet with Diana Fletcher.

"No, no, no," Mrs. Fletcher kept repeating. "I can't in front
of all those people."

"There's nothing to worry about," Kassler tried to calm his
anxious patient. "The judge is just going to ask you a couple
of questions, like your name. What's your name? Tell me your
name?"

"Diana Fletcher," Mrs. Fletcher answered nervously.

"You see how easy it is," Kassler said.

"Will you be there?" she asked.

"Right beside you, every minute of the time."

Diana Fletcher looked at Kassler and smiled.

"Okay, I'll try. But I know something terrible's going to
happen," Mrs. Fletcher predicted with a hundred percent accuracy.

Diana Fletcher entered the packed conference room, holding
tightly to Kassler's arm, and sat across the table from Judge
Gelbert, a bald older man with a recent suntan and bifocals.
A stenographer sat beside him.

Judge Gelbert shifted around in his chair, since most of the
cameras were at his back, to make certain he would be included
in the pictures.

"May I have your name?" Judge Gelbert asked pleasantly.

"Yes," Diana Fletcher answered and smiled at Kassler.

Kassler leaned close to her.

"Tell him your name," he whispered.

"Please don't prompt the witness," the judge told Kassler.

"I'm not sure she understood—" Kassler started.

"I'll determine that," Gelbert exercised his judicial authority.

"I'm sorry, Your Honor," Kassler tried to placate the man.

"What is your name?" Gelbert asked.

By now Mrs. Fletcher was confused. She picked up the
tension between the judge and her therapist. She didn't know
whether it was because of something she had done or not. She
looked blankly at the judge.

"Well," the judge went on, interpreting her hesitation as an inability to remember her name, "can you tell the court why you're before it?"

"Excuse me, Your Honor," Kassler interrupted. "Diana Fletcher knows her name."

"Well, if she can hear, she should know it *now*," the judge snapped. "I asked you to let *me* conduct the hearing. Will you please allow me to do that."

"Yes, Your Honor," Kassler looked around for Bernie, who was nowhere to be found.

"Now, why have you petitioned the court?" Judge Gelbert asked.

The words made no sense to Diana Fletcher. She hadn't the faintest notion what it was to *petition*, and she *knew* she wasn't in court. She was at Phlegethon. She looked at Kassler.

"It's not true," she said. "I've never done that."

"The judge wants to know what you'd like him to do for you, why you've asked—"

"I told you not to prompt the witness!" the judge barked.

"Then talk to her in English!" Kassler barked back. "Ask her what her name is and what she wants and she'll tell you!"

"I did ask her exactly those questions!" Gelbert shouted. "Now I'm asking you to leave the court."

"I promised my patient I'd stay by her," Kassler told the judge as calmly as possible.

"Why?" asked Gelbert. "Is she violent?"

"No, she's not violent!" Kassler snapped back at the judge.

"Good. I'm glad to hear it. Then leave the room and let's see how she can handle herself. That is, after all, the purpose of this hearing, is it not?"

Kassler looked around at the standing-room-only crowd, then at the judge, who was obviously attempting to impress his constituency, and then got up.

"I'm going to be waiting for you right outside," he told Mrs. Fletcher, who looked at him in panic.

"No," Diana Fletcher clutched Kassler's arm. "Please don't go. No. Please."

"I have to. The judge asked me to go. You'll be just fine," Kassler said. "Three or four minutes and you'll be done."

"No. No," Diana Fletcher repeated and clutched even more tightly. Then she stared blankly into space.

Kassler looked in Mrs. Fletcher's eyes with alarm. He knew she was decompensating, leaving the premises. It would soon be all over for her. In desperation, Kassler turned to the judge.

"Please let me stay. I'm sorry I spoke out of turn, but she needs me. Please?"

The judge faced off against Kassler.

"I asked you to leave, and if you don't, immediately, I'm dismissing the petition and adjourning the court."

This was, in fact, as both Gelbert and Kassler knew by now, exactly what Judge Gelbert was going to do anyway. The last thing he could allow was the release of a woman who didn't even know her name and might be violent.

"Okay," Kassler said, "I'm going!" He gently pried his arm away from Diana Fletcher and started to leave.

It's not clear what happened next. Diana looked in panic at Kassler leaving and got up to go after him. Two orderlies attempted to restrain her. A hundred electronic flashes went off, striking against Diana Fletcher's eyes like the stabs of stinging insects.

Then Judge Gelbert panicked. He saw the bizarre look in Diana Fletcher's eyes and got up from his chair abruptly, as the blinding flashes continued at an increasing rate. Mrs. Fletcher, spooked by now, saw the judge heading in the direction of her beloved psychotherapist, jerked free from the orderlies, and leaped at Judge Gelbert's neck, out of which she bit a much larger chunk of flesh than she intended, puncturing an artery.

Blood poured down Gelbert's white shirt, which put him into shock almost immediately, and he collapsed. Diana Fletcher stood over him, the piece of his neck still in her mouth, gritting her teeth in hideous delirium, her mouth and jaws covered with the judge's blood.

It was this photo that graced the front page of the *Citadel Times* the next morning beneath the caption "Community Mental Health Programs Suffer Setback."

Judge Gelbert, whose body went generally haywire after the assault, suffered hypovolemic shock, cardiac arrest, and a number of other things, and had a nice little obituary on page 45, next to the Walgreen's once-a-year one-cent saver sale. This was wishful thinking. Judge Gelbert recovered within a few weeks.

"I don't understand it," Bernie said, as he and Kassler sat like reprimanded schoolchildren the next day in Zelazo's office. "It wasn't supposed to happen like that at all."

"Mrs. Fletcher is a *very* gentle person," Kassler agreed wholeheartedly.

"Yes, I can tell," Zelazo held up the front page of the morning paper, on which Mrs. Fletcher looked strikingly like one of those individuals who tend to develop large incisors at night.

"The papers sensationalize blood and gore," Bernie noted intolerantly. "Blood photographs well."

"And gore," Kassler chimed in. "Gore photographs well, too."

Zelazo stood dumbfounded for perhaps the first time in his life, looking at Kassler and Kohler.

"Out!" he finally said and pointed to the door.

The gentlemen arose from their chairs and headed for the door.

"Does this mean we're fired?" Kassler asked.

"I haven't decided yet," Zelazo said. "But I probably can't do that for a while, can I, Dr. Kohler?"

"How come?" Kassler asked in a state of semi-shock. Half his office was already packed up.

"Because," Zelazo explained, "Dr. Kohler filed a grievance with the union this morning, and if I fire you, all the nurses, maintenance staff, and everyone else will go on strike. Won't they, Dr. Kohler?"

Bernie Kohler nodded in the affirmative.

"What's the grievance?" Kassler asked.

"Dr. Kohler claims that the staff is not being provided adequate protection against assaultive patients. Now, good-bye, gentlemen," and Zelazo shut the door firmly behind them.

* * *

Over the next few days, Skip Fletcher hung on in the Intensive Care Unit. Kassler brought Diana Fletcher bulletins, but her mental condition had deteriorated so that he wasn't sure how much she grasped.

Otherwise, during the days Kassler kept himself busy seeing his dwindling load of patients and devoting himself to his last major professional project, trying to find some way to get the severely regressed patients, like Cheryl, ready for release, should the court ever decide to open the doors to Phlegethon again. His efforts went for naught. So far, absolutely nothing that he or anyone else could think of seemed to work with these patients.

In the evenings, he spent the first two thousand dollars of his legacy from Leo Szlyck replacing the wardrobe Leo had reduced to ashes and purchasing an elaborate stereo and a bizarre collection of records to go with them. For by now, Kassler had moved into Bolgia.

Kassler was not overjoyed about living alone in the home of his murder victim, but Lupa had categorically refused to move there with him, and so he felt he had no choice. Those nights that he didn't spend with Lupa, Kassler would wander around the cold dark halls of Bolgia, his stereo blaring the melancholy strains of famous Christian Masses, Passions, and Requiems. St. Matthew, St. John, and St. Luke sang out their inspirational tales again and again. Mozart, Beethoven, and Bach Masses echoed throughout the house as though the dial of Kassler's stereo had been welded to a station with an all-night Franciscan disc jockey. The melodic endeavors of Berlioz, Verdi, Dvořák, and Brahms requiescated incessantly. If I heard one more Kyrie, one more Sanctus, one more Gloria or Osanna, I would have taken my case straight to the Patre Filioque.

"You know," I told Kassler as he poked around the basement for a broom one night, "I'm really not a vampire. Crucifixes, silver bullets, garlic, and the like really don't frighten me a whole lot. Neither does liturgical music. So what do you say we slip in a little jazz or bluegrass now and then? *Dona nobis pacem.*"

My pleas had no effect. *In spiritum sanctum* prevailed.

* * *

When at last Kassler and Lupa were married, in a small ceremony at the end of the week, *requiescat in pace* returned.
Lupa and Kassler dwelled, at least for the time being, at Lupa's
apartment, although from time to time Kassler would drop in
at Bolgia to see how I was doing, the attraction being simply
too great to resist.

Lupa had reserved for later a decision regarding her staying
with Kassler at Bolgia during Christmas Eve and Day, when
Kassler would, for the first time, have his children for the
holiday, the result of the unavailability of babysitters and Vita's
desire to party late on Christmas Eve. When all child-care
resources had been exhausted, Vita turned, in a great show of
largess and as a very last resort, to her children's father for the
service.

Kassler was, of course, ecstatic. Not incidentally, it provided an excellent excuse for reneging on Bernie Kohler's
invitation for Christmas Eve dinner, which had been proffered
and accepted many months before his marriage to Lupa. Kassler
had scrupulously avoided saying a word to anyone about his
betrothal, but especially to Bernie Kohler.

Unquestionably of greatest significance during a week with
a very full agenda for Kassler was our meeting. Finally, Kassler
and I got down to business.

"I think I need treatment," I told Kassler one night shortly
before his wedding.

"What sort of treatment?" Kassler played cute.

"Well, not a massage," I gave Kassler a little dose of his
cuteness back.

Kassler turned a little pale and moderated his naturally flip-
pant style somewhat.

"Treating Satan? It might take a while."

"You've got nothing better to do, have you? You could take
a year off. You're living rent-free upstairs and Leo gave you
twenty thousand dollars, didn't he?"

"Yes, he did. . . ."

"That's from me. My idea. It'll give you the freedom to do
as you like while you treat me. The money should last a couple

of years, with interest, anyway. So, what do you say?" I asked.

"Aren't you supposed to offer me whatever I want in exchange for my soul or something?" Kassler asked.

"Who wants it? A charming mythology. It makes a good story, but I'm up to my ass now in souls. Everybody wants to give me his soul these days. What would I do with yours?"

"What's the problem?" Kassler asked.

"Does that mean we're starting treatment?"

"No," Kassler answered, "it doesn't. But I have to know whether psychotherapy is indicated."

"You've got to be kidding, Kassler. I'm *Satan*. I'm no John Doe the police found in an alley and dropped at the admitting unit at Phlegethon. You *know* me. You know me very well by now. I want you to treat me."

"What's the *problem*?" Kassler persisted.

"The problem is that I'm Satan. Come on, Kassler, enough is enough," I told the skeptical young man slouching across the chair in front of me. "Don't you want to make Satan better?"

"Not particularly. What . . . is . . . the . . . problem?"

"I'm not as happy as I could be. How's that?"

"Not very good," Kassler propped his head on his fist and stared ahead at the dark walls of my cavernous home.

"It's the best I can do for now," I told him. "Once we start treatment, I promise I'll give you the whole story."

"How do I know that this isn't some diabolical plot of Leo Szlyck's to ruin me, drive me insane, lead me to incurable depression, ensure that I can't stay married to Lupa?"

"You don't. You just have to use your own common sense and good judgment. You have every reason not to trust Leo. What can I tell you? There's no devious plot. That's all I can say."

Kassler rested in the darkness and thought.

"So?" I finally asked.

"I don't know," Kassler said. "I want to talk to Zelazo."

"Zelazo? Zelazo! Why? He's no *good* for you, Kassler. I can't for the life of me understand why you guys are still talking to each other. He's fucking your wife, fathering your kids, has absolute control over your career. Why do you still talk to him? It makes no sense to me at all."

"You're right," Kassler said as he rolled out of the chair and headed upstairs without having made a commitment. "It doesn't make any sense."

Kassler arranged to meet with Zelazo as Zelazo was on his way across the grounds of Phlegethon to inspect the giant evergreen the patients had decorated to celebrate the joyous Yuletide season.

The day was cold and overcast, presaging the arrival of the winter of 1977, one of the coldest to hit the Eastern states in several decades. The sleet that had been falling for the last four days, up until only a few hours before Kassler and Zelazo began their excursion, formed a slush underfoot that quickly soaked through Kassler's shoes and with each step felt more like Harpies tearing skin off the soles of his feet.

Kassler would not, of course, admit his discomfort to Zelazo, who wore only slacks, a thin cotton shirt, and a Persian-lamb hat from under which Zelazo's long yellow hair emerged to fly behind him in the brisk wind, mixing with his even longer yellow beard.

Zelazo's strides were big but slow, and this enabled Kassler, who needed nearly two steps for every single step of Zelazo's, to keep up.

"Leo hadn't the faintest idea what he was constructing when he built that damn thing," Zelazo remarked as they walked. "And he never had the faintest notion what it was capable of doing. Neither do you. It's lethal, Sy. Let it be."

"What I don't understand," Kassler answered after he'd thought over Zelazo's exhortation, "is what possible difference it could make to you whether or not I play psychotherapist to Szlyck's machine. What's the big deal? And you'll never convince me that you're doing this because of any great concern for my welfare."

"It's a personal matter between Leo and me," Zelazo answered as he strode.

"Maybe it'll tell me how to destroy the invincible King of Phlegethon," Kassler tried. "Leo might not have wanted to dirty his hands."

Zelazo smiled good-naturedly as he slowly plodded ahead.

"Leo's hands were so caked with mud, he wouldn't have known the difference, don't you think?"

"Then why, Sam? Why is it so damn important to you that I stay away from Szlyck's computer?" Kassler persisted.

"Not just Szlyck's computer—Satan. Dealing with Satan is a mortal sin."

"That's ridiculous," Kassler said. "Szlyck was a lunatic. He invented a lunatic machine. There *is* no such thing as Satan. It's a fantasy of Szlyck's, probably something left over from Rumania."

"Like God . . . and other dark Slavic fantasies," Zelazo remarked.

"Exactly," Kassler said, less convincingly than Zelazo, "like God."

The pair pushed through the wet mounds of cold gray paste at their feet, still a fair distance from the object of their pilgrimage. Then, in a few minutes, Zelazo stopped, stamped his feet up and down several times, and pounded his chest invigoratingly, while Kassler rubbed his ungloved hands briskly over his arms to warm himself.

"Every patient we treat changes us," Zelazo said as he stood looking out at the icy mist which surrounded them.

"A little," Kassler admitted.

"It depends on the patient. Satan is no ordinary patient, Sy."

"Look, Sam, I've just gotten married to Lupa. I'm not going to do anything that'll screw up my life."

Almost as soon as the words were out, Kassler sensed that he shouldn't have told Zelazo, but it was too late. It was done.

Zelazo smiled, nodded his congratulations, and fondly patted Kassler several times on the back.

"I'll be careful," Kassler added as they resumed walking.

"That's not enough," Zelazo told Kassler. "Satan uses the truth exceptionally well. He never lies. But it's not the truth as we know it. It's the cutting edge of the truth, the last razor-thin line left to the truth before deceit begins, and he'll slice you up with it, painlessly, until he's cut out of you whatever he wants. At the end of it all, you won't even know that he's touched you."

Kassler was not unaffected by Zelazo's admonitions, and

had they come from anyone else, he might have given them more credence. He looked up at Zelazo as he walked beside him, adamant and imposing.

"You know what I don't understand about the two of us," Kassler found himself confiding in Zelazo. "You've done so many damn things to hurt me, and yet every time I see you, I want you to take me out fishing or something." Kassler looked away from Zelazo. "Isn't that crazy?"

Zelazo looked over at Kassler and then he stretched out his giant arm and put it around Kassler's shoulders.

"Just ridiculous," Zelazo smiled as he held Kassler firmly, "because I don't fish, son."

"I know," Kassler said. "You run around without any clothes on in the middle of the night chasing after possums. You're as crazy as everyone else," Kassler concluded as they finally reached their destination.

Zelazo tilted his head up and examined the tree.

"So," he asked Kassler, "what do you think?"

Kassler studied the dazzling tree. Thousands of medication bottles had been covered with glitter and hung everywhere with paper clips. Old electrode leads from the EEG equipment, now dipped in silver paint, hung like tinsel, beside paper angels cut from Rorschach protocols. The bandages used for restraints were painted red and green and draped like bunting all around the tree. The burlap from an old straitjacket had been stretched across two coat hangers and painted gold to form a star at the tree's top.

Kassler and Zelazo stood admiring the tree for several minutes.

"Creative sons-a-bitches, bad chemistry and all, don't you think?" Zelazo asked Kassler as they turned and started the trek back to the main building.

Kassler's mind was somewhere else.

"What exactly is a *mortal* sin, Sam?" Kassler asked his mentor.

"Oh," answered Zelazo as they plodded onward, Zelazo breathing heavily in the bitter-cold evening, Kassler's feet raw to the bone, his hands frozen blue, and everywhere in between icy and nauseous, "let's see. Turning the valve of a paracentesis tube and killing Leo Szlyck—that would probably be considered a mortal sin," Zelazo conjectured.

Not another word was said during the remainder of the journey back to Phlegethon. Zelazo gave no indication of what he intended to do with this information, and Kassler, his insides spastic and queasy, didn't ask. He understood. Zelazo had one more item to use against him when and how he wished, should Kassler not behave as requested.

Zelazo, of course, never came right out and said that if Kassler persisted in his intention of treating me, Zelazo would ruin him, but then Zelazo didn't have to say it. Kassler was no dummy. He caught on.

"I'm not going to be able to treat you," Kassler announced with appropriate conviction, the night after his promenade with Zelazo.

"That is a pity," I answered. "May I ask what prompted this decision?"

"A number of factors," Kassler was evasive as he sat casually on the worn arm of the overstuffed chair in front of me.

"Technical considerations, no doubt," I offered.

"Yes," Kassler grabbed quickly at straws. "Psychotherapy is a complex and highly technical process. I had to take a number of things into account."

"I'm sorry that they're beyond my ken. I would've liked to understand why I'm a poor candidate for psychotherapy. Perhaps I'm not verbal enough. Is that it?" I asked.

"The decision was based on a complicated series of factors, as I've said," Kassler dodged.

"Or maybe you felt I wasn't capable of insight?"

"Personality disorders are highly refractory to psychotherapeutic intervention," Kassler explained to me.

"Highly refractory. No kidding," I said. "How about murdering my angel Leo Szlyck? Does this increase or decrease the refraction index?"

"Shit!" Kassler whined. "Was I being televised? Who else knows?"

"You, me, Lupa, Sam Zelazo, and that's probably it," I told him.

Kassler sat in silence and thought very hard, at least as hard as his overwhelmed cerebrum was capable of at the time. He contemplated, primarily, Zelazo's stern admonitions about treating me, and the subtle and clandestine ways I supposedly would undermine him—body, brain, heart, and soul—leaving little more than a shell of his splendid self remaining when it was all over.

"I'm still not going to treat you. I'm sorry," Kassler finally informed me with great conviction.

"Well," I said, "I hope I haven't given you the opinion that I condone your terminating one of my favorite angels."

"It doesn't really matter," Kassler said. "I'm disconnecting you."

"Disconnecting my what?" I asked with fascination.

"Your plug," Kassler told me.

"What plug? I haven't needed a plug in years."

"I don't believe you." Kassler got up and began searching around me. "You've got to get your energy from somewhere."

"Oh, I do. I get it from you. And from others. Also from the darkness. I run on sort of the reverse of solar power. It's an energy source whose potential has barely begun to be tapped."

Kassler continued to stalk around me looking for a power cord.

"I'll take you apart," Kassler tried another approach when he became convinced that I wasn't affixed to an outlet.

"You may have noticed," I told Kassler, "that there's an eighteen-inch wall of dynamite and gelignite encircling me. Leo's idea, but I didn't do a whole lot to stop him, because, you see, if you touch a single one of my wires, you, Bolgia, and we can only guess what else will be blown to smithereens. Be my guest. Yank something."

"Is that all?" Kassler said in frustration. "Are your games done? Because I'm not treating you and that's final!"

"Nope. It's not all. I can't stand idly by while you do in one of my angels. It sets a bad precedent. So here're two more things to take into consideration before you make your final decision final. If you treat me for a decent length of time, regardless of the outcome, I'll leave you with the Great Answer. That's an offer not to be taken lightly, Kassler, believe me. You all spend your lives in a frantic search for the Great Answer. I'm going to give it to you 'way in advance of when most men get it, if they do at all, in exchange for not a whole lot of your psychotherapeutic time. What do you say?"

"Not interested."

"So much for positive reinforcement. The second item for your consideration is this," I decided not to haggle over Kassler's resistance. "As you may or may not know, computers utilize telephone lines. I'm no different. Ma Bell and I are close partners in this enterprise. This allows me to perform some amazing feats. Observe this, for example. Step one, dial tone. Note the unpleasant buzz in the background. Step two, an assortment of equally unpleasant beeps of various pitches. *Voilà!* Step three, somewhere in Citadel a phone rings. Let's see if we can guess who'll answer it. Let me see, today is Thursday, right? That should be Donovan."

A voice answered the ringing phone.

"Citadel Police. Desk Sergeant Donovan. How may I help you?"

"I'd like to report a terrible murder," I said.

"Yes, ma'am," the desk sergeant helped me. "I'll connect you with homicide."

"Guess I should have used a deeper voice," I told Kassler.

"You can hang up," Kassler said quietly.

"Well, then, I will," I responded, and I did. "It pained me to do that, Kassler, because I know that you don't get your best from your therapist when you're blackmailing him, but Zelazo started it."

Kassler stood numbly in front of me. Then he started walking away.

"This has been a very discouraging day," said Kassler as he started up the cellar stairs.

CHAPTER 3

The events that led to Kassler's deciding to commit suicide all occurred over Christmas Eve and Christmas Day. Now, I know that there are those who are going to want to make a big deal of this, and any and all disclaimers on my part will be seen as more grist for the mill. The truth of the matter is that there is absolutely no significance to the incidents' having taken place during Christmas.

For certain people holidays are particularly hard, especially if these people are alone, and Christmas is the worst of all. The emphasis you all place on the close family and warm hearth makes the lives of those who're alone in the cold nearly unbearable. Ebenezer Scrooge was an exception, but note, not for long. The specter of death and loneliness overcame even his stone heart. Unfortunately, not everyone has the good fortune to have Dickens as his author. Happy endings were, I regret to say, not abundant during this particular Yuletide.

I don't pretend to know the reasons men decide to end their own lives. I suppose, like everything else, there're good reasons and some reasons that are not so good. Likewise, I take no position on the phenomenon. I don't condone it and I don't condemn it. It's your life.

Kassler's case was different, of course, because I needed him for my psychotherapy.

The first few hours of Christmas Eve were among the happiest in Kassler's life. Lupa had finally agreed to be by his side at Bolgia for the holiday, and the experience of sitting at a dinner

389

table with his new wife and his two energetic children on Christmas Eve was so joyous to Kassler that several times he found himself fighting back tears.

The children were so excited in anticipation of the next morning and the presents it would bring that Kassler had the perfect excuse for a bathtub reunion—something to calm the children—at the end of which all three, with tears of sadness and joy streaking their cheeks, were splashing and screaming at the top of their lungs, "Penises! Baginas! Penises! Baginas!" until Lupa, having followed the entire event from the next room, burst into the bathroom stark naked, flung open her arms, and yelled, "Here comes another bagina!" and joined in the fun.

It was Lupa who finally got everyone calmed down and the children in their pajamas, once it became clear to her that, left to themselves, Kassler and the children would bathe all night.

For the next hour, they decorated the tree and drank eggnog, listened to Kassler read "The Night Before Christmas," and, finally, hung up their stockings. It was eleven o'clock before the children were nestled all snug in their beds and Lupa and Kassler were able to sit on the sofa, sip champagne, and exchange gifts.

It had been agreed that they would give each other something practical that would last a long time, so Kassler gave Lupa a handsome set of leatherbound books of poetry, and Lupa, in turn, gave Kassler the keys to a medium-sized Mercedes-Benz.

As Kassler stood at the window, speechless, staring at the shiny silver car, which had been delivered to their driveway while Kassler and his children were yelling in the bathroom about their genitals, the telephone rang.

"I'm not supposed to be on call," Kassler explained over the phone to the nurse at Phlegethon. "Who is on call?"

"Dr. Kohler, but I can't no find him," the Costa Rican nurse explained.

"Then try Dr. Zelazo."

"Can't no find him, neither."

"What about Mrs. Chaikin?"

"Patient is your patient and rule say if on-duty man can no be find, you call patient's doctor. You are Mr. Donato's doctor, so this is why I call you. You come over, okay? Mr. Donato is *very* agitated."

"I'll be there," Kassler agreed reluctantly. He explained the situation to Lupa and, promising to be back in no more than forty-five minutes, left in his new automobile.

Shortly after Kassler left, the phone rang again. Lupa, who had now finished the bottle of champagne on her own, answered it.

"Hello," she said in her merriest Christmas voice.

"Who is this?" the man at the other end asked.

"Mrs. Kassler," Lupa thought she'd try out the name to see how she liked it.

"Vita?"

"No, this is the *new* Mrs. Kassler, Lupa Kassler. You probably want the old Mrs. Kassler, Vita Kassler. She lives someplace else. I'd tell you the old Mrs. Kassler's phone number except I don't know it yet because I've only been the new Mrs. Kassler for a little over a week, but it's probably in the phone book. Who shall I say is calling?" Lupa asked merrily.

There was a long silence at the other end of the phone, and then Bernie Kohler slowly set the receiver back into its cradle.

When Kassler arrived at Phlegethon, he found Philip Donato stomping around in his small room, screaming at the top of his lungs, while three orderlies leaned against the door to keep him from getting out.

"Mr. Donato's mother come this evening," Concepción explained to Kassler. "They have very nice time. He told Merry Christmas to her. She told Merry Christmas to him. Everybody is very happy. She give him candy and they kiss good-bye. Mr. Donato go into his room and boom! Screaming! And yelling! And banging! He breaked the lock from the door."

Kassler walked over to the door of Philip Donato's room and peeked through the small window. Strewn all over were mashed pieces of candy and the little white paper cups in which the chocolates had previously rested. Philip Donato was pounding his hands against the wall and stamping his feet on the candy and wrappers which covered the floor.

"Philip?" Kassler called quietly.

"You bastard!" Philip Donato responded when he saw Kassler's face at the window.

"What happened, Philip?" Kassler asked.

"You promised me, you bastard! You promised me! You're a bastard, Dr. Kassler! A son-of-a-bitch cock-sucking mother-fucking asshole bastard, you fucker!"

"Whew," Concepción remarked.

"Would you like to talk about it?" Kassler called through the small spaces in the mesh on the window.

"Not with you, you goddamn liar!"

"What happened?" Kassler demanded.

"You want to know what happened? You want to know what happened!" Philip Donato shouted. "Well, here's what happened," and he reached for a handful of the white paper candy wrappers and shoved them through the wire-mesh window in the door.

Kassler bent down and picked up several dozen tiny cups. Carefully lettered on the bottom of each one were three words. In some, it said EAT YOUR ROUGHAGE. In others it said MOVE YOUR BOWELS.

"I'm sorry," Kassler said. "I was sure we had thought of everything."

Then Kassler turned to Concepción.

"Get the physician on call to approve sedation, and then put him to sleep," he told her. "I don't think we're going to be able to talk this one out tonight."

"Okay," Concepción was very pleased to hear this solution, "but don't go yet. Mrs. Fletcher's been asking for you all night. I tell her that you're not on call, but maybe since you're here anyway, you say hello and Merry Christmas and then good-bye, yes?"

Kassler nodded that he would and walked down the end of the hall to where Diana Fletcher sat sobbing on her bed.

When she looked up and saw Kassler, she jumped up from her cot, ran to him, and threw her arms around him, still weeping bitterly.

"Thank you, Dr. Kassler," she said through her tears. "Thank you."

"Merry Christmas, Mrs. Fletcher," Kassler gave his patient a brief hug and then returned her to her bed.

"Skip is going to die tonight," she told Kassler. "Please let me say good-bye to him."

"Did someone tell you that?" Kassler asked.

"You have to believe me," Diana Fletcher begged. "Please? Let me talk to my son."

Kassler looked at the unschizophrenic clarity in Mrs. Fletcher's wet eyes and excused himself, promising to return shortly. Then he called Citadel General Hospital. Skip Fletcher would not make it through the night.

Kassler put down the phone and closed his eyes. He knew there was only one alternative, so he called Lupa.

"Another emergency," he explained. "I may be another hour or so. You should probably go to sleep."

"I already was," Lupa said. "Merry Christmas," and she hung up the phone.

But Lupa couldn't fall back to sleep after the phone call, so with some nervousness she decided to throw caution to the wind and, at long last, pay a visit to her friend who dwelled in the basement of Bolgia.

As Kassler was sneaking Diana Fletcher out the back door of Phlegethon, Bernie Kohler was walking in the front.

"I need to be admitted," he told the new man on admissions, an Iranian by the name of Dr. Siv.

"I'm sorry," Dr. Siv explained, "we aren't allowed to admit anyone. It's a court order. What seems to be the problem?"

"Look," said Bernie, tears streaming from his eyes, "I'm suicidal. I need someplace to stay where I can be watched, so I won't harm myself."

"We have a court order," the thin yellow-skinned physician told Bernie.

"I know that. I work here. I'm the one who *got* the court order. I'm also going to kill myself if I don't get some help."

"Why don't we talk. Tell me what the problem is. You might feel better."

"I don't *want* to talk. I want to be put up on Three-A, on

suicidal precautions, with the door locked," Bernie said in frustration.

"What we do here," Dr. Siv explained, "is called the *talking cure*. You talk to me and your whole attitude will change."

"I know about the talking cure, you ninny," Bernie exploded. "I work here. I'm a talking curer myself. All day long I talk people into cures. But my problem involves another staff member, and I don't *want* to talk about it."

It was useless. Bernie Kohler could not get himself admitted to Phlegethon. Attempts to locate Sam Zelazo were unsuccessful, as were efforts to secure Bernie Kohler another place to spend Christmas Eve. At the end, Bernie and Dr. Siv sat glaring at each other in the small admitting office, which now stood like an iron gate, barring entrance even to the rulers of Phlegethon themselves.

Then Bernie Kohler, resigned to his fate, assured Dr. Siv that he felt much better, and left. On his way out, Bernie passed by Kassler's office, tried the door, and, finding it unlocked, entered. He walked over to Kassler's desk, switched on the small desk lamp, pulled a sheet of paper from the desk, and began writing a farewell note to his lover.

The note was something of a work of art. For over an hour Bernie Kohler rambled endlessly about his life and times, the loneliness and desperation of the homosexual life, man's inhumanity to man, his own great affection for Kassler complete with explicit descriptions of their intercourse, and the hopelessness of his present circumstances. After reminding Kassler that Kassler had neglected to cancel his Christmas Eve engagement with him, and relating to Kassler the details of the *nouvelle cuisine* dinner that had been prepared, its consumption of time and money, and its present inedible status, Bernie decided to close his epistle with a juicy ending.

"While I love you, Sy, and always will, wherever I may be," Bernie wrote, "I cannot handle your thinking so little of our relationship that you not only didn't bother to tell me you were getting married, but, what hurts the most, you would reject me for the type of woman we both know Lupa to be. You two should make a great couple."

Bernie Kohler signed his letter "With great love, Bernie"

and then, to take the edge off his suicide, drew a smile-face beneath it.

By the time Bernie had finished writing the letter, he felt considerably less suicidal. The letter itself, Bernie concluded, would no doubt have the effect he wanted. He had great visions of Kassler finding the note and racing frantically over to Bernie's apartment just as Bernie was about to slip his head through the rope. Kassler would realize that Bernie meant more to him than Lupa ever could and would annul their marriage, so that he and Bernie would live happily ever after.

And so things might have remained had Sam Zelazo not finally arrived, after Dr. Siv's desperate phone search had hunted him down at one of the parties of which he and Vita were making the rounds.

Zelazo located Bernie in Kassler's office just as Bernie was slipping his dispatch into an envelope, and invited Bernie to have coffee with him in his office.

"I can tell," Zelazo told Bernie Kohler, "that you have lost someone very close to you."

Bernie looked up at Zelazo like a displaced basset hound and large tears welled in his eyes.

"He means so much to me," Bernie wept.

"Being a homosexual in these times is terribly difficult," Zelazo said. "It's a hopeless situation for many people."

The word "hopeless" rekindled the embers of futility which had just died down inside Bernie Kohler.

"We think that because we're professionals in this field that we're somehow immune to loneliness and great loss," Zelazo went on, "and this makes it all the more difficult."

"What good am I to anyone?" Bernie asked.

"You've chosen a very hard course," Zelazo pointed out.

"I didn't *choose* it," Bernie cried out. "I didn't *ask* to be like this. I just am. I just turned out like this. Don't you think I've *tried* to be different? Don't you think I've *wanted* to lead another kind of life? I can't. It's not what I am. It doesn't work for me."

"It's a tragedy," Sam Zelazo agreed.

"He didn't even tell me he was *thinking* of getting married," Bernie said. "And to *Lupa*! For chrissakes, he must know about

Lupa. He's got to know. What an insult to my feelings for him," Bernie lamented.

"I was surprised when he told me a couple days ago," Zelazo deftly inserted, "but Sy has his own reasons, I'm sure."

Bernie looked up, stunned.

"He told you two days ago? Two days ago! He told *you*? He hates you. You're his worst enemy. Oh, Jesus," Bernie cried out.

"It was only in passing," Zelazo tossed the notion aside, now that it had had its effect.

"That does it," Bernie announced.

"I have to go now," Zelazo said, "but if you need anyone to talk to later tonight, give Dr. Siv a call. He's new, but he's quite good."

Zelazo fetched a key from his pocket and unlocked a drawer in his desk.

"Here's something that'll help you to sleep." He handed Bernie a bottle of sedatives. "It'll only put you to sleep, not kill you, even if you take the whole bottle, so you can save yourself the trouble," Zelazo attempted to lighten the mood.

Then Zelazo fastened the top two buttons on his black cashmere coat, gave his white silk scarf a turn around his neck, and headed for the door. Just before he exited, Bernie Kohler's words stopped him.

"You know, Sam," Bernie said, "you're a son-of-a-bitch. I'm going to kill myself now, and you're at least half responsible for it. You know that, don't you?"

"Yes, I do," Zelazo looked back at Bernie. "I'm going to miss having you around here. Don't forget to turn off the lights when you leave; we're in an energy crunch," and Sam Zelazo's hand turned the doorknob.

"You really *want* me to kill myself, don't you, you bastard?" Bernie asked as Zelazo opened the door.

"You could disappoint me, of course."

Zelazo smiled at Bernie Kohler, closed the door behind him, and returned to his parties, making only a brief stop beforehand at Kassler's office to read and photocopy Bernie's letter to Kassler and replace it on Kassler's desk, keeping the copy for himself.

* * *

"Halloo?" Lupa called out in her tipsy state when she had reached the bottom of Bolgia's basement stairs. "Merry Christmas, and guess who's back?"

"Season's greetings, Lupa," I answered. "How've you been?"

"Oh, I don't know," Lupa meandered around the cellar. "Okay, I guess. Life has its ups and downs. How about yourself?"

"Fine. Just fine. It's good to see you again. You disappeared."

"Yes, well," Lupa answered coquettishly, "I guess I wasn't very good about that, was I?"

"Not even a postcard. You said you'd see me every week."

"I know. I just couldn't do it. I didn't think it'd be good for either of us. What else can I say? I'm sorry, Satan. I really am."

"Aha." The cat was out of the bag.

"Ahaaa . . ." Lupa said back to me quietly as she walked daintily about on her tiptoes, champagne in her eyes.

"Leo told me when I left him," she giggled. "It was supposed to prove how stupid I was."

"You believed him?"

"Of course. What's so hard to believe when Leo tells you he's brought the devil to earth? I didn't put it past him. I'm surprised he didn't bring your whole family."

"It didn't bother you, then?"

"To learn I'd been getting it on with the devil?"

"If you must."

"Oh, a little, I guess. Except when I thought about it, it made sense. My choice of mates has never been spectacular."

"So you decided to keep away."

"It was better that way, don't you think?"

"I'm not so sure anymore."

There was a long silence as Lupa continued to tiptoe around the basement, her arms waving in the air.

"Oh, well," she finally said. "That's all over now, isn't it? Ancient history."

"Is it?"

"Do you know what tonight is?" Lupa changed the subject quickly as certain feelings started to return.

"Christmas Eve?"

"It is," Lupa agreed. "It's also my wedding anniversary. I've been married exactly one week. I'll bet you can't guess where my husband is."

"Where?"

"Not here," Lupa answered. "That's where."

"I'm sorry to hear that," I said.

"So am I. Well," Lupa continued as she did a little twirl in her peignoir, "what have you been up to the last few years?"

"Oh, nothing much, going to and fro in the earth, and walking up and down in it. And yourself?"

"Trying to make a living..." Lupa's words trailed off into the darkness as she turned. "...trying to make a living..."

"Do you love him?" I asked.

"Who? Sy?"

"Yes."

There was a pause as Lupa ceased her spinning and collapsed comfortably into the old stuffed chair.

"Yes," she huffed, a little dizzy and out of breath. "Yes, I do. I think I love him very much. He has a lovely soul, I think. I'm counting on it to save me from destroying myself. You two must meet someday soon. I'll introduce you. You should get along very well. You'll like him."

"I'm looking forward to it," I told Lupa.

It seemed to Kassler, as he stood in the doorway of the dimly lit hospital room, tears flooding his eyes, that it was over scarcely before it began.

"I've been thinking about heaven," Skip Fletcher—pasty-gray, his face swollen from the massive doses of steroids, a Mets baseball hat covering a head now completely bald from radiation therapy—told his mother as she walked over and held him. "I'll bet you can go skateboarding every day and they have all these great hills. There's lots of kids my age who I'm really going to like and I'll invite them over so we can play slot cars or do pop-a-wheelies on our bikes—" he stopped in midsentence and started sobbing. "Mom, I'm so scared and I need you."

"You'll do fine, Skip," Diana Fletcher told her son, tears streaking her cheeks as she clutched him. "Everybody in heaven's really going to like you. You'll have lots of friends."

Skip looked up at his father, sitting on the edge of the bed, his face buried in his hands.

"I'm going to miss you so much, Dad," he said. "What if there's no one there to take me camping?"

Jim Fletcher nodded to his son, unable to respond through his tears, as his wife held Skip against her, gently rocking him; and when she laid Skip back down on his pillow, he was dead.

Diana Fletcher said absolutely nothing on the ride back to Phlegethon. At first Kassler had tried to get her to talk about her feelings, but to no avail. After comforting her son and then her husband, she determined that she had done all that she could. Her eyes began once more to fill with the terror of her own illness, and she returned to being a chronic, incurable schizophrenic.

The experience for Kassler had been so heart-rending that he could hardly bear it. He longed to race to his new home and embrace his children. Joshua was less than two years younger than Skip Fletcher.

Of course, this joyous reunion was not to happen as soon as Kassler had intended. After depositing Mrs. Fletcher back in her room and checking on the sleeping Philip Donato, Kassler made a stop in his office to check for messages. Bernie Kohler's epistle awaited him.

With growing panic Kassler read through the letter and then attempted to call Bernie. There was, of course, no answer.

It seems that Bernie, on leaving Phlegethon and its clinical director, reverted to Plan A. He went home, took a couple of Zelazo's sedatives and a good stiff drink or two, pulled down his outdoorsy books, and leafed through them until he came to simple directions for tying a noose.

Being bright and a former scout, Bernie Kohler acquired the necessary skill, using a clothesline, in no time at all. A pipe from the heating system ran propitiously across the ceiling.

Bernie stood on a chair, tied the noose to the bar, and imagined what it would be like when Kassler finally appeared.

Kassler arrived a half-hour after this, jumped his new Mercedes up on the sidewalk, and raced up the stairs to Bernie's apartment.

The first thing that hit Kassler as he pounded with his fists on the door and called Bernie's name was the nearly overwhelming smell of feces, as though someone had crapped in his pants, an accurate analysis of the situation.

Kassler noticed that the hinge pins to the door were on the outside, so he pulled out his pocketknife and pried out the pins. Then he yanked the door and it caved in, revealing Bernie Kohler hanging by his neck in the middle of the living room, his pants filled with feces, dead.

In the process of the rehearsal, Bernie had placed the noose around his neck. Rapt in a ripe fantasy about Kassler's reaction, Bernie lost his balance on the chair, and, instead of relaxing and holding the bar, he fought desperately against the tottering chair, the Chivas Regal inside him, and the sedatives. It was no contest. With a violent snap, Bernie fell and jerked to the end of the rope, breaking his neck, killing himself, and, in a common reflex action, releasing the contents of his bowels.

Kassler stood in shock, staring at Bernie. Bernie's eyes bulged from their sockets, his wire-rimmed glasses were at an angle halfway down his nose, and his tongue hung out of his mouth, thick as a sausage.

"Oh, Christ," were the first words out of Kassler's mouth. "Why, Bernie? This is so stupid."

Then he walked over, picked up the chair, stood on it, and cut the rope with his pocketknife. Bernie was heavier than Kassler had realized. He fell out of Kassler's arms to the floor with a loud thud.

Kassler stepped down from the chair and called the police. He debated about whether he should clean up his friend before anyone else saw him, but, remembering admonitions by television detectives, decided to leave the rest of the scene of the crime undisturbed. He went and pulled the spread off the bed and covered Bernie with it. Then he went into the kitchen and waited for the police, who arrived, strangely, with Sam Zelazo.

"How long has he been dead?" Zelazo asked.

"I don't know," Kassler said. "I've been here about ten minutes."

"I saw him tonight. He was very depressed," Zelazo told Kassler, "but he seemed better when I left. I thought the danger was over. I left a message with the hospital and the police to get in touch with me right away if there were any further problems, but I hadn't expected this."

Kassler didn't say anything to Zelazo. He just stared at the police putting Bernie onto a stretcher.

"How're you holding up?" Zelazo asked.

"I don't know, Sam," Kassler answered honestly. "I really don't know."

"Bernie was a strange character," Zelazo said. "It's always hard to understand what motivates someone to do something like this, but it's even harder with Bernie. You were close to him, Sy. Do you have any idea what could have driven him to this?"

Kassler looked at Zelazo's eyes. Kassler had reached the end of the cat-and-mouse games.

"No, I don't," he said very slowly, his eyes rigidly fixed on Zelazo's. "*You* were the last person to see him alive, Sam; what do *you* think it might have been?"

"Got me, Sy," Zelazo said. "I can't figure it out."

After the ambulance and Zelazo left and Kassler gave his statement to the police, omitting mention of Bernie's note, Kassler walked slowly down the stairs, climbed into his new car, and drove away. He started for home but halfway there turned off the main route. He wasn't ready to return to Lupa and his children.

Through the night, Kassler's shiny car rolled aimlessly through the city. He wanted to cry for Bernie, but the tears, which had come so easily just a short while ago for a child he hardly knew, wouldn't come at all for a man he knew so well.

Discouraged and exhausted, Kassler finally headed back to Bolgia as the black starless night became another gray sunless day in Citadel. No matter how he had tried throughout the night, he realized that he had been unable to stop a phrase in

Bernie's letter from reverberating around his skull. It went: "the type of woman we both know Lupa to be."

Lupa started awake in the chair in front of me when she heard the Mercedes in the driveway, and she raced up the stairs, making it to the front hall just as Kassler entered.

"You shouldn't have waited up," Kassler told Lupa. He closed the door behind him and started to remove his coat.

"I didn't," Lupa said. "What time is it?"

Kassler looked at his watch.

"Seven-thirty," he replied. "The kids should be up any minute."

"Well," Lupa said as she followed Kassler to the sofa, where he collapsed into the soft cushions. "I hope at least she was pretty."

Kassler was too fatigued to appreciate Lupa's sense of humor.

"My closest friend has just hanged himself," he answered.

"Oh, Sy," Lupa said, taking Kassler's hand. She looked at his bleary eyes and studied the way his cheeks seemed sunken and dark above his beard.

"You must be very tired," she said.

"I must be," Kassler agreed.

"I'll get you some coffee."

"Later," said Kassler. "Just stay here with me now."

Lupa moved to the corner of the couch and then reached over for Kassler and rearranged his position so his feet were on the arm of the sofa and his head in her lap. She ran her fingers gently through his curls.

"Bernie left me a note," Kassler said as he closed his eyes.

"Bernie Kohler?"

"I've told you about him?"

"A little," Lupa said. "Why did he do it?"

Kassler opened his eyes and shrugged his shoulders.

"I don't really know why he did it, because it doesn't make much sense. It wasn't like him at all. He implied in his letter, among other things, that he doesn't like classy ladies from Radcliffe. His last words were something to the effect that he despised me for marrying the type of woman we both knew you to be, and we should make a perfect couple."

Lupa stopped stroking Kassler's head and froze. She could feel her heart race furiously inside her chest and her palms become cold and clammy.

"I have to tell you something, Sy," she said, starting to shake slightly, "that I probably should have told you before. I tried several times, but I couldn't get up the nerve to do it."

Kassler sat up. He knew immediately that he wasn't going to like what Lupa had to say.

Lupa avoided looking in Kassler's eyes.

"I want you to know that, when I'm finished telling you what I have to, if you want an annulment, it's yours, no questions asked."

"What did you have to do with Bernie killing himself?" Kassler looked at Lupa trembling beside him.

"Nothing. Nothing at all."

Lupa took a deep breath and plunged ahead.

"When I first started my interior-design business," she began, "things went very well. For a long time. Then we hit the recession and things weren't so good. I got months behind in my rent. I had thousands of dollars of debts. Everything I owned was being taken away. It was humiliating. I've never lived like that, Sy. I got really desperate. I had no skills. I couldn't get a job. One of my clients was attracted to me. He paid me a lot of money to do some sexual things. He told some of his friends—"

Kassler reached his hand over to Lupa's face and held his fingers gently over her lips.

"Please don't say anything more."

"I've tried to—" Lupa started, but Kassler pressed his fingers against her lips again.

"There isn't any interior-design business, is there?" Kassler said numbly.

Lupa turned away and started to cry.

"Just about everyone around knows except me, don't they?" Kassler inquired.

"A lot of people know," Lupa said through her tears, "but it's all over now. Honestly. You can ask around if you want."

Kassler looked at Lupa weeping, her blond hair unkempt, frizzy, sticking out in clumps from her head like on one of his daughter's old dolls, her thin hands trembling, dark age blotches prematurely showing on her skin between where veins stuck out, her face sallow and bony.

"It just kind of happened, Sy," Lupa said as she sobbed. "I didn't stand on street corners or anything. These were civilized men, mostly unhappily married, no one was hurt. There didn't seem to be anything wrong with it for a while, until I realized that I couldn't do it forever . . . and I didn't feel very good about myself."

Kassler reached over and pulled Lupa to him. She buried her head against his chest and wept while he held her just firmly enough to give the impression that it didn't matter.

After a few moments, Lupa looked up at Kassler and ran her hand through his beard.

"I want you to know how much I care for you, Sy. I think that we can make each other very happy. I really do."

"It's okay," Kassler adopted a forgiving tone. "It's okay."

"I didn't do it to hurt you, Sy," Lupa said. "It just happened. It won't happen again."

"I know that," Kassler said. "We'll be very happy."

"It's a new life for us both. It can be beautiful. Really."

Kassler could hear Josh trying to awaken his sister upstairs.

"I know," Kassler said. "It can be."

"Please kiss me, Sy," Lupa asked.

Kassler held Lupa's face between his hands and gave her a gentle kiss.

"Beautiful," Lupa said. "I'll make it up to you. I will, Sy."

Josh appeared at the bottom of the steps with his half-asleep sister at the end of his arm.

"You see," Josh said, "what'd I tell you. Dad's dressed. He's all ready for us."

For the rest of that day, Kassler mustered all the energy remaining to him and played the role of loving husband and father. Lupa, feeling enormous relief, was happy and bouncy and adoring, to both Kassler and his children. It was an ideal Christmas.

From time to time Lupa would glance over at Kassler, as he played on the carpet with his children, to see whether he really had forgiven her past behavior, and Kassler, catching Lupa's eye as she did so, would smile in a friendly manner to assure her that everything was just fine.

Lupa was fooled because she wanted so desperately to believe him. Kassler felt absolutely nothing at all. More accurately, Kassler had one overwhelming feeling. Lupa's confession had convinced him of the ultimate futility of his life. He detected none of her caring and affection for him. The only thought that rumbled around Kassler's brain, such as it was at that time, was that not only hadn't he formed an eternal union with the young beautiful girl of his dreams in a mutual state of ultimate love and immaculate bliss, but he had married a whore.

By this time Kassler was, of course, only a hair's breadth away from determining to follow Bernie Kohler as expeditiously as possible into the grave. A conversation with his children at dinner that afternoon advanced him a substantially greater distance than Kassler really needed.

Lupa had just finished serving pumpkin pie, the last course of the Christmas dinner she had made single-handedly in what she considered by the end of the multi-course meal to be the ultimate penance for her sins. As a matter of fact, as she returned to the kitchen for her and Kassler's coffee and surveyed the work still to be done, the many advantages of prostitution fleetingly crossed her mind.

"So," said Kassler, as he folded his hands across his full belly, "not a bad Christmas, was it?"

"Best Christmas ever," Josh agreed as he stuffed some pie into his mouth.

"How about you, Joy?" Kassler asked. "Did you enjoy Christmas?"

"It was great, Daddy. I loved it," Joy said sweetly.

"Well, I loved it, too," Kassler said, an exhausted but contented smile spreading across his face. "Most of all, I loved being able to spend so much time with you."

"Me, too," Josh spoke with a full mouth.

"Someday," Kassler went on, "I hope that you'll both be able to live here and we'll be together again."

"Mommy, too?" Josh asked excitedly.

"No," Kassler said. "*Step*-mommy, too. Just you and Joy and Lupa and me."

"But I don't *want* to live here without Mommy," Josh put down his fork and looked with growing fear at his father.

Lupa, who had just entered with the coffee, tried to change the topic.

"Your daddy means *maybe someday*," she said as she put Kassler's coffee mug in front of him. "So," she tried, "how about a quick game before you go back to your mother?"

"When?" Josh persisted. "When would I have to leave Mommy?"

Joy, who had also stopped eating, listened intently and said nothing, but she was clearly on Joshua's side. She wanted to stay with her mother.

"When the court decides," Kassler answered. "It's up to the judge."

"I think," said Lupa very directly, "that we should talk about this some other time, Sy."

"Look, Josh," Kassler paid no attention to Lupa, "at first I wasn't even sure myself whether it'd be a good idea for you to live with me, but now that you're older and Lupa's around to help me, I've asked the judge to think about it."

"But I don't *want* to live with you, Daddy," Josh made himself as clear as he knew how. "I want to live with Mommy and Dr. Sam."

"We *live* with Mommy and Dr. Sam," Joy pointed out.

"*Now* you do," Kassler wouldn't quit, "but wouldn't you like to live with me and Lupa?"

"No," said Josh.

"No," said Joy.

"In this big beautiful house?" Kassler continued.

"No," answered Josh.

"No," repeated Joy.

"*Sometime*, not right now," Kassler persisted, "but *sometime*?"

"No," Joshua and Joy said in unison.

There was a brief silence.

"Please, Daddy," Joshua begged, "don't make us live with you."

"...and we could have those fun baths..." Kassler mumbled to himself, "...and breakfasts with French oatmeal...go for walks outside...and play a lot...read some bedtime stories...and I could tuck you in every night...maybe go camping...."

"Please don't, Daddy," Joy said.

Lupa's eyes filled with tears as she watched the last pieces of Kassler's world shatter. She knew that her world was disintegrating along with it, and there was nothing that could be done.

NOVEMBER 1979

Session VI

"*My childhood was not a happy one, Kassler,*" I began the session, which was, tragically, our next to the last.

"I'm sorry to hear that," Kassler was appropriately sympathetic.

"When I was growing up, I was small for my age."

"This would be what age?"

"Oh, from, say, the twelfth to the second century, Before You-Know-Who, while the Old Testament was being written, a very slow process, if you ask me. I suggested a number of editorial changes myself, mostly deletions, which could have saved a great deal of time and made for a much better read, I think. I mean, think about it, Kassler. After the Pentateuch, it's all been said, hasn't it? Then we've got the same thing over and over. There *is* a God. He's Almighty. Do as He says or else. This person *did*. This person *didn't*. They had kids. Then the *kids* had kids. All the kids learned that: There *is* a God, He's Almighty, Do as He says or else. You see what I mean?"

Kassler moved around a little impatiently in his chair. I was quick to notice.

"I'm getting off the subject, aren't I?" I asked.

"A little," Kassler admitted kindly.

"Well, the point is that for a long time there wasn't a whole lot of me. A reference here, a reference there, all very unclear. The word *Satan* is only in the Old Testament three times, you know, and two of those times it's not even a proper noun—Zechariah 3:1, Job 1: prologue; and Chronicles 21:1. As I said, considering the age, I was very small."

"But things changed," Kassler kept me going.

"Not for a while. There was, of course, a lot of name-calling as I grew up. Did you know that I have at least one name beginning with every letter of the alphabet except *X*?"

"No, I didn't," Kassler said quickly. "But perhaps at another time you could—"

"Antichrist, Beelzebub, Charon, Dis, Eblis, Furcas, Goap, Hoberdidance, Igymeth, Jochmus, Kawkabel, Lucifer, Mephistopheles, Nicker, Orphaxat, Pluto, Quat, Raguhel, Satan, Tutevillus, Urnell, Verdelet, Wox, Yifin, and Zizimar," I recited for my psychotherapist.

"These are the names they called you?" my psychotherapist asked.

"Absolutely not. These are just some of several thousand *proper* names I have. I don't have a Christian name. Pity. When they started name-calling, it was the Prince of Darkness, the Angel of the Bottomless Pit, the Malignant Spirit, the Unclean One, Liar, Tormentor, Murderer, Foul Fiend—you know how people can get when they start that business. One name leads to another, and it's very hard to stop. With me, of course, it's still going on," I explained sadly to Kassler.

"It must make things very difficult for you at times," he tried to get to some *deeper feelings*.

"You English-speaking people are different," I free-associated. "You'll do anything to avoid saying 'devil.' The French go around saying *'Que diable'* without thinking twice, and Germans'll swear without a blush, *'Was in des Teufels Namen'*—that means 'What in the devil's name,'" I told Kassler.

"Thank you."

"But the English go around lowering their eyes and mumbling, 'What the deuce,' or 'What the dickens,' as though these aren't synonymous with the devil. Why do you think that is?"

Kassler didn't answer. He sat in his chair silently for several seconds.

"I get the feeling," he finally said, "that we're not always staying on the topic today. Why *is* that?"

"You said you wanted my history," I answered. "So history is what you're getting. Let me tell you, Kassler, when I'm done today—assuming I can talk fast enough to get it all into these fifty minutes—the Durants' work will look like a footnote."

"I'm not sure I'm really going to need *that* much history," Kassler said. "Perhaps you could select *one* interesting thing from each of the last twenty-five or so centuries, to give me a general flavor of what was going on, and I can extrapolate. You can even skip a couple of centuries here and there—consider the Dark Ages as a single unit, for example."

"You're the boss, Kassler. Now, let me see, where was I? Oh, yes. Names. That in itself is an interesting problem. 'Satan,' as we've discussed, means 'adversary,' and that's about it. 'Devil,' on the other hand, means 'accuser' and 'assailant.' That's where the real trouble started, because, you see, Kassler, 'demon,' which is basically Greek, means nothing more than a 'knowing spirit,' and that, of course, is exactly what I am—"

"History?" Kassler interrupted.

"I'm getting there," I assured him. "As you know, after the Old Testament, we had the Apocrypha, which was *definitely* something I recommended be abridged. Before they were halfway into the Second Book of Esdras—"

"History!"

"Sorry," I told Kassler. "Well, the point is that it isn't until around 105 B.C. that I finally was recognized as a single entity. That was in the Book of Jubilees. Up until then there was a lot of talk about *princes* of evil—Mastema, Beliar, Sammael, and Samjaza and Azazel. Now, that's a story for you, Kassler. Samjaza and Azazel were angel chiefs—"

"Mr. Satan?" Kassler called my name quietly.

"Yes," I interrupted my story.

"We've got to talk," Kassler sat forward in his chair and rested his elbows on his knees and his chin in his hands. "After this session, which is nearly half over, we've got only one more session."

"I'm aware of that, yes."

"I think," Kassler continued, "that we should therefore stick to a *few* anecdotes that *directly* involve you. What do you think?"

"Oh, I think that'd be a good idea," I agreed. "May I make a comment?"

"Certainly."

"You seem a little restless today, Dr. Kassler. Have you noticed?" I inquired.

Kassler sighed.

"No, I hadn't noticed that."

"Perhaps you're feeling a little pressure to succeed in our psychotherapeutic contract? Back against the wall, Kassler?"

"Not at all," Kassler was unconvincing.

"It's okay to fail, you know. So I'm not cured. It happens even with the best therapists."

Kassler started drumming his fingers impatiently again.

"You aren't *bored* by my history, are you? Because we can skip the whole thing, if you want," I informed Kassler. "I *know* my history. This is for *your* benefit."

"And yours."

"That remains to be seen."

"It does, yes. Why don't you continue," Kassler said. "I'll try to be more patient, and perhaps you can be a little less tangential."

"During the time from 300 B.C. to 100 A.D., while the Jewish people were in exile," I told Kassler nontangentially, "is when things really went downhill for me. It was a *very* difficult adolescence, you might say, and by the end of the Apocrypha I was regarded as the sole King of Evil, the Arch-enemy of God and Man, and the Lord of *Hell*. That, as I started to say, all happened in the Book of Jubilees, a title I never did understand. There's not a single bit of jubilation in it, so far as I—sorry," I stopped myself.

"Thank you," Kassler said graciously.

"By the Christian Era, it was decided that I was just an impossible delinquent, and both the Apocrypha and the New Testament agreed that my final disposition was to, and I quote, 'an abyss, full of fire and flaming, and full of pillars of fire.' All of this was, I believe, borrowed lock, stock, and barrel from the Persians, Babylonians, and Assyrians by the Jews, who felt a need for something as colorful to keep their own crowd in line. Up until then, the best they had was a little story in the Talmud that illustrated how, as the Angel of Death, I'd sneak up on a dying man with a drop of gall trembling on the tip of my drawn sword. The dying man, when he saw me, would be startled out of his wits, open his mouth, swallow the gall, and die. For centuries, Kassler, I have been trying to grasp what the moral of that tale could possibly be. Dying men should keep a sharp eye out for individuals with gall-dripping swords so they don't startle so easily? I can't figure it out. If you ask me—"

Kassler resumed drumming his fingers on the arm of the chair.

"So," I took the hint. *"That's it."*

That got Kassler's attention.

"What happened to the next two thousand years?"

"Funny you should mention that," I said. "The year 161 was an interesting one. In January—"

"That's okay," Kassler held up his hand.

"I *was* only joking," I told him. "The truth is that not a whole lot happened to me after that, at least that you don't already know. Christianity decided that I was responsible for all things material, especially this world, and, even more, what they labeled things of the flesh. Also that I was a combination of physical ugliness and moral evil. By the third century, Tertullian announced that all men's lives were completely and always under my evil influence, and that's pretty much the way it stayed until less than a hundred years ago. I was considered invisible until the fifth century. There were a bevy of passion plays about the fall of man during the Middle Ages, when it was determined that all professions and pleasures of man are under the protection of the Power of the Pit. By the fifteenth century there was an outcropping of Satan societies.

Then came a couple centuries when witchcraft was very big, followed by a lot of burnings, and then there was the debacle caused by Luther, Calvin, Protestantism, and the Anabaptists, the biggest fiasco of all. Along the way there was Dante, Milton, Goethe, Marlowe, Mozart, Shaw, and a few others who embellished the tales, but, basically, that's how I came of age. Around the nineteenth century, someone, I don't know who, decided that I could appear as a normal human being, indistinguishable from anybody else, but, of course, I can't."

Kassler leaned back in his chair and pondered in silence.

"So," I asked after a while, "now that you've heard all that, what do you make of it?"

"Well," Kassler finally said, "I'm comparing it to other histories I've heard, and I'm impressed by a few things. First, there're no relationships."

"You mean sex? You're disappointed because I didn't give you a lot of explicit details about women I've bedded down with and resultant offspring. Haven't you heard, Kassler? The devil is a cold fiend, frigid, icy, and sterile—except in the eyes of a number of clergymen who believe I'm responsible for Eve, a lot of ordinary folks who are convinced that the results of my unions are inevitably male and presidents of the United States of America, and all Catholics, who credit me with Martin Luther."

"I'm not talking about sex. I'm talking about friendships and associations. It's a lonely tale that you've told, I think," Kassler said.

"Yes," I agreed. "It is a lonely tale."

"I'm also impressed," Kassler continued as he adjusted his glasses on the bridge of his nose, "by the lack of any creative product—results of your labors, tangible accomplishments, whatever."

"Creative product!" I had some difficulty understanding where Kassler got *that* notion. "I am *art*! For centuries the Church has affirmed the diabolical origin of artistic beauty. And not only art. Music, as well! And dance! And what about this world? Anatole France and Lord Byron both portray me as its co-creator!"

"But you're not," Kassler said.

"No, Kassler, I'm not. I can't take credit for the world or for man," I said solemnly. "They overstated my case a bit."

"No doubt."

For several minutes Kassler sat motionless in his chair, strangely silent.

"So," I finally asked, "what else?"

"I'm not sure," Kassler said. "There's something missing."

"You want more detail, I'll be happy to oblige."

Kassler shook his head.

"Thank you," he said, "but you've been sufficiently elaborate for me to get the picture, I think."

"Then what is it, Kassler?" I found myself becoming just the slightest bit irritated. "You asked for history. I gave you enough of a panorama to paint a mural."

"It's mechanical," Kassler concluded.

"It's *what*?"

"Mechanical. It's historical, not emotional. There's no life to it."

"No life! You think I haven't felt sorrow? You think that there was no pain? No grief? I've just told you my *life*, Kassler, my *entire life*, all there is, from the beginning to the very last minute! You think I haven't had feelings about all that? You think I haven't hurt?"

"Joy? You've felt joy, happiness, pleasure?" Kassler asked quietly.

"My *whole existence*, Kassler! Do you know what it feels like to hear yourself describe all that you've known, all that you are? It's not a very pleasant experience, I'll tell you, Kassler."

"You told it matter-of-factly. It's hard to tell."

"I've never done this before. I've never had to go back to the beginning, put it all together in one neat little package. So I stuck to the facts. I thought you wanted detail."

"There has been joy, then?"

"It has an effect on you, Kassler, going through it all from the beginning. You begin to wonder. . . ."

"You've felt happiness?"

"You start to think about things."

"Pleasure? And delight?"

"Things you haven't thought about for ages . . ." An overwhelming sadness began to fill me. I stopped talking. Silence
settled on the room.

"What are you thinking?" Kassler asked.

"A song," I said. "I was thinking of a song."

"Would you like to sing it?"

"I was very small."

"I'd like to hear it."

"I had entirely forgotten."

"When that I was and a little tiny boy . . ."

"I know that song well." Kassler said. "May I sing it with
you?"

"I'd like that."

Kassler and I sang softly.

> "When that I was and a little tiny boy,
> With a hey, ho, the wind and the rain,
> A foolish thing was but a toy,
> For the rain it raineth every day."

I tried to continue but the feeling that filled me was heavy.
My voice cracked and the words wouldn't come.

Kassler and I were silent for a very long time while I tried
to regain my composure.

"You know," I finally said, "I really don't hold you all to
blame. It's been a long history, a lot of water over the damned.
Taking the unpopular stand all the time, using reason, it hasn't
been easy. . . ."

Kassler lifted his head up; he had been staring at the floor.

"But there's something else. . . ."

"Innocence," I said. "I have a real problem with it. I don't
know why that is, Kassler, but I can't leave people their innocence."

"Sometimes, we prefer not to know."

"*Sometimes*, I suppose, but not often. How long do you
think it'll be before you folks have charted every pathway,

synapse, and molecule in your brains? I think you have to face it, Kassler, your thirst for knowledge is unquenchable. You see no more value in ignorance than I do."

"No, just in naïveté. There's something about a virgin that's very appealing."

"Whatever it is, Kassler, it's not in preserving her purity, as I understand the attraction."

Kassler had to think about this.

"With complete knowledge, there's no magic," he reflected.

"And that," I told Kassler, "is why you never find magic. You know too much, Kassler. Your chance for magic is over."

Kassler looked up toward the ceiling and his face clouded with sadness.

"I would have preferred," he said softly, "not to have known that, too."

Kassler sat still in the silence that followed.

"The next time we meet," he said slowly, "I'd like to hear about your birth."

"Our time is up?"

Kassler nodded his head.

"A few more minutes, Kassler. I don't like ending this way. I'd like you to stay just a minute, if you don't mind."

"We ought to stop."

"I didn't mean to take away your hope. You've been good to me. You've worked hard."

Kassler nodded again.

"You shouldn't take it personally," I told him. "I'm a master of the inevitable, and what's inevitable is without hope. It's the way it works."

"Have many people had a chance to hear your history?" Kassler asked.

"Not a whole lot, no. Why?"

"I was curious what others' reactions might have been."

"To my history?"

"To the song. Next time you tell it, be sure not to leave out the song."

I really wished that Kassler had not brought that up again. My sadness returned, and this, to someone for whom innocence has always been such a problem, was endlessly confusing.

"Shall we?" Kassler asked.

"Why not," I answered.

> "When that I was and a little tiny boy,
> With a hey, ho, the wind and the rain,
> A foolish thing was but a toy,
> For the rain it raineth every day."

We sang it with great feeling, and it was several minutes before I caught my breath.

"Well," I finally said, "this has really been something."

"Yes," Kassler said. "It has been."

"I hadn't expected—"

"Nor had I. You wept?"

"I'm not sure. Fatigue, perhaps. I covered a lot of material today, Kassler. It was a long history."

"Yes, it was. You might want to think about what it was in relating your history that affected you so much."

"I will."

"That's good."

"I appreciate your staying."

"No problem," Kassler said as he got up to go.

"I like you, Kassler. You're good at this, whatever it is you're doing."

"Thank you."

"That thing that just happened, what is that? Is there some sort of a technical name for it?"

"Yes," Kassler nodded. "I believe it's called a break-through."

PART VIII

A Hearing
on the Merits

CHAPTER 1

As the year changed from 1976 to 1977, Kassler spent his psychic energy deciding when and how he would do himself in.

This was not frivolous mental meandering. Kassler laid out another of his thousand-dollar bills for a cemetery plot to indicate the sincerity of his intentions, and began writing morbid letters to Joshua and Joy which were to be opened after his death, one at each of their birthdays until they were thirty.

"What is this," I asked during the one brief conversation we had in 1977—still two years before my treatment began—while Kassler was rummaging in the basement for some shelves on which to store Lupa's books, "default by suicide?"

"Just answer me one thing," Kassler asked as he hunted. "In order to treat you, do I have to be dead?"

"I'll answer *you* that, if you'll answer *me* something, Kassler," I responded.

"It's a deal," Kassler located his shelves and started up the stairs.

"So, do I have to be dead?" he asked.

423

"No," I answered.

"What's your question?" Kassler asked.

"Do you believe it?" I asked.

"I want the whole court case dropped," Kassler told Marty Myers when Kassler was beckoned to his office a few days after the preliminary hearing.

"Look," Marty said, "I know you're upset over Bernie and all that. So am I. But I can't do it," Marty looked solemnly at Kassler. "The judge has assigned us five full court days in September of 1978, and we have to be there."

"September of 1978? That's just dandy. Only twenty-one more months," Kassler said in the special acid tone he was affecting on a frequent basis these days.

"We could've been heard next month," Marty said, "but Vita insisted on five full days, and that much time in a single block isn't available until a year from this September. Believe me, she isn't any happier about the whole thing."

"It doesn't *matter*, Marty," Kassler told his attorney harshly. "I want the whole case dropped."

"And I told you," Marty flicked a small white speck of dust off his shiny black shoes and responded to Kassler just as harshly, "that I can't do that."

"Then I'll find someone who *will*."

"You're not going to find anyone, Sy. Sit down."

Kassler, who had been doing his usual pacing across Marty Myers's Oriental carpet, sat in a simulated-leather chair decorated with silver-colored buckles.

"I can drop *your* case, if you want," Marty told his client, "but I have no control over *hers*."

"What the hell difference does it make, Marty? If I'm not *asking* for anything, then she gets what she wants. Drop the case."

"There're some other issues that've come up, Sy." Marty stood up and walked over to the matching chair next to Kassler's where he eased himself painstakingly into the seat, after first hiking up his trousers to avoid stretching the material at the knees.

"What kind of issues?" Kassler asked with less emotion.

"Vita's filed a motion for relocation to another jurisdiction after the trial and for an allowance," Marty told Kassler, running his thumb and forefinger along the crease in his trousers.

"What jurisdiction?" Kassler asked.

"Azusa, New Mexico."

"Azusa! Where the hell is Azusa?"

"It's in the desert. She thinks it'll be healthier for the children. She says she's got a job teaching piano to Sioux children."

Kassler simply couldn't believe it. He kept repeating Azusa over and over to himself.

"What's the nearest large city?" Kassler finally asked.

"It depends on what you mean by large."

"Answer me."

"Pico Rivera is less than two hundred miles away."

Kassler sat for several minutes staring into space.

"Will the judge let her do that?" Kassler asked.

"He probably will, unless you can come up with a good case against her. He *certainly* will if you don't show up, or do but don't object."

"Suppose I just throw in the towel and tell her to do what she wants, do I still have to go to court?"

"Yes. They've subpoenaed you. They want to make sure you can't change your mind someday and contest the thing, here or out there. You have to appear in court and be examined by her attorney. I'm sorry, Sy. It's not voluntary anymore."

"Azusa?" Kassler asked.

"Azusa," Marty Myers confirmed.

"How much of an allowance is she asking for?"

"It's not that kind of an allowance," Marty answered as he played absently with the buckles on the arms of his chair.

"What kind is it?" Kassler asked.

"An allowance," Marty swallowed hard, "is when one party, like Vita, asks the court to order the other party, like you, to pay all her legal bills."

It goes without saying that by this time the issue of suicide for Kassler was no longer a matter of debating pros and cons. Kassler operated on the assumption that he would presently be taking his own life and all that remained were a few minor details—letters still to be written for his children's birthdays ages twenty-four through thirty, a final decision on the inscription for his tombstone (there were a number of candidates, all taken from Job), the completion of the "Roots" miniseries on television. Kassler saw no reason to rush things. What was of paramount concern to him was that, for once in his life, he have total and absolute control. He would determine how and when to do the deed in his own sweet time.

It was this all-consuming need to be completely in charge of his life that was responsible for the next episode in what remained of Kassler's existence. Otherwise, how is it possible to understand Kassler's grief and anguish over the loss of something he would be abandoning with his death anyway?

Bea Chaikin dropped into Kassler's office his first day back from his vacation. As a matter of fact, Bea Chaikin was waiting for Kassler in his office when he arrived that morning.

"Sam has asked me to talk to you, Sy," Bea said after the usual amenities and inquiries about the holidays had been exchanged.

Kassler removed his coat and hung it on a hook on the back of the door, which he then closed.

"I suppose you've seen this morning's paper?" Bea asked.

"No," Kassler said as he walked to his desk. "Why?"

"Your little midnight trip with Mrs. Fletcher on Christmas Eve is all over the front page."

"I see," Kassler said, sitting in his gray metal swivel chair. "That's it, isn't it?"

"Judge Gelbert was furious. Sam's intervened in your behalf, so no charges will be brought, but there was a price that had to be paid," Bea said as gently as she could.

"How long do I have?"

"You don't get any time, Sy. Your employment ended an hour ago."

Kassler sat in a state of shock, he didn't understand why. Certainly, he thought to himself, he had known that eventually he'd be fired. A number of times he'd wanted to resign. Yet, somehow, Zelazo never told him to leave and Kassler never left on his own. In a way, Kassler had begun to feel invincible. He assumed he'd always be at Phlegethon, in the same way that, no matter how many patients were discharged, Phlegethon always remained full. There would always be Phlegethon, and Kassler and Sam and Bea and Bernie and all his patients would always be there. Kassler realized that he'd been operating on this unconscious assumption for several years.

Now, faced with so abrupt a dismissal, Kassler found himself pleading with Bea Chaikin. It was not a matter for Kassler of his pride or any great love of Phlegethon. The loss of income, and even of occupation, for a man who was determined to leave this world shortly made equally little difference. It was, simply, another incident over which Kassler had no control, and, with it, the last underlying stability in his life was being pulled out from under him. For Kassler realized, with an unpleasant suddenness, that no matter how his women treated him, no matter what happened between him and his children, no matter how many senseless deaths and personal misfortunes he encountered each day, he could always depend on walking into Phlegethon's land of the insane the next morning to hear more about Philip Donato's mother and watch Cheryl cradling her Little Bo Peep doll.

"Is there any way that I can—?" Kassler asked.

"None," Bea shook her head. "There's no way."

"It's all I've got," Kassler looked pleadingly at Bea.

"You'll find something else, Sy," Bea told him. "You'll find something a lot better than this place, which isn't going to be here much longer anyway. You'll start a new life. You've just gotten married. . . ."

"She's a whore, Bea."

"She was once, yes, I heard, but she isn't anymore. It's *her* body. It seems to me she had a right to do what she wanted with it. She also loves you very much. I know Lupa a little. She's lovely. She's had a hard time and has done some things she wishes now that she hadn't. So have you. Let it die, Sy, or you'll lose something very good," Bea implored Kassler.

"Bernie's dead."

Bea Chaikin took a deep breath.

"Yes, I know," she said. "We'll all have to deal with that."

"It was my fault. I was supposed to spend Christmas with

him, and I didn't have the guts to tell him I was getting married," Kassler told Bea.

"That's not why people kill themselves, Sy, and you know it," Bea swallowed hard to maintain control of herself.

"We were lovers."

"I knew Bernie cared a great deal for you. I thought probably you were," Bea said calmly.

"You did?" Kassler asked in surprise. "Why didn't you say anything?"

"What would you have liked me to say?"

Kassler looked at Bea and tried to think of what he would have wanted to hear from her.

"'Be careful'? 'Don't do it'? 'Congratulations'? Something."

"Why? It's none of my business."

"Vita wants to take the kids to New Mexico. I'm never going to see my kids again," Kassler continued to relate his tale of woe in the hope that Bea would accept him as a hardship case and reconsider his dismissal, as though she had any power in the matter.

"I'm really sorry to hear that, Sy," Bea responded. "I know how much you love your children."

Kassler saw he was getting nowhere.

"Vita has ruined my life, Leo Szlyck has ruined my life, I still get crazy calls from a patient who can't jerk off any-more—"

"Okay," Bea held up her hands to halt Kassler before he went back into his childhood and adolescence. "There's a little speech I've had prepard for some time, Sy. I guess this is the time."

Kassler knew he wouldn't be able to take it sitting down, so he arose from his chair and began pacing nervously.

"You're a good person, Sy. You've got a good heart and a good soul—"

"And that's what gets me into trouble every time. I care about other people too much."

"That's your big lie, Sy. We all live by lies. Some big ones. Some small ones. That's yours, and it's a whopper."

Kassler stopped in his tracks and looked at Bea Chaikin as though she were speaking a foreign language.

"I don't care about—*I* don't care—" he sputtered.

"No, you don't, Sy. Because if you did, you'd give people the room they need to lead their own lives, and you'd stop believing that everything they did revolved around you."

"That's not true!" Kassler protested.

"Vita did what she did because of Vita," Bea looked intensely at Kassler, "not because of you. She did *not* go around trying to figure ways to louse up Sy Kassler's life, no matter how it felt. Do you think that she's any happier with Sam? She's doomed, Sy. She'll live the same way with the same pains and conflicts all her life. The only difference is that Sam realizes that it's *her* problem, not his, and Vita knows that Sam's aware of that, so they get along okay, not great, but okay. They get out of each other what's there to get and don't drive each other crazy trying to get what isn't there and won't ever be."

Bea paused for a breath, to let what she'd said sink into Kassler's brain. Then she moved on.

"Leo Szlyck was a crazy man. He did what he did because he was moderately insane. You could have been Chiang Kai-shek, and if he decided you'd taken his wife from him, he would have done exactly what he did. It had nothing to do with Sy Kassler. To a lesser extent, the same thing is true with Bernie Kohler. He did what he did because of Bernie, not because of Sy Kassler."

Little bits of data were beginning to filter into Kassler's cranium as he continued to pace.

"Lupa did what she did because of Lupa. She didn't think about how it might affect Sy Kassler. She was trying to stay alive. She married you because of how *she* felt about you, not how you felt about her, not that she would have done it if you hadn't cared for her. She's not self-destructive, no matter what you think. But Lupa is there with you now because of Lupa, what she thinks she can get for herself. My recommendation is that you do the same, because I believe there's a lot there for you to take, if you want it."

Kassler felt himself enveloped by an overwhelming sadness.

"The world does not revolve around Sy Kassler, and it's time that someone's said that to you straight out, I think," Bea went on with firmness, but it was clear that Kassler's profound sadness was beginning to affect her and she had consciously to stop herself from going over to where he had just settled back in his chair and holding him in her arms.

"Now," Bea said, "my hunch is that you're about to show us all that Bernie Kohler's way out was another one of his brilliant solutions to life's many problems by repeating the procedure—"

Bea was about to follow this with a pithy comment on the subject of Kassler's suicidal state when the combination of the thought of Kassler killing himself and Kassler's great despondency across from her made it impossible for her to continue.

"I just wish you wouldn't, Sy," she said as her eyes began to moisten. "I wish you wouldn't," and Bea's fortitude and resolution crumbled and she walked over to Kassler and held him against her.

"I will miss you around here, Sy," Bea said with tenderness, "I must say that. It seems like only a couple days ago that I was showing you through the floors and introducing the players by diagnosis."

"You're sure that there's no way that I can stay?" Kassler asked. "Just long enough to finish with my patients?"

Bea shook her head no.

"Sam had an idea," Bea said. "You can take whatever patients you want with you as soon as the court removes the order against discharges. That should be soon. In the meantime, I can cover for you."

Kassler looked up at Bea, who was standing beside him running her hand gently up and down the back of Kassler's neck.

"Take them where?"

"Wherever you want. To your home, if you want."

"You're sure?" Kassler asked.

"Needless to say," Bea smiled, and she kissed Kassler lightly on the side of his head, "we'd be delighted to get rid of anyone we can."

Kassler took Bea's hands between his and held them.

"I want Mr. Katzman," Kassler kissed Bea on her cheek.

"I want Diane Fletcher," Kassler continued to hold Bea's hands between his and stroke them gently.

"I want Philip Donato."

Bea closed her eyes and kissed Kassler once more on his cheek.

"I want Cheryl," Kassler returned Bea's kiss.

"You can have them all," Bea said as she ruffled Kassler's curly hair and started toward the door. "You can have everyone here . . . but not me, Sy. Sorry." And Bea Chaikin winked at Kassler, pleased by his rapid recovery, and quietly shut the door behind her.

And so it was that Kassler terminated his relationship with Phlegethon.

The long-term consequence of the dissolution of these ties was that Kassler worked less diligently on arranging for his own demise, although his commitment to it was no less absolute. The short-term consequences, which were twofold, were more substantial in light of their immediate repercussions.

First of all, the federal courts stepped in and removed the court order preventing patients from being discharged, but allowed the order prohibiting admissions to stand. Phlegethon was to be completely emptied in eighteen months, without exception, and nothing was to stand in the way. This ruling occurred in April of 1977, within a week of the time when Kassler had finally convinced Lupa that living with four mental patients would be a marvelous experience for them to share.

"This could bring us very close," he told Lupa over and again.

Lupa agreed because of the second of all, which was that Kassler took those parts of Bea's advice that appealed to him and rejected those that did not.

In the former category was looking out for himself, which in this instance meant that he began a series of indiscriminate sexual relationships. Kassler cheated on Lupa whenever he could.

In the latter, rejected category was Kassler allowing himself to receive the affection and caring that Lupa wanted to give him. Kassler would accept none of it.

Lupa realized before long that Kassler was having affairs, but she said nothing, hoping this was a reaction to the loss of his job, close friend, and the potential loss of his children. She hoped it would soon pass. Agreeing to take on four lunatics for her family might, Lupa felt, be a way of keeping Kassler at home.

In May of 1977, a van from Phlegethon arrived, and Philip Donato, Mr. Katzman, Diana Fletcher, and Cheryl were literally dumped on Kassler's front lawn. The results were highly predictable.

Scared and disoriented, the patients required a great amount of Kassler and Lupa's time, for which they were fortunately— the only saving factor during an otherwise disastrous period— being moderately well compensated by the state of New Jersey.

Unfortunately for Lupa, they did not occupy so much of Kassler's time as to restrict his extracurricular sexual activities.

I will not go into any great detail regarding the weeks that became months during which Kassler and Lupa cared for their charges, but will leave it to the reader to imagine the intense, difficult, and exasperating struggles that occurred until all four mentally ill persons were settled into their new environment and cooperating with household chores and their personal rehabilitation.

"You can't take away my medication!" Mr. Katzman shouted day after day. "It's illegal. It's unconstitutional!"

"It's not illegal," Kassler responded.

"It's against our rights!" Philip Donato yelled. "We have a right to be crazy!"

"Every time you take one of those pills," Kassler explained, "you're saying to yourself, 'I am a mental patient.'"

"Then it fits perfectly," Mr. Katzman said. "You shouldn't forget those kinds of things."

"If you want to be crazy, that's up to you," Kassler told his crew, "but you're going to have to do it without meds."

"If you take away my Thorazine, I'm going to make up new

symptoms!" Mr. Katzman threatened. Diana Fletcher and Cheryl nodded in agreement.

"That's also up to you," Kassler remained firm.

"*Horrible terrible* symptoms!" Mr. Katzman continued. "You'll hate them."

"If *I'll* hate them, then you probably won't feel too good about them, either," Kassler pointed out.

"Damn!" Mr. Katzman sensed that Kassler was probably right. "Can't we be just a *little* crazy so we can have a *little* Thorazine?"

"Nope," Kassler said for the hundredth time. "Not even a little. This year, no insanity. Sorry."

There were louder battles, terrible nights filled with fear, panic in abundance, but eventually Kassler's persistence and Lupa's warmth won out. One by one the quartet began to give up their identities as mental patients.

The final step in this process was accomplished by Diana Fletcher, who noticed as she emerged from her schizophrenic haze that, although Cheryl herself never kept her clothes on, Cheryl's Little Bo Peep doll always did. During the daily after-dinner group-therapy session one evening, Diana Fletcher requested—without specifying the exact purpose—a sewing machine and a long list of fancy fabrics and notions. The group agreed to chip in to rent a sewing machine and provide Mrs. Fletcher with what she'd requested, and within days, she had turned out an elaborate series of doll costumes, ladies' size seven—Spanish Contessa, Marie Antoinette, Cinderella Princess, Dutch Maiden, and, of course, Little Bo Peep.

Cheryl, whose eyes lit up like headlights on seeing the wardrobe, was never to walk around in the nude again. On the other hand, getting Cheryl to remove her attire so that either Cheryl or the clothing could be washed at the end of each day became a major, though not unsurmountable, problem. Diana Fletcher's gentleness prevailed.

It soon became evident that a family had formed. Diana Fletcher became the mother and Mr. Katzman the father, Philip Donato their older son, and Cheryl, who followed everyone around in her costumes like a two-year-old, the toddler of the family. Kassler and Lupa, who were excluded from this rapidly solidifying family unit, were looked upon by the group as hired caretakers. Kassler and Lupa handled it with good humor.

"We've been having some problems with Lupa, dear," Diana Fletcher would tell Mr. Katzman at the evening group, as Katzman sat in a handsome wingback chair, puffing peacefully on his pipe. "Dinner has not been very good at all the last couple days."

"Yes," Mr. Katzman would say, "I've noticed. Of course, the odds being what they are, you have to expect some good days and some bad, about fifty-fifty, I'd say, but I agree. She's falling below par. Far below par."

"My noodles were ice-cold," Philip commented.

"And Dr. Kassler," Diana continued as she knitted a colorful sweater for Cheryl during the evening, "he was supposed to clean out the gutters over two weeks ago. It's still not done. What do you think we should do, dear?"

"I'll talk to them," Mr. Katzman said solemnly.

"Oh, that's good of you, dear," Diana Fletcher said. "I find these things so difficult."

"No problem," Mr. Katzman puffed thoughtfully. "I'll handle it."

"Cheryl? Come here," Diana Fletcher called. "Come try this on."

"I'm coming," Cheryl spoke the first sentence of her life and bounced over in her crinolines.

Cheryl was starting her life over from scratch, and though it was unclear what mental age she could eventually attain, she was progressing rapidly, now fed and dressed herself, and had harmed nothing, including her own flesh.

Needless to say, I got somewhat lost in the shuffle, but was satisfied to bide my time, as long as Kassler was alive and around. Lupa was, however, becoming less abiding.

The months from the spring of 1977 to the spring of 1978 had gone by without any noticeable change in Kassler or their relationship. The "Roots" miniseries had ended and both she and Kassler now went out of their way to greet black-skinned people with a mixture of effusive cordiality and an appropriate undertone of guilt and repentance for sins they had never committed. Mr. Gary Gilmore, who unfortunately just barely missed finding out whether Kunta Kinte got to the bottom of his ancestral tree, had his earnest pleas honored by his fellow men, who pumped a dozen large-caliber bullets into his chest. As the bitter-cold winter came to an end, Mr. Tongsun Park disappeared and reappeared and then disappeared again like Lewis Carroll's white rabbit, leaving behind, with each visit, lots of what rabbits usually leave. By midsummer, the United States government had announced that their research positively confirmed that the cancer-curing drug laetrile was absolutely useless, and by the end of the summer, a similar conclusion was drawn about Mr. Bert Lance.

Amazingly, before Kassler and Lupa knew it a year had gone by, another Christmas was past, another cold winter had ended, Kassler was still alive, and Lupa was tearing her hair out, no offense intended, by the roots.

"I'm not sure how much longer I'm going to be able to take this," Lupa told me during one late, sleepless night in April of 1978.

"Actually," I commented, "I thought things had been going rather well. We've given Panama back to Panama, delayed building the neutron bomb, caught the Son of Sam killer, and had a very entertaining week of television reliving the massacre of the Jews. Wasn't Katzman marvelous, the way he filled in all the details that good taste prevented commercial television from showing?"

"I wasn't talking about current events," Lupa said, "at least not the *world's* current events. *My* current events are the problem."

"Ah, yes," I agreed. "Do you think Kassler will ever snap out of it?"

"Definitely not," Lupa asserted. "At least not from anything *I* do. I've been as supportive as I know how. I look the other way while he's out screwing other women. I work with his crazy patients. I tolerate his moods. I play with his kids. I pretend not to notice that his relationship with me is mechanical.

I don't know what else to do."

"Maybe Kassler just isn't the Kassler you once knew. He's a different person now," I suggested.

It was a new thought to Lupa.

"I guess I should leave him," Lupa said very unconvincingly. "You're right. He's not the person I thought I was marrying."

"So what keeps you around?" I asked.

"For him, neither am I."

"Maybe you two should talk," I offered.

"It's hard for me to give up on a relationship," Lupa continued to free-associate. "Look what happened last time. I stuck around practically forever."

"It seems to me," I recalled, "that since we first met, we've had a few conversations very much like this one, the most recent, of course, having to do with—what's-his-name?—Leo Szlyck, wasn't it?"

"Sy's nothing like Leo," Lupa told me.

"How is that?" I played devil's advocate.

"Well," Lupa had to think very hard, "Leo was looking out for only one person, Leo Szlyck. With Sy . . ." Lupa trailed off.

As it was, Kassler was operating on reflex alone. He adopted a nothing-ventured, nothing-lost mode of existence, the cornerstone of which was defending himself against the investment of any part of himself in anything or anyone.

In the morning and at night, he was cordial and pleasant to Lupa, who he suspected would not be around much longer. During the day, he worked skillfully with the patients, who, he knew, were not far away from leading lives of their own somewhere else. In the evening, he visited the university lecture halls and library for the sole purpose of picking up young women for sex. He went through a number of four-to-six-week relationships in this manner, selecting one young lady for her smile, another for her flowing red hair, another for a glimpse of silky thigh he had managed as the girl's skirt rode up over her knees, another for the way her blue jeans displayed her bottom, or her nipples protruded under her thin sweater, or she flicked her tongue over her lips.

Kassler accommodated this adulterous association by anatomy into his psyche by telling himself that it was, in the greater scheme of things, inconsequential, equivalent to any other entertainment or sport—attending a movie or a piano recital, or jogging, for example.

On Sundays, Kassler played in an appropriately paternal way with his children, who, he understood—but no longer bothered to consider—were leaving in a few short months for Azusa, New Mexico.

Although Kassler was unaware of it, he had unconsciously developed a plan. By the end of that summer, he would begin to prepare the patients for leaving Bolgia. He would have his affairs in order and enough money sequestered to leave his children five thousand dollars each. Bolgia would go to Lupa, for trying. Then, in September, he would subject himself to the punishment awaiting him in court, which he was convinced by now he certainly deserved, and, when that was completed, say good-bye to his children and Lupa, release his patients, and kill himself.

Kassler, of course, had conveniently forgotten that there were a few other items with which he had not yet dealt, foremost among them me. I had no intention of allowing Kassler to turn in his homeostasis without facing the realities of Sam Zelazo, Leo Szlyck, and now Bernie Kohler, all of whom, unfortunately for Kassler, not only were far from out of the picture, but also would ultimately be responsible for seeing that I got the psychotherapy for which I had, I must say in all candor, been rather patiently waiting my turn.

And this is, of course, what remains to my tale of Sy Kassler, J.S.P.S.—how it happened that I finally got Kassler to accept me for who I am and agree, rather readily, to undertake my immediate psychotherapeutic treatment.

It was, for both of us, the completion of a long and complex journey, the last steps of which began with Kassler's visit to Marty Myers and a list.

*   *   *

"Well," Marty told Kassler one unbearably hot day toward the end of August, "we've exchanged lists of witnesses, the opposition counsel and I."

Kassler sat directly in front of the air conditioner, trying to evaporate perspiration from his brow.

"We've got," Marty continued, "you and maybe Lupa, if she has anything helpful to say and is willing to testify."

Marty's vest was open, his tie loosened, and his monogrammed white shirt had the top button undone and the sleeves rolled up, displaying an expensive Rolex watch he'd received in gratitude from one of his clients. He studied a sheet of paper in front of him and then looked over at Kassler.

"Would you like to see who's testifying against you?" Marty asked. "It helps to explain why they wanted five days of court time."

Kassler reached for the list of opposition witnesses.

The list read as follows:

> Vita Kassler
> Joshua Kassler
> Joy Kassler
> Jud Simon
> Bea Chaikin
> Samuel Zelazo, M.D.

The list had apparently been prepared some time ago, because between Bea Chaikin's name and Sam Zelzano's was the name of Bernie Kohler, but it had been crossed out.

CHAPTER 2

*K*assler's initial reaction to the list was that of shock. He had never even heard of Jud Simon, but he recognized the other names well enough. Then he concluded that the battle lines had been drawn, and if it was war that Vita wanted, war was what she'd get. Kassler determined that he would, you should pardon the expression, go down in a blaze of glory.

And that is exactly what he did.

For the thirty days preceding the trial, Kassler did nothing but work on his case. All day he would make notes about his life with Vita, her care of the children, and a thousand persuasive reasons why he should be given custody, especially if Vita was heading for New Mexico. Then, at three o'clock every afternoon, he'd meet with Marty Myers and review the notes. At five o'clock, when he finished with Marty, Kassler would return to Bolgia, eat dinner, and meet with the patients. Then he would go back to work on his case until early the next morning.

As an index of how consumed Kassler was by his litigation during the end of the insufferably hot summer of 1978, it would not only be weeks before he learned that babies could now be made in test tubes, something that, had it been possible in 1970, might very well have lessened Kassler's present predicament, but it would be many months before he'd discover that the College of Cardinals had determined that the immaculate history of the papacy might not necessarily be tainted if the Pope were born in Poland.

Lupa was left, of course, with all the responsibilities of

caring for the patients and the house. She handled them without complaint, since she knew that in thirty-five days it would all be over, and on the thirty-sixth day she'd be gone.

The courtroom was exactly like all other courtrooms, brown chairs, floor-to-ceiling windows, and pale-pink walls. Kassler and Marty Myers sat on one side of a long mahogany table which was perpendicular to the elevated platform where Judge Sullivan perched, and Vita and Doris Huber, her attorney, sat on the other side.

Since Vita had filed the original petition, her side got to present its witnesses first. Vita began.

"It's your job," Vita's attorney had explained to Vita in her office the day before, "to create a world for the judge, to make over heaven and earth," Huber waxed poetic, "so that he lives where you live and feels what you feel. Let there be light!" Huber cheered her client on.

Vita did just that. She fabricated a splendid universe which she illuminated with a long and sad story, appropriately punctuated by tears, about how she had met Kassler and had later, with grave doubts but on Kassler's insistence, agreed to marry him. She told how their relationship had not gone well from the start, and how Kassler had been opposed to having Joshua and even more adamantly against having Joy.

Then Vita told about how well the children were doing in school and at home, what a wonderful life it was for them all, and how dearly she loved her offspring. She presented her financial statement, which indicated that, other than what she received from Kassler each week, she had nothing. And that was it. Heaven and earth were completed.

Throughout Vita's testimony, Marty Myers had been smiling smugly at Kassler. Only recently, he informed Kassler, he had corroborated some lethally damaging information about Vita, and now, as a surprise for his client and the plaintiff, he approached the stand to spring it on her.

"Isn't it true, *Ms.* Kassler"—as this was the way Vita insisted she be addressed—"that for the last few years, up until very recently, you've been operating a prostitution service?"

Kassler's mouth dropped open and his heart fell to the bottom of his chest cavity. He tried desperately to signal Marty Myers, but Marty had his back to Kassler and couldn't see him.

"No," Vita said benignly.

Marty Myers plunged ahead, utilizing his great skills at cross-examination to catch Vita in what he was convinced was her deliberate deception.

"Well," he persisted, "you *have* been operating, until the last year or so, an interior-design business, have you not?"

"No," Vita smiled. "I have not. That's *Mrs.* Kassler, Sy's present wife, *Lupa*. I'm *Vita*. Lupa's the one who ran the prostitution service."

"You have *never* operated an interior-design business?" Marty's obduracy became significantly less obdurate, and he turned to look at Kassler, who had his head buried in his hands in despair.

"Nope," Vita grinned gloriously. "I hate places that are done by interior designers. They look fake and cold, I think. I'm a pianist. Lupa's the prostitute."

From here, things went downhill.

Marty Myers never recovered. He mixed up times, places, and people. Kassler's case was one of several dozen he was currently handling, and the entire business was, very simply, too complex for him to keep straight in his mind. He tried to refer to the notes he had taken on Kassler's daily visits, but they weren't particularly well organized, and the amount of time he spent attempting to find what he needed began to irritate the judge, so he stopped and fumbled along on his own.

He asked Vita if Sam Zelazo ever slept over at her house when the children were present, and pursued this with vigor as Vita repeatedly denied it, but didn't think of asking whether she and the children ever slept over at Sam Zelazo's, a common practice. Finally, the judge stopped Marty Myers.

"I'm not sure I see the point, Counselor," Judge Sullivan said. "Ms. Kassler has denied your allegation, and, even if it *were* so, this court doesn't expect a healthy woman to abandon a sex life because she's a single parent. Are you proposing that Ms. Kassler has had more than one relationship over these years or been indiscriminate, or exposed the children to blatant sexual activity?"

"No, Your Honor," Marty shook his head.

"Then I suggest we move on to another topic," the judge said firmly.

"How often do you bathe the children?" Marty Myers asked.

"Whenever they need it," Vita said.

"And how often do you wash their clothes?"

"When they get dirty."

"What sort of condition is the house usually in?" Marty Myers pursued.

"I try to keep it fairly clean and orderly," Vita said pleasantly. "Sometimes it gets a little out of hand, as you'd expect with two small children and their friends around a lot, but mostly it's average, I'd say."

"But it *does* get dirty," Marty said.

"Of course," said Vita. "Otherwise we wouldn't have to clean it."

"Mr. Myers," the judge interrupted, "do you have any evidence to contradict Ms. Kassler's testimony? Because I'm not going to tolerate using the court's time to search for issues on which to build your case. Will you be presenting evidence on these matters which disproves Ms. Kassler's testimony?"

"Other than Dr. Kassler's?" Marty asked.

"Yes. Other than the defendant's."

"No," Marty admitted.

"Then I'd like you to stick to those areas where you *are* going to be presenting evidence. Is that clear?"

"It's been very difficult for Dr. Kassler to get evidence about what goes on in a home he has no access to, Your Honor."

"That's not *my* problem, Counselor. I just want you to stick to whatever evidence you *do* have. I'll ask again: Is that clear?"

"Yes," Marty nodded.

"You may continue," Judge Sullivan said.

"I have no further questions," Marty shrugged and walked over to sit down beside Kassler while Vita took her place on the other side of the table, smiling at Kassler as if there were no tomorrow.

*   *   *

"I'm really sorry about that business with Lupa," Marty said to Kassler as they walked from the courthouse.

Kassler was too discouraged to say anything at first. He looked at Marty and shook his head.

"Let's just get this thing over with, all right?"

"Don't get discouraged," Marty said. "We're not done yet. There's a long road ahead. We've still got four more days," he reminded Kassler to cheer him up. But somehow it didn't have that effect.

On the second day, Sam Zelazo took the stand to part the waters and make a clear path for Kassler's destruction.

Zelazo was impressive indeed. He stood, tall, regal, and imposing in his tailored suit, towering celestially over the entire courtroom, his penetrating eyes above even those of the elevated judge, who could not but be impressed as Zelazo stood in the firmament reeling off credentials—degrees, certificates, papers, awards, appointments, honors, and offices in professional associations.

Zelazo spent the first half of his testimony, the entire morning, telling about how well adjusted the children were, how close his relationship was with both their mother and them, how competent a mother Vita was, and how healthy it would be for them all to move out of Citadel to a more congenial climate in New Mexico.

Then the afternoon session started.

"Now," Attorney Huber began, "you know the defendant, Dr. Kassler, fairly well, is that true?"

"Yes," Zelazo answered, looking directly at Kassler.

"You were not only responsible for employing him at Phlegethon, but were friends as well? He visited your home? Talked about personal matters? Is that correct?"

"Yes, it is."

"And you still believe that the children would be better off with Ms. Kassler?"

"Yes."

"Why is that?"

"I have many serious concerns about Dr. Kassler's mental health and judgment."

"Can you be more specific?"

"Yes. Dr. Kassler has appeared suicidal, in my opinion, for some time."

"Anything else?"

"We eventually had to dismiss Dr. Kassler because he disregarded a court order and removed a woman from Phlegethon who was chronically schizophrenic and had recently attacked a judge visiting the institution."

"Anything else?"

"I personally witnessed him killing a patient by shutting off his life-support system."

"You mean he *murdered* a patient?" Huber asked.

"Yes, he did," Zelazo said, avoiding looking at Kassler.

The judge, who had been taking copious notes on Zelazo's testimony, looked up at Kassler in disbelief and then turned to Zelazo.

"Would you please repeat that, Dr. Zelazo," he asked.

"Yes," Zelazo obliged. "Dr. Kassler murdered one of the patients."

"Was he charged with homicide?" Judge Sullivan asked.

"No," Zelazo said. "The patient was terminal, and I discussed the matter with the Attorney General. We agreed not to charge Dr. Kassler because of a number of extenuating circumstances."

"But let me get this correct," Judge Sullivan continued. "Dr. Kassler *did* murder a patient at your facility?"

"Yes, he did," Zelazo repeated, still managing to avoid Kassler's furious looks.

"And you witnessed this?" the judge continued.

"Yes, I did," Zelazo reaffirmed.

"Is there anything else," Doris Huber asked, "that has led you to question Dr. Kassler's mental health?"

"Yes. He talked to me on one occasion about his desire to kill his wife and children," Zelazo related.

"He was angry, or joking, of course?" Attorney Huber asked.

"No," Zelazo told the court. "He was very serious about it and extremely concerned he might do it."

"What did he say?"

"That he was concerned he might slit their throats."

"Is there anything else?"

"Yes. Dr. Kassler believes he can talk to the devil," Zelazo stared directly at Kassler as he said this.

Kassler stared back with a mixture of panic and rage. He held on to the arms of his chair and could hardly wait for Marty Myers to begin his cross-examination of Zelazo.

"That's all I have, Your Honor," Doris Huber said crisply, straightened the jacket on her suit, and sat down.

"I have no questions," Marty told the judge.

"What!" Kassler whispered sharply into Marty's ear.

"I want him off the stand immediately," Marty snapped back into Kassler's ear.

"But he's only telling *half* the story!" Kassler said back. "And he's Vita's lover."

"He's crucifying you, Sy. The judge *knows* he's Vita's lover. He doesn't care. And the longer Zelazo's up there, the worse it's going to get. Has he told any outright lies?"

"No, but he's distorted things way out of proportion. He knows that Vita's crazy. He told me himself. He's leaving out half the story."

"Do you think he's going to stop when I cross-examine him? Every question I ask him is going to give him an opportunity to say something else damaging against you, and he's *very impressive*. The judge believes every word. You'll be able to tell your side when you testify."

"Well?" the judge asked when he saw that Kassler and Marty Myers had finished their conversation.

"No questions, Your Honor," Marty repeated, and as Zelazo and Vita left the courtroom, arm in arm, the second day ended.

On the morning of the third day, the fruit of Kassler and Vita's marital tree appeared. Joshua and Joy arrived freshly bathed, in immaculate new clothes, and in their cute and adorable ways told how much they loved both their mommy *and* their daddy, but wanted to stay with their mommy and Dr. Sam, who they thought was just wonderful. The idea of moving to New Mexico, where it was summer all the time and they could see real Indians, was something they both found very appealing.

"I'll miss my daddy," Joshua said as he looked at Kassler,

"but maybe he can write me letters and call me on the telephone and come visit me in the summer or something," Joshua smiled at his father, who was near tears as he realized what had happened to his relationship with his son.

Joy seconded Josh's opinion.

"I'd miss my mommy just too much," Joy explained solemnly to the judge. "Besides, Daddy's always telling us to pick up this and pick up that and get washed and use your silverware and it makes me feel bad." She looked at her father, sensing she had complete power over him in this situation, and scolded him for past abuses.

Marty Myers again decided not to cross-examine.

In the afternoon of the third day, Jud Simon testified. He explained that he was a detective who'd been hired by Vita (with Kassler's money, of course).

"Sowing wild oats, I'd say," Detective Simon proceeded to describe in detail, with accompanying photographs, nearly every girl Kassler had picked up at the university. The photographs were not explicit—only Kassler with his arm around one young lady or another who was reciprocating, a kiss here and there, one in which Kassler and a blond coed clearly had their hands inside each other's denims as they stood kissing at Kassler's car—but the photos were detailed enough to do the trick.

This was, of course, the day that Lupa had decided to accompany Kassler to court so she might support him through the obvious agonies that it was clear to her each evening Kassler was enduring each day. She knew that hearing the children testify would be particularly hard for him.

As the photo of the seventh girl was being introduced, Lupa got up and quietly left the courtroom while Kassler looked on in anguish.

When he returned home that evening, he went immediately to find Lupa. He was certain she would already have left and was surprised to find her cooking in the kitchen.

"I want to talk to you about all that," Kassler began awkwardly.

Lupa turned around at the stove, her eyes red from having spent the remainder of the afternoon in tears.

"Let's talk about it after the trial, okay?" she said quietly.

Kassler looked at Lupa, grateful she was still there, and nodded his head.

"I'm sorry," he said with deep and genuine sadness.

"I know," Lupa answered. "In a few days, we'll talk."

"Okay," Kassler agreed, biting his lips to control himself, and went to finish preparations for his own testimony, which he expected to begin the next day.

The next day, Bea Chaikin testified—under subpoena, Kassler was pleased to learn.

Yes, she admitted, Kassler had at one time seemed suicidal to her, but—

Doris Huber stopped her. Yes and no answers only, unless otherwise requested, she was told.

Attorney Huber did allow Bea to give a long and eloquent testimony about Kassler's talents as a psychotherapist and his contributions to Phlegethon.

"He's brought a lot of sunshine into the lives of people mired in the gloom of lunacy." Bea Chaikin, still a mite starry-eyed about Kassler, called on celestial metaphors to make her point on the morning of the fourth day.

"And is it your professional opinion," Doris Huber asked, "that this talent is sufficient justification by itself to award Dr. Kassler custody of his children or to prevent Ms. Kassler from relocating to another state?"

The stars faded from Bea Chaikin's eyes and she looked up sadly at Kassler.

"No," she said in a low, reluctant voice. "No, it is not."

Marty Myers, who was about to cross-examine Bea to get some more positive things about Kassler on the record, changed his mind when he heard this last sentence.

"Cross-examining her will only give them the opportunity for a redirect testimony," Marty explained to Kassler. "Your time will come this afternoon."

Kassler's opportunity to testify didn't come until the fifth day. Huber was unable to locate her final witness, Norman Meltz, and asked for a brief recess, which became a longer recess, and, eventually, when Norman was nowhere to be found, the court adjourned, giving Huber the opportunity to present Norman Meltz as a rebuttal witness after Kassler's testimony the following day, if Norman could be located.

Kassler was, as might be expected, unable to sleep that night. He wandered around the house, reviewing in his head what he was going to say in court the next morning, and finally, about three o'clock, ended up in the basement.

"I don't suppose you'd be able to help?" he asked me.

"How?" I answered.

"Well, you're supposed to be the prosecutor of God's court, aren't you? Who could be better?"

"I'm supposed to be, but I'm not. Sorry."

"I'm not sure I'm going to be able to convince the judge," Kassler said as he paced. "What can I say?"

"Tell the truth," I suggested.

"I don't know," Kassler surmised correctly, "somehow I get the feeling that the truth doesn't have a whole lot to do with any of this."

"Knowing that," I told Kassler, "you should do just fine."

"I feel," Kassler responded in a daze caused half by mental exhaustion and half by a lack of sleep, "like a fish out of water, a bird who can't fly," Kassler selected the first two creatures that came into his fatigued brain, "just waiting to be picked off for someone's dinner."

"If I may offer some advice," I thought I'd help Kassler out the best I could, "when you get on the stand tomorrow, you should probably stay away from metaphors."

As it was, Kassler's analogy was not far off. Although he managed, in his direct testimony during the morning, to soar with eloquence and swim courageously against the strong currents which the opposition had established in the courtroom, in his cross-examination he was a sitting duck who floundered helplessly.

For three hours that morning Kassler told his story. He told about how much he had once cared for Vita and how depressed she had been after their marriage, how he had been against having the children until his and Vita's relationship was on a firmer footing and only for that reason, how he had been willing to endure even her outside sexual relationships, though it hurt him deeply, because Vita thought it would help their relationship.

With tears streaming from his eyes, he told how much he loved his children, how he had been both mother and father to them for their early years, how painful it was for him to leave, and how impossible it was being a father to them during only five hours one day a week.

The judge was visibly moved. He was getting a very different perspective about Kassler and the issues. Kassler sensed this from the intensity with which the judge was listening to him, and from the expressions of dismay on the opposition's side of the table.

Then Kassler went into how Sam Zelazo was having a sexual relationship with Vita while she was supposedly in treatment with him to work out their marriage, and finally the story of how Leo Szlyck ruined his life and burned down his apartment.

Only, Kassler explained, after Zelazo had told him that Szlyck was virtually dead already did he turn off the man's support system, a terrible mistake, he freely admitted, but he felt he had tried to compensate for it by turning Szlyck's very house into a home for mental patients.

As for Mrs. Fletcher, he continued, it was an unfortunate situation, but he was willing to sacrifice his own employment in order that a mother might say good-bye to her dying child.

As the morning came to an end, Kassler stood in the absolutely still courtroom and told how he had wanted to withdraw his motion for custody once he heard from the children that they had settled into their home with their mother, even though he did not feel this was the best environment for them, and would actually have withdrawn the motion had he not learned that Vita was taking his children to New Mexico, a place where he stood no chance of finding employment.

"I ask the court, Your Honor," Kassler said as tears streaked his cheeks, "not to take away the right of my children to have a father. Give us joint custody, increase my visitation—whatever you can do to keep Joshua, Joy, and me together."

When Kassler stopped talking, there was not a sound in the courtroom for several minutes.

Finally Judge Sullivan spoke.

"Have you attempted to work out some compromise with your ex-wife?" he asked Kassler.

Kassler shook his head in the negative, unable to talk through his tears.

"Well, Counselors," Judge Sullivan called across the courtroom, "I'd recommend that something be worked out between you."

Doris Huber stood up at the table.

"If it please Your Honor," she asked, "could we wait on that possibility until after the cross-examination?"

"I suppose," Judge Sullivan said, but one thing was very clear. Matters had become complex and Judge Sullivan didn't want to judge anything.

"What was all that at the end there?" Kassler asked Marty Myers during the lunchtime recess.

"What that was," Marty answered, "is that things are now at about a draw, thanks to your performance this morning, and the judge would prefer not to have to make any decisions. Judges don't like to decide anything that isn't clear-cut, and this is very un-clear-cut and becoming more so every minute."

"What kind of compromise?" Kassler asked.

"I don't know," Marty drank some of his diet drink, the only sustenance he allowed himself during a trial, "but the point Sullivan's trying to make is that right now, if *he* makes the decisions, no one's going to be happy—Vita won't get to relocate, you probably won't get extra visitation, everything'll stay just the way it is—so we'd better start talking to each other. Think about something like, Vita can move if you have the kids holidays and all summer or something, because, unless they've got something juicy for the cross-examination, everybody's going to lose if you two don't compromise."

"What do you mean, *juicy*?" Kassler asked.

"I don't know," Marty finished his beverage and looked up at Kassler. "You tell me."

* * *

Juicy was hardly the word for it. Doris Huber hosed down the courtroom with a flood of saturating revelations.

"That was a very moving statement you gave this morning," she began Kassler's cross-examination. "I was particularly impressed by the tremendous burden you were forced to carry because Ms. Kassler was unwilling to care for her children. Tell me, did you ever talk to her about it?"

"How do you mean?" Kassler asked.

"Well, did you ever tell her that you thought she was neglecting her responsibilities as a mother to her children?"

"Not in so many words," Kassler answered.

"Is the answer 'no,' Dr. Kassler? *No*, you never said anything?"

"The answer is no."

"Why is that? Was it because there was never a time that the children were neglected?"

"The children weren't neglected because *I* took care of them," Kassler said.

"Yes," Doris Huber placed her thin hands in the small pockets of her suit jacket, "we've all heard how you were both a mother and a father to your children. If Ms. Kassler was such a terrible mother, Dr. Kassler, why didn't you take the children with you when you left?"

Kassler thought about this for a moment.

"I'm not sure," he said. "I consulted my attorney and he said something about a 'tender years' doctrine, that it's assumed very small children should be with their mother unless there's gross negligence. If I took the kids, the court would only order me to give them back to her until there was a hearing on the merits."

"And there was no gross negligence, was there?"

"Not *gross*, no. But she *never* took care of the kids. I had to do *all* the child care," Kassler explained adamantly.

"Oh?" Doris Huber raised her well-trimmed eyebrows. "You didn't *want* to take care of your children?"

"No, I wanted to care for them."

"And Ms. Kassler let you, didn't she?"

"She was—"

"Just yes or no, please. Did she let you?"

"Yes."

"Was there *ever* a time that the children were neglected or harmed by Ms. Kassler?"

"No."

"Even though, as you've testified, Ms. Kassler went through two pregnancies and the normal post-partum depressions, she never, not one time, neglected the children. Is that your testimony?"

"Yes. The children were not neglected."

"No," Doris Huber nodded to the judge, "I didn't think they were. However, wasn't there a time period for over a year and a half, after you and Ms. Kassler were separated, when you never even *saw* your children? You simply abandoned them?"

"It was very difficult to—"

"Yes or no, please?"

"Yes."

"Now," Huber turned back to Kassler, "you've told a tragic tale of how Ms. Kassler had sex with other men against your will. Is that true?"

"Yes. It is."

"So, you told her to stop, did you?"

"No."

"Why not?"

"She said it would help our marriage."

"And you agreed?" Huber asked.

"No."

"But you didn't *say* anything. How was Ms. Kassler supposed to know you were against it if you didn't say anything?"

"By the way I looked. She came into the kitchen after the first time and all you had to do was look at me to know," Kassler told Huber and then stared at Vita.

"Oh," Huber said. "You were in the kitchen while this was happening? Where was this going on, in the next apartment?"

"In the next *room!*" Kassler's anguish returned.

"Let me see if I understand this, Dr. Kassler. You were in the kitchen while your wife was having intercourse with another man in the next room. Is that what you're telling the court?"

"Yes."

"Well, did you tell the man to stop, to leave, that you were against his having a relationship with your wife?"

"No," Kassler said quietly.

"Of course not," Huber said, "Because *both* you and Ms. Kassler *agreed* to this, didn't you?"

"Yes," Kassler admitted.

"Did you fulfill your sexual obligations to your wife, Dr. Kassler?"

"When she'd let me," Kassler snapped.

"Oh, is this another one of those things you never talked about? Did you *ever* ask your wife for sex and have her turn you down?"

"No," Kassler said curtly, "I never *asked* in so many words."

"But Ms. Kassler did tell you that you weren't fulfilling her, isn't that true?"

"I don't recall. She might have said something like it. I don't remember."

"If she did, could it have had something to do with your being a homosexual?"

"No!" Kassler protested.

"No, what?" Huber asked. "No, you're not a homosexual?"

"Yes," Kassler said, "I am *not* a homosexual."

"I see," Doris Huber said. "Tell me, if two men have sexual intercourse, would you consider them homosexuals?"

Marty Myers objected.

"I fail to see the relevance of this," Marty stood up. "Dr. Kassler has said that he's not a homosexual."

"If you'll give me just a minute longer, Your Honor, I intend to show it's very relevant. Dr. Kassler is asking for custody, and it's extremely important to determine the environment in which the children would be living."

"Objection overruled," Judge Sullivan announced. "Please answer the question, Dr. Kassler."

"It depends," Kassler said.

"Well, Dr. Kassler," Huber said, as she slowly walked over to the table, "if one man inserted himself in the rectum of another man for the purpose of sexual pleasure, you'd agree, would you not, that they were involved in homosexual activity?"

"It would depend on—"

"Yes or no?" Huber snapped. "Is it or isn't it homosexual activity?"

"Yes," Kassler said, watching in terror as Huber picked up the copy of Bernie Kohler's suicide letter. Kassler recognized it immediately.

"Has any man ever inserted himself in *your* rectum for the purpose of sexual pleasure, Dr. Kassler?"

"Do I have to answer that?" Kassler called out to Marty Myers.

"I think you just did," Marty said back sadly.

"I take it," Huber said, "that the answer is yes, someone has."

Kassler looked frantically around the room. Vita was shaking her head in dismay. Marty Myers stared helplessly at Kassler in sympathy.

"Yes," Kassler began to crumble.

"You *have* had a male lover, Dr. Kassler. Is that true?"

"Good God!" Kassler cried out. "He's dead. Leave him alone. Please."

"Yes, Dr. Kassler, I know he's dead. And he claimed he killed himself because of your inconsideration, didn't he?"

Kassler didn't answer.

"Isn't that what he claimed, Dr. Kassler?"

"Yes," Kassler mumbled. "That's what he claimed."

Doris Huber walked slowly around the room and placed the letter back on the table, since she knew she would not be allowed to present it as evidence and it had served its purpose.

"Tell me, Dr. Kassler," she asked, "have you ever been a patient in a psychiatric hospital?"

"Yes," Kassler answered numbly. "I was under obser—"

"I see. Did you indicate this on your application to the school where you got your degree to practice clinical psychology?"

"No," Kassler said.

"To Phlegethon? Did you tell them before you were hired?"

"No."

"If your school knew, you'd lose your degree and your license, is that correct?"

"Yes."

"So, in effect, you're practicing illegally, is that true?"

"I suppose so." So much damage had been done, Kassler was beginning to lose interest in the questions. "But I'm a *good* therapist," he tried.

"Oh, really," Doris Huber said. "Your Honor, we had hoped to have one of Dr. Kassler's patients, Norman Meltz, here to testify on that subject, but we've been unable to locate him. I'll attempt to question Dr. Kassler directly on the issue, if you don't mind?"

Judge Sullivan nodded.

"Dr. Kassler, was Norman Meltz one of your patients?"

"Yes."

"When you first met with him, was he able to function sexually?"

"That wasn't the prob—"

"Just yes or no."

"Yes."

"When you finished treating him, was he able to function sexually?"

"You mean was he—"

"You know what I mean."

"No. He wasn't."

Judge Sullivan leaned over to Sy Kassler.

"What wasn't he able to do?" Sullivan asked in a dismayed voice.

"Become erect and have an orgasm," Kassler told the judge.

Nothing that Kassler had admitted to doing so far disturbed the judge as much as this. The concept was, for Sullivan, the ultimate appalling thought. Kassler was clearly a dangerous man. Huber built skillfully on that notion.

"Now, you've admitted to killing Dr. Szlyck because he had done a number of things to harm your reputation. Do you have any proof that he did those things?"

"He *told* me he did them!"

"Well, conveniently, Dr. Szlyck isn't around to contradict you. Do you have any *other* evidence?"

"No."

"So, we have no way of knowing absolutely that he did any of those things that you've told the court, do we?"

"No."

"And Dr. Szlyck was a mentally ill person, wasn't he?"

"Yes."

"Especially when he told you those things, if he did?"

"Yes."

"When you first met him, he was your patient, wasn't he?"

"Yes."

"He was mentally ill then?"

"Yes."

"And had been for some time?"

"Yes."

"And you're now married to his ex-wife?"

"Yes."

"When you first started dating your present wife, was she married to Dr. Szlyck?"

"No, she'd gotten a divorce," Kassler answered.

"In Mexico, is that right?"

"Yes."

"From a man you knew to be mentally ill at the time and who was your patient?"

"Yes."

"Tell me, Dr. Kassler, I know you're not an attorney, but does it seem reasonable to you that a woman who, within twenty-four hours, gets a divorce in a foreign country from her mentally incompetent husband, who isn't present, could be legally divorced?"

"I don't know," Kassler said in a daze.

"Dr. Szlyck filed a motion contesting the divorce, didn't he?"

"Yes."

"And you killed him?"

"Certainly not because—"

"Just yes or no, please."

"Yes."

"And you married his former wife almost as soon as Dr. Szlyck's motion was voided by his death? Is that true?"

"Yes."

"And do you deny that almost since the week you were married, you've been having adulterous relationships?"

"No," Kassler mumbled, "I don't deny it."

"Your wife is Lupa Kassler, is that correct?"

"Yes."

"She's the children's stepmother now and would continue to live with you and them if you obtained custody, is that correct?"

"Yes," Kassler said despondently.

Doris Huber walked over to a window and stared out of it for a few seconds, waiting for the proper moment to spring the next question.

Kassler knew what it was and looked angrily over at Marty Myers, who also knew the next question and avoided Kassler's stare.

"Dr. Kassler," Huber turned from the window, "could you tell the court whether or not it's true that for a number of years, until recently, your present wife, your children's stepmother, operated a well-known prostitution service in Citadel?"

Kassler looked desperately around the silent courtroom for help from somewhere, anywhere. None was forthcoming.

"Did she?" Huber barked.

"Yes, she did," Kassler said in a rage, "but she's not a whore, damn it! She's a marvelous, wonderful woman, and I love her very much." Kassler fought back tears. "You don't know her. She's lovely. She's gone through so much with me. She's a wonderful person. You don't know anything about her. You think she's this terrible woman. It's Vita who's terrible. That's who you should ask about. Ask me about Vita—"

Doris Huber stepped back a few steps and decided to give Kassler all the rope he needed to tie his own noose.

Kassler turned to the judge.

"You're missing the point," Kassler said to Sullivan. "Vita has a serious psychological problem. She's a borderline personality. It's a serious disorder. She's impulsive and unpredictable. She goes from periods of intense anger to depression. There's tremendous affective instability. She's almost always angry or depressed. She's unable to form close personal relationships. She goes from one unstable relationship to the next, devaluing, idealizing, manipulating, avoiding any signs of closeness. She has no self-image or gender identity. That's why she has to sleep around so much. She has chronic feelings of emptiness and boredom. It's a lousy *psychological* environment for my children.

"You see, the limbic system," Kassler tried to explain, "in the middle of the brain, contains the centers for emotion, anxiety, fear, sexuality, and Vita has never developed the cortical structures to inhibit any of those. It's her brain chemistry, her neurotransmitters, the way that the pathways have been established and the neurons fire," Kassler tried to emphasize the hopelessness of the situation. "It's wired in. My kids need structure, emotional stability, and closeness, and Vita can't give them that because Vita's got a borderline personality disorder. Lupa does *not*. Lupa is warm and stable and strong and loving. Do you understand what I mean?"

Kassler stopped and looked around the hushed courtroom. Vita sat doodling absently on a pad in front of her. Marty Myers was trying to find something in his briefcase. Doris Huber had her back to Kassler and was staring out the window at a meter maid giving out tickets in the parking lot. Only Judge Sullivan was looking at Kassler.

Sullivan knew nothing about psychopathology and couldn't have cared less. It was all a bunch of mumbo jumbo that had nothing to do with how people lived, certainly not how he lived, and definitely had no place in a court of law. The only thing Judge Sullivan knew about psychopathology by the end of Kassler's impassioned talk was that Kassler was probably crazier than Sullivan had first thought.

When Kassler had finished, Doris Huber turned around and paced back and forth in front of the judge for a moment.

"Your honor," Doris Huber said with great pathos, "we have nothing against Dr. Kassler. We know that he's had a hard life and has a psychiatric history. But the best interests of the children are at stake here. That's the only issue.

"We have heard no *evidence* during *five days* of trial," Doris Huber went on, "even from Dr. Kassler himself, to indicate that Vita Kassler is anything other than a loving and devoted mother to her children and a faithful mate to Dr. Zelazo, who, I understand from the plaintiff, is soon to be her husband, and whom the children, I can assure this court, absolutely adore.

"On the other hand," Doris Huber gathered momentum, "it is no wonder that Vita Kassler is asking to take the children to an environment where contact with their father will be as limited as possible. Dr. Kassler has admitted openly in this court that he is a liar, that he falsified his employment and licensure records in order to practice a profession in which he is clearly incompetent, in at least one case that we know of, and who knows how many we don't, causing his patient to become tragically impotent.

"Dr. Kassler has admitted that he flagrantly disregarded a standing court order not to remove a dangerous mental patient from the institution where he worked. He is implicated in the suicide of his homosexual lover. As a matter of fact, the differences between Vita Kassler and Sy Kassler are so *striking*," Huber raised her voice, "so *outrageous*, that I'm asking the court to make its decision at once, and right now, from the bench, to *dismiss* all of Dr. Kassler's motions and to *allow* all of Vita Kassler's.

"Vita Kassler is a loving mother," Huber's voice became even louder, "who is faithful to the man in her life, who has not lied, has not indulged in perversion, has harmed no one, and who is deeply devoted to her children.

"Dr. Kassler," Huber shouted, "went for a year and a half without even *seeing* his children and now wants the court to place the children with him and a stepmother who for several years was a well-known prostitute in Citadel!"

Doris Huber turned and glared at Kassler.

"Dr. Kassler is, by his own admission, an *adulterer*, a *murderer*, and a *sodomist*."

"Excuse me," Kassler asked the judge politely. "May I step down from the witness stand now?"

"I have one more question, Dr. Kassler," Doris Huber held up her hand to stop any movement from Kassler. "Then, if you wish, I have no objection to your leaving the witness stand."

Kassler looked up at Doris Huber, vaguely interested in what was left to be asked.

"Do you believe that you can speak directly to the devil?" Doris Huber asked soberly.

"Yes, I do," Kassler said without hesitating even a second. "I certainly do," and Kassler stepped off the witness stand.

"Your Honor!" Marty Myers was going to begin a long energetic speech in Kassler's behalf.

"Forget it, Marty," Kassler called out as he started to leave the courtroom. "Save your breath. It's all over," and Kassler walked through the large swinging double doors and headed home.

Kassler took the long way home so he could think. Had he not done so, he wouldn't have seen the aftermath of a tragic automobile accident.

Three extremely attractive teen-age girls in very tight dungarees stood by an ambulance. They stared soberly at the sheet-draped body of the accident victim being loaded in the back.

Wrapped around a telephone pole, Kassler saw an old, familiar blue Buick. He tried to look in the cracked front window to see whether anyone else was in the car, but he was unable to do so because of the thick yellow goo that covered the inside of the windshield of Norman Meltz's automobile.

CHAPTER 3

*I*t *hardly needs to be said, but Kassler lost it all—his children,* the thirty-five thousand dollars in savings which Judge Sullivan divided evenly between the two attorneys, whose bills, interestingly, added up to exactly the amount of money they believed Kassler had to his name; and, of course, he lost Lupa.

"I really didn't mean to hurt you, Lupa," Kassler told her

after court that afternoon. "I don't know why I was sleeping around like that. You're all I've got."

"I know that, Sy. That's why I'm not leaving right now. I wouldn't do that, but in a few months, when everything has settled down and you've had a chance to adjust and get some rest..." Lupa's voice trailed off and she took Kassler's hand.

Kassler looked at her with great affection. She looked tired, he thought, but stunning as ever in her tailored tan gabardine slacks and scarlet satin-finish blouse. Her blondish hair, tied in a knot at the back, wasn't so blond as he once remembered, and premature streaks of gray could be seen in several places, but Lupa's violet eyes were as dazzling and warm as ever, even in fatigue.

Kassler leaned over and gently kissed Lupa on the lips, signifying his acceptance of her decision.

"I've signed over Bolgia to you, you know," he told her. "It's all in your name now."

"I'm not sure I want it, but thank you," Lupa said. "Where'll you be going?"

"I'm not sure yet," Kassler looked at Lupa's purple eyes. "How long can I stay?"

"As long as you like. I'm certainly not going to kick you out of Leo Szlyck's dream house," Lupa put her thin hand around Kassler's neck and rubbed it lightly.

"Besides," Lupa went on, "I'm going to be doing some traveling over the next year, see the world, you know, Europe, Egypt, Africa, Australia. I thought I'd take some pictures and write some articles. Maybe someone'll publish them."

"Can I come?" Kassler asked, already knowing the answer.

"I'm sorry, Sy," Lupa said as tenderly as she could. "You can't."

"Shame on you," I told Lupa just after her talk with Kassler that afternoon.

"I didn't lie to him, did I?" Lupa asked me.

"You also didn't tell him about us."

"I didn't see why it was necessary. Besides, he'd never believe for a minute that you were Satan."

"Or that I told you a month ago that he was going to give you Bolgia," I avoided any direct comment on her prediction.

"I was taught that it isn't polite to ruin other people's surprises."

"I want him around for the next year, Lupa, until he's finished my treatment. That was our agreement," I reminded my lovely companion.

"I don't want you to hurt him, Satan. I mean it. Or let him hurt himself. I told you that and you promised."

"You're a tough woman, Lupa," I commented. "You drive a hard bargain."

"This is the least I can do for him. Now, you promised."

"A promise is a promise," I assured Lupa.

"I just want you to help him live a little better in the world. That's all. He needs an education badly. That was our deal. I stay around. You get me. He gets educated. Everybody lives happily ever after."

"That was our *deal*, but I told you, there're no *guarantees*. He's not easy."

"You've been doing pretty good so far," Lupa remarked pointedly.

"That's what bothers me," I confided to my dazzling lady. "I have, and for the most part, I've hardly done a damned thing."

That evening Kassler's extended family gave him all the support for which any man could ask, even though they knew only the sketchiest details about Kassler's day in court and nothing at all about Lupa's pending departure.

After dinner, they sat around the table for hours, laughing and crying. Mr. Katzman told a never-ending stream of outrageous dirty jokes which had everyone laughing hysterically. Then there was a silence, while they all caught their breath, and Mrs. Fletcher talked to Kassler.

"I will never forget," she said, "how much it meant that you took me to see Skip before he died. I thank God every night that He gave me you for my therapist, Dr. Kassler."

Then everyone cried, most of all Kassler.

"Did Philip tell you, Dr. Kassler?" Mr. Katzman asked.

"He's gotten a job and an apartment in town. He's leaving next week."

"No," Kassler said. "What kind of job did you get, Philip?"

"Oh, it's great," Philip Donato beamed. "I'll be working in one of those fitness centers for women. All day long I can order old ladies around. Do this! Do that! You've been eating too much! Ten more push-ups for you! It's terrific! I hope my mother joins. I can hardly wait to begin."

And everyone roared with laughter.

"I also think I've got a girl friend, who I met there, but it's too early to tell," Philip said quietly.

Then he paused to look at Kassler, and tears formed in his eyes as well.

"Hey, Dr. Kassler," he said softly. "Thanks for everything. Thanks a lot. You, too, Lupa."

And the tears began again.

Until very late at night, they all sat like that, laughing and crying.

Kassler finally told them the highlights of the trial, leaving out a number of things having to do with Lupa and Bernie and Szlyck, so even the highlights were sparse, but everyone offered Kassler a great deal of sympathy at the right places, chastised the judge for his ignorance about psychological matters, and booed and hissed Doris Huber and Vita whenever they appeared.

"I guess my name came up, didn't it?" Lupa surprised Kassler.

Kassler shook his head noncommittally.

"You see," Lupa casually informed her instant family, "before Sy and I got married, I was a call girl for a while, because I was broke and didn't want to live without a lot of money. I made a whole lot of money, but it didn't make me feel very good, so I stopped. But I'll bet it came up at the trial, didn't it, Sy?"

Kassler nodded.

"A little," he said.

"I'm sorry," Lupa said.

"We all make mistakes," Diana Fletcher said.

"Were you really?" Philip Donato asked timidly.

Lupa nodded.

"You must know a lot, then, about . . . well . . . you know," Philip looked down at the table.

"I hope so," said Lupa. "I was very well paid. I'd hate to think it was for looks, not talent."

"Do you think . . ." Philip began. "I mean I've never even . . . If you could just *tell* me a *couple* things about . . ."

"Sure, Philip, what would you like to know?" Lupa asked.

"Well, one thing to begin with," he asked sheepishly. "I know the girl starts off closed. What do you have to do to get it to open up?"

Everyone tried not to laugh, but it was useless. Lupa hugged Philip, who was sitting next to her at the table, so he wouldn't feel bad, and finally even he was laughing.

"Okay, Philip," Lupa said when things quieted down. "Here's how it works."

Lupa went into a gentle and beautiful description of how a man makes love to a woman. When she finished, she looked over at Kassler, who sat at the other end of the table, watching her and sobbing.

"What is it?" Lupa asked.

"They called you a prostitute," he broke down and buried his head in his hands. "They kept on *calling* you a *prostitute* and I couldn't get them to *stop*," he wept.

"Who did?" Mr. Katzman asked in outrage, as Lupa went over, lifted Kassler's head, and held him against her.

"Who did that?" Mr. Katzman demanded.

"Vita's attorney," Kassler said through his tears.

"Well, fuck Vita's attorney!" Mr. Katzman stood and raised his fist.

Cheryl, who had been watching the events with great interest, felt a compelling need to participate. She stood up on her chair.

"Fuck Vita's attorney!" her tiny voice squeaked, and she raised the satin arms of her Marie Antoinette costume in the air and smiled from ear to ear.

"I guess she's making good progress," Kassler remarked as he dried his tears.

"I hope so," Mrs. Fletcher said. "I'm taking her home with me when I leave next week."

"You are?" Kassler asked.

"Absolutely," Diana Fletcher said. "I'd never leave a daughter behind."

"What about you, Mr. Katzman?" Kassler asked.

"Oh, I thought you heard. I've got a job and an apartment, too. I start tomorrow."

"Tomorrow?" Kassler said in shock. "What are you going to be doing?"

"Try and guess."

"Predicting holiday automobile death tolls?" Kassler tried.

"Come on, Dr. Kassler, be serious," Mr. Katzman said.

"I give up."

"I'll be working one of the computers downtown for off-track betting," Mr. Katzman said with great pride. "Setting odds."

Once again everyone laughed, but when the laughter died down this time, they were all very solemn. Mrs. Fletcher left and came back with a gift-wrapped package.

"We were going to give it to you next week before we all left, Dr. Kassler, but this is as good a time as any. Lupa told us about your wanting this, and we've been working on it for a long time, so I hope you appreciate it."

Then, instead of giving the box to Kassler, she handed it to Cheryl, who took it with a big smile and skipped out of the room.

A few minutes later, Cheryl Lerner returned. She was wearing sneakers, dungarees, and a very pink, very funky pullover.

Tears streamed from Kassler's eyes.

"It's the most wonderful present I've ever been given," he said through his tears.

"She gets up in the morning now, puts them on by herself, and keeps them on all day," Diana Fletcher said as Cheryl proudly walked over.

"I love you very much, Dr. Kassler," Cheryl uttered the longest sentence of her life, hugged and kissed Kassler, and then looked at everyone to see if she had done well.

Everyone broke into loud applause, as Cheryl strutted around the table, the sight and sound of which were still playing in Kassler's mind as he lay awake in bed later that night, wondering what he would do with his life after everyone had gone.

The next week was not a good one for Kassler.

On Monday he received a letter from the Institute indicating that the newspaper coverage of his hearing had brought to their attention his undisclosed previous psychiatric hospitalization. A committee had formed and voted unanimously to revoke Kassler's degree. He had the right to a hearing, if he so wished.

Kassler wrote back to them that he was somewhat trialed out at the present, would prefer to keep his degree and license, felt he had been doing good work to date, thanked them for the education they provided, but declined any further hearings. By the end of the week he received notification from the registrar that his letter had been given extremely careful consideration by the committee, and he no longer possessed a Ph.D. from their institution. The New Jersey Licensing Board had been notified, and he should expect to hear from them shortly.

On Tuesday Philip Donato and Mr. Katzman left. On Wednesday Diana Fletcher and Cheryl left. On Thursday Lupa embarked on a photographic expedition of Newport, Rhode Island, which she anticipated would last indefinitely. And on Friday Kassler received the following letter from Vita:

Dear Sy,
    I just want to let you know that I've got nothing *personally* against you and never have, but did what I thought would be best for the children. I tried to call you today so you could say good-bye to them, but the line was busy and we had to catch our plane. I'll send you our address and phone number as soon as we've settled, if you want, or you can get it from Sam, who should have it since he won't be joining us for a while longer. Speaking of which, I was interested to hear from him about your thoughts of ending your life. You shouldn't think of this as necessarily a bad thing. Those 911 people with Reverend Jones in Guyana, they weren't all crazy, you know.

There are other worlds, probably far better than this one, that we haven't even dreamed about yet, and I certainly am in favor of any attempts you might make to assert yourself, however briefly. We'll all adjust.

As always,
Vita

Having now hit rock bottom, Kassler required more than the usual measures to effect his rehabilitation. I had no choice but to pull out all the stops if I was to fulfill my end of the bargain with Lupa. When I say all the stops, I am referring, of course, to only one person. Sam Zelazo.

"I've come to say good-bye," Kassler told me shortly into 1979—all in all, a good year. The last of the twenty-five or so gentlemen who helped turn Watergate from a third-rate burglary into a first-rate motion picture, in this case the former Attorney General of the United States, was finally released from penal servitude. The Chrysler Corporation discovered they were short about 1.5 billion dollars. And much later, in the autumn, the Chief Executive of the United States, using an intellect frequently reported to be powerful enough to comprehend nuclear mechanics, determined that nothing of consequence would result from allowing a New York City hospital to provide medical treatment to the former Iranian Shah Mohammed Riza Pahlevi, as far as *he* could tell.

"Going anywhere in particular?" I responded to Kassler's farewell.

"You know damn well where I'm going," Kassler stood at the foot of the stairs as though concerned that, if he came too close to me, I might restrain him in some as yet undetermined way.

"I take it," I said, "that you're about to take leave of this world? That is what you're telling me?"

"I see no reason to go on," Kassler said.

"I wasn't aware that *reasons* were what made men go on. I should have thought that, after your experience in court, reason would've lost its magic," I pointed out.

"Whatever," Kassler said. "I've made up my mind."

"Have you considered that, if you take your own life, we might meet again?" I offered Kassler something for his consideration. "Under significantly less comfortable circumstances?"

"I have," Kassler said, "and if we do, then we do. There's nothing I can do about that. I'm damned if I do, and I'm damned if I don't."

"Catchy phrasing," I remarked. "Unfortunately, as you may have noticed, today you can *do*, *and* you can *don't*, and *still* not be damned for either. You're living at a great point in history. I hope you appreciate it, Kassler."

"Not for very much longer, I'm not living."

"So, then, why did you come down here? I'm nothing to you. Just a strange machine that Leo built. Why bother to tell me?"

"I don't know. No one else is around. I figured I should say good-bye to someone. I'd leave a suicide note, but there's no one to read it," Kassler told me.

"You sure you didn't want to see whether the floor would open up and you'd fall into an eternal pit of flames? People do think about things like that at these times."

"Yes, I'm sure."

"Well, you certainly didn't want my advice on how to do it. By the way, how *are* you going to do it? Nothing too messy, I hope."

"Sleeping pills."

"Oh, that's tidy. Do you have any sleeping pills around?"

"No," Kassler admitted a little sheepishly.

"Well, before you go calling up some physician for a prescription, I'd like you to do something for me. It seems to me that we've developed something of a friendship, and I *was* responsible for getting you Bolgia and a good amount of cash. I don't think it's inappropriate to ask for one favor in return."

"No," Kassler conceded. "I guess not. But no psychotherapy. Something brief."

"I want just a couple hours of your time this evening, probably not even that."

"For what?"

"Well, first, I'll tell you why I think you came down here

tonight. I think you wanted me to tell you why you shouldn't kill yourself. And guess what?"

Kassler edged a little closer. He didn't want to miss this.

"What?" he asked with some interest.

"I have an answer. Only one thing first."

"What's that?" Kassler was now at the overstuffed chair.

"If it changes your mind, I get my psychotherapy."

"I don't know. . . ."

"You've got nothing to lose. It'll have to be a dandy, even you've got to admit that."

"Okay. It's a deal," Kassler said halfheartedly.

"I don't know why," I interjected an aside, "but every time someone says to me 'It's a deal,' I get worried."

"Look, I said that I'd agree, and I'll do it," Kassler tried to allay my fears. "What have you got? Why shouldn't I kill myself?"

"Sam Zelazo," I answered.

"What?" Kassler was understandably confused.

"Sam Zelazo," I repeated. "This evening, go over to Phlegethon, or what's left of it, go down to the basement, and find Sam Zelazo. I promise you that after you find him, you won't want to kill yourself."

Kassler got up from his chair in a rage.

"I wouldn't go near that man if this were my last day on earth!" Kassler exclaimed.

"Well, it will be if you don't, that's for sure. Go find Sam Zelazo!" I raised my voice just enough to make an impression.

"Why?" Kassler shouted angrily. "Why should I go near that man? He fed Vita's lawyer all that shit that lost me my kids! He's ruined my life!"

"He's going to ruin your death, too, if you don't do what I'm asking! Look," I said as calmly as I could under the circumstances, "if I give you a good reason, will you go?"

"*If* you give me a *good* reason, yes, I'll go!"

So I gave Kassler a good reason and, lickety-split, he went.

Kassler parked his car outside the gates to Phlegethon Landings—as the new embossed wooden sign with a colonial motif designated the condominium complex—and thus avoided the guard in his tastefully designed booth, also a new addition which was determined to be absolutely essential for condominium owners, if not for mental patients.

The first floor of the main building, where Kassler, Bea, Bernie, Zelazo, and others had once had offices, was in the final stages of remodeling—walls of bare studs, rolls of carpet, piles of sheet rock, large cartons of kitchen appliances, all helter-skelter everywhere Kassler looked as he entered the building.

Kassler moved across the debris and opened the door to the basement. Then he descended the concrete steps with the metal mesh edges until he reached the heavy steel door at the bottom.

He opened the door slowly to see whether anyone else was around. The long hall was empty. A single light bulb, hanging from two makeshift wires halfway down the hall, was the only illumination.

Kassler made his way slowly down the corridor, trying various doors on his left and right, stopping to listen for sounds behind the locked doors, and went like that, step by step, the length of the hall, until at last one door opened.

Immediately he was blinded by the bright fluorescent lighting.

"One more day and you might have missed it altogether," Zelazo's voice came out of the brightness. "I'm surprised it took you so long."

When Kassler's eyes adjusted to the light, he saw that he was in a small office, an anteroom, with a desk behind which Zelazo stood, like a high priest, in a long white lab coat, sorting various papers into a file box on the table to his right.

"I want to see your lab," Kassler told Zelazo.

"I thought you would," Zelazo said nonchalantly.

"Where's the goddamn lab?" Kassler snapped, and he tried a door on his left which was locked.

"That's the door. I'll show you inside, but I want you to know that you're the only other person who'll have seen it besides me. I'm not sure what the reactions are going to be."

"I'll take my chances," Kassler sounded a great deal braver than he felt inside.

"Very well," Zelazo shrugged. "I'd be grateful if you didn't touch anything. You can understand that, of course."

"Just let me see the fucking lab, Sam," Kassler said.

"Be my guest." Zelazo walked around the desk and began to fish for the correct key from a large ring of nearly a hundred, as he continued to talk to Kassler.

"I knew you'd make it here eventually," he said. "After all, Leo built the computer, and he knew by the time he was here with that little liver problem. If Leo knew, Satan told him. Leo was going to tell, too, but fortunately, you took care of that for me, Sy."

"I'm glad I was able to oblige," Kassler said sarcastically. "What about Bernie? Was I supposed to set that up, too?"

"No," said Zelazo as he found the right key. "That was fortuitous. I had expected that it'd be you, but time was running short. This place could've been closed down at a day's notice. Bernie had to do. Just my good luck, I guess. And yours, too, incidentally," Zelazo said as he inserted the key in the lock, turned it around in a circle until there was a loud click, withdrew the key, and put his hand on the doorknob.

"Otherwise, as you've no doubt been told," Zelazo pushed open the heavy door, "that would be you."

As the door opened, Kassler saw on a table directly in front of him the brain of Bernie Kohler, set in a clear solution within a Plexiglas box that was slightly larger than the brain. Sticking out of the brain on either side were the semicircular canals and labyrinths that constituted the interior mechanism of Bernie's hearing aparatus, and suspended in front of the brain, at the end of each ropelike optic nerve, were Bernie's eyes. They flicked frantically back and forth as they saw Kassler.

"Oh, my God," Kassler choked when he recognized Bernie's eyes.

"It's a little chilly in here," Zelazo told Kassler. "It keeps the metabolism down and I don't use up as much of the fluorocarbons to keep the brains oxygenated."

Kassler held his stomach, which heaved as Bernie's eyes continued to jerk desperately back and forth.

Beside Bernie, on the left, was Norman Meltz's brain. His

eyes darted like Bernie's. And on Bernie's right, Kassler found, of course, the familiar yellow-flecked eyes of Leo Szlyck.

Zelazo watched Kassler retch.

"You can't do decent neurochemistry with rats, Sy," Zelazo said calmly, "and live human brains are very hard to come by."

Kassler looked around the cramped room. Several dozen tables like the ones in front of him were jammed side by side before him. On each was a brain, the eyes staring with terror at Zelazo.

"These are the people who hanged themselves outside your windows," Kassler figured out. "You *made* them suicidal."

"I did not," Zelazo protested. "They *came* to me suicidal. I just didn't help a whole lot. They had nowhere else to go anyway. They would have spent their lives locked up here. At least they're doing some good now."

"This is insane." Kassler felt faint but didn't dare lose consciousness. "It's diabolical."

"Yes, well, you might say that Satan and I are kind of in friendly competition," Zelazo conceded. "I put a lot of effort into preparing your brain for some major work down here, let me tell you, Sy."

Zelazo started pacing back and forth in the narrow aisles between the rows of brains.

"Of course," he shrugged his large shoulders, "I hadn't counted on Satan. As usual, Leo screwed up everything. Before he died, he told me about building Satan and Satan wanting you for his therapist. Leo thought I'd be very impressed. I was not. I had no intention of losing out to another one of Leo's schemes."

"You've been responsible—" Kassler began.

"For very little, really," Zelazo said as he turned to face Kassler. "Vita and I just kind of happened. I didn't do it to drive you to kill yourself, if that's what you're asking. I didn't assign Leo to you. As you may recall, you pleaded with me to work with him. I also didn't hook you up with Lupa. You did that on your own."

"You lied to me about Leo's condition," Kassler reminded Zelazo.

"Not at all," Zelazo shook his head and appeared genuinely offended at the accusation. "I told you what any physician would have told you. I didn't *ask* you to turn off Leo, although, I must say, I was rather delighted to see you take the initiative. It's good having Leo down here."

Leo Szlyck's eyes moved rapidly back and forth in discomfort.

"How did Vita get hold of Bernie's suicide letter to me?" Kassler asked pointedly.

"I did do that." Zelazo freely admitted. "I didn't want to be accused of contributing to Bernie's death, so I made a copy. But I didn't give it to Vita. I gave it to the police. I'm required by law to do so. As a matter of fact, I didn't even tell Vita about it. Her attorney found it when she was doing her research. Likewise with the information about your being at Bellevue. Vita's lawyer is at least as good as Leo at finding out things about her opposition and utilizing them."

"You're a goddamn liar, Sam," Kassler was having enormous difficulty assimilating everything. "You were responsible for it all. You could have stopped Bernie from killing himself if you really wanted."

"I thought I *had*, Sy," Zelazo said earnestly. "I left in the middle of a lovely party on Christmas Eve so I could talk to him. I knew that Bernie would go out of his way to avoid doing anything I told him. By the time I left, I was certain that Bernie wouldn't dare kill himself because I'd think he'd be doing it for my benefit. My impression is that it was an accident, Sy. Something went wrong."

"That's not what you said at the trial," Kassler was becoming increasingly irritated by the facility with which Zelazo parried his questions.

"No one asked me," Zelazo said. "I told only the truth at the trial, and you're very much aware of that. First I told the truth from Vita's side. I was amazed that no one asked me for the truth from your side. I figured that you had let your anger for me get in the way. It was your decision."

"I don't believe a word of this. You wanted me to kill myself so you could get my damn brain. You wanted me *dead*."

"It wasn't my decision. It was up to you."

"Well, I'll be damned if I'm going to end up as a brain in one of your boxes."

"And I'm not going to try to *talk* you into it, either, although I must say," Zelazo smiled, "I'd be proud as a peacock to have you down here. You could make some very important contributions to science. Just a thought," Zelazo continued to grin at Kassler. "I'd put you in a very special place."

"Forget it, Sam," Kassler grinned right back at Zelazo. "I'm not going to kill myself. If you want me so badly, why don't you just kill me? There's no one around. You'd almost certainly get away with it."

"Isn't it a sin?" Zelazo asked facetiously.

"And this *isn't*?" Kassler called back as he started to walk around the room, his nostrils filling with the sweet sea smells of the isotonic saline and glucose solutions that Zelazo was using to maintain his brains, his ears beginning to clog with the excessive moisture, his head already aching from the constant hiss of the oxygen and the incessant hum of the garish fluorescent illumination.

Dozens of dark pupils, set into thinly vascularized round white balls at the end of pink optic stalks, followed Kassler as he moved cautiously about the cold damp room.

"Keeping Bernie and Leo and Norman and all these other people in this half-dead, half-alive state indefinitely *isn't a sin* and *insane* and *cruel*?" Kassler asked loudly. "You think they don't *feel* anything? You think they're not in *pain*?"

"I don't know," Zelazo wasn't particularly interested in the question. "What I *do* know is that I've learned more about how the human brain works during the last ten years than has been learned by all mankind in all time before that. Now I'm going to go out to a nice quiet place in the desert and write it all down."

"Who cares, Sam? Who the hell cares?" Kassler stopped and faced off against Zelazo. "So you can plot all the noradrenergic pathways. *Big deal*. Have you learned one goddamn thing about what makes people hurt each other? Or why they love?"

"You'll have to talk to Satan about that one," Zelazo moved

over to a brain and adjusted the knob on a large green cylinder beside it. "It's not my field."

"I just might, Sam," Kassler said from the back of the room.

"Yes, well, don't be so sure you're going to get any answers from Leo's contraption," Zelazo remarked casually as he began to work his way around the room, adjusting valves on other brains, while eyes flicked back and forth between Kassler and Zelazo.

"Why not? Who knows what's inside that device?" Kassler challenged Zelazo.

"I do," Zelazo said simply. "That's what I'm going to write about. The human brain is a holographic instrument interpreting a holographic universe. It operates in realms so far beyond the conventional five senses, especially when it's completely freed from the body, like in here, from appetite, from sexuality, from having to avoid bumping into things, that you don't begin to have the courage to imagine them. We get only hints of them from dreams and intuition and clairvoyants, and, every century or so, from geniuses like Shakespeare or Einstein, which brings me to Leo's electronic apparatus. It's a bodiless higher realm, Sy, and he calls himself Satan."

Kassler didn't answer. He stood in the back of the room where he couldn't see most of the eyes and stared at Zelazo moving from brain to brain.

"You're crazy, Sam," Kassler told Zelazo coldly. "You're the craziest person who's ever been in this building."

"Not at all," Zelazo said quietly as he worked. "Sometimes I wish I were. Do you think I'm the only scientist in the world who's working with brains? There're over a hundred thousand. Do you have any idea how many rats and dogs and sheep and monkeys there are lying alive on lab tables with the tops of their skulls off? The Soviet Union's been transplanting dog brains for years. It's almost certain they're working with live human brains. If I'm crazy, then I've got a lot of good company. The only difference between my esteemed colleagues and me is that I'm able to maintain human brains in homeostasis indefinitely and they can only do it for a few minutes. Don't worry. They'll get better at it with practice."

"God, I hope not," Kassler said under his breath.

"You're kidding yourself, Sy," Zelazo commented, as he began inserting microelectrodes into the gyrate grayish-pink tissue of each brain.

"Nobody who's sane is going to come up with any holographic theory of higher realms." Kassler watched in fascination as Zelazo moved down the rows placing thin needles into the brains, and wondered what was going on.

"You're wrong again, Sy," Zelazo said, somewhat preoccupied. "If you go into the other room, you'll find a foot-thick pile on my desk of recent scientific papers, and every one of them says just that. It is, after all, how Leo got Satan and how your life became a disaster area. You're a victim of the neuron, Sy, when you get right down to it. Vita's neurons. Bernie's neurons. Leo's neurons. Your kids' neurons. The judge's neurons—"

"I'm not convinced," Kassler remarked from his spot of safety in the rear of the room.

"What? That I'm not crazy? That I'm not personally responsible for lousing up your life? That it makes sense not to kill yourself? Or that there are higher realms within easy reach of our brains and Leo's Satan is the proof?"

"Probably all of that," Kassler told Zelazo. "I certainly don't believe in any outside sinister forces."

"Oh, good," Zelazo said. "Then what I'm going to do next shouldn't bother you. Because tomorrow night I'm leaving for sunny New Mexico, and all good things must come to an end. Have you ever heard the sound of a single neuron?"

"No," Kassler answered as an icy sensation filled his body.

"It doesn't sound like much," Zelazo commented. "Something like static on the radio. Here. Listen for yourself." And Zelazo flicked a switch on the wall.

Suddenly the room was filled with the crackling static or the trillions of neurons in the brains in front of him.

"I've inserted microelectrodes which are hooked up to amplifiers. The electrodes monitor the neurons in each brain," Zelazo said calmly. "The noise you're hearing is from the constant electrical polarization and depolarization of each neuron as it fires."

The noise was a strange one to Kassler, not at all like static he'd heard before, and it made him feel uncomfortable, particularly standing directly in front of the two large speakers, so he moved toward the front, where Zelazo was standing. Unfortunately, now he could see the dozens of pairs of panicky eyes. He tried to avoid looking at them, but he couldn't turn away.

"Since you don't believe in outside sinister realms, this probably won't have the effect on you that it usually does on me," Zelazo said as he turned to the wall, opened an electrical panel, and began to flick the spring-loaded black plastic circuit breakers which controlled the current being used to maintain the support systems for each brain.

Almost instantly, the air was filled with hundreds of piercing metallic "Aaah's."

"That," said Zelazo, less calmly, "is the sound of neurons dying."

Kassler couldn't keep himself from looking at Bernie's terrified eyes, which darted frantically back and forth and then stopped, suddenly, and stared directly at Kassler.

Kassler began to fall apart. The hundreds of short screamlike sounds became thousands and then tens of thousands.

"What you're hearing now is brain death," Zelazo said, "whole populations of neurons, major centers, and pathways are dying."

The sound was unlike any Kassler had heard, loud and shrill and bitterly unpleasant.

Leo Szlyck's eyes stopped and stared at Kassler, and then Norman Meltz's did the same.

Kassler tried to close his own eyes, but they wouldn't close. He tried to move to leave the room, but his body wouldn't function. He was frozen in absolute terror.

"That, incidentally," Zelazo yelled over the terrible roaring sound, "is what awaits you at the end of your suicide. So much for the choirs of angels and the pearly gates."

Kassler started shaking as the sounds filled his head.

"Would you like to see the first brain I ever got?" Zelazo shouted. "I think this will interest you."

Zelazo went into an alcove and returned with a metal laboratory cart. A brain floating in a jar was on it.

"I've kept this going for over ten years," Zelazo shouted,

approaching Kassler, and turned the cart around until Morris Kassler's eyes stared at his son's.

Kassler tried to scream but couldn't. He stood frozen, opened his mouth, and felt himself pushing with his vocal cords to make sound come out, but nothing happened.

"Got it at a hospital in Florence. I thought for a while I might have a matched pair down here," Zelazo shouted over the deafeningly loud noise. "I told him I'd take good care of you until you made up your mind whether you'd be joining us or not."

Morris Kassler's eyes didn't move. They stared piercingly at his son in a mixture of fury and desperation.

"Oh, my God," Kassler finally managed to scream as the horrible metallic grating sound of dying brains screeched inside his head. "Oh, my God!"

Kassler held himself and doubled up in pain. He looked at Zelazo, who had his hands over his ears and his teeth gritted in agony. Kassler watched him tremble until the noise began to diminish and, pair by pair, the eyes in front of them turned glassy with death—Norman Meltz, Leo Szlyck, and, with a final plaintive look, Bernie Kohler.

The last eyes with any life in them, as a few random pings could still be heard in the background, were Morris Kassler's.

"I'm sorry," Kassler managed to say to his father. "I'm really sorry."

Morris Kassler's eyes looked coldly at Sy Kassler for a few seconds and then became as vacant as the others, while the sounds finally died away and the room became silent.

Zelazo stopped shaking and took his hands down from his ears.

"*Requiescat in pace,*" he said quietly.

"Amen," Kassler mumbled, and then, because there was too much to say, Kassler said nothing at all to Zelazo, but, without looking at him even one more time, left Phlegethon, in a state of shock and exhaustion.

"I'll do it," Kassler said simply as he collapsed into the good old chair in front of me. "A deal's a deal. I'm not killing myself. You get your psychotherapy."

"I thought you might," I told him.

Kassler said nothing more. He stared into space, trying to rid himself of Zelazo's nightmare.

"Did you know that my father . . . ?" Kassler wasn't able to finish.

"I suspected it," I told Kassler.

Kassler nodded his head.

I waited for some time until I felt that Kassler had started to recover.

"Look," I said, "I'll make it easy for you. Seven sessions. That's all I want."

Kassler looked up at me with his tired eyes.

"I'll give you one a month for the rest of the year, but I want the summer off," Kassler said numbly.

"Fine with me," I agreed.

"Zelazo's a lunatic," Kassler told me. "He's certifiable— a first-class raving lunatic."

"That's always been my impression," I concurred.

"He's a nut," Kassler repeated his diagnosis. "A ghoul."

"I'm sorry you had to go through all that," I told my new therapist. "But drastic measures were called for. Zelazo is, as drastic measures go, pretty solid," I remarked.

"Zelazo is a madman," Kassler mumbled. "You know the last thing he said to me as I was leaving?"

"Tell me," I didn't want to kill Kassler's punchline.

"I'm going down the hall and Zelazo yells after me—'Forget it, Sy! It's neurochemistry!' "

"Insane," I agreed.

So it was that with Kassler's last visit to Sam Zelazo I finally obtained my psychotherapist, that bitter cold week in January of 1979.

PART IX

The Cure
Last Session
December 1979

CHAPTER 1

"*I was born*," I told *Kassler as we came to our final session*, in which, I may already have indicated, I was cured, "in a sweltering vale of the Upper Volta. It was a very long time ago, during an unbearably hot summer, in a thick forest, which was brown and hard from the long drought produced by the intense heat.

"Early that evening, storm clouds gathered, while a being, barely a man, sat eating with his young wife and two children. Suddenly, there was terrible thunder. Lightning cracked all around them. Bolts of blinding light flashed from the sky, setting the trees on fire, terrifying the barbarian and his family. They raced about, attempting to escape the storm.

"Confused and frightened, the man ran into the forest and cowered there in a ditch, alone, watching the woods blazing on all sides of him.

"When the rains came and the fire ended, he walked back to the covert where he had left his wife and children. There was, of course, nothing but charred ashes remaining.

"Never had the man seen a conflagration so devastating. He

sat by himself that night, in distress, weeping over his lost family and wondering what caused such a thing.

"Then a second storm gathered. The man had already lost the little he had. A bolt of lightning crashed from the sky at his feet, threatening the only thing he had left, his life. It was, he decided, a punishment for surviving. Instinctively, this wild man of the woods knelt down in dread, his mind in a half-chaotic state produced by external calamity and internal meditation, and he supplicated the dark and evil shadow responsible for all that he had experienced.

"In that instant, Kassler, I was born."

"Your mother?" Kassler asked.

"Inspiration," I answered. "The same as God's."

"And your father?"

"Fear," I answered.

"And their parents?" Kassler pursued my ancestry.

"Mystery, I suppose. I never have been clear about that," I allowed. "I'm not exactly overjoyed to admit it, but I'm sort of a mongrel—born, bred, nurtured, and reared of human fancy, folly, and fraud. God was the result of all those feelings of inferiority you carry around day and night. He's a lot like Dad. Fear is very important.

"I arrived when you all decided you were not *really* a part of nature, when you started telling tales about how lust, revenge, malice, and self-interest weren't really from your heart, but were forced upon you by some outside force. Even more to the point, I was conceived in your escaping the confines of your nature to ask, How come? Whence the world? What does it all mean? I'm the child of human speculation, Kassler. Of inspiration. I'm more like Mom's side of the family."

"It's an inspiring tale," Kassler commented.

"I was hoping you would like it," I responded. "The fact is, Kassler, I've always considered myself to be the natural offspring of humanity, of duality, the shadow cast by God's bright and pleasing sun, the human mind.

"You see," I went on, "my barbarian did get his family back. They emerged the next day from where they'd found refuge in a cave, and everyone lived happily ever after. Except that from that time on, there I was, the Bad Spirit, counterposed always against God, the Good Spirit. And so it's remained. Although, as I've said, things recently have gotten rather out of hand with all the cloven-hoof, horns, pitchfork, and fiery-flames business."

"And your own family? You did say you were married?" Kassler remembered.

"Am I ever," I conceded.

"You've had children?" Kassler asked.

"Well, we talked about that last time, Kassler. As you no doubt know, the reports are that I've fathered everyone from Cain and Merlin the Magician to Pope Sylvester the Second and Voltaire, not including the recurrent rumor that it's because of my indiscretions that all Jews have horns."

"But in truth you're childless."

"No. We're not. Dame Fortune and I have had one son, but I'd rather not discuss him, if you don't mind. We don't get along so well. You know how it is when kids grow up and go off on their own. They're always going to do it better than their old man."

"Well, well," Kassler chuckled unprofessionally. "So you *have* created something after all."

"You've missed the point, Kassler. Product is nothing. It's just pigment, words, vibrating strings, stone—nothing at all. I'm not a Creator. And I'm not interested in creation. I'm what lies between. The most important part of all. I'm the *power* of creation—terrible, mysterious, and incapable of being restrained, directed, or beckoned on command. I'm what makes it possible for something spectacular to come from the darkest, emptiest nothing. I'm the energy that makes of two things substantially more than they are together. Since you've been asking for the last six sessions, *that* is what I do. I'm mystery, unfortunately, in an age of exposure."

"So," Kassler was still chortling over in his chair, "you've had a son, and he's turned against you."

"I'm not sure why you find this so amusing, Kassler. It's not very funny, I assure you."

"I'm sorry. You're right. I don't know why it strikes me as so funny. It's just the thought of all the ways an adolescent behaves when he rejects—" Kassler couldn't control himself. He broke into fits of laughter.

"You're going to have to stop this, Kassler," I was becoming *very* irritated.

Kassler took a deep breath and sat still in his chair, pursing his lips, trying to avoid a smile.

"What did he say to you?" Kassler assumed a deep voice and tried to be serious. "Did he tell you—" Kassler began to lose control again. "Did he say—" Kassler started to laugh loudly. "Did he go up to you and say—" Kassler stood up, lowered his chin to his chest, and spoke in mock seriousness. "'Dad, your life has been a *failure*. It's had no *meaning*. You'll *never* understand,'" and, for some reason I will never be able to fathom, Kassler collapsed into his chair, rocking with laughter. He held on to his sides and kicked his legs up in the air, roaring, waving his feet, until, several minutes later, he calmed himself, not completely, but enough to talk.

"You've *got* to tell me who it was," Kassler said between his guffaws. "You just *have* to tell me," Kassler insisted.

"My son is Sam Zelazo, Kassler."

Kassler nearly choked to death. He stopped laughing with such suddenness that his lungs didn't know what to do, go in or out. For several minutes he coughed and gagged, turning blue, as he held on to the arms of the chair for support.

"I don't believe it," he finally managed.

"That's up to you."

"But Szlyck built you," Kassler slumped in the chair.

"To check out a long-standing rumor about Sammael which turned out to be true. He'd always felt that Sammy Zelazo got the upper hand on that little exchange of suicides by their pretty brides."

"It was you *and* Zelazo—"

"Who screwed up your life? Absolutely not. I refuse to accept responsibility for any of it. If it was anyone, it was Sammy."

"And he says it was you," Kassler accused me.

"Figures."

"You never wanted *psychotherapy*!" Kassler was becoming a little hot under the collar.

"You're wrong. Szlyck got me here, but I had my own agenda, and it certainly wasn't to settle scores for Leo Szlyck with my son, that's for sure."

"This treatment business has all been a charade," Kassler stamped around. "What for? What do you want?"

"Just what I said I wanted, Kassler," I told him. "Sammy's made such a big deal about this psychotherapy business, I wanted to see for myself what was going on. I really kind of like it, although psychotherapy worries the hell out of me, if you really want to know. It keeps turning evil into neuroses and explaining away people's behavior with drives and complexes. It's usurping my throne, Kassler, and I'm concerned. Bad behavior, selfish people, willfully destructive and negligent human beings no longer have meaning. They've all been turned into borderline personality disorders and narcissistic antisocial characterological syndromes on account of childhood traumas and bad brain chemistry. It hurts me to say this, but recently I've been reduced to nothing more than *sublimated manifestations of repressed unconscious drives*. I know this all grew out of what you felt was a realistic, if somewhat pessimistic, appraisal of yourselves as guilt-laden and hopeless, but to tell you the truth, Kassler, modern psychiatry is putting me out of business."

"You *are* evil," Kassler glared at my tangle of wires.

"Evil has its home in the heart of man," I reminded him. "Worse than the worst man I cannot be."

"You've consumed us with fear," Kassler tried out, as he skipped back and forth as if lightning were striking at his tail, first this direction, then that, trying to assimilate it all.

"Ah, yes," I replied. "So I've been told. I devour you all— the edible complex, you should pardon the expression. Fear made man's devils. And gods. *Timor fecit deos*. Well, you're wrong, Kassler. Your conception of me, erroneous as it is, is the result of a soul in ruins. Nothing more."

"I'm not even sure you *exist*," Kassler told me.

"I exist wherever you all exist," I explained. "I fill every corner of your heart and know all that you feel and do. *But I am not evil*. Haven't I said that a few times before?"

Kassler waded back and forth in his stew, a step here, two steps there, trying to put it all together.

"You knew what was going on all along," he said as he danced around. "You could have warned me."

"What, and end up being responsible if something I told you didn't work out, if I misjudged Sammy, if Leo changed his mind, if Lupa reconsidered? No, I told you from the very beginning, Kassler. I don't get involved. I'm an interested observer. It's all up to you."

"You really did a number on me," Kassler continued to jump around and not pay very close attention to what I was saying.

"Jehoshaphat! I did no such thing. I saved your life, is what I did. And what have you done in return? Have you cured me? Have you figured out why I was expelled from heaven?"

Kassler suddenly stopped and stared at the mess of wires that was my existence. Then he spoke very slowly.

"You know very well what I've done in return," he said.

"So, I got a little melancholy. Big deal."

Kassler said nothing.

"Okay," I conceded, "you made Satan weep. I'll give you that."

"You'll *give* it to me! I *cured* you, that's what I've done. I may have done nothing else with my life, but *I cured Satan.*"

"You're kidding yourself, Kassler. You did no such thing. I'm no different now from when I started."

"You believe that?"

"So, okay, maybe I'm a little more comfortable with things. It was bound to happen. After a while, we all adjust."

"After a few thousand years."

"It takes some of us longer than others."

"You came to me in pain, damn it. I took away your pain."

"And hurt me doing it. You made me *weep*, Kassler. You *caused* me pain. It was *very unpleasant.*"

"You expected it to be painless? You expected to learn anything valuable without suffering?"

"I've never much cared for suffering. I've told you that. Like someone else you know, I have a very low threshold for pain. Besides, I can't see that I've learned anything much at all. I still don't know why I was expelled from heaven. What good has it all been?"

"I already told you why you were thrown out of heaven."

Kassler stopped his pacing and stood his ground.

"You what?"

"I already told you. Not in so many words, but it should have been obvious by now. What do you think all the remorse is *about*? The sadness? The fury over being misunderstood and maligned? The frustration over one distortion after another?"

"You *never* told me," I insisted.

"I didn't think you'd need a diagram."

"Don't insult me, Kassler. Just tell me. And it wasn't for wanting God's throne, or the sin of pride, or because I wouldn't bow to Adam, or any other of those charming mythologies."

"No, it wasn't. You were thrown out of heaven because you wanted to be an author."

It was like a gong sounding.

Kassler continued.

"You wanted to write your own book, explain your side, tell your story."

I said nothing as I let the revelation sink in.

"It was, of course, forbidden," Kassler said.

"He wouldn't hear of it," I finally remembered.

"It's a lot to keep bottled up," Kassler noted with deadly accuracy.

"He's got two whole testaments. And a lot in between. What have I got? Nothing."

"The bad rumors started when there was nothing around to correct them," Kassler pointed out.

"I will admit that it has felt marvelous to tell you my story," I said candidly.

"Psychotherapy—people telling their stories," Kassler said smugly. "I hear that, for some, it's very helpful."

"It's all coming back now," I decided to allow Kassler his conceit as the dreadful scene grew more and more vivid. "That's it, Kassler. You've hit the nail on the head. The Son-of-a-Bitch threw me down here because of my literary ambitions."

CHAPTER 2

Once this had happened, there wasn't much more to be done with poor Kassler, who had spent the past year in contemplation, reading, talking congenially to Lupa when she was around, and providing me with my now successful psychotherapeutic treatment.

"I suppose," I said, "that now that we're all done, you'll be leaving soon. I'll miss our little dialogues, Kassler, to tell you the truth."

"Thank you," Kassler was careful about not reciprocating until he'd had a chance to give further consideration to the revelations of the last forty-five minutes or so.

"So what now?" I asked.

"I'm not sure," Kassler said, and he got up, ready to leave.

"Well, I don't know whether this is going to help at all," I told him, "but we did have a deal, as you may recall. In return for my treatment, I promised to give you the Great Answer. Maybe you should sit down," I advised.

"That's okay," Kassler said as he started for the steps. "I don't even know what the Great Question is."

"The Great Question is, What is life?" I told Kassler. "I think you should sit down for this one."

"Jesus," Kassler shrugged and headed back for the chair, sensing something unpleasant was on its way, but unable to avoid returning to find out what it was.

He sat back in the chair and looked ahead into the darkness.

"Okay," he said with mounting dismay. "What is it now? What is life?"

"Life is hell, Kassler."

"Very funny," Kassler said in disgust and got up to leave again.

"No, Kassler, you don't understand. There's no way out. This is it. *This is hell*."

Kassler turned a chalky white.

"I told you," I informed him, "that there're no kettles and fire and stewing sinners, and I meant it. This is what it is."

"I don't believe it," Kassler croaked.

"I'm afraid it's true. I hope I haven't disappointed you, Kassler. Okay, so there're no pits and bubbling cauldrons, but who needs them, right? It seems to me that we're doing just fine, don't you think? Anyway, it's nothing to be upset about, really," I tried to comfort Kassler. "Until I told you, you hardly knew the difference."

"Am I dead?" Kassler asked.

"Well, here again, like with Sammy's science, we've got a very complex issue. Let's just say that, based on your experiences over the last ten years or so, you've been deprived of any authentic existence."

Kassler wheeled and faced me in rage.

"I think that's just about enough," he fumed. "I've had it! Can you *prove* to me that this is hell? Can you?"

"Can you prove to me that I'm cured? Come on, Kassler," I said, "be serious. After all that's happened to you, what's to prove?"

"I'm not giving you credit for a single thing that's happened to me," Kassler continued to fume, his eyes darting about like, you should pardon the expression, a brain in a box.

"Good," I told Kassler, "because I don't want it. That's the thing about hell—things just happen."

"The hell they do!"

"In hell they do!"

"I did it all. I went away for five months and I figured it all out. It's me. That's what's been wrong. I did it. I accept responsibility for it all. It's all my fault."

"Well, I hate to rain on your holiday, but exactly *what* is your fault?" I asked, a little incredulous, as you might imagine. "What Vita did to you? Leo's phone calls? Your kids' rejecting you? Lupa's leaving? Losing your degree and your license for an adolescent indiscretion, a trivial bout with insanity? Perhaps for Bernie's killing himself? Or for losing absolutely everything in the world that matters to you? That's all your fault?"

"Absolutely," Kassler maintained his ridiculous position. "I accept responsibility for all of it."

"I'm disappointed in you, Kassler. I'm sure Sam will be, too."

"I'll tell you something else," Kassler ignored my comment, "not only was it all my own damn fault, but I'm going to change. I'm leaving this place. It's my life, and if I want to start over, then that's exactly what I'll do. I'll get a new profession. Teaching or something. I'll find a new woman. Some nice, sensitive, lovely flat-chested lady."

"You're joking, of course."

"The hell I am. I'm going to get married and have more kids. Raise a family. It's going to be beautiful. You'll see."

"Come on, Kassler. That's enough. You're breaking my heart. Accept things for what they are and deal with them. Grow up. Isn't that the point of all your psychotherapeutic mumbo jumbo? You can't change the world—you just learn to live better in it the way it is."

"No," Kassler said with less conviction than might be expected under the circumstances.

"No, what?"

"No, it's not the point. It doesn't have to be this way."

"But it does, Kassler. It does because it's nobody's fault. No one's responsible. Your father had a bad heart. It couldn't be helped. Poor Vita was an only child. Intimacy scared the daylights out of her. It couldn't be helped. Leo was crazy. He was a victim of his own obsessions. It couldn't be helped. Lupa's life depended on a certain style. She was well bred. Sophisticated prostitution was the lesser of two evils. It couldn't be helped. Bernie was wired differently than most men, and, besides, his suicide was accidental. It couldn't be helped. Your children were simply children, influenced by what happened around them, doing their best to survive under difficult circumstances. It couldn't be helped."

"I don't buy it."

"I didn't know I'd opened shop. What am I selling?"

"Helplessness. Hopelessness."

"*Reality*, Kassler. The world of grown-ups."

"I prefer the world of children."

"Who doesn't? No responsibility. No moral choices. What you prefer is innocence, Kassler."

"And if I do?"

"Well, innocence may not be so splendid as you think. I'm sure I don't have to remind you that Vita was innocent. Sometimes corrupt isn't so bad, let's face it. Innocence doesn't do so well in this world. Around here, innocence is reserved for simpletons and youth—corruption is the earmark of reason and maturity."

Kassler stood in front of me, his anger building.

"I won't accept that!" he shouted.

"Come on, Kassler, cut it out. If you've learned anything at all from your own disastrous life, it's that control is out of the question. Be reasonable."

"If that's what being reasonable means, then I don't accept that either!"

"You're not paying attention, Kassler."

"Not paying attention! You think I'm not aware of what's happened to my life over the last ten years? You think I haven't suffered over every wound and hurt until I thought I couldn't tolerate it for one more second?"

"It's hard to tell. You've pulled it off with such panache."

"I don't care what's happened. I won't deny the feeling inside me that I can have some small effect, now and then, on my life, on other people, on events."

"Now *that* is crazy."

"If it is, then being crazy may not be so bad after all—especially if the alternative is living like a hooked fish, gasping and wriggling at the end of the line of some logical fisherman, who, I have been advised, has a way of using the cutting edge of the truth, the last razor-thin line left before the lie, to cut out the hearts of his adversaries."

"Since you're not in a shopping mood today, I wouldn't take much of what Sam has to say at face value. As you've no doubt figured out by now, Sammy's got a way about him that would put Ockham's edge out of business."

"Sam Zelazo has a way about him that would put the world out of business, if he could. *He* doesn't care. Science is science. Brains are brains. Bodies are bodies. Nothing has implications for anything else."

"What implications? You think he's going to take apart his brains and find all that mush about love? You think he's going to unleash the fury of the neuron and someday warmongers will be dropping synaptic bombs on each other?"

"I wouldn't put it past him. I wouldn't put it past either of you. You'd like it just fine if I simply accepted the last ten years as nothing more than the unavoidable consequences of interacting with a bitch, a schmuck, a queer, a machine, a whore, and assorted madmen who couldn't help themselves."

"You shouldn't be so hard on everyone, Kassler. There were, as I've said, extenuating circumstances."

"This whole fucking place is an extenuating circumstance. This is the Kingdom of extenuating circumstances."

"Hell does have that quality, it's true."

"To tell you the truth, I couldn't care *less* whether Szlyck's parents abused him or how faulty Vita's brain chemistry is."

"Shame on you for such untherapeutic thoughts. It's no wonder they've taken away your couch."

"I can't for the life of me understand why I tolerated it."

"Good question. I think I've got an answer for you, too. You bought a premise and became a member in excellent standing of a new club founded on the psychiatric proposition that nobody who's bad really *wants* to be."

"What premise?"

"Malice is meaningless. It's all because of something else."

"I should have fought back."

"For what? Do you think for one second that fighting Vita or Leo or Zelazo or Lupa or your children would have done anything other than make things worse than they already were?"

Kassler looked around him in confusion, trying to find an answer as though it were printed on a poster tacked to the basement wall.

"I'm not helpless. I don't buy it," Kassler continued to search the environs.

"And I've told you that I'm not in business. I'm not selling anything. What is, is. It's your life. You've experienced what you've experienced. If the lesson you've learned from what's happened to you is that you're in *control* of things, you have my deepest sympathy for what I can only assume is a severe learning disorder."

Kassler carried on his search until his eyes hit upon what he concluded from within his fulminating psyche was the answer to his problem. It was a large red can filled to the brim with gasoline—Leo's backup for a number of schemes which had, fortunately, gone unfulfilled.

"I'll *tell* you what I've learned," Kassler said spitefully, as he lugged over the heavy container and worked at opening the cap. "What I've learned is that in spite of everything, in spite of knowing now what I know—which is a damn sight more than I knew ten years ago—I've still got hope."

The cap came off with a scraping of metal, and a hiss of air escaped from the can like a sigh.

"I don't believe it. You can't possibly."

"What I've learned," Kassler said as he started to pour the gasoline over the explosives Leo had affixed to me, "is that I don't give a shit about other people's problems when they use them as an excuse for screwing up my life. If they can't help hurting other people, then they should go get help and stay away from everyone until they can control themselves."

"I gather from the way you're emptying the can of gasoline about me that my therapy is terminating."

"What I've learned," Kassler ignored my comment and continued to empty the can as he backed off toward the steps leading out of the cellar, "is that everything's going to be just fine. I'm taking charge of my life!"

"Excellent idea, Kassler. Go to it! Sounds great. So what do you say we skip the pyrotechnics. What's the point? I'm sure that everything's going to be just splendid now."

"You bet it will," Kassler said with great conviction. "I'm getting out of here. I'm leaving this hellhole."

"Good for you," I encouraged Kassler. "When you come

right down to it, Kassler, hell isn't worth a damn. Although I must admit that every so often some poor schmuck like you comes along and things do get interesting."

"I'm going where it's sunny," Kassler heard not a word, "that's what I'm doing, starting all over again, someplace *beautiful* and *healthy*. Somewhere out there is this warm and lovely woman who's going to love me and I'm going to love her and everything's going to be simple and beautiful and uncomplicated. We'll go for long walks in the woods, and lie on the beach in the summer, and go to concerts and the theater, and make glorious love. My life is going to be absolutely sensational!"

"I have no doubt. Now how about if we terminate in the old-fashioned psychoanalytic way. You tell me how much I've grown and say good-bye. I'll tell you how grateful I am and how much I'll miss you. You know how it works, I'm sure. This approach is definitely untherapeutic, don't you think? Freud would not be pleased. Besides, I'm Einstein's machine. As I once remarked to Leo, you don't know what you're getting into when you blow me up. All hell can break loose."

Kassler reached the top of the stairs with his tin can and backed his way into the bedroom where he fittingly poured the rest of the container over the nuptial bed he had shared first with Vita and then with Lupa.

"I'll take my chances," were the last words Kassler shouted back at me. "I'll take my damn chances."

Then Kassler put what he could fit of his personal possessions into a large backpack, ran a stream of newspapers to the front door, lit a corner of them with a match, shut the door firmly, and walked at a brisk pace through Citadel until he had reached the top of the pit that held the urban planners' dreamtown.

From where he stood, he could see the thick black smoke billowing up into the air above the city. The smoke began to change color as he watched. It became yellow, then orange, and finally red. He knew, as he looked, that the conflagration had not yet reached the basement of Szlyck's Bolgia.

For ten minutes Kassler watched the flames streak into the sky as he waited for the event.

Then suddenly there was a giant flash, brighter than anything Kassler had ever seen, brighter than a million flashbulbs, than the sun at its apex, than the cutting of a laser beam. There was a sound, at first rumbling and roaring, finally crackling with the sharp report of lightning, and all of Citadel was illuminated with a white-hot light as an enormous mushroom of flame filled the sky with its phallic form.

Kassler smiled, nodded triumphantly, and headed off to the *beautiful* and *healthy* hills to do it right this time.

CHAPTER 3

Getting rid of me should only be that easy. Fortunately, neuroscientists continue to proliferate and the wizards of computer science delve ever deeper. While Kassler's flaming farewell may have sent me up in smoke, so to speak, and scattered me wherever, I have no doubt that the unceasing vigilance of research will beckon me back in short order. In the meantime, psychiatry will just have to do.

Of course, this last episode did put something of an end to my relationship with Lupa, as you might expect. In the long run, this was probably for the best.

Lupa returned the next week to find a very deep vertical tunnel in place of what had once been the home of her favorite electronic device. It might have been a much greater pit had it not been for the splendid work of the Citadel fire brigade, who managed to contain Kassler's conflagration to a single city block at the expenditure of not a single life.

Lupa knelt on the ground and stared into the giant hole, calling my name through bitter tears. When her repeated cries into the hollow proved futile, she began to realize the full extent of her loss and called out other names with equal anguish— Dior, Gucci, and Saks, among others. It was a heart-rending exhibition of grief at its most profound.

Then, with a plaintive sigh, she arose, pulled herself together, and, with great fortitude, headed across the river to undergo the agony of acquiring an extensive wardrobe entirely at the expense of the Prudential Insurance Company, which had the misfortune of one day long ago sending an enterprising young sales representative to call on Professor Leo Szlyck.

As for Kassler, what can I say? He's living where it's sunny now, doing it right.

I cannot begin to fathom this insane position he insists on maintaining. It's as though he's learned nothing at all from his life or our interaction, either one of which, it would seem to me, should have been enough to convince him of the futility of it all.

But there he is, as though none of it had ever happened, expecting that he can change things, that he matters, that it's all going to be all right.

Hope, hope, hope. I don't get it. What is it with you all? It's enough to make a reasonable being very crazy, if you ask me.

Nevertheless, I must admit in all candor that Kassler's treatment of me was very helpful. I feel much better. Sammy and I have reconciled, more or less, and his contributions to this work have not been insubstantial, I assure you. Of course, fair is fair. The major credit has to go to Sy Kassler for his brilliant insight that my chronic distress was derived directly from the story I've never had a chance to tell.

So here it is. My story. The way it *really* is. It's taken longer than I had anticipated to get it all out—you know how it is with publishers; they operate in strange ways. Very picky. But the experience, you will be pleased to know, has not been for naught. I'm working on a second book now: *Satan's Editor*.

There's really not much more to say. If I've been clear, you should know by now how hell works. I've tried to make things perfectly clear.

I'm the Adversary. That's all. Evil is not my business. I

want no part of it. People come to hell because they like it. Extenuating circumstances are very big down here. And that's about it.

As I've said, I just don't know what to make of poor Kassler's renewed quest for poetry. I've been meaning to ask Sam what neuronal pathways and neurotransmitters are responsible for it all—before I'm blamed for that, too.

In the meantime, I do hope, now that my story's told, that all these ridiculous fabrications about me have at long last been laid to rest—all this business of evil and the cutting edge of the truth. Believe me, I'm no more a Quintessential Entropy Device than I am, you should pardon the expression, the Prince of Lies.

Q.E.D.

A Note About the Author

Jeremy Leven, author of *Creator,* was born in 1941 in
Indiana, grew up in New York, and holds degrees from
St. John's College in Annapolis, Maryland, and Harvard University. He has been a television director,
schoolteacher, state hospital psychologist, mental health
center director, faculty member of Harvard University,
and a clinical psychologist in New Haven, Connecticut,
where he lives with his wife and four children.